A
MAID
on FIFTH
AVENUE

ALSO BY SINÉAD CROWLEY

The Belladonna Maze

A MAID on FIFTH AVENUE

SINÉAD CROWLEY

An Aria Book

9 7 5 3 1 2 4 6 8

A catalogue record for this book is available from
the British Library.

ISBN (HB): 9781801105682
ISBN (XTPB): 9781801105699
ISBN (E): 9781801105668

Typeset by Divaddict Publishing Solutions Ltd.

Cover design: HoZ / Simon Michele

Printed and bound in Great Britain by
CPI Group (UK) Ltd, Croydon CR0 4YY

MIX
Paper | Supporting
responsible forestry
FSC® C171272

Head of Zeus Ltd
First Floor East
5–8 Hardwick Street
London EC1R 4RG

WWW.HEADOFZEUS.COM

To Bridget Crowley and Mary Anne Lyons

PART ONE

Prologue

The storm came out of nowhere, rattling windows, tearing washing off lines and calling a halt to the under-seventeen league final which was the closest the parish had come to glory in over fifty years. The villagers closed their windows, fired up the tumble dryers – ignoring the dire warnings from their younger children about global warming – and consoled their disconsolate teens, all the while raining curses down on the weather forecasters who had promised a decent weekend. But what did that shower above in Dublin know about Kerry weather anyway? With their charts and their apps and their winking at you after the news as if it was all only a bit of fun after a day spent behind a desk in their warm, dry offices. They hadn't a clue what it was like trying to get a tourist season properly off the ground for the first time in three years, when the weather itself was trying to get everyone to stay at home.

And up by the cliffs the wind blew stronger.

The pub owners and the restaurant owners looked at their sodden parasols, newly purchased and branded at great expense for the summer, and wheeled their outdoor furniture back inside. Because it was all very well those experts talking about ventilation and mitigation, but no one was asking them to feed a party of Americans bowls of stew and plates of fish and chips when the wind was blasting so hard down Main Street the fish themselves were in danger of being blown back into the bay, only wearing beer batter jackets this time around.

And out at sea the storm rose.

The parents in the holiday homes unpacked the Switches and the Xboxes and handed them to their children, telling themselves they could do the #makingmemories bit tomorrow and thanking the heavens they had shelled out extra for Wi-Fi, while the local families closed their curtains on the grey skies and squalls of rain and binge-watched *Stranger Things*. And next to the cliffs, a woman in a bedroom with panoramic views of the bay turned her back on its fierce beauty and, exhausted by confusion and pain, closed her eyes to the chaos.

She slept so deeply that she did not hear the rumble of thunder nor feel the power of the wind as it rose to a terrifying velocity; she did not see the clouds scudding across the water, nor the waves that had risen to a level not even the most confident surfer would risk. And she did not see the single bolt of lightning that struck the shore and caused a crack in over one hundred years of village faith and memory. The tree shuddered, then swayed, but everyone was at home now, insulated from the storm, and there was no one around to see its roots dragged from the earth, and with them the soil of the last century, the scurrying insects and the picked-clean gleam of the bones.

Chapter One

CO. KERRY

1908

Through the grey gloom came a whisper.

'Where are you off to, child?'

'I won't be long.'

Auntie Kathleen opened her mouth to speak but closed it again almost immediately, giving, instead, a brief nod. Annie pulled on the heavy wooden door, opened it a fraction and then squeezed her way through, anxious not to flood the cottage with morning sunlight. It had been a difficult night for all of them but particularly for her mother, and now that Eileen had finally fallen asleep Annie had no desire to wake her.

She stepped out onto the grass, dew soaking the soles of her feet, then stood still for a moment, relishing the silence, so thick it was almost tangible. For over a week now their little home had been filled with strange and unsettling noises, the heavy tread of footsteps in the darkness, the buzz of urgent conversations, the clack of her grandmother's rosary beads and, above it all, the raspy sound of her mother's laboured breathing. Last night had been the most frightening time of all, the kitchen bed Annie shared with her little sister Eve sent rocking in the darkness as visitors pushed past to get to the bedroom at the back of the house.

Their father's sister had urged them to say their prayers and to go to sleep and Eve had obeyed, at six years of age still young enough to trust that God, and Auntie Kathleen, would make everything better by morning. But Annie, two years her senior, had been unable to ignore the tension in her aunt's voice or the air of barely suppressed panic that was swirling around their home. Too scared of the answer to ask what was going on, she had shut her eyes tight but the darkness had served simply to amplify the sounds around her and eventually she had curled herself into a ball and jammed her fingers into her ears, as if by sealing herself off from the horror she could pretend it was not happening at all.

But now, for a short time at least, she was free. She dipped her hand into the pocket of her skirt to make sure the treasure she was guarding was still safe inside then ran across the patch of scrub grass that lay between the cottage and the road. The sky was blue and cloudless overhead, it was going to be a warm day and Annie made a mental note to collect rags later and soak them in seawater for her mother's forehead. But first she had a much more important job to do. Moving more quickly now, she continued along the dusty track for a few yards then stopped when she got to the crossroads, ignored the turning that would have taken her to the village and, raising her skirts, jumped over a low stone wall. Wildflowers dusted pollen on her bare feet as she trotted across the meadow, heading for the cliffs, and then she paused, as she always did as the sparkling waters of the Atlantic opened out in front of her. The sea was royal blue this morning, a light breeze raising foamy tips on the tiny waves, and as salt tickled the back of her throat Annie couldn't help but smile. But even as she did so an image of her mother's grey lips and shuddering chest flickered in the corner of her mind. She blinked the memory away then slipped her hand into her pocket and touched again the edge of the lace handkerchief she had hidden in here. Soon, there would be no need to worry any longer. Soon, everything would be in order again.

The hawthorn tree stood a few paces back from the cliff edge, squat and bent in places from the strong Atlantic winds but its trunk still thick and strong. As Annie began to walk towards it she felt her own breath skitter in her chest as anticipation and raw hope bubbled inside her. Annie knew her grandparents had not approved of her father's decision to build their home so close to the ocean, claiming the salt breeze made the soil inhospitable and that it would be far too easy for winter gales to find their way through the thatched roof of the cabin. But Pádraig Thornton had married an island woman and when Eileen had moved to the mainland for him he had promised her she would never live out of earshot of the waves. That was a promise, Annie knew, that meant far more for the two of them than the odd gust of wind. Especially now, with her mother—

Enough. She was not going to think of that now. This was a morning for hope. She stretched out her hand and touched the tree trunk gently, its bark rough under her small fingers. This was the other reason her father had built their home so near the sea – to seek the guardianship of this Fairy Tree that had stood here for as long as anyone in Ballydrynawn could remember. The field in which it grew was, in truth, part of the Lynches' farm, but not even Seánie Lynch would dare fence it off or prevent the other villagers from having access to it. Besides, how could he claim ownership over something that had existed long before he was born? All that mattered to the Thornton family was that it stood within easy reach of their cottage, summer and winter, between them and all harm.

Annie bent down to look at the strips of ragged material that had been knotted to the tree's dense, sturdy branches. She didn't dare touch them but examined them as closely as she could, thinking of the hands that had tied them, and their owners' fervent wishes for a child, or a husband, or a letter from a family member who had gone to live across the very ocean that now stretched out in front of her. And today, Annie had her own request to make.

'Boo!'

'Oh!'

Lost in thought, she hadn't heard the footsteps padding up behind her and she turned sharply, her hands flying to her throat in alarm.

'I'm sorry!'

May giggled at the startled expression on her friend's face, and then her expression grew serious.

'How is your mammy? We heard ye had to get the doctor again last night.'

'We did, we—'

But Annie's throat dried before she could finish the sentence. Despite their young age, both girls knew that to call the doctor from the town, with all of the expense

8

that decision entailed, was to admit just how serious her mother's condition had become. Then she swallowed, and her face brightened.

'I know how to make her better though. Look! I brought this to help her.'

She withdrew her hand from her pocket, revealing the square of material, its whiteness emphasised by her grubby, sunburned fingers. Her friend gasped.

'Does your mammy know you have that? She'll kill you if she…'

May's voice tailed off as she realised the insensitivity of her words, but Annie simply smiled.

'I took it yesterday morning but this is the first chance I've had to use it.'

May hesitated for a moment, and then, the innate curiosity of an eight-year-old girl getting the better of her, she stretched out her own hand.

'Can I hold it?'

Annie shook her head.

'You'd better not. It mightn't work if too many people handle it. But you can look.'

She balanced the handkerchief in her palm, flattening it with the tips of her fingers, and May, tucking her hair behind her ears, bent over to take a closer look.

'It's so beautiful.'

The girls stared at it for a moment, taking in the fine cotton weave, the delicacy of the lace at the edges, before May spoke again.

'Where did your mammy get it, do you know?'

'There was a new teacher in her school, a lady teacher.'

Annie had heard the story so many times that telling it was

a comfort and even the horror of the night before receded as she touched the edge of the lace before continuing.

'She gave the pupils a spelling test at the end of every week and my mammy got every one of them right.'

'Every one?'

May screwed up her face in doubt; she herself was no fan of schoolwork, but Annie simply nodded, beaming with inherited pride.

'Every single one. Some of the boys said she must have been cheating, but she wasn't. She was just the best. In the end the lady teacher gave her a pair of handkerchiefs for her very own.'

'She never used them though?'

May's voice was solemn, as if imagining the danger that could come to such delicate objects during the roughness of day-to-day life in a busy home. Annie shook her head vigorously.

'No, no. She keeps them folded away at the back of the dresser. Me and Eve aren't allowed to touch them even.'

'So when did you get this one?'

'Yesterday morning, when everyone was asleep.'

It was only part of the story, but even though Annie loved her friend like a sister, she couldn't bear to tell her the truth, which was that although she had had to tug the heavy wooden stool across the kitchen floor and climb up onto it to locate the hidden treasure, the rest of the household had been gathered in the bedroom, their heads bowed in prayer, too preoccupied to notice her.

'Won't she miss it?'

'No, she—'

And suddenly the lump was back in Annie's throat again,

bigger than ever this time. The truth was, of course, that her mother was locked in a fierce battle for every breath and past caring about lace handkerchiefs or even the whereabouts of her beloved children. May reached over to grasp her free hand, and the two children stood silently for a moment, in the shade of the tree, thinking thoughts too terrible to be spoken aloud.

And then Annie pulled her hand away from her friend's and took a decisive step forward.

'The tree will look after her.'

She bent down and tied the handkerchief to a low branch, taking care not to snag the lace on the thorns. It was foolish, she supposed, to take such care, as the ocean wind would leave the material tattered within days, but it seemed important, somehow, to respect the handkerchief as much as possible.

May stared at her in horror.

'You can't mean to leave it here. Your mother—'

'She's very sick, May. I'm asking for her to be cured. The doctor said she might die...'

It was as if finally saying the words loosened the knot in her throat and Annie burst into loud, hot sobs. Her friend threw her arms around her and with the empathy of the very young began to cry too and they held each other tight, tears soaking the shoulders of their thin dresses. Such was their misery, it was several minutes before they heard the name being called.

'Annie!'

They turned then and Annie's stomach seemed to shrivel up inside her when she saw the slender figure of her aunt, waving frantically from across the field.

'You're to come home now, child. Hurry!'

The tone in Auntie Kathleen's voice allowed for no dissent, and Annie dropped May's hand without a word and ran. By the time she had reached the cottage, her aunt had gone back inside. Annie allowed the door to close behind her, walked across the floor to the bedroom and then stopped, unable to move any further. Her father stood between her and the bed. He was holding her little sister in his arms and his shoulders were bent and shaking with silent sobs.

'Go to her, a stór.'

Her aunt reached over and tugged gently on her arm but Annie couldn't move. Every inch of her wanted to turn and run in the opposite direction, back out of the door and across the fields, past the tree and further still, into the ocean even, any place that was far from this room and from the words she had been dreading. She had tried so hard, so hard, had said her prayers every night and visited the Fairy Tree, petitioning everyone from Holy God to the fairies to save her mammy and not to take her away. But now here they were, and the silence in the bedroom was far, far scarier than any noise she had heard the night before. And then her father turned to her and Annie was astonished to see a smile on his unshaven, tear-stained features. She looked past him to the pale figure in the bed and there she saw hope, weak, but determined. It couldn't be, could it? But it was, it was her mammy, propped up by pillows and extending a trembling hand.

'Come closer to me, alannah. I want to see you. I'm feeling so much better but I'm going to have to stay in bed for another while. You've been such a good, brave girl...'

Her aunt tugged at her sleeve again and now Annie could see that Auntie Kathleen was smiling too.

'Go over, child. She's been asking for you ever since she woke.'

In a moment, Annie was kneeling by her mother's side. She looked tired, but her eyes were bright, the sheen of sweat was gone from her skin and her chest was falling and rising quite easily. Around the room the adults had begun to mutter again and Annie could hear words float past, theories about medicine doing its job and an infection bravely fought. But Annie ignored them all and simply took her mother's pale hand in hers, and as her eyes blurred with tears she suddenly felt as if she was looking at the handkerchief too, fluttering and waving from the Fairy Tree.

Chapter Two

CO. KERRY

May 2022

A squall of rain hurled itself against the glass and Emer tucked her feet under her on the sofa, wrapping her hands a little tighter around her mug of tea. On clear days a ribbon of ocean could be seen across the fields from here but this morning, the only thing that was visible through the rivulets of rain running down the French windows was the patio, complete with wooden garden furniture and her father's pride and joy, a brick-built barbecue. A barbecue, would you mind? A camping stove had been good enough for Emer and her brother back in the day but her parents had renovated the Tigín since then, and their summer cottage now boasted a new kitchen, a flat-screen TV and even a power shower that was a serious improvement on the plastic bath attachment Emer had used to wash her hair during her teenage years.

Her phone told her it was seven o'clock but she had to take a second look out the window to make sure that referred to a.m. rather than p.m. Emer's body clock was utterly scrambled from two days of travelling; first the long flight from LA to Dublin, then what felt like an even longer drive down here to Kerry, fuelled only by petrol station coffee and a longing to see the sea. Stifling a yawn, she opened WhatsApp to find a photo of her parents, grinning self-consciously from the departures gate at Dublin Airport. Maura and George Molloy were all about the selfies now, two years stuck at home during the pandemic had seen them 'going digital', as her father put it, and Maura was even threatening to document their long-awaited holiday on Instagram, if she could persuade her husband it wouldn't cost them a second mortgage in roaming fees. Emer snapped her own photo, just to prove she'd made it down in one piece, then took care to crop last night's empty wine glass out of the picture before pressing send. It was crazy really, she was thirty-two years old but it still felt rather scandalous to be drinking alcohol at the Tigín.

The Tigín, pronounced Tig-een was the Irish word for 'little house' and when Emer had been very young the Molloys' holiday home had been just that, a two-room chalet built on land inherited from Maura's parents. Over the years, however, the house had been extended until it was now a very comfortable bungalow with both the beach and the village of Ballydrynawn within easy reach. And although Emer's schoolfriends had regularly returned from holidays abroad with suntans, exotic sweets and tales of even more exotic encounters, she had never felt like she was missing out. It was impossible to feel bored at the Tigín, where sunny days were spent with cousins on the beach, and rainy ones merely an excuse to select a book from Maura's stash and curl up on the lumpy sofa beside the turf-burning range. In later years there had been no shortage of boys either, mostly students from the local summer college which imported children from the cities and sent them home three weeks later with a good grasp of the Irish language and an even better grasp of the local teens. No, Emer had loved every moment of her childhood holidays. But that didn't mean she wanted to spend this summer at the Tigín, completely and utterly alone.

Emer hadn't told her parents she was returning to Ireland for the summer, assuming that after two years of Zoom calls they'd welcome the surprise. As commercial flights filled up post-pandemic, social media had been crammed with videos of adult children appearing on parental doorsteps to a soundtrack of heartwarming squeals and tears. But when Emer had arrived at her childhood home in Dublin the previous morning George and Maura had reacted not with delight, but with barely concealed horror. The sense that something was deeply wrong had only increased as George led his only daughter through a house which reminded her of the morning after the Christmas decorations had been taken down, weirdly bare and clean but with the odd ball of dust rolling out of unexpected corners. There had been piles of clothes everywhere too, and Emer had to lift a bundle from a stool in order to sit down, doing a double-take when she spotted a size fourteen bikini bundled up with her dad's neatly ironed polo shirts.

'It is really lovely to see you,' George had attempted, before glancing helplessly across at his wife.

'Oh, I'll do it.'

Maura had leaned back against the counter and sighed.

'We're thrilled to see you, darling, really we are. We just weren't expecting you back this summer.'

Suddenly Emer had found herself on the verge of tears. This was her first trip home in years, her folks should have been debating whether to serve mash or chips with the fatted calf, not acting as if her unexpected arrival was nothing but a terrible inconvenience.

And then the truth had burst from Maura, so suddenly Emer almost fell off the stool.

'But we are coming to see you!'

The sentence ended in a sound halfway between a snort and a wail.

'It's all organised, you silly goose! We're flying to LA tomorrow, it was supposed to be a surprise! We were going to stay for a month, let you show us around a bit and then head over to Australia to stay with your brother and Sadie until the baby is born. We've a car organised at LAX and everything, an SUV! That was all your father's idea, I thought a saloon would be fine but he said no, Emer might want to come with us for a bit of a drive and you couldn't stick her in the back of a smaller car, sure she'd need the legroom...'

At least the image of being ferried around the LA freeways like she was twelve years old again, with her mother handing sweeties back through the gap in the front seats, had been ridiculous enough to make Emer laugh, rather than burst into tears.

Still wondering if it would be better to unpack or head into town to do some shopping, Emer stood up and looked around the room for wherever she had tossed her car keys the night before. And then she felt warmth on the back of her neck and turned to see a shard of sunlight fall across the hard wood floor. A quick glance out of the window confirmed it – there was more blue than grey in the sky now, the Kerry weather was doing one of its legendary U-turns, and she knew from experience that despite the early hour she'd better make use of the sun before it disappeared again. Tying a sports top around her waist, an expensive piece of kit she'd bought for hiking the LA hills which cheerfully claimed to be able to both warm her up AND cool her down, she locked the door behind her and headed down the gravel path on foot, leaving her mam's Ford Focus to rest after its long journey. By rights she should be resting too, of course, preferably in her parents' sitting room, tackling her jet lag with pots of tea and home-made scones. But although, once the full extent of their scheduling error had been revealed, Maura and George had half-heartedly offered to postpone their holiday, Emer wouldn't hear of it. She knew how tough the last two years had been on them, her folks had retired from their teaching jobs just before the pandemic and had planned to spend the latter half of their sixties exploring the world, not sitting at home getting on each other's nerves and being called 'vulnerable' every time they switched on the TV. Besides, they'd timed their journey to coincide with the birth of their first grandchild. Emer's brother Niall and his Australian partner Sadie were due to welcome their baby in a little over two months and that wasn't exactly an event that could be put off for another time.

So Emer had done what she always did in their family, smiled and told her parents she'd be absolutely grand. She'd enjoy having the house to herself, she said cheerfully, she could take it easy, maybe catch up with a few friends – and then Maura had swallowed before admitting that a summer in Dublin wouldn't be an option either as the

Molloys had arranged a house swap with an Australian couple who were, even now, buying duty free in Singapore.

'No problem at all!'

Emer's smile was starting to hurt her now.

'I'll go to the Tigín.'

The truth was that, after more than two years of 'social distancing', a further three months of isolation in West Kerry was the exact opposite of what the doctor – or in this case a frighteningly efficient psychiatrist – had ordered for Emer. But in the Molloy family Emer was the one who coped with things and never ever made a fuss, so she didn't mention 'shrink' to her parents, or 'stress' or 'panic' or any of the other words that had become an irritatingly central part of her vocabulary in recent months. And all those years spent on set with actors in LaLa Land must have rubbed off on her because before she could say 'Covid Burnout' she had been handed the keys to her mother's car and waved on her way.

And now she was here, she thought as she wandered down the small road that would eventually take her to the beach, she might as well make the best of it.

Despite the sunshine, there was a stiff breeze coming in from the ocean and Emer tucked her hair behind her ears as she walked. It was still damp from the shower but the sun and the breeze would look after that. Emer never considered herself to be anything particularly special, looks-wise; she had inherited her father's height and her mother's pale skin which freckled rather than tanned in the summer and flushed, in her opinion, far too easily. But whenever she read one of those online surveys demanding she 'rate her best features' she had to admit, albeit privately, that her hair was a solid ten out of ten. Poker straight and dark brown, it sat just below her shoulders in a neat bob, glossily healthy no matter what supermarket shampoo she used on it, and given that she never bothered colouring it or getting anything done really, rather than the odd trim, she was one of the few people who had emerged from pandemic lockdown looking pretty much the same as when she had gone in.

She reached the crossroads, where a left turn would take her back in the direction of Ballydrynawn but turned right instead, following the route that would eventually lead her to the sea. There was no pavement, so Emer stuck as close as she could to the grass verge and was reminded as she did so that she had never actually walked this route before. Although the nearest strand was less than a kilometre from the Tigín her parents would never have countenanced heading there on foot, given all of the accoutrements – food, toys, deckchairs and windbreakers – that were considered essential for a family day out on an Irish beach. In fact, every car the Molloys owned ended up coated inside and out with a fine layer of sand which would reappear on dark clothes or sticky fingers in the depths of winter, a reminder of warmer, brighter days. Right now, however, following two days of cramped airline and car seats, the prospect of a stroll was irresistible.

Having reached a dip in the road, Emer heard the car's engine before she saw the approaching vehicle, and moved closer to the hedge to let it pass. The driver lifted his index finger in thanks and, although she didn't recognise him, Emer returned the salute. Not to acknowledge him would be a serious slight, it might have been years since she had last been down here but she was still Maura and George Molloy's daughter and therefore an ambassador for her parents, her extended family and, inevitably, the whole community of holiday homeowners too. Second homes were a tricky issue in this part of the world, there was no doubt that the yearly influx of visitors kept villages like Ballydrynawn afloat, financially speaking at least, but there was also no denying the fact that the holiday homes tended to occupy some of the best sites in the region and had pushed general house prices up far beyond what many of the locals could afford. Well, Emer couldn't sort out the Irish housing sector with a casual wave, but appearing friendly was, she reckoned, the least she could do.

There was no signpost for the strand but she found the turnoff easily, quietly proud that she still recognised the way. And indeed very little had changed since her last visit, almost a decade before. It was still the same narrow road, lined by tall, scraggly hedges with a strip of grass growing down the centre and the occasional indentation to let cars pass each other by. A cow looked over an iron gate and as a gust of salted wind caught her full in the face Emer felt the headache she had been carrying for as long as she could remember finally start to lift. Vitamin Sea, now that was something the therapist would approve of.

The road she was walking on soon morphed into a sandy track with coarse grass on both sides and, after walking past a red van which had been parked neatly in a lay-by, Emer climbed to the top of a small hill then stood, hands on her waist, as the blue-grey sea opened out in front of her and miles of empty sand merged beige to brown. With no specific direction in mind, she turned left and began to walk, enjoying the push and pull of her muscles as she moved across the undulating surface. She would take up running again as soon as she had settled in, she decided, but for now she'd be happy to take up 'sitting and relaxing' and she pulled her sweater from around her waist then dropped it on the side of a sand dune and lowered herself onto it.

It was then she noticed the shape in the water, gliding in towards the shore. A seal? Here? But no, it was a surfer she realised as he came closer, sleek in a black wetsuit, his white board balanced on the crest of a wave until suddenly it wasn't and he was swallowed up by the churning water. Emer pulled her knees towards her then rested her chin on them, keeping her eyes fixed on the man as he emerged from the foam, heaved himself up onto the board and paddled back out to sea. He turned, then sat upright for a few moments, almost motionless apart from the gentle bobbing of the water, and then something behind him seemed to capture his attention and he threw himself forwards until he was lying flat again. The swell, imperceptible at first, grew until it was a wall of water and then a foaming wave and all the time he used his arms to paddle ahead of it, moving faster and faster until some magic confluence of speed and momentum seemed to send him a signal and he sprang to his feet in one fluid motion, keeping his knees bent but his feet rock solid on the board which leaped forwards then angled downwards, carrying him quickly but steadily down the face of the powerful wave which he rode all the way to the shore.

It was only when the board ran aground onto the sand and the man jumped off it in a small, light movement that Emer noticed she had been holding her breath while watching him. It had been a long time since her attention had been so focused on something other than work, wonderful to feel her mind so clutter free.

Except now, having picked up his board, he appeared to be walking right towards her. Emer looked left and then right as if she might have missed a posse of surfers sitting nearby, waiting for their comrade but no, she was both alone on the strand and, it seemed, the surfer's sole destination. A minute later he was standing right in front of her, his wetsuit glistening with salt water. He was around her own age, she reckoned, with thick curly hair flattened against his tanned face and a slick of white sunscreen across the bridge of his wide nose. He didn't say anything, just nodded at her then placed the board on the ground and began to peel the wetsuit off his tanned and, she couldn't help noticing, very broad shoulders, then eased it down until it hung off his comparatively narrow hips. Still seated right in front of him, Emer could do nothing but stare, until he spoke, in a soft, unmistakably Kerry rumble.

'I'll just get past you there, please.'

Emer felt a sudden prickle of irritation. She mightn't be local, not strictly speaking anyway, but her mother's family had lived around here for generations and even if they hadn't, he didn't own the bloody sand. Stretching her legs out in front of her, she kept her voice steady.

'It's a big beach, plenty of room for both of us.'

''Tis big all right.' The man's voice was lighter now and definitely amused. 'But I need my towel, like.'

Too late, Emer turned her head to see the neatly folded towel just inches away, partly hidden inside the sand dune. Heat flooded her cheeks as she scrambled to her feet.

'I'm so sorry! God, I was only out for a walk, I didn't even notice—'

'You're grand!'

The man was definitely smiling now as he eased past her and began to peel the wetsuit further down his long legs revealing, thank Christ, a pair of swimming shorts underneath. Emer continued to gabble.

'I was just out for a walk and said I'd take a rest and—'

'It's no trouble at all.'

The man wrapped the towel around his waist and pointed at a plastic box which she could now see contained a pile of dry clothes.

'You might give me a minute now, though?'

'Of course! I'll just head off now and... right.'

Utterly flustered now, Emer turned and began to stride away. Within moments, however, it became clear that she was heading in the opposite direction to the road and, with no other exit in sight she'd either have to keep walking until the man left, no matter how far out of her way that took her, or risk further mortification by turning around and passing him again, trying to look as if she hadn't just flown in from America with the sole purpose of stalking six-foot-two broad-shouldered Irish surfers. She was just calculating how long she could keep going without food and water when the weather took another one eighty and fat drops of rain began to fall on her head. Of course, her bloody hundred-dollar thermo-controlled sweatshirt didn't come equipped with anything as practical as a hood so Emer turned and began to jog back, past the surfer and over the hillock that guarded the entrance to the beach, the ground beneath her feet turning to mud and silt. She heard a padding sound behind her then and turned to see the surfer, carrying the heavy board under his arm as easily as if it was a snooker cue.

'You've no car with you?'

Emer looked around as if the Ford Focus might have made its own way to the beach to rescue her, then had to acknowledge it had not.

'Do you want to sit in the van for a minute? You'll be soaked.'

The surfer slid the board into the back of the red van, then jumped into the front seat and reached across to open the passenger door. Emer's first instinct was to refuse his offer of shelter, less for fear of him being an axe murderer than the thought of having to make stilted conversation in such a confined space, but when water began to actually find its way inside her clothes and trickle down her spine she decided embarrassment was preferable to pneumonia, and heaved herself inside. The vehicle smelled so strongly of salt water sun-baked into upholstery that it felt like she was a kid back in her parents' car again, a bucket and spade on her lap and a cousin or two squashed in beside her.

'That came down quick.'

The man ran his fingers through his hair.

'It did, yeah.'

Emer turned to look out of the front window of the van but it had completely steamed up, leaving her with nothing to see and, therefore, nothing other than the weather to comment on. There would be no point in opening a window either, the rain was coming down almost vertically and they'd be soaked within moments. She'd have to think of something else to talk about, so.

'You looked great out there. I mean…'

She gave a small cough before continuing.

'It looked great, I mean. The surfing. It looked like a lot of fun.'

'Ah, it was a bit mushy out there today, no power in the waves at all.'

Without a clue as to what he meant, Emer simply looked across at him and gave what she hoped was a sympathetic nod.

'I'd love to try it sometime.'

It wasn't a lie, actually. A keen swimmer, Emer had often watched surfers in LA and thought the sport looked like a lot of fun but they were all so tanned, toned and professional-looking, the thought of actually taking a board into the water seemed completely out of reach. There was something about surfing in Kerry, though, that made the whole thing seem a bit more accessible. A sport she could do less than twenty minutes from her couch couldn't be that difficult, could it?

But the man was looking at her quite seriously now.

'I could teach you, if you like.'

OK, that was a bit impulsive, given that they hadn't even exchanged names. Starting to doubt her initial dismissal of the axe-murderer theory, Emer took a quick look around the van to make sure the doors remained unlocked before replying.

'Right, thanks, I mean I don't know you so—'

But the surfer was still talking.

'Saturday should be good, around ten? The swell will be gentle enough – great beginners' waves.'

Would he come after her, Emer wondered, if she ran? And

then the man turned slightly in his seat and she followed his gaze to see the rows of surfboards stacked in the back of the van together with racks of drying wetsuits, and exhaled.

'You're a surf instructor.'

'Well yeah, obviously.'

He stuck out his hand.

'I'm Rob, nice to meet you! I run Breaking Waves, we're based over the other side of the bay.'

'Emer. Good to meet you.'

Rob turned on the wipers and looked out of the windscreen with a frown.

'Look, I have to head off, I'm working at two. Can I give you a lift somewhere?'

'Ah no, not at all, I'll be grand.'

But even as she spoke, they both knew Emer was just being polite. The rain was bouncing off the roof now and she'd need to borrow one of his wetsuits if she was to attempt the walk back to the Tigín. When they reached the edge of the main road he slowed the van and looked at her.

'Where do you need to go?'

She pointed.

'The house is just a few minutes back that way, if you don't mind?'

'No bother,' he said again and eased the van forwards. 'Just down on holidays, are you?'

'Down for the summer, actually. It's my parents' house. We're not total blow-ins though, my mother grew up around here, we spent nearly every summer here when we were kids.'

'Relax!'

Rob gave a broad smile, his teeth white against his tanned face.

'Everyone is welcome in Ballydrynawn. Even Jackeens!'

Emer hadn't heard the slang word for Dublin people in years but decided to assume he meant it kindly.

'And can Jackeens surf?'

'I've seen a few of them give it a go all right. And sure you're half Kerry, like, you'll be fine.'

She'd like to chat further, Emer decided, and it was a lot easier to talk to Rob when she didn't have to actually look at him but they had reached the Tigín now so she just smiled as he brought the van to a halt on the grass verge.

'I really appreciate the lift.'

'No problem at all. So, do you want to give the lessons a go?'

Emer paused. Her plan, such as it was, for the summer, had been to do as little as possible, certainly nothing that required an alarm clock, or a schedule, and definitely not anything that needed lessons. But Rob had looked pretty happy out there and, given that she had also promised herself she'd get fitter this summer, learning to surf would probably be a lot more fun than trying to access workout videos through the Tigín's dodgy broadband. There was one thing worrying her though.

'Do you not have to be, like seventeen and super fit?'

Rob gave that wide smile again and shook his head.

'Not at all. Can you swim?'

'Yeah.'

'Well then you can surf, trust me.'

He grabbed a card from a pile that had been wedged into the front of the dashboard.

'The number is on there and—'

But Rob was interrupted by the peal of a phone and broke off to fish it out of his pocket. It wasn't that Emer was looking, exactly, but the angle of the screen made it impossible to ignore the word 'Alison'.

Rob's voice dipped slightly as he answered.

'Howerya. Ah yeah, I know, I'm just on my way, couple of minutes. You too.'

Replacing the phone in his pocket he turned to Emer again.

'I have to head away, but I'll tell Alison you'll be down Saturday morning, all right?'

He started the engine and, not needing to be told twice, Emer opened the door of the van and jumped down. The rain had lightened to a drizzle and she waited for a moment, just to be polite, as the van pulled off, then made her way down the path towards the Tigín, taking a quick look at the card as she walked.

Breaking Waves Surf School

Owner Rob Lynch

Underneath it a phone number, and a note scribbled in pencil:

For bookings, contact Alison

Surfing, really? Shutting the door behind her, Emer pulled her wet top over her head and tried to remember where she'd packed her mother's decidedly less attractive but undeniably more useful Dunnes Stores anorak. It all sounded a bit too energetic for her, but she was going to have to live in this community for the summer so she'd probably be wise not to turn down the first offer of human contact she'd received. Without giving herself the chance to lose her nerve Emer peered at the card then unlocked her phone and fired off a quick WhatsApp. One beginner's lesson, just to be polite, and then she could crawl back to the sofa again.

Chapter Three

WEST KERRY

1922

'Would you ever take those two amadáns out from under my feet? They're driving me demented, God bless the pair of them.'

'I will indeed, Mam. I've darning to do, I'll bring it with me.'

'Good girl yourself, Annie, and there's no need to hurry back, either.'

Annie opened the door of the cabin and watched as her twin brothers scampered ahead of her, racing out into the sunshine. At almost three years of age, Emmet and James didn't need that much minding any more but a walk outside on a day like this was a treat, and her mother knew it. Annie didn't begrudge the time she spent caring for her family, to do so would have felt like flying in the face of God, given how grateful they all were that her mother's life had been spared. But there were times when the list of tasks she had to do felt unending, the rewards few, and the offer of a bit of fresh air was not one she was going to turn down.

It was almost fourteen years now since Eileen Thornton's illness and, although her subsequent recovery was still referred to by the neighbours as 'miraculous', there remained a sense among the rest of her family that Mammy needed to be minded. No matter how much Eileen protested that she was fine, she was always served first at dinner, given the cream off the milk with her tea and allowed to doze in front of the fire afterwards regardless of what chores remained to be done. The Thorntons' concern had only swelled a few years previously when a bad flu had swept the country. It hadn't, thankfully, reached their door but a number of the neighbours had passed away, many of them fine young men, and, if Annie and her father could have kept Eileen locked up in the bedroom for twelve months they would have. But she had come through unscathed and now spring was here, with its promise of longer and brighter days, it felt wonderful to be outdoors again, even with a large basket of mending hanging over her arm.

The boys scampered along the road, then leaped over a low wall, James landing on top of Emmet in a way that was almost, but not quite accidental. Annie frowned, aware a misplaced blow or word could easily turn their play-acting into a full-blown row, then urged them to race each other across the field. When they got to the end they looked back briefly then began to scramble up a steep slope, small stones skittering down in their wake. Annie sighed, then picked up her own pace as she followed them, the rough edges of her basket digging into her side. She could have done with an easier stroll, given the amount she was carrying, but the views would be glorious up on the cliffs today and the sense of space a blessed change from their cramped home.

★

There were seven of them in the cabin now: Annie's parents, her four siblings and her father's mother, Granny Cáit, who had moved in after being widowed two years previously. Two more bedrooms had been built to accommodate the growing family but they were small, cold lean-to rooms with dirt floors and damp ceilings and the family still tended to spend most of their time in the flag-stoned kitchen where the large open fire pumped out heat and smoke in seemingly equal measure. That fire was where they cooked, boiling potatoes and turnips grown in the field behind the house in a large iron cooking pot, and it was also where they gathered to eat, the adults perched on wooden stools and the children on the floor. It was a happy home, for the most part, but a very crowded one and there was always one more job waiting to be done. Eve did her fair share while Bríd, born two years after her mother's illness, was now old enough to help out herself but the twins had brought a level of chaos to proceedings that Annie couldn't have anticipated. Blond-haired and blue-eyed, they quickly grew from curious infants into boisterous toddlers, and when Annie heard a shout from behind her she turned with relief, knowing she'd appreciate a second pair of eyes today.

May drew alongside her, panting heavily.

'Your mother said you had gone out for a while.'

'It's good to see you.' Annie smiled. 'I didn't think you'd be free today, though? I thought you and your mother were going to town.'

'We were supposed to. But Daddy wasn't – he wasn't well, this morning.'

May didn't elaborate and Annie didn't pursue the issue. She didn't need to. Instead, she looked straight ahead for a moment to allow May time to compose herself and thought, not for the first time, how little she really had to complain about. Her own house might be crowded, and the family's tempers prone to fraying, especially since her grandmother had taken up residence, but it was for the most part a place of love and refuge for them all. The same, sadly, could not be said for the neglected cottage occupied by May's family on the far side of Lynch's farm. May had twelve siblings still living, but most had moved away as soon as they were able and there were now just five of them remaining alongside her parents in two tumbledown rooms. May shared a bed in the kitchen with her younger brother and sister while the bedroom was occupied by her father, an ill-tempered man who brewed and sold poitín and was known to be his own best customer, and her tiny, thin mother whose habit of wearing a shawl pulled across her face was never fully able to hide the result of that ill temper. Annie also had her suspicions that May's mother wasn't the only family member who bore the brunt of her father's moods and indeed her friend seemed to be limping this morning. It wasn't proper to pry into the affairs of another man's family, but Annie could spare her friend a long walk if she wasn't feeling up to it, so she swapped the weight of the basket from one hip to another with an exaggerated sigh.

'I don't know about you, May, but I need a rest. Will you sit with me for a while? I'd certainly appreciate the company.'

Her friend flashed her a grateful look as they reached

the top of the hill and they both sank down onto the grass, gathering their heavy skirts under them as protection. Having liberated branches from a tree earlier in their journey the twins began a rambunctious game of soldiers and Annie pretended not to hear Emmet, the older of the two by twenty minutes, refer to his brother as a 'dirty Irregular'. Trouble had been raging throughout the country for months, a brutal fight which set family against family and was the cause of much anguish to people like Annie's father who had thought that the signing of a treaty in London and the establishment of the Irish Free State would bring peace to a land that had seen so much turmoil since the Rising in Dublin six years before. But although Annie's father and grandmother spent many an evening discussing Ireland's right to become a self-governing nation, she herself kept at a distance from the topic. It was difficult to care about who held power above in Dublin, she told her mother, while there were mounds of potatoes to be peeled and buckets of washing to be dried here in Ballydrynawn. The truth, however, was a little more complicated.

The sea breeze ruffled her hair and Annie sat up a little straighter, her gaze drifting towards the navy, foam-tipped waves visible just beyond the cliff edge. Oh she was busy, right enough, but that wasn't the real reason she shut her ears to political debate or news of vicious attacks, no matter what side they came from. In reality, Annie was far more interested in what lay on the other side of that ocean than any local matter. Almost every family in Ballydrynawn had someone in America now and Annie loved hearing the neighbours talk about their letters home, tales of buildings that stretched into the clouds and plates so crammed with food a grown man couldn't clear them. What use was there in bickering over a few muddy fields, she thought to herself, when there were railways stretching all the way across the United States and anyone with a few dollars in their pockets could hop aboard and find adventure?

Her thoughts had taken her further away than she had expected and Annie exhaled, then redirected her gaze towards May, afraid her silence would be perceived as rude. But her friend didn't seem to have noticed her distraction and had instead turned her head to search the expanse of countryside behind them. After another moment Annie opened her basket and took out a pile of darning, dipping her head to thread the needle before smoothing a blouse of her mother's out on her lap.

'Are you looking for someone?'

'Oh, no, not really.'

May coloured slightly.

'It's just Seánie Lynch said he might be working the upper field this morning but I don't see him.'

Annie bit off an inch of thread to hide her grin.

''Tis almost noon, Seánie's mammy will have his dinner on the table for him by now.'

May nodded, either not noticing or refusing to acknowledge the amusement in her friend's tone.

'He may well have his work completed true enough. 'Twas yesterday I met him going back the road and he said he'd be out early today if the weather held.'

Annie sewed, shrugged, smiled.

'Oh he's a great worker right enough, when the weather holds.'

This time May couldn't ignore her friend's caustic tone.

'You've a sharp tongue on you today!'

'Arrah, I'm only teasing you.'

Finishing the sleeve, Annie replaced the blouse in the basket and dug out a piece of grey wool that was by now more hole than sock. The truth was, she wasn't overly fond of Seánie Lynch, the only son of a widow whose farm separated May's home from her own. Seánie's father had died of influenza shortly before he was born and his mother had raised him to be 'man of the house', secure in the knowledge that unlike most of his peers he would inherit the farm in its entirety and not have to divide it between siblings. Now a tall, red-faced man in his early twenties, Seánie had not bothered to finish his schooling but didn't let lack of education – or indeed, Annie sometimes mused, intellect – prevent him from having strong opinions on every subject and an even stronger tendency to take offence. May, however, seemed to find him fascinating and blossomed like a flower if he so much as threw a word in her direction as he walked past.

At first, Annie had been amused by her friend's infatuation but was now beginning to find it concerning. Most of the families in the area, the Thorntons included, were small subsistence farmers, using the land they rented to grow vegetables for their own use and rear a goat for milk, and a pig if they could afford it. Seánie's father, however, had owned the land his family farmed and his son now was in possession of a herd of cattle as well as other livestock. When Seán senior had died, the local men had followed tradition and gathered around to help his young widow manage her land. Now Seánie was grown, though, he seemed rarely inclined to return the favour, always finding himself otherwise engaged when a neighbour's wall needed to be mended or a harvest gathered in the face of an imminent storm.

Seánie had a rough tongue on him too and a brutish way of dealing with his livestock and Annie worried he may not be much kinder to any woman he took to live alongside his mother in their fine, stone-built farmhouse. May was a tiny person who had barely grown since they had attended the national school together and her slim waist, fine features and long dark hair had attracted the attention of many young men in the village but so far she had refused to give any of them a second glance, preferring to take long solitary evening walks along the road in the hope of bumping into her loud-voiced neighbour. Annie feared her interest in Seánie lay more in her desire to leave the poisonous atmosphere in her own home, rather than in any real affection for the man himself, but thinking about Seánie seemed to please May and God knows, Annie often thought, she could do with some happiness. So today Annie simply bent her head to her work and allowed her petite, pretty friend to chatter about Seánie and his ambition to double his herd in the coming years.

Sock mended to the best of her ability she reached into the basket again and her fingers brushed against the slices of bread she had tossed inside before leaving the house. The boys must surely be getting hungry, she realised, and turned her head to call them. And then Annie's heart gave a double beat as she realised she could only see one blond head playing in the tall grass. She scrambled to her feet, her work falling unheeded to the ground, and felt one blissful moment of relief when she spotted the second head bobbing around fifty yards away. That relief soon turned to horror, however, when Annie saw that her little brother was heading straight for the cliff edge, and the sharp drop onto the beach below.

'Emmet!'

Flinging instructions at her friend to mind the other twin, Annie took off at a run, but she was hampered by her long skirts and felt her panic bubble over as she stumbled across the grass, watching helplessly as Emmet trotted closer and closer to danger. Then, just as she was about to lose hope of ever catching him in time, the child stopped, raised his head and began to waddle with determination, that would have been funny in any other circumstances, back across the field. Still running, Annie had almost caught up with him before she noticed what had captured his attention. Emmet had made his way to the Fairy Tree and by the time Annie reached his side had already pulled something off one of the lower branches.

'You little divil you!'

Annie swept her brother into her arms and buried her face in his hair, tears and perspiration dampening the fair curls.

'No!'

The little boy pulled away and stared at her crossly.

'Mine!'

He raised his hand to his mouth and began to chew vigorously on whatever he had liberated from the tree's thick branches. Almost laughing now with a mixture of relief and exasperation Annie placed him back on the ground, tugged his hand away and unfolded his fingers to rescue whatever was inside. The scrap of paper was so yellowed and tattered it was almost illegible but then as she peered closer she realised with a sobering jolt that she was looking at her own mother's slanted handwriting. She squinted, moving the paper around until she could make out a few words.

'... *my dear ones ... that I live ... see them grow...*'

She was already flushed with exertion but Annie's face grew even redder as the thought dawned on her that she was reading her mother's innermost thoughts, written down and obviously placed on the tree some months before. This was worse than reading a diary, even; it was like overhearing a prayer, a plea to the heavens that Eileen Thornton be granted good health to look after her family. As May reached her side, James clutched in her arms, Annie scrunched the paper up in her hand, caring less about saving the document than about protecting her mother's privacy.

'He's a demon, that one!'

May placed James on the grass while Emmet reached for a branch and began to tug at it, as if eager to restart the earlier war. But before they could do any more damage to the tree, or indeed the tokens that had been tied to it, Annie grabbed both of her brothers around the waist and dragged them backwards, not stopping until she reached a smooth patch of grass a safe distance away. Emmet's lower lip began to tremble but before the tears could fully take hold his attention was caught by a clump of daisies and he began to tug them from the earth instead, joined within seconds by his brother who added to the fun by smearing mud all over his face and hands. Finally satisfied they would now come to no harm the two girls sank down beside them to catch their breath.

'I was sure it was into the water he was headed!'

May brushed her hair away from her forehead.

'The Fairy Tree was keeping an eye on him today for sure.'

She reached down to pluck her own handful of daisies and began to thread them together as Annie stared at her.

'You don't really believe in all that rubbish, do you?'

But her friend just shrugged.

'And why wouldn't I? There's smarter people than me has faith in the Fairy Tree. You've left messages on it yourself in your time, Annie Thornton!'

The girls fell silent for a moment, remembering a morning long ago, and a daughter's frantic prayer for her mother. But they had been children then, Annie thought, little children who believed in magic. She was a grown woman now, old enough to know that her mother had been saved by a combination of the doctor's skill and her own good fortune and that her recovery had had nothing to do with a scrap of handkerchief attached to a bush. She turned to May with a snort.

'That's only an oul piseog, surely you don't believe...'

But her friend didn't look at her. Instead, head bent, she worked deftly on the daisies until she had completed a small, neat chain, then rose and walked back to the hawthorn, reaching up to hang it on an uppermost branch, far away from destructive little fingers.

She did believe in it, Annie realised. May did have faith in the power of the tree and, given their earlier conversation, it was not difficult to guess what she was wishing for.

May finished arranging the daisies and stood back from the tree for a moment to admire her handiwork, but just as she did so the day suddenly darkened. A cloud had passed over the sun and seconds later a gust of wind blew directly through the meadow, causing the twins to look up from the game and James, the smaller of the two, to whimper. Annie reached over to comfort him but as she did so she heard a sharp exhalation and turned to see May reach up, attempting but unable to stop the wind from lifting the flowers from the tree and carrying them away in the direction of the grey foaming ocean.

'Bad luck of the year go with them!'

She made a brave attempt to smile but as she turned and made her way back to the group, Annie could see that her friend was fighting back tears. And then, just as soon as it had arrived, the cloud rolled away again, illuminating the meadow in sharp sunlight once more. But the joy had gone from the day now and when May announced it was time to leave Annie didn't argue, just handed her brothers the snack of bread to shorten the road towards home.

Chapter Four

WEST KERRY

2022

A massive tour bus, its windows almost completely obscured by camera-wielding tourists, appeared on the road ahead of her and Emer found herself holding her breath as she drove past, as if by doing so she could suck the car in a little too. The Conor Pass was one of the most scenic routes in the country but its narrow roads made circumnavigation a challenge, even for drivers who weren't operating on minimal sleep and driving a manual for the first time in years. The road ahead finally clear again, Emer exhaled then watched in the rear-view mirror as the coach pulled over to discharge its passengers. They had a treat in store, the earlier rain had disappeared leaving a cool but clear afternoon and with the sun glinting off the navy lakes the view down into the velvet valley would be spectacular. Right now, however, the only view Emer wanted was the one from under her duvet.

After she had returned from her walk, and the unexpected encounter with the surfer, it had taken all of her strength not to climb into bed there and then, but Emer knew from experience it was best to tackle jet lag by working with the time zone you were in, so she'd set off for the nearest town instead to do some shopping and keep herself generally occupied until a more respectable time to hit the hay. That was what this holiday was about, after all. Or break, or time out, or whatever her therapist wanted to call it. Emer had come to Ireland to rest and recuperate and hopefully recover some of the joy in life she seemed to have misplaced sometime over the last two years.

Haven't you a great life! Tell us, have you met many film stars? Will you smuggle me over in your suitcase next time...?

Emer hadn't kept in touch with many people from school but the odd time they connected online their comments all tended to follow a similar pattern. And sure, when viewed through the lens of her mother's Facebook updates, she did seem to have it made. She was a film director, based in Los Angeles – OK, so she worked on TV commercials rather than actual features but it was still good going for someone whose first encounter with the silver screen had been in a south Dublin shopping centre. It wasn't a life that allowed for anything as indulgent as 'evenings off' or 'weekends', let alone proper vacations, but in the ten years since graduating from college she had learned not to care about that, allowing her work to merge with her social life until there was no boundary at all between the two. Until spring 2020 had arrived, and with it the Covid 19 pandemic, the thirtieth birthday present Emer Molloy definitely hadn't asked the universe for.

During the first lockdown, like the rest of the world Emer tried to persuade herself she'd enjoy a bit of downtime but a month spent redecorating her studio apartment, burning banana bread and failing to learn Duolingo Spanish had left her climbing the freshly painted walls. And even when the pandemic restrictions eased just enough to allow her to return to work, life hadn't returned to anything approaching normal. There was no real fun to be found on set any more, no communal meals or post-deadline beers, and Emer even had to go on her treasured hikes alone, scurrying to the other side of the path if she came within breathing distance of another human being.

It was a peanut butter commercial that finally broke her. After a fourteen-hour day, mostly spent trying to make three actors look as if they weren't standing a full two metres apart from one other, Emer had been just about to call action on the final shot when a cloud arrived to block out the sun and brought with it torrential rain. Cast, crew and the former basketball star who'd been persuaded into a seven-foot-high squashy peanut costume had all looked on in horror as their director screamed at the sky, cursed the weather app on her phone then burst into loud, uncontrollable tears. Thankfully the client hadn't been on set that day but the cameraman, a Hollywood veteran, had taken Emer aside and tapped his therapist's email address into her phone.

'Covid Burnout' had been the official diagnosis and seeing it written down had been weirdly reassuring. If something had a name, Emer assumed, then surely it could be easily fixed. But towards the end of her six weeks of counselling the therapist, whose bangles could be heard jangling even over a dodgy Zoom connection, had issued an unexpected prescription. Emer, she felt, needed a complete change of scene. Had she ever thought about going back to Ireland for a while? The fact that the very thought of her mother's cooking made a sob well up inside her seemed to answer that question and so, for the first time in her working life, Emer finished one contract and didn't start another, sublet her apartment and booked a flight home. But home had decided to take a holiday too so now here she was, in a part of Ireland so beautiful people flew in from all over the world to see it, utterly free of all responsibility and utterly alone.

Her ears popped as she reached sea level and Emer swallowed, waiting for the fuzziness in her head to recede. Suddenly uncertain of which road to take next she reached across for her phone, a movement which only took a split second, or so she thought, and then the sound of a horn blared through the windscreen and she looked up to see another huge tour bus travelling at speed towards her.

'Jesus!'

Wrenching the wheel to the left, she felt the car wobble then veer dangerously close to the ditch as the tour bus sailed past. Shaking now, but too afraid of causing an accident to stop in the middle of the road, she drove on for a few more metres then spotted with relief a sign for a 'viewing area' just ahead. Heart racing, she brought the car to a shuddering halt and then sat motionless, the blood pumping so loudly through her body she could feel it thrum in her ears.

To hell with them anyway, she thought suddenly, anger replacing the tears that had threatened to overwhelm her. To hell with Maura, and George, and most of all Niall, still locked into the role of little brother and inviting his mammy over to hold his hand when he was on the cusp of becoming a father himself. Damn them all for not being here for her, the one time she needed them, for fecking off to the other side of the world and leaving her alone.

Then a movement on the car caught her eye, and Emer looked up to see an enormous seagull, with what looked like an entire burger gripped tight in his beak. Perched on the bonnet he looked at her, cocked his huge head to one side for a moment then flapped lazily away, heading for the sea. The viewing area, Emer saw now, had been perfectly positioned to provide a glorious view of the Atlantic Ocean which stretched out from here for miles, the water a blueish purple this afternoon, an island outlined in navy further out in the bay. Emer rubbed her eyes. She should, she supposed, get a blast of fresh air before attempting to drive home again. Unclipping her seatbelt, she hauled herself out of the car and then—

'Oh. Oh wow...'

Back in LA, her therapist had recommended online yoga classes but although Emer had given them a half-hearted go she'd never quite managed to get the hang of the whole deep-breathing thing. Here, however, it was simply instinctual to straighten her shoulders and inhale a lungful of air so crisp it felt like it was spring cleaning her entire circulatory system. She took another breath, and then another and then Emer found herself coming to a decision. OK, this wasn't the summer she had planned, but that didn't mean she couldn't have fun, did it? There was an awful lot to look forward to down here: a daily swim, a bag of chips to warm her hands afterwards, that incomparable smell of sand and seaweed baked into the interior of the car. And there was magic in West Kerry too, it was a place where even the sensible Maura saluted the magpies that landed in the tree outside the kitchen window and announced, if she heard a lump of coal fall in the grate, that a stranger was going to call.

Poor Maura. As Emer's head cleared it dawned on her that she was being unfair to her parents. It was a bit much, really, to expect them to know exactly what she needed from them when she had been keeping them at arm's length for years. It was a long time since they had even considered offering her help because it was longer still since she had asked for it so maybe, she thought as she stretched her arms high above her head, feeling the tension in her shoulders ease and disappear, maybe being in Kerry, even on her own, would give her frazzled brain a chance to heal. This glorious air might even kick-start her own creativity too, help her light a fire under that screenplay she'd been threatening to write for years.

Good humour almost totally restored, she turned back to her car and then realised this wasn't the first time she had been in this very clearing. The picnic tables were new, certainly, and someone had built a sturdy wooden rail at the edge of the car park to make sure eager tourists didn't selfie themselves over the edge, but she had been here before, all right, many years ago in the days when health and safety was taken a lot less seriously, and a sudden memory washed over her of holding tight to her mother's hand as they stared out to sea.

And if this was the place she was thinking of... Curiosity combined with the bracing air had caused her weariness to lift a little and Emer turned her back to the water then made her way to the far edge of the clearing, where an area of scrubland rose sharply from the road. The fence ended where the hill began, and of course it did, Emer thought, because Maura always said no local would ever fence off the path to the Fairy Tree.

She took one quick look back at the car to make sure she

had parked it safely then stepped up onto a large boulder and began to climb. The Fairy Tree. There was no signpost, of course, there was no need for one because the tree wasn't really a tourist attraction; in fact, if it wasn't for Maura the Molloys wouldn't have known about it at all. But Maura had brought the children up here for a visit every year when they were small.

'You don't actually believe in fairies, do you, Mam?' Emer had asked her mother one summer, the year after other childhood beliefs had been poked and discovered to be full of holes.

'The question is, do they believe in me?' had been the response.

Emer was breathing more quickly now – the climb was steeper than she had remembered, her limbs stiff after days of travel, and she kept close to the left-hand side, aware, despite the tall boulders and hedgerow that lined the path, of the sheer drop on the other side. She took three more steps then rounded a corner and stopped, placing her hands in the small of her back to ease her knotted muscles. And there it was, a couple hundred metres away across the wide field. The Fairy Tree. A bush really, a squat hawthorn bush which had been standing on this ground for more than a hundred years, standing guard over the cliffs and the sheer drop below. People used to leave offerings on its branches, Emer remembered now, prayers or little mementoes, and when they were younger, despite their obvious scepticism, Maura would never allow her or Niall to make fun of anything they saw hanging there. She took another step forward then stopped when she saw movement from the far side of the field. The woman was wearing a moss-green coat, which was why Emer hadn't noticed her at first, and its large hood obscured her features.

Was it a witch? As soon as the word entered Emer's head she banished it – where on earth had such a foolish, childish question come from? It was the jet lag, that was all, she needed a proper night's sleep. And then the woman raised her hands to her face and it became obvious that she was crying, her shoulders shaking under her thick coat. Not a witch then but a human being, and one who appeared to be in complete despair.

A gull shrieked and Emer jumped, then turned and strode back around the corner and out of sight of the tree. Not because she was unnerved, she told herself firmly, but just to give the woman, who was clearly distraught, some privacy. There was a boulder jutting out from the side of the track and Emer sat down on it, gathering her thoughts. She didn't want to go back to the car, it would be foolish to climb all this way and not actually visit the bloody tree, but she didn't want to disturb the poor woman either, so she'd wait until she was finished before finishing the climb herself.

But one minute's wait turned to two, and then five and the woman still didn't appear on the path. Emer was growing cold now, and stiff, and feeling a little like the frog in the song, neither halfway up nor down. And maybe sitting here had been the wrong thing to do, anyway, she thought to herself; maybe the woman would get a fright when she began her descent and found Emer perched on the path like some sort of insane busybody. She stretched, then coughed loudly and, making as much noise as possible, began to climb again, mindful of the need to alert the woman to her presence and save both of them unnecessary embarrassment.

But when she turned the corner there was nobody there. Emer stood stock-still, taking in the field, the tree, the cliffs beyond it. The cliffs beyond it... Her heart thudded as she jogged across the open space, fearing what she might see when she got to the edge, but there was no sign of any disturbance there and, when she bent carefully forward and looked out, nothing below other than calm waves washing against the rocks.

She took a shaky breath then returned to the tree, searching for clues as to where the woman might have gone. But what exactly was she expecting to find? It was just a bush, a rather tattered bush, its branches weathered yet still sturdy, rooted in a muddy field that was lined on two sides by large, thick hedges. She must have missed the woman, that was it, she must have walked past her on the path when she was looking in the other direction. But, as Emer left the clearing and began the climb down to the car park, she knew, in her heart of hearts, that couldn't have been the case. The path was simply too narrow, no one could have got past her without being seen. And she hadn't imagined the woman either, she was sure of it, she could still see her now, head bent, utterly lost in her own misery.

It was only when Emer reached her car and climbed inside that another element of the puzzle revealed itself. Hers was the only vehicle in the lay-by, just as it had been when she had arrived. Emer didn't believe in witches, or fairies, or magic bloody hawthorn bushes but there was no denying it. Whoever had been up on those cliffs had, quite simply, come from nowhere and then disappeared.

Chapter Five

KERRY

1923

It rained the morning of the wedding, thick sheets of it falling horizontally across the mountains and hiding the bay from view. Everywhere was grey, and sodden, and Annie's heart broke for May who had always dreamed that her route to the church on her wedding day would be lined by well-wishing neighbours, waving her towards her future.

Instead, she and the young bride had to scurry along the lanes, heads bent, sticking close to the hedgerows for protection, a sack thrown over May's head and shoulders to protect her new blouse from the downpour. May had sewn the blouse herself, saving her egg money to buy lace for the collar and unpicking her own mother's yellowing bridal outfit to rescue tiny seed pearls. She had made a two-piece costume as well but had changed her mind about wearing it a fortnight before the ceremony and asked Annie, in a stiff, almost offhand way, if she could borrow her good red skirt instead. Annie had agreed without question, and if the thought had crossed her mind that she was a good four inches taller than her friend and her skirt far roomier at the waist than May's, she decided now was not the moment to voice it.

It should have been May's parents walking her to the church, of course, or one of her siblings. But her mother would, Annie guessed, have enough to do ensuring her father turned up to the ceremony on time. Meanwhile, May's brothers and sisters were all working in England and although some of them had sent letters of congratulations, none had included a wedding gift – the implication being that she would not need their support now she was to be a Lynch of Ballydrynawn. So it had been left to Annie and her own mother to fuss over May that morning, to tie ribbons in her long dark curling hair and convince her that to take a sup of water wouldn't break her fast before mass. And now it was Annie alone who walked with her friend down the stony boreen that led to the village, and the church, and her new life as Mrs Seánie Lynch, mistress of the finest house for five miles or more.

But despite the weather, the lack of familial support and May's pale complexion, tinged almost green now in the grey morning light, the young bride's eyes were shining, pure happiness beaming out of her just as it had been on the night she called to Annie's house and told her she was to be wed. May had always been a pretty girl, the prettiest in the parish, but she had been beautiful that night, her head held high and her back straightened by the knowledge that she was to marry Seánie and her future was secure.

And even though it was known that Seánie's mother didn't approve of the match, had taken to her bed the day the engagement was announced and was said to be still too unwell to attend today's ceremony, and even though Seánie's first cousin Joseph had been heard in the village making a caustic remark about how easy it was to trap a foolish man, and even though Seánie himself had developed the habit of striding ahead of May on the rare evenings they walked out together, leaving the young woman scurrying three or four steps behind, none of these things had dimmed the light in those blue eyes and they were still shining now as the clouds finally parted and a single ray of sunshine pierced the grey morning. The church lay at the bottom of the hill and Annie paused for a moment at the top to give May, who appeared a little breathless, time to compose herself. To their right, the ocean was almost obscured by mist but the scent of fresh seaweed was as good as a tonic and Annie looked in its direction, then smiled at her friend.

'It looks like the rain might clear.'

May nodded.

'I prayed it would be fine, last night. I wanted to visit the tree, too but...'

She didn't finish the sentence and Annie looked at her curiously. Most of the people in the Ballydrynawn had a healthy respect for the Fairy Tree but May's faith in its ability to grant wishes was as firm as it had been when they were little girls. In fact, although it would possibly be blasphemy to voice the thought, Annie had a fair idea that May had more faith in that tree than in the church located less than two hundred yards from where they were standing.

'And what stopped you?'

May addressed her answer to the rosary beads she was carrying in her right hand.

'Seánie – he doesn't think it's fitting for women to be roaming the roads alone.'

'Roaming the roads?' Annie snorted. 'A walk across to the Fairy Tree is hardly "the roads" – and anyway, that tree in on Lynch land and you'll be a Lynch yourself in a couple of hours.'

May looked up at her sharply.

'Do you know, I hadn't thought of it like that at all. But Seánie – well, he was just looking after me, that's all. He knows I get... tired easily these days.'

'Hmm.'

Such was Annie's love for her friend and her desire to see her happy, she really wanted to believe in this new caring Seánie Lynch but she couldn't help thinking the man's reluctance to have his betrothed seen in public was less to do with worry about her welfare and more with his desire to limit the number of people who spotted the gentle swelling beneath her skirts, which was becoming more apparent by the day. But until May herself brought up the matter Annie didn't feel as if she could make reference to it so instead she just listened as the young woman continued.

'Besides, no one really owns the Fairy Tree.'

Annie grinned.

'I'm not sure old Mrs Lynch would agree with you!'

May giggled, then clapped her hands to her mouth as if to restrain her mirth.

'She's not well, the poor woman. I hope she's recovered enough to join us for the wedding breakfast.'

'I'm sure she will have.'

Annie refrained from mentioning the fact that she, along with her mother and sisters, had spent several weeks preparing food for the same feast and that when they had carried it over to the Lynches' the night before, Seánie's mother had been sufficiently recovered to leave her sick bed and comment on the fact that the fruit cake looked dry, and a little sunken in the middle. She had also attempted to begin a conversation about May's father's inability to provide a dowry for the new bride but Eileen had cut her off, claiming she had to rush home to look after her small children. Annie had almost laughed, thinking of the 'small children' who were at that very moment nestled on their father's lap listening to a story, but her smile soon faded as she remembered that from the following day onwards May would not be able to leave this house nor turn her back on this bitter woman's caustic comments ever again.

But surely, she thought to herself now as she looked at the joy on her friend's face and the pearls on her collar, shining now in the weak morning sun, surely no one could fail to love May, not even the sour Mrs Lynch or her red-faced, boorish son. And although she herself didn't believe in the Fairy Tree, not to any great extent at least, Annie sent a silent prayer in its direction, asking it to watch over this young dear hopeful woman.

And then the clouds rolled back and the sun disappeared again.

'You'll have another slice of currant cake?'

'Oh, it wouldn't be polite to refuse, I suppose.'

You've already had two slices' worth of politeness, Annie thought but didn't say as she handed the plate to May's brand-new mother-in-law who was sitting in a high-backed armchair in the best position in the room, close enough to the fire to enjoy its warmth but still within listening distance of all the important conversations. That seat should have been Seánie's, or even May's, but Annie hadn't seen the groom since the wedding ceremony ended and, come to think of it, hadn't seen the bride for a good while either.

Using the plate of cake as an excuse she took another turn around the crowded kitchen but May wasn't sitting with the group of neighbours on the far side of the hearth, nor was she attending to her father who was hovering near the window, ill at ease in a borrowed suit but still, Annie saw with relief, relatively sober.

Having been up since dawn attending to the bride, she herself was starving now so, after making sure everyone within reach had been looked after, she moved across to the table and filled her own platter with eggs, potatoes and ham from the pig Seánie had finally been persuaded to kill the week before. And then Annie felt a small draught on the back of her neck and looked over to see May creep in through the back door, her pallor more pronounced than ever. Sensing the young woman didn't want to be the centre of attention just at that moment, she made her way over to her but kept her voice low.

'You must be exhausted, alannah, sit down now and have a bite to eat.'

May couldn't suppress a shudder and closed her eyes for longer than a blink.

'I couldn't, no. Maybe later...'

'You have to eat.'

Annie grasped the bride firmly by the elbow and steered her towards an empty stool at the far end of the room, depositing her on it before leaving and returning moments later with food and a fresh cup of tea.

'I know you think you can't face eating but you'll feel much better if you do. My mother was the exact same way with Emmet and James.'

May shot her a fearful look but Annie just shook her head gently.

'And what matter? Aren't you a married woman now, darling? There's nothing to be worried about. Sit down there and rest, you'll start to feel better soon.'

May hesitated then offered her a watery smile.

'I hope so. I thought I was going to faint in the church this morning. It was only fear of what the priest would say kept me upright.'

She took a tiny bite of potato and, after a moment, a slightly larger one.

'Do you think the day went well?'

Annie looked around the room, foggy now with pipe and turf smoke. Ned Gorman had taken out his fiddle and was playing a slow air and it was clear from the way her own sister Eve was sizing up the other guests that he would shortly be asked for a jig or a hornpipe. Meanwhile most of the food had been eaten but there was still plenty of bread and cake left aside for late-comers as well as jugs of beer and bottles of whiskey, although these were standing, not on the table but on the floor by the mother of the groom who was taking every opportunity she could get to remind the gathering that it was her largesse they had to thank for the celebration.

But May, Annie decided, did not need that amount of detail.

'It couldn't have gone better! Even her ladyship has little to find fault with.'

The two young women looked across at Mrs Lynch who was now being persuaded by Annie's father to take a glass of whiskey herself 'for medicinal purposes'. May giggled, and the sound was so delightfully childlike Annie couldn't stop herself from reaching out and touching her hand.

'This is your home now, your table. I hope you'll be happy here. You – and your family.'

A spot of colour had returned to May's face and she took a sip of tea then looked Annie straight in the eye for the first time in what seemed like a long time.

'Annie, I have to ask you. Do you think it's normal if—'

But before she could continue the back door swung open again and the kitchen became even more crowded as a group of men strode into the room, a braying Seánie at its centre. Annie recognised most of the newcomers, one was a cousin of the fiddler, another was Phelim Murphy, a gormless but harmless oul divil who made his living working as a labourer on the local farms. And then she caught sight of a head of dark curly hair and felt her smile fade.

Colm O'Flaherty had started school the same year as she had but his ambition and razor-sharp intellect had seen him finish a year early, aged just eleven but top of the class in every subject. He had left the family farm then, and moved to town to live with his aunt and uncle and attend the Christian Brothers' secondary school. But Colm's Uncle Pat, a publican by trade, was also known to be heavily involved with the Republican Army and his nephew, it was said, had learned far more under his roof than Euclid and how to pull a pint of porter. It was no surprise to Annie that Colm had not been at the wedding service, the church was vocally opposed to the anti-Treaty-ites and Canon Moroney wouldn't think twice about refusing communion to any man he suspected of being a follower of Mr De Valera. But it was just like Seánie, she thought bitterly, while not principled nor indeed brave enough to take a stand on the issue himself, to be in awe of the likes of Colm and invite him to the wedding breakfast, regardless of how others at the gathering might feel. There had been little talk of politics so far this afternoon. Some of the neighbours, like Annie's own father, still believed that Mr Collins' Treaty had been the country's best chance of achieving lasting peace while others shared the O'Flahertys' viewpoint that remaining within the British Empire, albeit as a 'Free State', was too large a price to pay for an end to the conflict. Despite this, and out of respect to the bride, the chat that afternoon had remained on neutral subjects – the weather, the floweriness of the spuds, whether Kerry would take part in the football championships this year. The arrival of Colm O'Flaherty, however, seemed to send a silent signal to the rest of the room, and many of the older couples, Annie's parents among them, gathered their belongings and headed for the door, pausing only to shake Mrs Lynch's hand and congratulate her on a wonderful celebration.

The groom himself was unperturbed by the reaction, making use of the exodus to gather stools for the new arrivals and encouraging them to make themselves at home. As Colm warmed his hands by the fire, Annie stole a closer look at her former classmate. The good-looking child had grown to be a handsome man with a prominent nose and tanned features but he was thinner than would be usual for a man of his height and build and there was a watchfulness about him that marked him out from his farming companions.

'Ye'll have a drink! Ye will, surely.'

Answering his own question, Seánie pushed his way over to the table, picked up glasses and a jug of ale then distributed them amongst the newcomers, urging them once again to make themselves comfortable before looking around with a frown.

'May? Jesus Christ, woman, where are you? These men will think their throats have been slit.'

With a start, May hopped up from her seat and hurried over to the table but the length of the day had caught up with her and exhaustion caused her hand to shake as she cut the bread, the knife slipping sideways and piercing her skin. As she sucked the blood from her finger, her face flushed with embarrassment, and her new husband glared at her.

'A man can't even ask for a bite to eat on his own wedding day.'

'I'll help.'

Annie made her own way over to the table, furious at the way her friend was being spoken to but aware, given Seánie's bloodshot eyes, that the drink in his hand was far from his first and that to tackle him now would be to risk inflaming the situation. So, she helped her friend cut bread and pour beer and carried the plates over to the men who were now sitting in a circle, Phelim Murphy shuffling a deck of cards.

'Thank you.'

Colm's voice as he accepted the food was low but clear and Annie could tell by looking at him that he hadn't had half as much to drink as Seánie, or at the very least could hold it a lot better. As he began to tear apart the bread she noticed that although his hands were clean his nails were broken and ingrained with dirt and that he was falling on the food as if he hadn't eaten properly in a long time. A Free State soldier had been shot in the town a couple of weeks before and although no one had been arrested, it was said the men responsible had been on the run ever since, sleeping outdoors and depending on safe houses for food and water. She shivered, then turned away before he could notice her reaction.

Night was setting in now and the fiddler and the dancers, led by Annie's sister Eve had moved outside and were attempting a half-set on a patch of scrub grass in front of the kitchen window. Having made sure all their glasses were full, Annie moved away from the men and settled herself on the arm of a chair on the far side of the fire to Mrs Lynch, nodding at May to take the seat. Her intention was to support her friend by keeping a close eye on Seánie and his cronies but the early start combined with smoke from the fire soon caused her eyelids to droop and within moments both she and May were leaning against each other, drowsy, drifting, and starting to dream.

'And am I not to taste a bite of cake on my own wedding day?'

'I'm sorry!'

Annie almost tumbled to the ground as May shot up off the seat again and darted towards the table, but she was still half asleep and clumsy and dropped the remaining cake onto the flag-stoned floor. Embarrassed, she sank to her knees, shoved the slices back on the plate again and then hovered for a moment as if unsure what to do before rising and beginning, hesitantly, to offer it around.

Her husband rose to his feet and roared.

'By Jesus, woman, you might have been reared in a pigsty but you won't serve guests dirty food in my house!'

'Reared in a pigsty, what! Reared in a pigsty by Dad.'

Phelim Murphy's broad face creased into a foolish smile and beside him, Seánie's second cousin Jack, who had always been in thrall to his older and wealthier relative, let out a scornful cackle. Annie looked around the room for support but the only other woman present now was Mrs Lynch, and she appeared to be sound asleep, her empty glass still clasped tight in her fist. Annie's silence and May's stricken face seemed only to irritate Seánie more because he took a step closer to his bride, spittle falling on her face as he continued his barracking.

'I'd a right to send you back to the barn you came from, you dirty bitch.'

May was mortified now, tears swelling in her eyes as she stood stock-still in the middle of the floor, the plate still gripped tightly in her hand, incapable of movement or, it appeared, any independent thought. And then Colm O'Flaherty stood up and gently took it from her.

'That'll do me no harm. I've been sleeping in ditches this past week, I've had far worse to eat than food off a clean floor. And congratulations on your marriage, Mrs Lynch.'

The last words were said mildly enough but a slight toss of Colm's head directed them at Seánie, who sat back heavily on his stool, turned his back on his new wife and addressed himself to the card game again. But Annie had caught a glimpse of the fury in his eyes and knew that any reprieve for her friend would be a brief one. The two women went back to their chairs but there was to be no dozing now, no contentment; instead they sat as close to each other as they could without touching, their backs poker straight, staring into the centre of the room, afraid to speak or make any movement that might further anger the groom.

It was Colm's turn to deal the cards this time and Annie prayed Seánie would get a good hand, anything to lighten the tension that was as thick as turf smoke in the too-warm room but it was immediately clear from the look on his face that the game was not going his way. Colm won the first hand, Tadhg Daly the next, but it was when Phelim, a sleepy smile on his doughy face, relieved Seánie of the remainder of his coins that the host's temper finally boiled over.

'You cheating bastard.'

Annie didn't dare to look at her friend but could feel May stiffen in the seat behind her. On the far side of the fireplace Mrs Lynch jerked, but kept her eyes shut tight.

'I'm no cheat!'

Phelim's voice was thick with drink but his retort was mild, and he smiled lazily at the company.

''Tis only a run of bad luck, nothing to do with me.'

'You'd a card hidden!'

Seánie's stool toppled over as he sprang from his seat and Annie could feel May flinch as Phelim, too, rose to his feet. Phelim was a good head taller than Seánie but his sloping shoulders made him appear off balance and the smaller man rocked forward and back on the balls of his feet, as if deciding whether or not to land a blow.

And then Colm O'Flaherty rose too and put a hand on Seánie's shoulder.

'It was a fair hand. I dealt those cards and it was a fair hand.'

Seánie's mouth opened and closed but such was Colm's presence, and yes, Annie thought, the intimidation he was able to convey in those few words, that the groom seemed incapable of arguing with him. For a moment the ticking of the clock in the corner was the only sound in the room and then Seánie snorted and threw his cards on the floor.

'To hell with ye anyway, ganging up on a man on his wedding day.'

'There's no one ganging up on you.'

Colm's voice was steady and for a moment Annie thought he had done enough to defuse the situation. And then a smile broke out on his tanned face and she remembered that, although he was able to hide it better than the rest, he too had been drinking heavily.

'You're some eejit, Seánie Lynch, if Phelim Murphy is able to get the better of you. 'Twould take more than a feed of drink to let him take money off me.'

'A feed of drink,' Phelim agreed, not sure of the joke, but anxious to be seen to be joining in with the merriment and, most importantly, to be on O'Flaherty's side.

Seánie was sweating now, fury coming off him in waves. 'He'd a card hidden, I'm telling ye.'

But the other men were all laughing now, and although Annie's stomach was tight with tension, she could understand why, as Seánie reminded her of nothing other than her small brother James throwing a tantrum as he rocked back and forth, his hands balled into fists, his whole body shaking with temper.

Colm grinned again and gave the others a sidelong glance.

''Tis a terrible thing to be a sore loser.'

'He won't like this.'

May's whisper was so tiny, Annie thought she must have imagined it but then Seánie's head turned slowly, his glare piercing the stuffy, smoke-filled room.

'What did you say?'

Beside her in the chair Annie could feel May begin to shake.

'Nothing, I didn't say anything, I—'

'Are you laughing at me as well?'

With one bound Seánie crossed the floor then grabbed his new wife by the arm and dragged her to her feet.

'I said nothing, Seánie, you must have misheard, I—'

'Misheard? So you're saying I'm deaf, as well as a fool, are you? Or I'm a liar maybe. Sure ye're all laughing at me now, what's one more insult, ha?'

'Leave the girl alone, Seánie.'

Colm reached out a placatory hand.

'It's late. We've all had a feed of drink, sure there's no one laughing at you. It's late, that's all. We'll head away home—'

But Seánie had left rationality far behind now and was grasping his wife so tightly she couldn't stop herself wincing in pain. Annie made a move towards her but May shot her a look, imploring her not to interfere.

Seánie gave another low growl.

'I'll show you laughing.'

And then he strode across the room, driving his young wife in front of him with the same rough speed he used when moving cattle from one field to the next. Unlike with those recalcitrant beasts, however, he had no use for a stick, because May walked steadily ahead of him, looking neither left or right and making no attempt to go against his wishes.

Finally, Annie found her voice.

'May—'

'No, Annie.'

Her voice was small but, as the newly-weds made their way through the door at the back of the kitchen, May held her head high, a prisoner walking to the gallows with nothing left to wear but her dignity. Notes from a gay hornpipe drifted through the open window as the door closed behind them and the men in the centre of the room took out their cards and began their game again.

'You'll see me to my bed.'

After Seánie and May had left, Annie spent a while tidying the kitchen, anxious to do anything she could to spare her friend more work the following morning. She had intended to leave then, to sneak away without a word, but just as she moved towards the door the old woman opened her eyes.

'You'll see me to my bed before you leave.'

Too exhausted and upset to even consider arguing, Annie helped Mrs Lynch to her feet and steered her through the door at the back of the kitchen. It opened onto a corridor with several doors leading off it and despite her upset Annie couldn't help thinking how much bigger this house was than her own, how much grander. The first door had been left open a crack and as they shuffled past, the old lady leaning heavily on her arm, Annie heard from within an animal grunting and beneath it, a stifled sob. But the old woman kept walking, her head bent until she reached a second bedroom at the end of the corridor. A pair of heavy curtains kept out any moonlight and Mrs Lynch remained so silent, even when Annie sat her on the side of the bed and bent to help her remove her heavy shoes and thick woollen stockings, that she began to wonder if she had in fact fallen asleep again. And then, after she had eased Mrs Lynch onto the pillows and turned to go, a sentence floated towards her through the blackness.

'Seánie Lynch is his father's son.'

Annie turned, but the older woman was facing the wall now and didn't speak again.

She waited for one more moment, then backed out of the room, pulling the door gently shut behind her. There were no windows on this side of the house and Annie paused for a moment in the blackness, trying to get her bearings, wondering if she could find her way to the front door without having to pass through the kitchen again. Then she heard a cough and a scraping sound and she shrank back against the wall as the door to the first bedroom opened and Seánie stumbled out, tucking his shirt back into his breeches. He paused to give a long, liquid belch and Annie shuddered, but the darkness protected her and he didn't look around before lurching back in the direction of the kitchen. She waited a moment, but he didn't return and so, using her fingertips as a guide, Annie felt her way along the corridor then reached the room he had just vacated and pushed open the door. There were no curtains on the window here and enough light flowed in from the moon outside to allow her to see a shape, covered by a patterned quilt. Annie's stomach churned as she remembered the hours May had spent working on the quilt, how proud she had been to bring something so beautiful to her new home. The room stank of beer, and sweat, and another, less familiar, smell that heightened her nausea and she held her breath as she tiptoed towards the bed, then placed her hand lightly on her friend's shoulder. The figure jerked in fear, but Annie hushed her.

'It's me, darling, only me. I came... to check on you.'

Were those the right words, even? You checked on a sick child, you took their temperature, nursed them with love until they felt better. May was not a child, she was a married woman and it was normal, natural that her new husband should have taken her to his bed. But despite Annie's lack of experience in such matters it had been obvious to her that there had been nothing natural about the scene in the kitchen that evening, and certainly nothing loving. There was a pause, and then a hand emerged from under the quilt and Annie climbed up onto the bed and grasped it, tightly. Another pause and then May's voice emerged too, brittle and defeated.

'I was trying to ask you earlier – when your mother told you about how she felt, with Emmet and James I mean – did she... did she tell you how much it hurt?'

May was clutching Annie's hand so tightly now it was as if they were on a boat and feared a wave approaching. Annie returned the pressure before answering.

'The birth, you mean? I was there when Emmet and James were born and it was painful right enough, for a while. But don't think about that now, a stór. I'll stay with you when the time comes and it will be worth it, to see your baby.'

'Not the birth.'

May's voice was muffled, her throat thick with tears.

'Before it. What you do – to make the baby.'

Annie opened her mouth, but no words came. When her mother's waist had begun to thicken, years after the Thorntons assumed their family was complete, she had been old enough to understand that babies weren't the straightforward 'gift from Holy God' she had been led to believe and had even overheard her grandmother reprimand her father about the impending arrival. But Eileen and Pádraig had never declared themselves anything other than delighted with the news that their family was to expand. Annie knew, although she did not have the language to express it, that her parents took great joy in each other's company, over and above the love they felt for their children even, and there were many nights when she heard whispers coming from the bedroom at the back of the house, laughter and rustling that she instinctively knew were not meant for their offsprings' ears. There had been none of that joy in evidence between May and Seánie this evening. But they were married now, maybe things would change? She took a deep breath, trying to think of what her own mother would say in this situation.

'I suppose – anything can be difficult at the start, anything new. But it's God's will that when a couple are wed...'

The words died in her throat as the hand in hers began to shake.

'I thought it would be easier, the second time. The first time, we were outside in the field below the house. Two of the hens had escaped and I was searching for them, and Seánie found me there.'

Oh, May. Annie's heart lurched in her chest. Her friend had spent most evenings of the past two years wandering the roads near the Lynches' farm, living for the odd moments when she would see Seánie in the fields or be granted a word or two as he walked by, and a lost hen was just one of the many excuses she used to place herself in his presence. She had been so certain in her desire to be his wife, so sure that she loved him – tears sprang to Annie's eyes as the new bride continued.

'He said that I drove him to it, that men can't control themselves, and that it was obvious all along what I wanted. And I suppose it was, really? Only not like that. I never thought it would be – like that.'

May's voice trailed off. Annie wanted her to continue speaking, to unburden herself if that was what she needed to do, but it was as if there was a thread between them, light and fragile as a spider's web, and she was afraid that if she said the wrong thing she would lose her friend's confidence altogether. And then a cloud must have crossed the moon because the room grew darker and May began to speak again, more quickly this time, her words tumbling out into the night.

'I knew what we were doing was a sin and I thought maybe that was why it hurt so much. Seánie said I didn't deserve any better. And then, when I realised there was going to be a child I came to the house and when his mother overheard us talking she told him he had to marry me. I was happy that night, God help me, I was so happy when she said that. I called to you after, do you remember?'

The girl couldn't see her but Annie nodded anyway,

incapable of speech but holding tight to the small warm hand as she remembered how full of joy May had been that evening, how optimistic about the future.

'But tonight...'

The girl shifted in the bed.

'I thought it would be different now we are man and wife, but tonight it hurt more than ever. So I'm asking you, Annie, is this how it is always going to be?'

'Well maybe—'

But Annie's words were interrupted by a sudden banging on the door and Seánie's voice, thick with irritation and drink, floated through.

'The fire's gone out, woman! Will you come away up here and tend to it.'

Annie shook her head.

'Don't go to him. Stay here, rest.'

But May sat up, removed her hand from Annie's and began to arrange her clothes around her.

'He's my husband, Annie. I have to go when he calls.'

There was no light in her eyes now. The storm had hit, her friend was being swept into the ocean and Annie couldn't hold on tight enough to save her.

It would have been shorter to go by the road, but Annie headed home through the fields instead, taking the path that would lead her along the cliffs, craving sea air to flush the smell of that dank bedroom from her nostrils. She had assumed the rest of her family would be asleep by now but as she crossed the field her mother's shape materialised out of the darkness.

'A thaiscí, I wasn't expecting you home so soon. I was sure the young people would be dancing till dawn.'

Annie, who had never felt as old as she did at this moment, shook her head.

'I'd say you won't see Eve till sunrise but I've had enough. I'm away to my bed. You're abroad late yourself?'

'Arrah, I couldn't sleep. The boys were giddy tonight and even when I got them settled I had to talk to your grandmother and answer a hundred questions about who was at the wedding and what they did. She's snoring now, and I'm wide awake.'

The women exchanged a conspiratorial smile. Cáit was too lame now to go visiting, or even to mass, but her mind was as sharp as ever and, given her desire to extract every ounce of 'news' from the most innocuous of social occasions, a celebration such as a wedding would keep her going for weeks. Annie linked arms with her mother and the two women began to stroll together, Eileen leading her daughter in the direction of the Fairy Tree.

'I've been meaning to talk to you anyway, daughter. You've been on my mind.'

'Oh?'

The tree was grey in the moonlight and as they approached it Annie could see that several fresh tokens had been tied to the branches. One of them had probably been left by May, she realised, and tears filled her eyes as she thought of her lovely friend's hopes and dreams put through a mangle by a boorish man who did not deserve her. As if reading her thoughts, her mother looked at her.

'You're worried about May.'

'*Don't bother your mother.*'

73

Although her illness had been many years ago, that instruction was stitched so tightly into the fabric of the family that none of the children were used to turning to Eileen with even the most childish of complaints. But there was something about the velvety darkness – and indeed the novelty of being alone with her mam – that made Annie speak more freely than she usually would.

'I'm... a little concerned right enough.'

That small phrase had to carry a lot of weight but Eileen understood its meaning.

'There is to be a baby, I think?'

'Yes, before Christmas. She's not feeling very well but I told her... I told her that would get easier, with time.'

Eileen nodded.

'God willing. There's plenty of room in that house for a child anyway and sometimes – sometimes it settles a man down to become a father.'

Annie bit her lip. She was so tempted to tell her mother everything about Seánie's anger, his rough treatment of his new bride. But what could Eileen do with that information, what could any of them do? May had longed to marry Seánie Lynch, had wished for him on this very tree, and her wish had been granted. And even if marriage had not turned out as she expected, what option did she have? She had spent years trying to escape her father's house, she would never go back there now, and to leave Ballydrynawn, especially with a baby, was unimaginable. No, she and Seánie were joined together now in the eyes of God and there was no way to break that bond.

Eileen had been looking at the tree, but turned now to her daughter.

'I know you're worried about her, you're a good friend, Annie. But have you given any thought to your own future? A wedding can be a good day to make plans.'

Annie shook her head, so disturbed by what she had seen earlier that her own future hadn't even entered her mind. But her mother was persistent.

'Did you dance at all yourself the night? I saw Mike Begley take the floor.'

Annie gave a wry smile.

'You did, and Íde Rourke next to him. They've been walking out for months, Mother, they're only waiting for Íde's sister Mary Kate to marry because she made Íde promise she wouldn't go before her.'

Eileen let out a peal of laughter.

'And is Mary Kate walking out with anyone herself?'

'No, that's the awkward part of it.'

Annie was laughing now too.

'I think Mike will persuade one of his brothers to set his cap at her if she doesn't hurry up.'

'Oh that news will keep your grandmother amused for weeks, I'm delighted I asked you now. And Jack Duggan?'

'Mam.'

Annie glared at her mother.

'Perhaps you'd like me to make a match with Phelim Murphy? Or Colm O'Flaherty – I could join Cumann na mBan and we could go on the run together.'

'Ah, you're teasing me now.'

Still laughing at her daughter's indignant expression Eileen leaned over to retie a miraculous medal that was in danger of falling from one of the tree's lower branches. But Annie's own smile faded quickly. The truth was, there was no man at the wedding who interested her, no man in the parish or, she suspected, further afield. Seánie was a thug right enough but May had seen something in him – something that had proved false, in the end – but *something* nonetheless that had kept her walking the fields, hoping for a stray word or glance. And Annie could see the same thing happening to her sister Eve, practical, intelligent, level-headed Eve who stuttered and blushed scarlet every time the name of the new schoolmaster came up in conversation. Sometimes Annie felt as if all of the women in her life had crossed to the opposite side of a road and she couldn't imagine following them there, nor did she want to. To marry a man, to do with him what May and Seánie had done that evening? Annie knew from her parents that May was unfortunate, that married life could in fact contain great love and affection, but every time she thought of being with a man in that way her mind simply snapped shut. And even if by some miracle she found a man who made her feel the way her mother felt about her father, wouldn't that simply tie her here, to Ballydrynawn or the few parishes around it, and put an end to all of her other hopes and plans? It had been many years since Annie had made her own wish on this tree but the flame of it still burned inside her – she wanted to travel, to see America, to meet new people, see new things.

To marry any man would be to admit that this would never happen.

And then Eileen reached into her pocket.

'Your sister Eve is getting on great at the school. Father Drohan says she's the best assistant he's ever employed.'

Eileen was addressing her remarks to the leaves now.

'Bríd is a fine seamstress, and a great help to me now.

And the boys will settle down, they'll be working alongside your father before we know it. I only pray we will see peace before they come of age.'

She pulled her hand from her pocket then and Annie was astonished to see a white handkerchief, the sister of the one she herself had hung on the tree so many years before. She blushed then, remembering where the original had gone, and her mother laughed.

'Did you not think I'd miss it? I did, a stór, but I knew you would make good use of it.'

She reached out and touched Annie's shoulder gently.

'But that was many years ago. Tell me, daughter, what dreams have you now?'

Annie looked at the hanky, too surprised to speak as her mother continued.

'We'd be fine, you know, if you left us. I've watched you, my darling. I've seen the way you look when people talk about travelling to America, or make any plans to go away.'

'I can't leave you.'

'Ah now would you whisht!'

Eileen's voice rose in frustration.

'Sometimes I think all any of ye are short of doing is putting me away in the dresser like this handkerchief here, and what use would I be to anyone, hidden away? I'm as healthy as a trout, Annie, that's what I'm trying to tell you. And even if I wasn't – shush now – even if I wasn't that's not your concern. I've a fine family around me who want to be here. But you, my darling...'

Her voice softened.

'I know you're not happy, avourneen. And there's no shame in admitting it. There's plenty of people have left this parish and cried all the way to the boat but I don't think you would be one of them, would you? You want to take your chance in this world and I'm not going to stand in your way.'

'But I'd never see you...'

Annie's voice trailed off but her mother remained firm.

'Wouldn't we have letters? Wouldn't you write us big fat letters filled with everything you see and do, and wouldn't we read them over and over and think of you there, in New York or Boston? We'll miss you, my darling, but you're not happy. You've no notion of settling in Ballydrynawn, you wouldn't be happy here.'

Annie's grandmother said island people had the gift of seeing what others could not. She said it under her breath, like it was a bad thing, and Annie always ignored it; it sounded too much like a criticism of Eileen. But right now, standing in the darkness with the tree squat and steady beside them and the waves audible behind the leaves, she wondered if in fact Cáit had been right all along.

'There's no shame in having dreams, my darling.'

Eileen reached over and placed the handkerchief in Annie's hand.

'Make a wish, and see where life takes you.'

'You don't believe in all that...'

But there were tears running down both of their faces now as Eileen helped Annie knot the handkerchief to the highest branch she could reach, then stepped back and took her daughter's hand again.

'The Lord only gives us one life, my daughter. I came awful close to losing mine, and that's why I can't stand to see you throw yours away. Make a wish, my darling. And when you've made your wish – remember. It's good to have faith. But you can make your own luck in this world as well.'

'I can't leave May.'

Her mother's voice was quiet, but firm.

'May is a married woman now, Annie. She has her own journey ahead of her.'

'But, Mammy...'

She hadn't called her mother that since she was a very small child.

'But, Mammy, you nearly died. And that's why I can't leave you.'

'But, my darling, that's exactly why I want you to go.'

Chapter Six

WEST KERRY

2022

Emer yawned, heaved herself out of bed, pulled back the curtains then winced as light flooded in. Ugh. Or maybe the sun was just being magnified by the windows, or something? She pulled on her dressing gown and walked hopefully into the hall but a quick look out the front door confirmed her worst fears. It was, quite simply, a gorgeous day, bright, dry and already warm even though it was just gone eight a.m. In was in fact a perfect day for surfing and there was absolutely nothing stopping her from pulling on a wetsuit, jumping into freezing cold water and attempting to keep her balance on top of a thin foam board.

The sun was still shining as she started the car and pulled away from the house, the glare through the windscreen making her scowl. Fine, so she had persuaded herself that spending the summer down here mightn't be a total disaster, but what on earth had possessed her to book an actual surfing lesson? Oh, she was fit enough, she supposed, she went to the gym when she could and could run 5k if she really wanted to, preferably on a nice clean treadmill, but surely she was far too old to start a brand new sport, especially one she strongly suspected came under the heading of 'extreme'. Besides, the fact that she was still carrying around at least half of her Covid stone made the thought of wriggling into a wetsuit in front of Rob – in front of anyone, she corrected herself quickly – very unappealing.

But then as she drove through the village of Ballydrynawn Emer felt her mood begin to lift. It was lovely to see how familiar it all looked despite her long absence. There was a new set of traffic lights, all right, but the Hitching Post pub looked unchanged, apart from a large canopy which she suspected constituted an 'outdoor dining area', and although the corner shop had been replaced by a huge Spar there was still, she was delighted to see, a revolving stand outside it packed with brightly coloured buckets and spades.

It really was a gorgeous day, the clouds fluffy in the blue sky, and as Emer left the village behind and made her way towards the other side of the peninsula she couldn't help but think of how envious her US colleagues would be to see her here, miles from any stress or deadlines. When she spotted the turnoff for the beach where the lesson would take place, a properly signposted one this time, her spirits rose even further in tandem with the road. Green fields, dotted with sheep and low stone walls fell away on either side, and as the car crested the hill then began its descent a grey-green ribbon of water shimmered on the horizon before coming fully into focus. By the time Emer reached a cluster of newly built holiday homes, their picture windows turned opaque by the sun, she was feeling just as excited as she had been at the start of the school holidays all those years before.

The road narrowed slightly as passed on the left a

hotel where she and her family had sometimes gone for a toasted sandwich after a swim. Instead of the rather dull brown cladding Emer remembered, though, the building now boasted shining white walls and a long tiled terrace on which groups of people dressed in designer sportswear and sunglasses were enjoying possibly one of the best views in the country with their full Irish. It would be nice to join them, she thought, to leaf through a newspaper and make a pot of tea last an hour, but she had no time to kick back, it was already a quarter to ten. Sand crunched under the car's wheels as she rounded a final bend then turned into a public car park, its entrance marked by a retro silver coffee van, a handwritten sign outside boasting that it sold everything from flavoured coffees to a selection of fruit teas. Despite the early hour, the car park was already filling up, every roof-rack piled high with surfboards, paddleboards and kayaks, and it took her almost ten minutes to find a space between an SUV with a Dublin reg and a bright orange VW van. You didn't have to travel to Malibu to get the full Beach Boys, experience any more, it appeared, it was already here.

The sun had burned away the few remaining clouds and Emer grabbed a tube of sunscreen from her bag and began to rub it into her face as she made her way down the broad sandy track that led to the strand. A bright red metal container with 'Breaking Waves' stencilled on the side in yellow paint had been parked on a patch of hard-packed sand and she found herself growing nervous again as she approached. She hadn't a notion of what to do next, didn't even know what size wetsuit to ask for – but just as she was considering fleeing back to the car a blonde head poked out of the container and greeted her.

'Hey, are you here for the lesson?'

Given the location, she had been expecting the sun-streaked hair and golden skin, but Emer was surprised to hear that the woman's accent was closer to Denver than Dingle. She smiled nervously and nodded.

'That's right. Ten o'clock? I'm a beginner so—'

'Yeah, that's cool.'

The woman jumped down from her metal perch and looked Emer up and down, frowning slightly.

'What are you, like, a twelve?'

'Well yeah, I guess, or maybe a ten on a good day but...'

But her answer was lost on the woman who jumped back into the container and emerged, moments later, wetsuit in hand.

'Try this on, OK? And if it doesn't work we'll—'

'Hey, you came!'

Emer turned to see Rob striding across the sand, drops of water sparkling on his broad, rubber-clad shoulders.

'It's a perfect morning for it, just a small swell, great for beginners. Get suited up and we'll make a start, OK? You've met Alison?'

Emer nodded but the blonde had turned away and was dealing with what looked like a family group consisting of a mother, father and dark-haired, surly teenage boy. At least, Emer thought glumly, she wouldn't be the oldest person in the water, although she couldn't help noticing that the mother was at least a dress size slimmer than she was herself and had made time to apply – presumably waterproof – mascara. In hope, rather than anticipation, she looked around for a changing room but there was none, of course, just a beach full of people at various stages of pulling on and peeling off skin-tight rubber suits without, it seemed, an ounce of self-consciousness. Thankful she had at least remembered to put her swimsuit on under her clothes, Emer shed her tracksuit bottoms and tackled the wetsuit which was damp and smelled unpleasantly of seawater and disinfectant, the entire endeavour reminding her of a documentary she had once seen about the production line in a sausage factory. After a few false starts she eventually emerged, sweating, and almost entirely encased in black rubber.

'I'll just give you a hand...'

Alison walked behind her and Emer had barely time to wonder if it was possible to suck in back fat before the American girl yanked her zip upwards, taking her immediately from a feeling of 'vaguely uncomfortable' to 'verging on claustrophobic'. She hadn't time to protest though, as Alison handed her a long blue and white surfboard.

'You can make your way over to Rob now.'

But even that simple task proved impossible as Emer fumbled with the light but surprisingly wide board, trying to wedge it under her armpit and then almost dropping it before Alison gave her a pitying glance and showed her how to hold it by the handle built into the side. Bright red now, and not just from the wetsuit's thermodynamic properties, Emer made her way down the beach to where the dark-haired family, now chatting animatedly in French, were waiting for her. She grew warmer still as Rob gave them a lecture on water safety and something called a 'rip' which sounded utterly terrifying, and then watched as he placed his board flat on the sand. At least, Emer thought, getting into the water could cool her down – but to her horror Rob remained on the beach and lay down on his board, instructing the others to follow suit. Feeling more like a beached seal by the second, Emer did what she was told and found herself flat on her face, nose and hip bones grinding into the board's hard surface.

'Is that lady asleep?'

A couple of metres away, a family with young children had apparently decided that a beginners' surfing lesson would be the ideal floor show to go with their picnic but before she could think of a smart answer, Rob had pushed himself into a kind of press-up, which then flowed into a bunny hop and ended with him standing on his surfboard. It all looked sleek, impressive and absolutely impossible and Emer was about to ask what the Ladybird version was when the teenage boy executed a wobbly but ultimately successful version of the same thing. It took his father two goes but eventually he too had carried out his little bunny hop and was standing smugly on the polystyrene. His wife muttered something under her breath and although it had been years since she had studied French Emer got the gist of what she was saying and offered her a sympathetic smile. Maybe they could call it quits, grab a coffee on that lovely-looking terrace while the men played at being the Beach Boys? But Rob seemed to guess what they were thinking and shook his head.

'Don't worry. It's easier for people with good upper body strength to get the hang of it but it won't take you long. There's a modified version too, look...'

He lay down flat on the board then popped up again, as easily as if he was made of helium. Emer and the

Frenchwoman lay down, pushed with their arms, barely moved. Lay flat again, pushed again, still nothing. Oh, this was useless! And then Emer looked up to see the French kid shoot his mother a patronising grin. Little shit, shouldn't he be in school? She'd bloody show him... taking a deep breath, she placed her arms in front of her, pushed hard and found herself hovering over the board in a shaky plank. Rob walked over to her.

'That's right, now right leg forward...'

Summoning strength she had last used in a yoga class on the far side of the Atlantic, Emer flung her leg in front of her, curled upwards and found herself standing on the board, wobbling but definitely upright. Maman too had finally executed the move and the two women exchanged a gleeful high five.

'Great stuff!'

Rob was smiling broadly now.

'Now we do it in the water.'

The shock of the sea on her toes made her gasp but the wetsuit was a good one and kept out the worst of the cold. Even when the ribbon of water snaked its way inside the wetsuit and down her back it was soon warmed by her body heat and Emer found the sensation of being in the Atlantic, yet not freezing cold, almost dreamlike. The five of them walked forward until the water was at waist height, then Rob instructed them to turn their boards around until the noses were pointing back towards the shore.

'What now?' the French father asked in the tone of voice

of a man who had booked a two-hour session and wanted to get his money's worth. But Rob just gave him a lazy smile.

'Now? We wait.'

The surfboard, which was now connected by a leash to her left foot, bobbed harmlessly by her side. Emer was starting to feel almost affectionate towards it and was tempted to give it a quick pat, but then Rob called out to her.

'This one's yours, Emer!'

Emer looked over her shoulder to see a wave forming a couple of metres away. She dragged herself up on the board and got into the now familiar face-down position, before hearing Rob's voice in her ear.

'Paddle now!'

She felt the water swell under her, paddled with her arms for a moment then pushed up from the board – and promptly tumbled headfirst into the water. She stayed under for a moment, keeping her hands over her head to avoid being struck by the board, then doggy paddled to the surface. Seawater streamed down her face and she had to choose between wiping her eyes or clearing a suspiciously runny nose and by the time she could see again, Rob had moved onto the French teenager and was helping him to catch his own wave. Or at least, to try and catch it. It would have been childish, of course, to laugh when the kid also took an immediate tumble into the briny deep and, if Emer caught his mother's eye and they both grinned, well it must have been the West Kerry scenery and the joy of the good weather that was making them feel so cheerful.

All five continued in this vein for another ten minutes, waiting for a wave, being encouraged by Rob to catch it and then almost immediately pitching forwards into the sea. It wasn't at all unpleasant, they were warm, and it was a beautiful day for a swim, even with a seven-foot flotation device tugging at their ankles. And then Rob beckoned Emer over, pointed out another incoming wave and winked.

'Don't try and pop up this time, just enjoy it.'

The sea swelled and before she could ask him what he meant Rob had given Emer's surfboard a shove from behind. As it picked up speed, all she could do was lie flat and cling on and suddenly the water was pushing her forward at a pace she hadn't anticipated, the shore was rushing towards her now but her prone position on the board was solid and although she could feel the power of the wave, this time she wasn't fighting against it, instead she relaxed and rode it for as long as she could until she felt sand scrape against the bottom of the board.

Emer exhaled, then rolled over into the sea, the board bobbing gently beside her.

Rob looked over.

'You get it now?'

Yeah, she got it.

Emer caught three more waves that way, just lying flat, learning the rhythm of the sea, how to harness its power. On the fourth occasion she tugged the board back out to waist-high water, then climbed up and waited for her moment. One again a swell of water rose, and once again she began to paddle in front of it, waiting for it to pick up speed. And then she glanced over to see Rob looking at her.

'Pop up this time.'

The water was under her now, the board beginning to fly. Not allowing herself time to think or get scared, Emer pushed up with her arms, held herself in a plank for a moment then dragged her right foot forwards until it landed in the centre of the board. Afraid to breathe in case it disturbed her balance, she steadied herself and then pushed up and away from the board, allowing her front foot to take the strain while her back foot found stability. She wobbled – but she was still standing, unfurling now from her crouch and the shore was rushing towards her but she was still there, she was standing, she was bloody surfing, she was doing it! She heard a howl of delight and then realised it came from her and then the sudden intake of breath unsettled her and she found herself plunging backwards into the salt water.

'You OK?' Rob paddled over but Emer's triumphant grin as she emerged said it all.

Twenty minutes, three wipeouts and two more definite stands later, the session was over. The French mother, having successfully caught one wave, left the water first and stood on the shore, phone outstretched to capture her husband and son as they emerged, the teen grinning in a very uncool way and appearing to ask his father if they could do it all again tomorrow. Emer's lips were chapped, her arms felt like cooked spaghetti and she didn't think she'd be able to climb onto the board again even if there had been time left in the session. Before she left the water, however, she stood still for a moment and looked back out to sea. The breeze had picked up and the waves were larger now and she found herself trying to read them, to spot which ones would best suit her ability. Then she let her gaze drift further to the mountains on either side, noting how the clouds created sun patches on the green grass ensuring no two fields looked the same. She hadn't thought about anything other than surfing for more than two hours, she realised; not work, nor her family, the pandemic or any of the other dreadful things that were happening in the world. She had been entirely consumed by waves and water, and flying and falling and getting up again. It had been magnificent.

And now she was cold. Emer began to push her board towards land, allowing the water to take the weight until she reached the shore. When she finally picked it up she had a sudden flash of how astronauts must feel when they returned to earth – the rigid foam structure that had seemed so light in the water might as well have been made of rock and she fumbled with it for a minute before finding the knack to picking it up again. But although Rob was just a few steps ahead of her, chatting to the French family, she didn't call out to him for help. If she was going to surf regularly then she'd have to learn to deal with the equipment herself and even as the thought crystallised in her head she knew that yes, she was going to surf again. Taking a firmer grip on the board she trudged back up the beach towards Alison who was now sitting on a deckchair outside the Breaking Waves container, talking to another wetsuit-clad surf instructor, who was older, and slighter of build than Rob but had the same deep tan and sun-bleached hair.

'Did you have fun? You looked good out there!'

Alison eased herself out of the deckchair, took Emer's board then hopped into the van, returning moments later with her sports bag. The other instructor gave the women a brief wave.

'I'll see ye later, so.'

'Bye Mark.'

Alison nodded at the instructor, who made his way across the sand to where a small group of teenagers were dressed for a class in bright blue 'Breaking Waves' T-shirts. Moving slowly now as fatigue gripped her limbs, Emer began to peel off her wetsuit. It was a laborious and slightly ridiculous process but as she extracted herself from the tight rubber casing she suddenly realised she didn't give a damn who could see her hopping about on the wet sand. It didn't matter what her body looked like, it had held her up in the water for the entire session, the greatest couple of hours she could remember spending in years, and that made it the perfect body for her. She freed one leg, then another, then wobbled slightly as she uncurled to standing again.

'You OK?'

Alison gave her a concerned look but Emer simply smiled.

'Head rush. I'd better get something to eat – that's more exercise than I've taken in a long time!'

The blonde woman grinned.

'Bet it didn't feel like that when you were in there though, right?'

She retrieved Emer's suit and threw it into a barrel which was filled, by the smell of it, with water and disinfectant.

'Would you like to book another lesson?'

'Yes please!' Emer's answer came so quickly that both women laughed.

'That's no problem! You might want to give it a day or two though, you'll be exhausted tomorrow and the forecast isn't great. Drop me a WhatsApp later and I'll send you a time. You can check out our website too for tides.'

Unlike earlier, Alison appeared to have time to chat and

her flow of questions continued as Emer grabbed her towel then began to wriggle into her clothes.

'So, you here on holiday?'

'For the summer actually.' Emer poked her head through the neck of her fleece then raked her fingers through her hair. 'I'm staying in my parents' place, a few miles out the road.'

'Nice. You on your own?'

Alison's accent might have marked her out as a foreigner, Emer thought in amusement, but she appeared to have the Kerry habit of asking all of the questions she wanted to ask without a hint of embarrassment.

'I am, yeah.'

'Cool. Hey – why don't you come for a drink later?'

Emer paused in the middle of shaking a mixture of salt water and sand from her ears and looked at her.

'A drink?'

'Sure!'

Alison's eyes were friendly.

'There's usually a good gang in the Hitching Post on a Saturday night, plenty of blow-ins like me – that's what they call us, round here. Come join us! Honestly, you'd be doing me a favour. It's mostly guys – it'd be good to water down the testosterone a little.'

Emer's instinct was to say no – she was tired, she wasn't great in groups of strangers, she needed to call her folks – and then she paused, and wondered what her therapist would say. Her therapist (and she still internally squirmed when she said the phrase, even silently) – but THE therapist had been very keen on early nights and working out but she had mentioned that Emer needed to have fun too, especially after two years when most of her socialising had been done over Zoom. And after all, she had said yes to the surfing, hadn't she, against her better judgement, and look how well that had worked out? Before she could change her mind she nodded.

'Yeah, OK, that'd be lovely. Thank you!'

'Fantastic!'

'What's fantastic?'

Rob strolled towards them, carrying a surfboard casually under each arm. Alison smiled.

'Emer is going to join us in the pub tonight.'

'Sure we'll see you then, so.'

He moved past them, trailed by the French family who were also collecting their dry gear, and Alison turned her attention to Emer again.

'Any time after eight o'clock is good. I'm telling you that because I'm American. I mean, the boys will say seven o'clock and then turn up at nine, if you know what I mean?'

Emer laughed.

'Irish time, I get it. I've actually been living in the States for a while so I'll readjust my expectations.'

Alison tugged her sunglasses from where they were holding back her hair, and placed them on the end of her nose.

'Really, what part?'

'LA mostly.'

'I'm looking forward to hearing about it! I have to tidy up here now before the afternoon session, but I'll see you later, OK?'

'Sure.'

But Emer didn't leave, one more worry prickling at her.

'As long as you're sure – I mean, I'm not barging in or anything. I don't want to be a third wheel.'

'Wheel?' Alison looked puzzled and then gave a bark of laughter.

'Oh no! Rob and I aren't a couple or anything if that's what you mean—'

'Hi, we've a booking for twelve?'

A shadow fell over Emer and she turned to see a group of pale and rather shaky-looking young men stumble across the beach towards them. Alison groaned.

'Bachelor party, the worst,' she muttered, under her breath.

She reached down to grab her clipboard from where she'd left it on her deckchair and Emer took the hint.

'I'll leave you to it.'

Just as she was about to walk away, however, the American girl turned to her and removed her glasses again.

'Please tell me you'll come tonight. It would be really nice to have someone else to talk to, someone who is not from around here. It's a gorgeous place, but it can be hard to break in sometimes. Especially when—'

But the stag party had reached them now and even in the open air Emer caught the whiff of stale beer. She winked at Alison.

'I'll leave you to it. Eight o'clock, you said? I'll be there.'

Then she turned and walked back in the direction of the car park, her legs heavy with fatigue but the rest of her feeling lighter than she had done in a long time.

Chapter Seven

KERRY

1924

Even though they had known it was coming, the rattle of the cart's wheels outside the window still startled them and they looked at each other in silence for a moment. It was time, then. Eileen was the first to break, stepping backwards with a small cough.

'Right. Will you take the trunk, Pádraig? And tell John James we'll be out in a minute.'

'I will, I will surely.'

Annie's father gave Annie an almost puzzled look, as if, despite all the planning, her departure had come as a surprise to him. Then he shook his head slowly before walking into the pre-dawn, calling out into the darkness.

'She'll be with you shortly, John!'

'No bother, no bother at all.'

John James Rahilly travelled to Tralee on the first of every month and it was widely known that he valued company on the road, excuse enough for Annie to ask him to take her on the first leg of her journey to the boat. It would be too hard on the younger ones, she had told her parents, too distressing to haul them all the way into town or onwards towards Cork even, simply to wave goodbye. In truth, it was her own feelings she had been sparing. Annie had been dreaming of this day for almost as long as she could remember, and saving for it for almost a year, but now it had finally arrived it was all she could do to stop herself from jumping back into the still-warm bed in the corner of the kitchen and declaring she wasn't ready for adventure after all. But it was too late for that now, the ticket to New York was booked, her trunk was on John James's cart, the horse outside snickering in the grey light.

'Will you send us sweets?'

The twins wrapped their arms around her waist, and squeezed her tightly.

'Will you, Annie, the minute you get there? Pat Fogarty's aunt sends him nothing but clothes.'

'I will, I will surely.'

Laughing, Annie untangled herself and looked from one brother to the other. Emmet and James. The twins, but no longer the babies. They had no clue how much she would miss them and maybe that was just as well.

'Your sister sends her love.'

Eileen looked over from the settee, where she was straightening out a blanket that was not in any way crooked.

'She would have loved to have come over this morning but—'

'I know.'

Annie had not expected to see Eve this morning, her sister had moved more than twenty miles away when her new husband had been given his own school on the far side of the peninsula, and now in the early stages of pregnancy, it would have been too much for her to make the journey back to Ballydrynawn just to say goodbye. Annie would miss her sister, miss her dreadfully, but Eve had her own life now and her absence this morning was further proof that her siblings were moving on and that it was time for Annie to do the same. Bríd had a job now too, in the creamery near the town, and even the boys were getting bigger, tormenting the lovely but very mild-mannered teacher who had replaced Eve.

'What time is your train?'

Eileen could find nothing else to tidy, and looked across at her eldest child.

'Not for hours yet.'

Annie checked her slim silver watch, yet another reminder of how much things had changed this past year. Although she had seemed in reasonable health, Cáit had divided her belongings between her grandchildren the previous Christmas Eve and two days later, on, on St Stephen's Day, the woman who had been such a central part to their lives had simply faded away in front of the fire. Now Annie would carry a piece of Cáit across the Atlantic and the thought was a great comfort.

A sharp rap came at the door and Eileen frowned.

'John James must be in a hurry after all.'

But the figure who entered was much smaller than John James and even more welcome. As Eileen went outside to warn their neighbour that Annie would need a few more minutes, Annie took a step forward and enveloped May in a warm embrace.

'You didn't have to come.'

'Did you really think I wouldn't? Careful now, you'll smother the little man.'

May took a step backwards and peeled away her shawl, revealing a small red face, fathoms deep in blissful slumber. Annie leaned over and stroked the baby gently on the cheek.

'Harry, my darling. Are you being a good boy for your mammy?'

'He is in his eye!'

May snorted.

'He had me up half the night, he only fell asleep on the walk over here. But he wasn't going to stop me saying goodbye.'

'And what about my goddaughter?'

'Muireann is fast asleep in bed beside her grandmother. Sure that one isn't a lick of trouble.'

'And this fella won't be either, the little face on him.'

Annie gave the baby one last caress then glanced at her friend.

'And how is his mammy?'

May gave her a direct look.

'I'm grand.'

'There's no news, so?'

'Not a word.'

Just three short words but the story they told contained months of upheaval. Baby Harry was two weeks old now so it must have been more than eight months, Annie calculated, since any of them had heard from his father. May hadn't even been aware of her second pregnancy on the morning that Seánie headed off to sell two cows at a fair in the next town, and never returned. Most of the neighbours, Annie's own parents among them, had initially assumed Seánie had gone on a skite, a drinking binge in Tralee maybe, a not unusual occurrence for a young man with money in his pocket and the pressure of a new family at home. But a day had passed, and then a week, and Seánie had still not come back. His cousins had searched the county for him and sent words to friends further afield but there had been no word from May's husband, not even when his son, John Henry – Harry – was born.

Annie took a quick look over her shoulder to make sure her parents were out of earshot before addressing her friend again.

'And you've never told anyone what happened, the week before Seánie left?'

May shook her head.

'You're the only one who knows, Annie. And it's not like there is much to tell. Colm O'Flaherty turned up on our doorstep one night, just like I told you. I was terrified, you heard about so many things happening those days, men being attacked and bridges blown up and all sorts, and I hated the idea of Colm bringing that sort of trouble to our door. But you know Seánie, he always acted the big man around Colm and he insisted he come in, fed him half our dinner too. Mrs Lynch was asleep, she didn't hear a thing. Well, when Colm asked for a bed for the night Seánie didn't give it a second thought, just handed him a blanket and settled him in front of the fire. We went to bed ourselves then and when we got up the next morning he was gone. I had to throw out the good blanket too, it was crawling.'

May wrinkled her nose at the memory.

'But I didn't see sight nor sound of Colm O'Flaherty after that, and a week later Seánie was gone too.'

Annie nodded. May had told her the details before but it was good to hear the story once more before she left. She dropped her voice even lower before continuing.

'And now Colm is back.'

May shrugged.

'He came back as soon as the trouble ended, striding around Ballydrynawn like he owns the place. Sure there's talk of him going for politics next, getting a Dáil seat above in Dublin. But not a word from Seánie.'

Annie gave her a searching look.

'And do you still think Colm is the reason Seánie left? That he got into trouble, somehow, for helping him?'

Her friend shrugged and pulled the blanket up around her baby son again.

'I can't think of any other reason.'

Annie nodded.

'Even though Colm himself is fine.'

May sniffed.

'Colm O'Flaherty is the type of man who will always be fine.'

He is indeed, Annie mused, her thoughts taking her back to the wedding and those watchful, intelligent eyes. When she spoke again, her voice was brighter.

'And you're doing well yourself? You and the babies?'

'We are, we are surely.'

And it was true that May, although clearly tired, seemed more at ease within herself than she had been for some time. Annie had been planning her trip to America for almost a year but had held off until after May's baby was born, afraid her friend would not be able to cope with such a burden alone. But although the petite May had grown so huge in her second pregnancy that her mother-in-law was heard to remark that 'it would be as easy go over her as go round her', her face had lost that haunted, drawn look it had worn while she was expecting Muireann, and Harry's eventual arrival, on a warm summer's evening, had been a mercifully quick and relatively calm affair with Annie and her mother on hand to support the labouring woman and even old Mrs Lynch persuaded out of her bed to keep an eye on her older grandchild. Now, just two weeks later, May was back on her feet again, and the farm seemed to be running as efficiently as it had been before. As if reading her thoughts, May dropped a light kiss on her infant's head then looked up at Annie with a smile.

'Billy Madden has been lending a hand on the farm, and even Seánie's mother has been doing a bit, more than a bit to be honest with you. And I'll be able to do more myself when this one is weaned.'

May looked down again at the baby in her arms, who was drifting awake in the cold morning air.

'We'll manage fine.'

You will, Annie thought. I have no doubt in my mind.

'Annie.'

The baby whimpered, and May lifted him against her shoulder then spoke into his soft black hair.

'There's just one thing that's worrying me.'

The morning was so quiet, Annie could swear she could hear the wash of waves although the shore was almost a mile away. Her friend swallowed, and started again.

'The thing is, a few weeks before Seánie vanished I went to the Fairy Tree and wished – oh, Annie, it feels awful even to say it out loud! But I wished for something to happen to him. Not anything bad, I swear to you, I'd never do that. But just that he'd be nicer, that things would be more like before we were married. That he wouldn't – that he wouldn't hurt me, any more.'

Harry's tiny eyelids fluttered as she clutched him more tightly.

'Did I make this happen, Annie? Is it my fault that he's gone?'

'Oh, sweetheart.'

Annie reached out and squeezed her friend's shoulder.

'I know that tree gives you comfort, but it's a fairy story, no more. You had nothing whatsoever to do with what happened to your husband.'

'But whatever happened to him it has left this little man without a daddy, and that's bad luck, surely.'

Annie shook her head then looked directly at her friend and spoke in a fierce whisper.

'My mother says you make your own luck in this world. And this fella has a very fine mammy.'

'Annie.'

And then her own mother appeared in the doorway.

'I'm sorry, girls, but Annie has to leave now. JJ is worried ye'll miss the train.'

'I know, Mam.'

Annie bent down and kissed baby Harry on the forehead, marvelling once again at the sight of May's fine features picked out in miniature. Harry was his mother's son, all right, and she couldn't think of a finer compliment.

'Slán Harry, a stór.'

She bent closer still and whispered in the tiny, perfect ear.

'Look after your mammy for me.'

And then it seemed as if Annie only had time to draw one last breath before she found herself in the cart, perched up front beside John James. Her parents and Bríd waved, and the twins ran beside her, squabbling and laughing in equal parts, and then May lifted Harry's tiny paw and made him wave too and the sight of that small hand meant it was laughter and not tears that swept Annie Thornton away from Ballydrynawn and out on the road to a new home.

John James talked all the way to Tralee, which at least kept Annie from fretting about the journey ahead of her, but when he left her at the train station, dropping her trunk beside her before driving away, talking to the horse now for entertainment, she stared after him as if her best friend in the world had just been snatched away. The train journey went in a blur, the unfamiliar speed of the engine leaving her too afraid even to look out the window, and when she finally fell into an uneasy sleep she woke in Cobh with a cricked neck, a headache and an overwhelming fear of being late for the boat. Neighbours had instructed her on the best place to hail a cab for the quayside and she followed their instructions so methodically it was not until she paid the driver and was finally looking up at the giant ship that the magnitude of what she was doing rushed over her and she sank down on her case before her legs could give way. What in God's name was she doing in Cobh, when she could barely remember it wasn't called Queenstown any more? Who was she to think she could sail alone across the ocean? She, Annie Thornton, who had never been further from Dingle in her life?

And then a hand fell on her shoulder and Annie looked up to see an angel looming over her.

'Are you taking root there or what? Hurry now, or we won't get a place at the railings.'

Not an angel then, but a young woman with a strong west of Ireland accent and more self-possession than Annie had ever encountered in one person. Even in her travelling cloak and with soot streaked on one smooth cheek the woman was strikingly beautiful with strands of red hair escaping from a moss-green hat sitting atop pale skin and sparkling green eyes. She reached out again and offered Annie her hand.

'Are you travelling alone too? Well, if we go together then neither of us will be alone, will we?'

Unsure of how to answer, but with nothing better on offer, Annie allowed the young woman to lead her over to the gangplank and up and onto the ship. Handwritten signs indicated the way to the cabins but the woman, who Annie could see now was only around her own age, strode off in the opposite direction, leading her up a set of stairs and then out on deck.

The two women stood still for a moment, watching their fellow passengers swarm on board, the scene reminding Annie of how Seánie Lynch would move his cattle from the lower field to the upper after a heavy shower of rain. In fact, she thought, if an official from the ship had appeared behind the crowd to poke the slower ones with a sharp stick she would not have been particularly surprised. Every sort of person emigrated to America, it appeared: whole families, the women carrying babies and men leading dazed-looking children, as well as members of the gentry in long travelling cloaks who had porters to wheel their mountains of luggage on board behind them. There were other solo passengers too, of course, most of the women sobbing, the men aiming for studied nonchalance but Annie could see, even at this distance, how tightly their cases were grasped in their red scrubbed hands. Although Annie had lived beside the sea all of her life, she had never been on a boat larger than her uncle's currach and the view of the quayside from here was so foreign, and the gentle movement of the huge vessel so alien she felt excitement bubble up inside her to counter the earlier apprehension. The ship's horn sounded and the girl beside her took a white handkerchief from her pocket and began to wave. She looked across at Annie and winked.

'Come on! We're on our way!'

Despite her excitement Annie found fresh tears welling up in her eyes.

'I've no one to wave at.'

But the girl just shrugged and waved even harder.

'And what matter? Neither have I, but sure waving is half the fun. We're going to America, girl, and that lot back there are going nowhere!'

Her exuberance was so contagious that Annie found herself raising her arm and fluttering it shyly, but the other woman reached across and tugged on her sleeve.

'Come on, put a bit of effort into it. Like this, look!'

She threw back her head, and yelled.

'Bye! Bye – take care now – I love you!'

And the image of the young woman directing her affection towards a seagull flying overhead was so ridiculous that Annie couldn't help but laugh, and then she too was screaming and waving and before she knew it she felt a jolt, and then a gliding motion and they had set sail.

★

Annie had heard that life at sea seemed to move at a different pace to life on land and it must have been true because within hours it felt like she had known Nora Carey forever. Once the quayside had receded and the journey was properly under way the young woman led Annie, still clutching her suitcase, across the crowded deck and back down the steps. Nora was from County Mayo, she told Annie, from a small village miles away in the north-west, far too far away for any of her family to have come to see her off.

'They'll hardly notice I've gone, anyway,' she told Annie with a shrug.

Annie stared at Nora's vivid hair, gleaming white blouse and patent shoes which, although far from new, had been polished until they shone, and decided she couldn't imagine a more unforgettable person.

'I doubt that.'

'You'd be surprised.'

They made their way to a small narrow corridor then stopped at a cabin door, onto which had been pinned a handwritten note.

'There are twelve of them still at home, they'll just be glad of more room at the table. Come here to me though, this won't do, this won't do at all.'

She took a pencil from her pocket, drew a line through a name on the note and turned back to Annie.

'They had you in with a family, sure you'd be driven demented with the children crying all night. I'm sure you had enough of that at home.'

'Well yes...'

A sudden image of the twins' blond heads joined together on one pillow rose up in her mind and Annie's voice wobbled into nothingness. Nora frowned, then took her by the arm and led her down the corridor, stopping in front of another wooden door.

'I'm in here so you, my dear –'

She scribbled extravagantly.

'Now, Annie Thornton, you can bunk in here with me.'

She threw open the door and, although Annie could now see that her own name had replaced that of another passenger, such was the speed of Nora's movements she didn't have time to either protest or worry about the newly homeless woman. Instead, she followed Nora into the small but clean cabin and watched her throw her case onto the top of one of two matching bunkbeds.

'I'll go up here and you climb up there, onto the other side. It's best to be up off the floor, it can get messy down there, if you follow me.'

Annie stared at her.

'Have you travelled to America before, Nora? Only you seem to know so much about it!'

Perched neatly now on the side of her bunk, Nora opened her suitcase, extracted an ivory-backed brush and matching hand mirror then unpinned her hair before starting to brush it in long smooth strokes.

'My cousin Bridget is in New York these past five years, she wrote me a letter telling me everything I needed to know. I'll let you read it too, when we're settled. She sent me the money for the fare, God bless her, and I'll be staying with her and her family until I get myself sorted out. They run a small hardware store on the Lower East Side. Have you somewhere to stay yourself?'

Annie opened her mouth, ready to tell her new friend about how the parish priest had put her in contact with nuns in New York who found girls to work in the kitchens of the gentry, when suddenly she became very aware of the swaying of the floor under her feet. She placed her hand on the side of the bunk to steady herself but the bed was swaying too and a cold sweat broke out on her forehead.

Nora looked down at her and shook her head.

'Now you're not to go getting seasick on me, Annie Thornton. We've three weeks to put in on this ship and I don't intend to spend them mopping your brow. Come up on deck now and we'll get some air.'

Annie shook her head but the action only increased her misery and she sat down suddenly on the bottom bunk instead.

'Maybe if I just stay here for a while—'

'Not a chance.'

Nora jumped down from the bunk, and Annie gave a low groan as the action made the floor shake beneath her.

'Bridget said that was the very worst thing you could do. You have to come and look at the horizon.'

Annie didn't think she'd be able to find the horizon, let alone look at it, but by now she was too miserable to put up any resistance as Nora grabbed her by the arm and led her back up the stairs again. The breeze on deck was sharp and sent small sprays of water across her face but after a few moments she was amazed to find herself feeling a little better, as if the very force of Nora's personality would not allow her to be ill. She followed her new friend around the side of the ship until they came to a small, secluded area which was packed with ropes and cases, leaving just enough room for the two of them to stand together and look out to sea.

Nora took a deep lungful of air and smiled.

'That's better. So tell me now, Annie Thornton, what do you plan to do with this fabulous new life in America?'

Annie drew the words together with pride.

'I've an interview for a position as kitchen maid. On Fifth Avenue.'

But Nora simply shrugged.

'A kitchen maid? It'll do for a start, I suppose.'

Producing pins from her pocket, she began to dress her hair again, this time in elaborate coils worn low on the nape of her neck. It was as if she had harnessed the breeze as an assistant, Annie thought, as it blew stray strands of hair back off her face to reveal her high cheekbones and that milk-white skin. She really was extraordinarily beautiful, she realised, and, in an effort to stop herself from staring, gave the horizon her full attention for several minutes before speaking again.

'And what are your own plans, Nora? Will you work at your cousin's shop?'

Nora gave the final pin a satisfied pat.

'I will for a while, until I get settled. But not for too long. I'm going to be in the movies.'

Any remaining queasiness evaporated as Annie's mouth gaped open in surprise.

'The movies? What do you mean?'

'What do you think I mean? The films, of course. You have been to the cinema, haven't you?'

Annie had in fact visited the small cinema in Dingle the previous year, to accompany Eve who had saved for months for the treat. But although her sister had been captivated by the spectacle, Annie had found the space too dark and disorientating. The bright flickering screen had given her a headache while the newsreel, which showed pictures of disturbances in Dublin, had frightened her in a way that reading articles in her father's paper never did. There had been a made-up story afterwards, a silly thing about a man in a hat who kept trying to kiss a lady in a long white dress, but Annie's head had been splitting by then and she had only wanted to leave. And that was just watching a film – to want to be up there? Actually be up on that big screen? Annie stared at her new friend. Nora Carey seemed capable of almost anything but surely this would be beyond even her.

As if she could read her mind, Nora simply laughed.

'Someone has to be in them, don't they? I mean, when Mr Chaplin was born, it's not like they put a little hat on him and said, "This one is for the films anyway!" I'll save up my money and then I'll go to Hollywood, that's where all the studios are, Bridget says. You'll be watching me up there one day, Annie Thornton. Now!'

A sudden spray of water blew into their faces and Nora grinned.

'You're feeling better, aren't you? I told you so. We'll see about some tea now, and then take another walk before bedtime.'

They did walk that evening, and the next and indeed there were times, Annie thought afterwards, that it felt as if she and Nora walked all the way across to America. The weather worsened shortly after they reached open seas and, when it became clear their room-mates had not had the benefit of Nora's cousin's wisdom it became far more pleasant to avoid the dank and fetid atmosphere of the cabin and spend as much time as possible out on deck. On one particularly stormy night, when the noise of the wind was drowned out by the sound of their bunkmates retching, the women even slept outside, huddled together under Nora's coat in the little storage area they had come to think of as 'their' part of the ship. The following morning they skipped past the purser and made their way all the way to the first class deck where the tall and elegant Nora looked right at home and even Annie felt a little grander just to be in her company. And as they walked they talked, and shared their hopes and dreams for their grand adventure in the new world. Once she had made her fortune, Nora told Annie she might marry, but only to a man who would allow her to work and not force her to have more than one baby. Eventually Annie herself shyly admitted that she too had ambitions beyond a Fifth Avenue kitchen, plans to save enough money to buy a train ticket and see more of the city, the country, the world.

'And you will!'

It was late afternoon and the two were back in their favourite corner, perched on top of two packing cases.

'You can do anything you set your mind to, Annie Thornton. In fact I think—'

But Annie never found out what Nora thought because just at that moment a cry went up from the other side of the ship.

'Land!'

Just as she had done on their first day on board, Nora grabbed Annie's hand then pulled her upright to face the water. At first there was nothing but mist, but then a dark shape seemed to form out of the grey and the two women stood, fingers intertwined, as it grew larger and more imposing and finally solidified into Lady Liberty herself, her arm outstretched, beckoning them forward. It was the first time Annie had seen tears run down Nora's perfect face and she had to lean closer to her friend to hear her muttered words.

'We're here, Annie Thornton. We're bloody well here.'

After so many unchanging days at sea everything seemed to move in a blur after that. First there was the gathering of belongings and the brief goodbyes to the others they had met on board, and then the long queues at Ellis Island where the ground felt like it was swaying under their feet and Annie felt sure she would have stumbled if it were not for the solid presence of Nora by her side. The officials asked a lot of questions but cousin Bridget – God bless cousin Bridget! – had prepared them for that too and before long the women found themselves fully processed and free on American soil.

And to think Annie had thought of Cobh as a busy place! America was a solid wall of heat, noise and people and it was as if the breath was being squeezed from her lungs as she fought for a place to get her bearings on the busy quayside. Then they heard someone calling Nora's name and Annie watched sadly as the only person she knew in America was pulled away into a crowd of equally red-headed people who bombarded her with hugs and questions about how her journey had been and what news she had brought from home. Annie swallowed, then turned away. She should have expected this, of course – Nora had made it clear from the outset that she was travelling to meet her family. Annie had been a pleasant companion on board ship but there was no reason to believe they would still be friends, or even see each other again now that their new lives had begun. She was on her own now and that was fine, it was just the way things had to be.

She picked her suitcase up from the ground and turned, eyes searching the quayside for markings or a path that would lead to the city centre and the convent that had promised her lodging for her first two nights. Then suddenly her coat was grabbed from behind and she turned to see Nora, her hair in disarray, two bright patches of colour on her high cheekbones.

'I thought I'd lost you! Here...'

She pressed a piece of paper into Annie's hand.

'I have to go now but this is Bridget's address, I told her you'd be calling for me once you're settled. You'll have an afternoon off, maybe an evening if you're lucky. We'll go to dances together, we're going to have a fine time in America, Annie Thornton!' And then Nora was swallowed up by the crowd again but Annie, the piece of paper still warm in her hand, found herself feeling a lot less lonely than before.

Chapter Eight

KERRY

2022

'I hope you've the horse tied up somewhere safe?'

'What? Oh, right, yeah. Ha ha.'

Aware that she was indeed walking like John Wayne after several hours in the saddle, but not overly happy to have attention drawn to her bandy legs in the middle of a crowded pub, Emer felt her cheeks flare. But Alison came to her rescue and gave Rob a dig in the ribs.

'Leave her alone!'

The pair of them were sitting on a circular leather bench in a corner of the Hitching Post, the table in front of them laden with half-drunk pints and crisp packets, torn open for ease of sharing. Two other men were also crammed into the small area, chatting animatedly, and Alison raised her voice to be heard over the general hubbub.

'You should see how bad I was the first time I surfed, honestly, I could barely walk for a week. You did really well today, can I get you a drink to celebrate?'

'I'll get it.'

Rob heaved himself out of the seat, the movement

drawing attention to the broad expanse of his shoulders underneath a tight-fitting Breaking Waves T-shirt. Well, it drew Emer's attention, anyway, and she tried not to stare as he approached.

'Sure you know I was only slagging you. Let me get you a beer. Great for sore muscles, and I've years of research to back that theory up.'

'Just a water, thanks, I brought the car.'

The door behind her opened, bringing with it another wave of animated customers and forcing Emer to take several steps forwards until she could feel Rob's arm hairs brush against hers.

'Water's a bit dull for your first night out in Ballydrynawn. I could get you one of the zero yokes if you like?'

'Well, sure, that'd be great, thanks.'

It really was very warm in here this evening. Emer waited for a moment for the heat in her cheeks to die down before making her way over to where Alison was sitting. As she lowered herself gingerly onto the seat the American girl mouthed a sympathetic 'ouch'.

'It's tough, right? You really feel it after a few hours. Don't worry though – it's just a sign you had a good time!'

She turned slightly in an attempt to draw her table mates into the conversation.

'This is Paudie and Cian – say hi to Emer, guys! She took her first lesson today and totally killed it!'

'Howerya, Emer. Nice one, yeah.'

The other two gave vaguely friendly grunts but Emer had clearly arrived in the middle of what sounded like an intense conversation about waves, or wind, or a combination of the two and she was happy to leave them to it, shifting around on the leather seat until she found a position that was in some way bearable for her aching back and shoulders. She'd have loved some alcohol to help ease the pain – and her entry into the conversation – but having napped after her lesson, she had woken up with every muscle on fire and hadn't been able to face the two-kilometre walk to Ballydrynawn or, worse still, the hike home.

'There ya go.'

A brown arm reached over her shoulder and placed a bottle in front of her, before the rest of Rob appeared at the edge of the seat.

'Squoosh up there, so.'

Emer and Alison squooshed as Rob manoeuvred his considerable bulk into the small space they were able to vacate. The table rocked dangerously as the others grabbed their pints, slurping enthusiastically then replacing them in what looked like a well-practised move. Trying to ignore the fact that Rob's jeans-clad leg was now wedged against hers, Emer took a closer look at his friends, who looked around his age and wore the same uniform of jeans, faded T-shirts and deep, weather-beaten tans.

'There's no point in trying to interrupt those guys when they are arguing about conditions. No point in trying to follow what they are saying, either.'

There was a wistful note in Alison's voice and Emer turned to her.

'Are you not a surfer too? I thought you'd be an expert.'

The American girl shrugged.

'I mean, I can surf a little but nothing like them, especially Cian. He's won, like, competitions and stuff?'

Emer nodded.

'And how long have you been working with Rob?'

She was aware she might be coming across as nosy but Alison seemed genuinely pleased to have someone – or more to the point, another woman – to talk to and took a sip from her own pint glass before continuing.

'It's kind of a long story. I'm supposed to be travelling across Europe. I came to Ireland first and figured I'd go to London afterwards, and lots of other places. But when I saw this place...'

Alison's voice tailed off and she took another sip of her drink before continuing.

'There's something about West Kerry, isn't there? Something – oh, I'm going to say magical and you can laugh if you want.'

But Emer, who hadn't quite been able to forget her experience on the cliffs and had been checking all of the local news sites daily, just in case there was any word of a missing woman, simply nodded and waited for her to continue.

'I was staying in a hostel in the village when I met the lads and when I mentioned to Rob I was running out of cash he said he could do with a hand now things are getting busier. The school was shut during Covid, obviously, so there's quite a bit to be done to get it up and running again. I help him take bookings, hand out wetsuits, that sort of thing. I'm not technically allowed to work on my visa but...'

'I get you.'

Emer being Emer, she'd made sure she had a Green card before moving to the States but you couldn't be Irish in America without knowing someone who was earning money 'under the table' and it would be hypocritical, she decided, to criticise an American for doing something similar. Given Alison's obvious discomfort however, she decided to move the conversation along.

'You must have relatives over here then? Or why did you come to Ireland in the first place?'

It was, she thought, a simple question but to her surprise Alison seemed unable to answer it. The girl pursed her lips, then shook her head.

'Not really, I guess—'

But before she could continue the door to the pub opened again to admit a large and boisterous crowd. Rob's friend Paudie raised his head and roared.

'Here's trouble now!'

The newcomers were a mixed group, four men and three women, all in their mid-thirties and all obviously at the midpoint rather than the start of their evening. There was no way of squeezing one extra body let alone seven into their packed corner so Paudie stood up and began to briskly reorganise the space, dragging over tables and requisitioning chairs from other parts of the bar. Within moments, Emer found herself perched on a low stool beside Cian, with Alison now several feet away across the table. She briefly considered fighting her way back across to the American woman again, but then from the opposite corner of the pub a fiddle rang out, closely followed by the twang of guitar strings, and it soon became clear that any sort of involved conversation would have to be put on hold.

'You wouldn't get this up in Dublin, I'd say.'

Cian's face was serious, but his eyes were bright and as the music grew louder Emer wasn't quite sure if he was laughing at her or not.

118

'Well we do have music in pubs, yeah.'

'Ah, not like this.'

Cian folded his arms and regarded Emer with a slight frown. With sandy, thinning hair and small round glasses he reminded her of one of her tutors back in college; that is, if a tutor had worn a T-shirt that proclaimed, in loud purple, 'Surfers do it standing up'. At least he was making an effort to talk to her though and so Emer leaned in, mimicking his deadpan tone.

'So, you're saying this is special Kerry music, yeah?'

'Oh no.'

Cian's frown deepened.

'It's special West Kerry music. The best kind of all. Do you see that man?'

He nodded across the bar to a young accordion player whose fingers were moving so quickly, Emer wouldn't have been surprised to see steam rise from the white buttons into the air.

'Five generations of music in that family and it's only better they are getting.'

'And do you play yourself?'

Cian shook his head.

'I don't. I just sit back and admire the talent.'

'I hear you're pretty talented yourself though. At surfing I mean.'

'Yerrah.'

As Cian pulled his arms tighter against his body, almost folding himself away, Emer realised she had made a rookie error. She had been away from Ireland too long, and from Kerry longer again. The streets of Ballydrynawn might be flowing with alcohol-free beer and soy lattes these days but it was still a place where compliments were treated with the utmost suspicion and direct questions barely tolerated. In America, if you wanted information you asked for it, and if you liked someone's work you praised them for it, but down here it was more customary to bat away direct enquiries like a tennis player returning a serve and the phrase 'I will, yeah' meant 'most certainly not'. Distracted, she glanced across the table to see if Alison could come to her rescue but the American girl was now deep in conversation with Paudie and seemed oblivious to the rest of the group. Cian, however, had followed her gaze and as his face flushed Emer realised she had made it very obvious who had been talking about him. He rubbed his hands across his face as if to wipe away his reaction then turned to her again.

'You're staying above in your folks' place?'

As he cocked his head to one side Emer knew Cian was marking her cards, letting her know she wasn't the only one who had been listening to gossip. Fifteen love. She hesitated for a moment and then decided it would be easier to let him win the rally.

'Yeah, for a few months. Just taking a break really.'

'No better place, sure.'

This time Cian's smile was genuine and Emer felt as if she had passed some sort of test, albeit one she hadn't wanted to sit in the first place. A sudden wave of weariness came over her – being sober always got harder as the evening grew later – and she rose slowly to her feet.

'I'm just going to stretch my legs.'

A surge of lactic acid made her wince and although she had only planned on grabbing a glass of water Emer began to wonder if she might be better off calling it a night after all. And then Rob rose from his own stool and came to stand beside her.

'You're not heading off yet, are you? Let me get you another one.'

Or maybe she should hang around for a little while longer. Just to be polite, obviously.

'It's my round.'

Before Rob could put up any resistance Emer turned and made her way across the now packed bar behind which a small, industrious man, his white shirt escaping from a pair of too tight black trousers, was taking orders then sliding drinks across the counter in one seamless movement. It was a system the staff at her local coffee shop in LA would marvel at, Emer thought. There was no need to ask for names here, in fact some locals simply had to mutter 'Same again please, Shay,' before fresh drinks appeared in front of them. When her own turn came, she carried the drinks carefully back to the corner only to find that Rob had moved, and was now standing on his own by the wall. There was a wooden ledge by his elbow and when she placed the drinks on it he thanked her, then nodded across at his friends.

'Hope they haven't been bending your ear too much, the surf talk can get a bit wearing if you're not into it.'

'Not at all!'

Emer shook her head, but couldn't help a faint flicker of satisfaction that Rob had clearly been keeping an ear to how her evening was going. She took a sip from her drink, her tired muscles making the bottle feel as if it weighed a tonne. Rob noticed her grimace and grinned.

'Was my famous beer cure no use to you in the end, so?'

'Not much, I'm afraid. I'll have to chance the full-strength version next time, I think.'

'Well, that can be arranged.'

He clinked his glass against her bottle, drank and then exhaled happily.

'This, now, is the nectar of the gods. We'd two other groups in after you this afternoon, I'm fairly shattered myself.'

Emer couldn't help laughing at the pure contentment on his bronzed face, which looked relaxed and as far from tired as she could imagine.

'Are you teaching tomorrow?'

'Nope. We're just doing three days a week at the moment.'

'How many work at the school?'

'There's just two of us at the moment, myself and Mark, you might have seen him earlier?'

Emer nodded, remembering the older man she'd seen on the beach with Alison.

'We'll have three more instructors when the schools break up, we'll have kids' camps every day then. But I usually try to keep Sunday free no matter what, I'd never get out myself otherwise.'

'So that's what you do when you have a day off from surfing? You go – surfing?'

Rob looked at her, eyes wide in mock indignation.

'Well, obviously! Sometimes we drive up as far as Clare too, we wouldn't want to get predictable.'

Emer grinned.

'It must get frustrating though, spending your days watching beginners like me fall off.'

'Not at all.'

Rob was still smiling but his eyes, she noticed, were now entirely serious.

'You get the odd time in a school group or a summer camp when a kid clearly doesn't want to be there and that can be hell for everyone. But most of the time people are into it and when you can help them catch their first wave, there's no better feeling really.'

'It was incredible.'

The hum of conversation in the pub was growing louder and Emer took a step closer to him so he could hear her properly.

'I have to tell you, I nearly turned and ran when I got to the beach this morning, I thought it would be a total disaster. But when I got in the water – God, it's just the best feeling, isn't it?'

'It is. You did really well for your first time, too.'

Emer raised her eyebrows.

'I'm sure you say that to all the beginners.'

Rob was standing so close to her now, the sound of his voice was making her eardrums thrum.

'I don't really. I mean you try to encourage people, obviously, they're on their holidays, most of them, and you want them to have fun. But you really got it, didn't you? Towards the end there you were flying. You'll see, the next time you go out you'll be straight up on the board.'

'It was the speed of it.'

Emer glanced away for a moment, then looked back at him, remembering.

'I just wasn't expecting it to feel so fast, does that sound stupid? I've been swimming in the sea all my life but this was a whole other sensation, it was like flying. I had no idea how powerful the waves would feel, and they were only small, I mean I can't imagine what it must be like to be out there when the swell is big and—'

She stopped, suddenly self-conscious, but Rob held her gaze.

'Come out with me again some morning, and I'll show you. You'll be flying then all right.'

He was clean-shaven this evening, Emer noticed, and she could smell a light, citrussy aftershave.

'I'll definitely book another lesson.'

'You could. Or you could just come out with me. Whatever suits, like.'

'That'd be great.'

There was another layer under the aftershave, Emer realised, a subtle tang of salt and sea, and she allowed herself a moment to think about the power of the waves and the joy of doing something new, how glad she was that she had been brave that morning. Smiling, Rob leaned his elbow on the shelf until their eyes were almost level. It would be easier if she was drinking; easier to go with the flow and give in to the flirtation she was absolutely sure she wasn't imagining. But she was sober, and tired, and hadn't come to Kerry for a holiday romance, or any other kind.

Those shoulders, though.

'So.'

Rob held her gaze for one more moment then lifted his pint to his lips, raised it in her direction and took a small step backwards. It was as if he had read her mind, Emer thought, and suddenly found herself far more flustered than if he had actually made a move.

'So,' she responded and cast around for some way to

continue the conversation. A roar of laughter came from the table behind them. Emer glanced over to see one of the newcomers slap Paudie on the back, and then Cian rose and walked towards them. Rob gave him a sympathetic smile.

'Paudie is in flying form tonight anyway.'

'That's one way of putting it, I suppose.'

Cian placed his bottle of beer on the ledge beside Rob's, anchoring his place in the conversation.

'He'd drive you mad, that fella. Going on with the usual shite about me "gracing the place with my presence".'

Sensing her confusion, Cian looked at Emer.

'I'm teaching below in Cork but my parents run a guesthouse up on the cliffs and I come home every weekend to help them out, and during the summer. It's only a two-hour drive, like, but you'd swear from the way Paudie goes on that I parachute in from Vegas.'

He gave a mock grimace and Emer laughed along with him. Cian was slightly built in comparison with his friends but there was something very attractive about his open, friendly face and he was much less intimidating than the garrulous Paudie or even Rob, with whom she was finding it increasingly difficult to maintain eye contact. The three of them chatted for a moment, inconsequential stuff about the crowd in the pub, Emer's summer plans and her day job, and she didn't even mind when Cian asked her if she knew any film stars, because he did it in such a good-humoured way. And then the music, which had faded slightly into the background, stopped completely and Emer felt a shift in the atmosphere. She turned, craning her neck to see a small woman with a pale face and long thick red hair slide a flute from a wooden case. As they watched, she lifted the instrument to her lips and began to play a slow, haunting air, the other musicians resting their instruments on their knees and giving her their full attention. Emer watched, rapt, as the woman breathed music into the flute, the notes soaring out and over their heads then dissipating into the warm moist air of the pub. A final note faded away, there was a beat of absolute silence and then, as if working from an unspoken cue, the others took up their instruments again, grasping the melody and galloping away with it until it became something else entirely, a jagged, living thing, while the woman took the flute away from her mouth and replaced it with a smile, her job complete.

Emer continued watching them for a moment then turned back to the men.

'That was beautiful.'

Rob nodded but Cian didn't seem to have heard her, his attention focused once again on his group of friends. Or, to be more precise, one friend, Alison, who was, now the music had ended, deep in conversation with Paudie again. Rob gave him a sideways glance.

'Why don't you see if she wants a drink?'

Cian flushed.

'No, I think she—'

'You lousy piece of shit!'

And now everyone in the pub was looking at the corner table as Alison rose from her seat, took Paudie's almost full pint of Guinness and poured it over his head.

'How dare you speak to me like that!'

Even the music faltered as the musicians craned their necks to see what was going on. Paudie rose from his seat, his face brick-red with anger, and wiped as much of the beer away as he could with one hand. The extent of his rage was visible even from where she was standing and Emer shivered, despite the heat of the pub. Then she heard a rustle from behind her as Shay the barman darted across the floor. Rob, who up until now had appeared vaguely amused by the spectacle, replaced his own pint on the ledge.

'We'd better rescue Alison before your man throws her out.'

All of the corner drinkers were standing up now, some sympathising with Paudie and others teasing him, but they moved aside as Shay and then Rob approached. Unsure of what else to do, Emer followed them and heard Rob's urgent whisper.

'I'll take her home, Shay.'

'I've the right to bar her.'

'I know you do, but if you just let me look after her now I promise it won't happen again.'

Rob was standing still now, his palms outstretched in a gesture of easy friendliness, but there was toughness too and just enough authority in his tone to make the barman pause and consider what he was saying. It was no wonder Rob was drawn to teaching, Emer thought, then flinched as Paudie hissed at him.

'I could have that bitch done for assault.'

His hands were by his sides but the fists were tightly clenched. Rob must have noticed because he looked around and caught Emer's eye.

'Give us a hand here, will you?'

Emer grabbed her jacket from where she'd left it on her seat then between them they half led, half carried Alison towards a door at the back of the pub. Shay followed but Paudie was restrained by a stony-faced Cian. The words 'two-faced bitch' accompanied them out into the air and as the door shut behind them, Shay glared at Rob.

'I can't have shit like that in my pub, Robbie, you know that.'

'I'm really sorry.'

They were the first words Alison had spoken and came out as little more than a sob as Shay continued.

'Jesus, man, I'm only after opening back up, I can't afford any trouble now!'

Rob shifted Alison's weight until it looked like she was almost standing on her own feet again and only Emer, wedged on the other side, realised how much support she still needed as he returned Shay's gaze.

'I know, man, I get you. We'll take her home, it won't happen again. And if it does you can call the guards, all right? Just give her one chance.'

'I shouldn't.'

There was a layer of worry under Shay's annoyance now and he peered closer at Alison, whose eyelids were fluttering as she struggled to focus.

'I wouldn't have served her, either, if I knew she was in that state.'

'I know you wouldn't, sure.'

Rob's tone was light, placatory.

'That's Yanks for you, that stuff they call beer over there is only water, they can't hold their drink at all.'

The barman paused, and then gave a heavy sigh.

'You'll look after her?' He included Emer in his gaze. 'Both of you? You won't leave her alone?'

'Of course not.'

'Go on so,' the barman muttered, but not unkindly, then turned on his heel and disappeared back into the pub. Rob waited until the door had shut behind him before exhaling and releasing his grip on Alison who sagged forward onto Emer's shoulder.

'Jesus, she's in some state.'

Moving slowly, they walked the girl over to a low wall which connected the pub with the village's large public car park. Emer could see her Ford Focus from here but had a feeling it wouldn't be carrying her back to the Tigín any time soon. As if he could read her mind, Rob looked at her, and crinkled his lips in a half smile.

'I don't suppose there is any way you could drop her home? I know it's a big ask but I'm not sure what else we can do. There's taxis, but I can't see any of them wanting to carry her in this state.'

Emer sighed.

'I will, I suppose. She'd better not puke in the car though.'

'I'll make sure she won't, promise. That is, if you don't mind me hopping in too? And I can show you the way.'

'Go on, so.'

'You're a gem. Give me five minutes, I want to sort out that dickhead Paudie and then we can hit the road.'

Rob turned and jogged back to the bar while Emer sat down beside Alison, preparing herself for a cold and silent wait. But the cold air seemed to have revived the American a little and she moaned and then struggled upright, covering her face with her hands.

'I am so sorry.'

Emer gave her a quick, one-armed hug and when she

released her was relieved to find she was more or less able to remain sitting upright on her own.

'What happened, sweetheart? Did Paudie do something to you? Because if you want to make a complaint or anything...'

'No.'

Alison shook her head slowly.

'He's a creep but he didn't touch me or anything, not like that. It was just what he'd call banter. He's married but he likes to pretend he still has it, you know? But when I didn't play along he started to come out with the usual shit, that I'm only hanging around here because I fancy Rob, or Cian, or somebody. Because of course it must be a man keeping me here, there's no way I'd stay here just for me, I mean because I want to be here, because I am happy...'

A look of intense concentration came over Alison's face as she struggled to put her words in the right order.

'He kept saying there must be someone, because why else would I stay here? And when I told him I wasn't interested, he basically called me a liar. And that's when I, well...'

'Gave him a well deserved Guinness shower.'

Emer gave the younger woman a tighter hug.

'I don't bloody blame you.'

'I know, right!'

For a moment Alison sat upright, triumphant. And then she sagged against Emer again.

'Is Shay ever going to let me back in the pub?'

The final word turned into a wail.

'It's the only place the guys like to hang out; if he says I can't come back I'll have nowhere to go...'

'It's OK.'

Emer tried to sound cheerful.

'Rob's gone back in now to sort it out.'

Alison looked at her, alarmed.

'He doesn't know, does he? What Paudie said?'

'I don't think so.' Emer shrugged. 'He just said he was going to "sort him out", whatever that means.'

'Rob's so nice.'

Alison's voice took on a dreamy quality which made Emer wonder if Paudie hadn't been on the right track after all, but then the American girl turned and did her best to focus on her.

'He likes you.'

'Ah now here...'

Emer felt a prickle of irritation. This was a way heavier conversation than she wanted with a stranger, or anyone really. Sure, there had been a bit of flirtation back in the bar but that was as far as it had gone and she certainly didn't appreciate feeling Alison, or anyone, had been keeping tabs on her.

But the other woman had gone into full-on drunk talk mode.

'He's super-hot. But take care, OK? He's like a total player. I mean, God, have fun, but don't expect anything serious from Rob Lynch—'

'Alison, I think you have the wrong end of the stick.'

But the American was still talking.

'I love him so much and I can't tell him.'

'Right.'

Totally confused now and not a little irritated Emer pulled away.

'But what you said to Paudie—'

'I love him because he's family!'

Alison sniffed and then began to sob extravagantly.

'He's family and I haven't told him yet. And I feel like I'm lying to them all, and I can't—'

'Can't what?'

The two women looked up to see Rob towering over them. Although she could feel Alison tense beside her, Emer was fairly sure he had only heard the tail end of the conversation.

'Can't wait to get home, isn't that right, Alison?'

The American woman looked at her gratefully but didn't speak and Emer looked up at Rob.

'Did you talk to Paudie?'

'I did. He'll get over it.'

All of a sudden Emer felt another wave of exhaustion hit. It was almost eleven, she was both stone-cold sober and stone cold and the low concrete wall was doing nothing for her aching muscles. Hot surfers and pub fights and long-lost relatives – she had been in Kerry for less than a week and had already encountered more drama than in any film she'd ever worked on. On another night, or with a few beers on board herself, she might have found it mildly entertaining but right now she just wanted to get the American girl sorted and then head to bed herself.

She eased herself up from the wall then dragged Alison to her feet.

'Let's just get this one home.'

Chapter Nine

NEW YORK CITY

1924

'Watch where you're walking!'
'I'm so sorry...'
But Annie's apology was lost in the roar of the automobile engine. She clambered up onto the pavement and clutched the collar of her thin jacket to her neck, feeling her pulse leap under her fingertips. She had been trying to be careful, she really had, but there were just so many people here and so many vehicles, black motor cars belching out smoke and green double-decker omnibuses that looked like they could topple over at any moment, that she found it impossible not to get in the way.

Heart still racing, she ducked into a shop doorway then watched with envy as the rest of the world simply strolled by. Messenger boys, members of the gentry, young working women like herself, it didn't matter what business had brought them to New York City, each person seemed to be able to find a gap in the crowds and pass on through without breaking stride. No one made room for anyone else on these streets, Annie thought to herself. She would have to find her own way.

The piece of paper with the address on it was wedged deep into her pocket but there was no need to look at it, she had already memorised the words.

Mrs Peter Cavendish, Chateau D'or,
5th Avenue, New York City.

Her interview was at noon and her grandmother's wristwatch told her it was already a quarter past eleven so, with as much determination as she could muster, Annie took a deep breath and plunged into the crowd again. A man in a long white apron smiled at her from behind his wooden cart, he was selling what looked like boiled sausages wrapped in a floury bun but although Annie had coins in her pocket, she didn't feel in the slightest bit hungry. The nuns had given her a fine breakfast that morning, and they had been very hospitable the night before too, feeding her a dinner of stew before leading her to a spotlessly clean dormitory room. The mother superior, a tall woman with a west of Ireland accent similar to Nora's, had been brisk but kind, showing Annie where she could wash and iron her best blouse and preparing her for the type of questions that she might be asked at today's interview. She had also reassured her that, being a Catholic herself, Mrs Cavendish was always willing to allow her staff time off to attend mass. Despite the sisters' kindness, however, Annie had barely slept and only worried down the food out of politeness.

Now it was time to stop fretting and let her new life begin in earnest. Annie reached the end of yet another street and crossed the road that would finally bring her on to Fifth Avenue. The nuns had given her excellent directions but she deserved a little bit of praise too, she decided, for navigating these wide and crowded streets, so utterly foreign to anything she had experienced before. With fifteen minutes still remaining before her appointment she slowed her pace and allowed herself a moment to look upwards, to where the buildings, some of them bedecked with advertising hoardings, loomed over her. Annie had known to expect 'skyscrapers' in New York City, the letters she had read at a neighbour's house had spoken of structures so tall they stretched into the clouds, but no one had told her how beautiful the buildings were, how much care had been taken with every brick and railing. One window ledge boasted ornate stone flowers, on another a steel balcony had been attached, its function as a fire escape eclipsed by the artistry of its intricate metal swirls. Back in Ireland Annie's family kept their home as neat as they could, of course, and her mother painted their wooden front door bright red every May to mark the beginning of summer. But these American buildings were magnificent, other-worldly constructions and yet another very visible sign of just how different Annie's new life would be over here.

The houses grew bigger and even more splendid the further Annie walked until she finally came to a halt in front of the grandest of them all, a pale yellow palace that seemed to glow golden in the afternoon sunshine. There was no name on the gatepost, no number hidden in the golden swirls on the huge wooden door, but this had to be the Cavendish home, the Golden Castle of Fifth Avenue, looking for all the world as if it had been lifted by magic from the French countryside and deposited onto the side of a grey Manhattan street. A flight of stone steps connected the castle with the street but Annie walked straight past them – the nuns had warned her to use the servants' entrance but even without their guidance she knew she would never have had the courage to march straight up to the door and grasp that polished brass knocker. Instead, she made her way down an alleyway at the side of the building and towards another smaller wooden door. Her cautious knock elicited a shuffling sound and then the door swung open to reveal a tiny woman, as broad as she was tall, with pince-nez perched on the end of her long nose, and black hair streaked with grey scraped back in a low bun from a ruddy, pleasant face.

'You're on time anyway, I'll say that much for you.'

The woman spoke as if they had already been in the middle of a conversation. It was a habit her grandmother had had too and Annie immediately felt a little more at ease.

'You'll be Annie, that the sisters sent. I'm Mrs O'Toole, I'm housekeeper here at the Chateau.'

She pronounced it *Shadow*, in an accent that was not American but not familiar to Annie either. Mrs O'Toole seemed to sense her confusion.

'I'm a Belfast woman myself, Annie, but I've been in New York this fifteen year. The girls the nuns send over are usually good workers, are you a good worker? I hope you are. Follow me now down here...'

Despite her tiny stature, the woman moved at a brisk pace and, tired after her long walk, Annie found herself struggling to keep up as they made their way through a huge kitchen, dominated by a large wooden table in the centre of the room. At a sink by the window, two blonde girls stood, heads bent over a huge mound of potatoes, chattering in a language Annie definitely didn't understand, but she didn't get the chance to listen properly as Mrs O'Toole ushered her through a huge wooden door covered in a green felt material. It shut behind them, gentle as a whisper, and they were suddenly plunged into near darkness as Annie followed the housekeeper up a set of narrow wooden stairs. A door at the top led them into a giant hallway, and as Annie blinked rapidly it became clear the sunlight was not the only difference up here. Oh, she was in the land of the gentry now, no doubt about it. Polished wooden floorboards were covered by ornate woollen rugs and as they scurried across Annie found herself wondering if it would be her job to keep them in that pristine state. But there was no time to take in any more details, they were still moving, trotting up another flight of stairs now, this one covered by a light blue carpet. Images from the house were flashing past her now, so quickly she could barely absorb them: a huge picture window, a highly polished table in an alcove, a vase of fresh flowers. They reached a landing and headed off down a long corridor – were they still in the same house, even? It seemed impossible to have walked this far and not reached their destination – and then Mrs O'Toole pulled up so suddenly Annie almost bumped into her, and muttered.

'She's no fool, Mrs Cavendish, but she's a fair woman, so speak up, Annie, and you'll do fine.'

Then the older woman gave a gentle knock on the door and turned the handle.

It needed a good dusting, was the first thing Annie thought about the room. It was grand of course, this one single room bigger than her entire house at home, but although the sofas arrayed under the windows were deep and comfortable-looking, streams of dustmites were visible in the light pouring through those windows and Annie found herself itching to take out a cloth and run it along the dark, heavy furniture. Lost in thought, she didn't see the figure sitting on the far side of the room until Mrs O'Toole gave her a gentle nudge.

'Annie Thornton, madam. From the nuns.'

Annie dipped her head but not before noticing that the woman was sitting not on one of the deep sofas, but on a narrow, high-backed chair covered in pink velvet atop wooden, but equally dusty, legs. Although it was a warm day a fire had been lit in the grate and Annie felt her cheeks burn as Mrs O'Toole pushed her forwards.

'This is Mrs Cavendish, Annie.'

Although she had never done so before, Annie bobbed a curtsy and heard Mrs O'Toole give a quick murmur of approval. From her pink throne, the woman extended a long, thin hand.

'Come closer, Annie. You're a tall girl, aren't you? When did you arrive in New York?'

'Just yesterday, madam.'

Her voice felt wobbly and small and the woman frowned, as if sensing her hesitation.

'Fresh off the boat! And what sort of experience do you have, Annie? Have you done this sort of work before?'

Annie gave a quick glance around the room and felt her stomach clench with tension. This type of work? Surely the woman could guess she had never stepped inside this kind of house before, let alone cleaned one. Were they expecting

someone else? Would they send her straight back to the nuns
if she admitted this was her first position, and, oh Lord,
would the nuns allow her to stay if she did so? She didn't
have the money yet for the fare back to Ireland... And then
an image of Nora drifted into her head and Annie thought
of what her tall, confident friend would do in this situation.
Act her way out of it, more likely. She took a deep breath
then threw her shoulders back and spoke as confidently as
she dared.

'I'm the eldest of my family, ma'am, and my mother
was unwell when I was younger so I took over most of the
housework. I minded the children, kept the house clean, did
all of the cooking...'

The vision of herself sweeping the flagged kitchen floor
then boiling potatoes over the open fire almost made her
smile but she held her face still as she continued.

'I know you are looking for a kitchen maid, ma'am, and
I can assure you—'

'I need a general maid.'

Mrs Cavendish sounded bored.

'I don't know what those nuns told you but I need a
general maid. You'd clean these rooms, and wait at table,
and be available when we call at other times. Will you be
able for that?'

Given that the alternative involved heading straight back
to the boat again, Annie nodded eagerly.

'Yes, ma'am. That sounds perfect, madam.'

'Very well.'

The woman shifted on her chair as if her lower back
ached.

'Mrs O'Toole will give you the rest of your instructions.

I would like a cup of coffee now though, so if that could be arranged—'

Mrs O'Toole stepped forwards.

'Certainly, Mrs Cavendish. Annie will bring it up presently.'

Within moments they were back out in the corridor and then descending the stairs. When they got to the kitchen, Mrs O'Toole walked towards the range and moved a kettle on to the heat.

'I'll help you set the tray, Annie, but make sure you watch what I'm doing as I won't have time to show you the next time. Those two...'

She nodded her head towards the blonde girls who were now attacking a pile of carrots, longer and somehow more orange than any Annie had seen before.

'They're German, great little workers but not a word of English between them. So they'll do the work down here and you'll go between here and upstairs, do you understand?'

Annie didn't, but nodded anyway.

'And who else is here – on the staff I mean?'

Mrs O'Toole was cutting and buttering scones as she spoke.

'We're a small household, considering.'

Considering the amount of work we have to do, was what Annie felt was missing from the sentence.

Mrs O'Toole made a harrumphing sound before continuing.

'There's Mabel, the cook, but today is her free afternoon so I'm looking after her duties and she will do the same for me come Friday. Mr Lawrence is Mr Cavendish's man really but he looks after the front door as well, greets the visitors. There's Tim, who looks after the stables and he's just learned how to drive Mr Cavendish's automobile too – my goodness you should hear the din it makes when he starts it up! And we have Millie, who helps with the pots, but she stays down here. You'll mainly go between the kitchen and upstairs – don't look so scared, child!'

The older woman placed the scones on a plate, poured boiling water into a coffee pot then reached out and placed a hand gently on Annie's arm.

'You're a bright girl, Annie, I can tell just by looking at you. You'll be busy but the Cavendishes are good people. Now, we're ready…'

With the same efficient movements she placed the food and drink on a tray and handed it to Annie with a wink.

'Go back up to the room you were just in, don't spill anything, put this on the small side table, ask her if she has everything she needs and leave as soon as she dismisses you. I'll show you to your room then. Welcome to your new life, Annie! Welcome to your new home.'

Chapter Ten

CO. KERRY

May 2022

'If you take the next left so – no, not this one, the next one. That's it.'

Rob pointed, then settled back into his seat as Emer executed the turn, moving slowly and carefully to avoid the ditch at the side of the road. It was almost irrelevant, she thought grimly, that she was still getting used to driving on the left again – down here you hugged the middle of the road and hoped for the best.

The village of Ballydrynawn now far behind them, she checked once again that the car lights were on full beam then glanced across at her passenger who seemed completely relaxed, despite the fact that his large frame was spilling out of the front seat of the Ford Focus.

'How's Alison?'

His seatbelt strained as Rob twisted round to look at the back seat, from where gentle snores were now emanating.

'Out for the count, but grand, I think. I'll keep an eye on her anyway.'

Emer nodded, reassured by his matter-of-fact tone.

'Has this happened before?'

Rob shook his head.

'Honestly, I've never even seen her drunk before. She usually only has a couple of beers on a night out and, you know, that could be part of the problem. We had a late class this evening and she mightn't have had time to eat before she came to the pub. And then Paudie and the lads were doing shots – sure they would have floored her.'

An insect flew out of the darkness straight into the windscreen and Emer flinched, then flicked the corpse away with the wipers before continuing.

'You don't think he could have spiked her drink or anything?'

'Ah God, no.'

Rob shifted in his seat.

'Paudie can be an awful arsehole but he wouldn't do that. He's all talk, that fella, nothing more. Sure he has a wife and two kids at home. Cathy, the missus, usually comes to the pub with him on Saturdays to keep an eye on him but her mother isn't well so they'd no babysitter tonight. She'll give him awful shit when he comes home half drowned in porter.'

'He probably deserves it.'

Emer's tone was designed to convey exactly what she thought of men who needed their wives to 'keep an eye on them', and Rob's answer was a low chuckle.

'He probably does. Have you any idea what he said to Alison? To make her so upset?'

'Not really.'

The road narrowed even further and Emer slowed the car, concentrating both on her driving and the need to respect the American girl's privacy. Before she could fumble an answer, however, a gap in the hedge on her left revealed an old stone cottage, exactly the sort of house she imagined Rob would live in.

'Is this you?'

'No, we've a while to go yet.'

It was a good thing he had offered to accompany her back to Alison's place, Emer thought, as otherwise she would be desperately lost by now, and even if road signs existed around here there was no public lighting to read them by. They drove past two more dwellings, another traditional cottage and a larger, 1960s bungalow through whose front window the blue flicker of a television set could be seen, but each time Rob indicated she should keep on driving.

'Does she live very near you then, Alison?'

Emer came to a temporary halt at a T-junction then followed her passenger's instructions to take the right-hand turn.

'She's staying at our place, actually.'

Rob pressed his large, tanned hand against his mouth, stifling a yawn.

'There's a kind of a granny flat out the back of my mom's house, Alison is hanging out there for summer.'

'Your mom's house?'

Emer wasn't surprised to hear Rob refer to his mother as 'Mom'. It wasn't an Americanism, the word was traditionally used in this part of Ireland too, possibly related to the way 'Mam' was pronounced in the Irish language. But whether he called her Mom, Mam or Mommy Dearest, she was a little taken aback to find he still lived with her. Rob, though, didn't seem to have noticed her change in tone, or if he had didn't seem to care.

'That's right. Left here, now...'

Following his instructions, Emer indicated then turned onto yet another narrow, unlit road. Here, gaps in the hedgerow to her right revealed silvery glimpses of sea and she imagined she could hear, over the sound of the engine, the gentle slosh of the waves. This would be a stunning journey during the day, she thought, but she was very tired now and decided to risk sounding nosy just to keep the conversation going and herself alert.

'So have you lived in Kerry all your life then?'

'I was born in America, actually.'

'Oh?'

'Yeah, Mom was working over there when she had me. My father – well, he wasn't ever in the picture, put it that way. Mom looked after me on her own for as long as she could but it was impossible really, with work and that. So when the time came for school she sent me back here to live with my grandparents.'

'And did you start surfing down here then? Or in the States?'

'Here, when I was around twelve. Cian and I started together, and Paudie a little while after. There was an older guy in the village who taught a lot of the local lads. There was nothing as formal as a surf school back then but he was a great teacher, and a bit of a hero to us really, he'd surfed in Hawaii and that, we thought it was fierce exciting! It was all I ever wanted to do, to be honest with you. Mom wanted me to do the whole college thing so I went up to Sligo for a bit but I still spent more time in the water than out of it and after a few years I went travelling and ended up in County Bondi.'

Emer laughed, having heard the Irish nickname for the Sydney suburb before.

'Is it really that bad over there?'

'It's ridiculous.'

Rob grinned.

'Next left, please. Yeah, it's all Irish over there. It's a drawback really, you end up hardly meeting any Australians at all, you're socialising with Irish, living with them. Living with one, in my case. But that ran its course so I moved home. No place like it, as they say! Just up here now, on the left.'

Emer resisted the urge to probe more into what had 'run its course', which was a good thing because the road she turned onto was, incredibly, even narrower than the one they had left behind and, as a branch scraped against the side of the car, she suddenly found she needed to keep all of her attention on the road. Sensing her nervousness Rob continued to chatter gently.

'I opened Breaking Waves five years ago but sure when Covid hit I had to put everything on hold – just here.'

Emer stopped, too quickly, and the car skidded on some loose stones. She looked around for a house but could see nothing, just tall hedgerows on one side of the road and on the other, a low stone wall beyond which fields dropped away to the sea. But just as she was starting to question her willingness to ferry a giant Kerryman and an unconscious Yank into somewhere far past the back of beyond, Rob extracted a set of keys from the pocket of his jeans and pointed a plastic fob towards the windscreen. There was a gentle humming sound and then Emer stared in amazement as the darkness ahead of them seemed to shift and solidify, revealing two huge solid gates which slid apart to expose a long silver driveway. Rob replaced the fob in his pocket.

'You can head away in here now.'

Emer eased the car forward then blinked as a set of security lights blazed on. The vehicle was travelling smoothly now, the rough stony road replaced by smooth tarmacadam with manicured lawn on both sides. But her surprise at the driveway was nothing to the shock she felt when the house itself came into view, an expanse of angles crafted from wood, glass and steel, dominant in the darkness yet somehow also nestling into its surroundings rather than diminishing them. To hell with the country cottage of her imagination – Rob's 'Mom' appeared to live in a cross between a luxury hotel and a Bond villain's country lair.

'What did you say your mother did again?'

Rob's answer was gruff, almost embarrassed.

'Computers, that sort of thing. Could you follow the path around the back, please? And we'll get this lady home.'

Silent now, Emer eased the car around the side of the magnificent building then brought it to a halt at a freestanding structure some metres away, which was much smaller but of a similar design to the main house. From the back seat came a groan and then a shuffling sound as Alison pulled herself into a sitting position.

'I guess we're home.'

Rob and Emer looked back at her. Alison, although bleary-eyed, seemed far more alert than when they had left the village and, as if to prove their point, gave a weak smile.

'Thanks for the lift.'

Rob gave a short, satisfied nod then turned to Emer.

'I might leave you to see her inside? If you don't mind.'

He lowered his voice.

'I mean I'm technically her boss, as well as her landlord so...'

'Sure.'

Rob opened the car door, hauled himself out then crossed around the front and waited till Emer rolled down her window.

'Call by the house after and I'll give you directions to get back to your own place. And thanks again, Emer, I owe you one.'

He gave the roof a short solid tap then disappeared into the blackness. Emer sat for a moment, conscious of how empty the car suddenly seemed without him. Then she turned to the girl in the back seat who seemed to be working hard on bringing the world back into focus.

'Come on, let's get you inside.'

Rob had called it a 'granny flat', which always made Emer think of overstuffed rooms and violently patterned carpets but the inside of this house was light years away from that particular design cliché. Closing the heavy front door behind her, she made her way across light wooden floorboards and guided Alison towards a pair of low grey sofas, arranged not in front of a television but a large picture window. The view from here would be stunning in daylight, Emer thought, and was spectacular even now, with the moon rippling light onto the sea and a pair of islands further out in the bay. She didn't have time to appreciate it, however, as Alison had flopped onto the nearest couch and seemed to be on the verge of nodding off again.

'Tea?'

Emer paused for a moment, then answered her own question.

'I think so, yes.'

An alcove at the top of the room led to a small but impeccably equipped galley kitchen and after some foraging Emer found bread, a stainless steel toaster and a set of gorgeous handcrafted mugs, each one bearing a stylised painting of a cow and the signature of a local artist whose name she recognised from the Sunday supplements Maura loved to leave scattered around the house, in the hope that some of their tasteful contents would magically transfer themselves onto her walls. There wasn't a mass-produced item in the place, Emer thought, wondering how much the 'granny flat' would fetch on Airbnb and, more to the point, how well-off Rob's mom had to be to be able to hand it over to a summer worker without a second thought.

The toast popped up, disturbing her musings, and she buttered it, then brought it and the tea back into the sitting room where Alison fell on it with enough enthusiasm to indicate that Rob had been right about why the drink had gone so spectacularly to her head earlier that evening. After chatting to her for a while to make sure she was sober enough to be left alone, Emer rose to her feet.

'You'll drink more water before bed? And you'll go to the loo if you feel you're going to throw up?'

'Yes, Mom. I promise, Mom.'

Emer raised an eyebrow at the young woman who was now wiping crumbs from her mouth with the back of her hand.

'Very funny. I know I sound like a pain in the arse but

you were pretty far gone earlier, do you know what I mean? If I'm going to leave you here I just want to be sure you'll be OK.'

Alison's look of embarrassment was further proof, Emer thought, that she was on the road back to sobriety.

'I'm sorry, I didn't mean to be a bitch. I really appreciate you bringing me home. I'm just embarrassed I got myself in such a state.'

The woman's rumpled hair and pale face made her look around twelve years old, and Emer felt a jolt of sympathy.

'We've all been there, hon, I'm just worried about you. But you look a lot better now you've eaten. So tell me, what day is it? Who is the President?'

'Here, or at home? They both seem like decent guys anyway, they like dogs. And it was Saturday when I went to the pub but I'm pretty sure it's Sunday now. Oowww...'

Alison winced.

'And my headache is telling me this hangover is going to be spectacular.'

She clambered up from the sofa and headed out of the room, returning a few moments later with a blister pack of supermarket paracetamol.

'I'll just take two of these, and then I'll hit the hay. You don't have to worry about me, OK? And I really am grateful.'

'It's no problem.'

Emer walked towards the door and then paused.

'And are you sure you're OK about – about everything that happened?'

She still wasn't sure if Alison remembered anything of

the conversation they had had, and was left none the wiser when the American woman simply shrugged.

'Paudie said some shit, I overreacted, and you and Rob hauled me out of there, I think that's the crib note?'

Emer nodded but didn't move and after a moment the other woman continued, frowning now as the evening came back to her.

'I'm gonna say I warned you off Rob, too? Which is totally none of my business but you know, I felt like I owed you one. And then I started to tell you about – why I'm really here?'

Emer nodded.

'Yeah. You did. And why you are here is none of *my* business but I just wanted to make sure you remembered what we were talking about. There's nothing worse than waking up in the horrors and not being sure what you've said.'

'I remember.'

Alison's voice was quiet, and she looked out of the window for a moment. When she turned her head back to meet Emer's gaze, her expression was impossible to read.

'I guess I have a lot to think about in the morning. But right now I just need to sleep. I really can't thank you enough, and I'll see you around, OK?'

It was unmistakably a dismissal. A bit rude, given that the woman had been barely able to stand without assistance a few hours before but further proof that her role as Good Samaritan was no longer needed.

'Yeah, see you.'

She reached once again for the door but was interrupted

by a muffled sob and then nearly knocked off her feet as Alison ran towards her and enveloped her in a hug.

'Whatever happens next, don't think badly of me, OK?'

Emer hadn't a clue what she was talking about but it seemed simplest just to return the embrace before heading, once again, for the door.

Wood, chrome and steel – as Emer eased her car away from Alison's Insta-perfect cottage she couldn't help thinking how much Maura would love to see this place and how she really should be taking mental notes to make sure she had plenty of gossip for their next phone conversation. But her eyes were watering with tiredness and all she could think about was her own bed at the Tigín, if she was able to find her way back at this hour. As she approached the main house, a glass door to the side of the building slid open and a tall figure emerged and waved at her to stop. Rolling down the car window, Emer felt yet another assumption evaporate into the warm May air. As Rob was around her own age – and still living with his mammy – she had assumed that his mother would be a dowdier version of Maura, solid and comfortable with a sensible hairdo and cardigan although, given the house, one that probably came from Prada rather than Penneys. This woman actually looked a little older than Maura but was far more glamorous and dressed in fantastically expensive-looking grey silk pyjamas, while her close-cropped white hair and red-framed glasses made her look like a professor of cultural studies about to go on TV to give a learned yet witty take on the latest social media craze. She walked around the car until she reached the driver's side then bent her head through the open window.

'Hello, I'm Siobhán. Rob says I've you to thank for bringing the pair of them home.'

Emer smiled.

'It was no trouble.'

The woman sniffed, then pushed her glasses higher onto her nose.

'I can't see why he couldn't call a taxi, John Joe down in the village has seen a lot worse than that in his day. But I suppose it was good of you anyway.'

There wasn't any way she could think of answering that so Emer just nodded and waited for her to continue.

'I'd invite you in but it's far too late – I'm sure you're dying to get away.'

It was, in fact, the exact opposite of an invitation and Emer was starting to wonder if she had done something in a former life to really piss this lady off, when a shadow loomed over the car and she looked up to see Rob approach.

'Is Alison all right?'

Emer smiled with the relief of seeing a friendly face.

'She's grand.'

'I'll see you back as far as the main road, so.'

Rob opened the door and climbed into the passenger seat, the car dipping to absorb his weight. He had exchanged his T-shirt for a Breaking Waves fleece and Emer couldn't help noticing that lemony aftershave again, this time with a faint undertone of mint toothpaste. It felt good to have him back in the car, and somehow right, as if the space belonged to him now and she had been waiting for him to fill it. And then she gave herself an internal wrist slap – in vino veritas and all that – and Alison's drunk talk had made it quite clear Rob Lynch would flirt with the wall. She needed to go home, and get some sleep. Possibly a cold shower too, if it came to it.

Rob's mother, however, didn't seem quite ready to let them go.

'You're just down for the weekend, are you, Emer? Heading back tomorrow?'

'No, I'm here for the summer!'

The look that crossed Siobhán's face made it clear she wasn't a member of any Ballydrynawn welcoming committee.

'The whole summer? I see.'

'I'm staying at my parents' place. The Molloys – you might know them? We have a house out the other side of Ballydrynawn.'

'I don't think I know any Molloys.'

'My mam was Maura Delaney before she married.'

For the first time in the conversation the older woman's face softened.

'Ah, Maura! Of course, she was a few years behind me in school but I knew your uncle Tom well.'

Siobhán studied Emer for a moment.

'You have the look of the Delaneys all right. How is Maura? Well, I hope?'

'She's great, thank you! She and my dad have gone to Australia to see my brother, his girlfriend is expecting a baby soon.'

'I see—'

'We'd better get going.'

Rob shot his mother a look.

'Emer has been ferrying us about all night, she needs to get home. But I'll tell you what...'

There was a definite note of amusement in his voice now.

'Why don't you come up for lunch tomorrow, Emer? I'll cook, you two can catch up then!'

A flicker of something not unlike horror crossed Siobhán's face.

'Oh no, I'm sure Emer has plans—'

'I don't, actually!'

Emer wasn't usually one to push herself in where she wasn't wanted but the prospect of seeing the inside of that magnificent house was impossible to turn down. It would be nice to see Rob again too, of course, but it was the house, obviously, that was the real draw. Rob's mother didn't say anything else, just gave the same firm rap on the roof of the car as her son had earlier before stepping away. And that wasn't the only thing about her that was familiar, Emer thought as she started the car then made her way slowly down the driveway. In fact she had the strangest feeling she had met Rob's mom before, although in a completely different setting. There was no point in trying to puzzle that out now, though, her brain was too tired to pull out the relevant file while there was the journey home to think about and that smell of toothpaste to ignore. Rob zapped the gates open and allowed Emer a moment to get used to the narrow roads before breaking the silence.

'I hope that's all right about tomorrow. I mean – you don't have to come to lunch if you don't want to.'

Emer stole a look at him but he was staring straight ahead,

concentrating on the road as intensely as if he himself was driving the car.

'Oh no, I'd love to.'

She hadn't intended her response to sound quite so enthusiastic and reddened, grateful for the dark interior of the car which seemed to have suddenly taken on the charged atmosphere of a secondary school disco. In fact, Emer thought if she turned on the radio right now she wouldn't have been surprised to hear that awful song that was playing the night she kissed Stephen Fennelly after being asked to do so by his best friend. What was it called again? But the silence turned out to be no less embarrassing than the initial enthusiasm, so she tried again.

'I mean, if it's OK with you. I don't want to intrude or anything…'

'It's OK with me, Emer.'

That slightly amused tone again.

'I would love to see you tomorrow.'

'Right. Great!'

The silence in the car thickened further and even the bloody road had widened so Emer couldn't pretend she had to concentrate on driving. She cast around for something neutral to say, eventually landing, despite her better judgement, on Siobhán.

'By the way, have I met your mother before? I mean, sorry. Of course you don't know if I met her before. It's just she looked really familiar…'

'Yeah, she gets that a lot.'

For the first time since she met him, Rob sounded hesitant.

'She would have been on TV a bit over the years, with her job and that.'

And suddenly Emer found the information slotting into place in her brain like a record in an old-fashioned juke box. Siobhán Lynch. Siobhán Lynch, holy shit. The hair had been brown, not silver, that was what had thrown her, but Rob's mom wasn't the only woman to have abandoned dye during the pandemic. In every other way, however, she hadn't changed from the woman Emer had been reading about in the business pages of the newspapers for over thirty years. Emer hadn't actually ever met Siobhán in person but in her early days in LA had worked as an assistant editor on a documentary about women in tech, and Siobhán Lynch had been one of the stars. Oh, it was all coming back to her now. Siobhán had been one of Ireland's first tech entrepreneurs but had the good sense to sell her first company before the dot com bubble burst in the nineties, and since then had been operating as an 'angel investor', specialising in women-led start-ups. She was well known for her charitable donations too and Emer was pretty sure she'd find a 'People of the Year' award lurking around that magnificent house if she looked hard enough. Siobhán bloody Lynch. No wonder her home looked like that, she could probably buy the entire peninsula if she had a mind to it.

'Of course. It took me a minute, but I recognise her now.'

They had reached the same viewing area Emer had stopped at earlier in the week and she indicated left, then turned into the clearing. Rob's face was impassive.

'That's right.'

And it must have been a pain in the ass, Emer realised suddenly, to have grown up with a mother like Siobhán. Sure, the money must have been nice, especially for someone who basically wanted to spend his life on a beach, but Rob was so low-key, she really couldn't imagine him enjoying any of the other trappings of serious wealth. It made perfect sense now too that Siobhán had sent him back to Ireland to go to school. Emer's own job had brought her into contact with enough wealthy people in the States to know what their lives were like, raising children in gated communities, panicking about school shootings, the drives from private school to music lessons to carefully curated playdates without a breath of unconditioned air. Siobhán might have given her son fabulous wealth but her greatest gift to him, Emer thought, had been this life back in Ballydrynawn.

They sat for a moment, looking at the sea. Wispy clouds drifted across the moon and tiny waves slopped onto the shore before disappearing into the sand and giving Emer the cue to return to a more neutral topic.

'Not a good night for surfing.'

Rob shook his head.

'Not tonight, no. Should be a decent swell tomorrow afternoon though.'

'Does it take long to learn? Not just the surfing but the tides, that sort of thing. I saw figures written down on a board by the beach, wind direction and that. It looked kind of complicated.'

Rob shrugged.

'You get a knack for it. And there are apps now, obviously, all sorts of tech. But the Kerry weather doesn't always do what an iPhone tells it to.'

'I can imagine.'

'You'll give it another go so?'

Emer didn't have to fake the warmth in her response.

'Absolutely. First chance I get.'

There was a pause and then her gaze fell on the clock on the dashboard and despite herself she had to fight a yawn.

'Thanks a million for coming this far but I'll be all right from here.'

Rob stretched, his hands brushing against the roof of the car.

'You sure?'

'Certain. No point in making you walk back for miles. I'm only, what, about ten minutes from Ballydrynawn?'

'About that, and it's a straight road.'

'Brilliant.'

Another pause. At least if this had been a secondary school disco, Emer thought, there would have been a DJ to give some direction to the evening but tonight they were on their own.

'I'll head off so,' Rob said, and didn't move.

'Grand so,' she replied and didn't either. And then...

'James Blunt!'

The words popped out before she could stop them and Rob sat back, a look of utter confusion on his face.

'I'm sorry?'

'I was just...'

There was no way around it, she had to explain.

'I was thinking of a song they used to play in the school disco... I must have heard it on the radio earlier. You know, one of those earworms.'

'Right.'

Rob's grin told her he knew exactly what she had been thinking about.

'I was more of a Green Day man myself. "Good Riddance" was a great one if you wanted to ask a girl to go with you.'

Emer was laughing now too.

'And did she?'

'Did she what?

'Did she go with you?'

'She usually did, yeah.'

'I bet. He's actually supposed to be fierce sound, you know.'

'Who?'

'James Blunt. He's a gas man on Twitter.'

There was a beat, and then Rob sat back and exhaled.

'I'd better make tracks. I've a Yank coming for lunch tomorrow, they're supposed to be awful picky.'

'I'm looking forward to it.'

'Me too. Around one?'

'Sounds good.'

That rap on the roof of the car. The bulk of him disappearing into the night. Emer was glad of the driving now, it gave her something to focus on and as catseyes flickered under her headlights the day's events unspooled in her mind. Rob. Alison. *Don't think badly of me.* Siobhán Lynch. Billionaires and Breaking Waves. To think, she reflected as the shuttered shops of Ballydrynawn suddenly materialised outside her window, to think she had feared this summer would be a boring one.

Chapter Eleven

NEW YORK

1926

'A dam and Eve on a raft!'

The waitress put the plate down in front of her and Annie smiled her thanks, then picked up her knife and fork. Across from her, Nora rolled her green eyes heavenwards and gave an exaggerated sigh.

'You're stone mad, Annie Thornton, do you know that? It's just two eggs on a bit of bread, no matter what fancy name they put on it. Honest to God, I don't know why you waste your money in places like this, what's the point of taking a live-in job if you're going to go out and spend every penny you have on your afternoon off?'

'I like the sound of it.'

Annie broke the yolk of her egg and watched in satisfaction as it spilled out on to the golden toast.

'I like the sound of it, and I like eating food I didn't prepare myself and I like not having to clear up afterwards. It's my money anyway, Nora Carey, I don't know why you're so bothered about what I spend it on!'

'It's Noreen now, I've told you often enough. Noh-REEN.

Nora makes me sound like some old hag just down off the side of the mountain.'

Nora took a sip of coffee and gave a pointed look at Annie's blouse which, though clean, had been heavily darned.

'And if you're going to be throwing around your few dollars, why not start in a dress shop?'

'Sorry, NorEEN.'

Annie gave a saintlike smile, then took a sip of scalding black coffee, relishing the bitterness on her tongue. She had never tasted coffee before arriving in New York and had almost spat it back out the first time she sampled it, longing for the lukewarm, heavily sugared tea her own family drank with every meal. But now, almost two years after arriving in the city, she craved the drink, relishing the jolt it gave her, the feeling of sophistication, the very aroma proof that she, Annie Thornton, was a young woman who lived in New York and ate and drank whatever she pleased – on one afternoon a week, anyway.

The rest of her time was, of course, spent at the Cavendish family's beck and call, but really, Annie mused as she took another sip of coffee, there were far worse places to be. Mr and Mrs Cavendish had three children but the oldest two, men now in their early twenties, were currently touring Europe meaning only their parents and younger sister were in permanent residence in New York. Oh, the days were long, right enough, Annie was woken at six every morning by the shouts from the delivery boys beneath her window and often didn't get to bed until after eleven but to be fair to her employers, sometimes the long hours were of her own making. Annie's work ended once the family dinner was cleared away around nine, but rather than go to sleep she often stayed up reading, or writing letters or going for a walk with Noreen or one of the other maids who lived nearby, all relishing a breath of fresh air before turning in.

There was certainly no time for idleness during the day. Annie's first task every morning was to serve Mr Cavendish breakfast in the room the family referred to as the 'pink dining room', a warm and sunny space located just off the second-floor landing which was smaller than the main dining room on the floor below. Mr Cavendish liked to be at his office at eight and therefore ate breakfast at seven, before his wife and daughter rose for the day. It was his preference, Mrs O'Toole had explained to Annie on her first week in New York, to spend that first hour of the day in total silence, which meant Annie had to make sure the breakfast was on the table before he arrived in the room and cleared away after he had left, and she herself had to use the back stairs at all times, even though it doubled the amount of walking she had to do, for fear of disturbing him.

But Mr Cavendish was not an unkind man and on the odd occasion that Annie was late, or he was early and already ensconced in the pink dining room when she arrived with his tray, it was not his nature to complain; in fact he would not look at her at all, merely stay silently barricaded behind his newspaper until she had placed the food in front of him and backed away. There were other homes in New York, Annie knew, where the doors in the family rooms were wallpapered over so that the maids would appear in the rooms as if by magic and disappear again just as rapidly and she had even heard of an employer who asked all of her 'girls' to buy expensive rubber-soled shoes, so that their walking up and down the wooden floors of the house would not disturb the residents – shoes, mind you, that had to be ordered from Chicago and paid for out of the maids' own wages. Annie knew all of these things because maids in New York City liked to meet up on their free afternoons and when they did they liked to talk, and what did they have to talk about, after all? Only their lives and the employers who moulded those lives. Sometimes Annie laughed when she read articles in Mr Cavendish's cast-off magazines about the 'problems' New York ladies had in finding 'good help'. If only they knew, she often thought to herself, that the 'help' gossiped so much among themselves that everyone knew which were the good employers and which were the bad, and if a lady was having difficulty in finding and then keeping staff the issue might well lie with her own management of the household rather than some deficiency in the girls themselves.

Once Mr Cavendish's breakfast had been cleared away the rest of Annie's day would unfold like a rug being brought outside for a beating – although that particular task was now, thankfully, less frequent since Mrs Cavendish had invested in not one but two metal carpet sweepers. Cleaning, laundry, the serving of food – the list of tasks Annie had to complete was long and some, she felt, even verged on the unnecessary, such as Mrs Cavendish's insistence on a real fire in her drawing room every day, even at the height of summer, meaning Annie would have to light the coals and then open the window for fear the room would become too stuffy. For Annie, however, the joy of living in New York more than compensated for any drudgery. She had a half holiday every Thursday and a free evening on Sundays and used that time to explore her new home, walking the length of the island with friends or alone, relishing the sights, sounds and particularly the smells that made this place so different from Ireland.

She was happy at the Chateau too. The staff was small, relative to the size of the house, but Mrs O'Toole was scrupulously fair in ensuring that they all got adequate food and the breaks they were entitled to. Meals, eaten at the kitchen table, tended to be good-humoured affairs, the table presided over by Mrs O'Toole herself at one end and the butler, Mr Laurence, at the other, who sometimes, after a glass or two of claret, would forget the British accent he adopted in the course of his work and lapse into his native South Dakota. Mabel the cook sat next to him and Annie herself tended to sit opposite Karla and Stefie, the two German kitchen maids, and had even picked up enough of their language to join in a little with their giggled conversations. They ate well, Mrs O'Toole insisting that their food was bought in the same stores the Cavendishes ordered from, and were served by Millie, the scullery maid who made sure they had all they needed before she sat down to eat herself. And if conversation ever faltered, or if anyone was particularly tired, Tim was always on hand to lift their spirits. Tim was around Annie's own age but had been living with the Cavendishes for so long, working first as a stable boy and now as the only person who could tame Mr Cavendish's automobile, that he claimed he could remember no other home.

Tim. Frowning slightly, Annie replaced her cup on the table. Tim was a handsome man, tall with a shock of brown hair that he wore too long and brushed to one side and

Annie knew a number of maids who attended early mass on a Sunday because that was the service attended by Mrs Cavendish herself, and Tim would wait outside for her, cigarette in hand, his lanky frame leaning against the door of the automobile. Indeed their very own Karla was unable to look at him without turning pink and had, Annie noticed, been making considerable effort to improve her English in recent weeks. But it wasn't Karla, nor any of the other Fifth Avenue maids that Tim had his eye on. Much to her surprise, he had in fact asked Annie to go for a stroll with him some months after she had arrived at the Chateau and, despite some reservations, she had agreed. Annie had never met a man back in Kerry who she could imagine walking out with, let alone anything else, but this was America, where everything was new and different, maybe the men would be different too?

But although Tim had been a perfect gentleman, taking care to walk between Annie and the traffic and buying her a lemonade as soon as they reached the park, and although conversation between them had flowed as easily as it did when they were seated at dinner, Annie had been left utterly unmoved by his company. At the end of the evening, when he leaned forward as if to kiss her she had simply stepped aside and covered the ensuing awkwardness with a comment about the weather and a suggestion that they buy ice cream. Tim had walked Annie home then and they hadn't spoken about the evening again and, when Annie had seen him dancing with a young woman from Co. Donegal at a social the previous month she had been delighted for both of them although a little worried at how poor Karla would take the news.

Noreen, who liked hearing about other people's entanglements, had laughed when Annie told her the story and informed her that there was no point in being shackled to a man too early in her American life and that there would be 'other Tims'. Annie had agreed, although she was not quite sure that the shackling part was the problem.

She looked across at Noreen, who was regarding her reflection with great satisfaction in the back of spoon. No matter what she wanted to call herself, Noreen had been a fantastic support to Annie over the past two years, as close as a cousin or even a sister, always first with news of a dance or a social and introducing Annie to a bewildering array of relatives and friends on their free afternoons. Of course Annie still missed her family and May, and pored over their letters, relishing every bite of news from home. But unlike many of the girls she met at dances who sobbed their hearts out and dreamed of returning, she was enjoying life in America too much to really miss home.

The fact there had been no news of Seánie Lynch had also eased her passage into this new life. May prayed for his safe return, she told Annie in her letters, but was keeping herself busy with the farm, and the children. Muireann was a bright girl of almost three now and Harry already a handful at two, and although May was not a fluent or particularly vivid writer, Annie could feel her love for them bursting out of every line.

News from Annie's own family tended to be equally positive. Eileen wrote long letters filled with local gossip and hilarious descriptions of the twins and their antics, epistles that maintained a careful balance between telling Annie how much she was loved while never making her feel guilty at having gone away. And Annie did likewise, never complaining about the length of her working day but instead sending her family lengthy descriptions of life in New York City and the excitement she found in the everyday.

And much of that excitement was generated by the vivacious redhead sitting in front of her who was right now staring at Annie's blouse as if she had just rescued it from a dumpster on the street.

'You will find something else to wear by the weekend?'

Annie shrugged.

'And sure, who'll be looking at me?'

'No one, madam, if you don't make a bit more of an effort!'

Annie smiled, but remained silent. It wouldn't matter, she thought, she could borrow a ballgown from Mrs Cavendish herself and no one would take any notice as long as Noreen Carey was at her side. It wasn't even that her friend made a huge effort to draw attention to herself either, it was just the way she had been born. There was a confidence about Noreen that attracted attention as soon as she walked into a room, an aura that made men straighten their ties and women pat their hair and regret not buying that new hat when they had the opportunity. Even after two years spent working behind the counter in her cousin's store, Noreen still had the soft hands and long, delicate fingers of a gentlewoman, and one of those fingers was now poking Annie's sleeve.

'It's not just a parish dance, you know. It's a county social, they're coming from all over to it.'

'Oh! Is that the dance on Sunday you mean?'

The words came from over Annie's shoulder. She turned

to see a young waitress approach, coffee pot in hand, and accepted a refill with a smile.

'Yes, it's in the St James's parish hall. I think I've seen you there at mass, haven't I?'

The girl nodded enthusiastically, her black curls escaping from under her cloth cap.

'Yes, that's right, I heard the Father talking about it last week. Are you both going?'

'We are indeed!'

Noreen beamed, all thoughts of darned blouses forgotten.

'We wouldn't miss it, isn't that right, Annie?'

'We wouldn't, I suppose.'

Annie picked up a crust of toast and chewed it, to save herself saying anything else. The truth was, she would quite happily forgo the dance, which would take up her entire and very precious free Sunday evening. But Nora – sorry, *Noreen* – had talked about little else since it was announced at mass the previous week and she would never forgive Annie if she didn't show at least some enthusiasm for the outing. It was a shame, she mused, that Noreen couldn't simply go with the little waitress, whose sallow skin was warmed by excitement as she continued to chatter.

'I only heard about it because I went to the eleven o'clock service on Sunday. We usually go earlier but my cousin was sick and I had to mind her baby so then I had to go to the Irish mass...'

Her voice tailed off as she looked from one girl to the other, worried she might have caused offence but Annie simply grinned. There were no masses at her local parish church specifically for the Irish, or for any other community, but the eleven o'clock service was indeed known locally as 'the Irish mass'. Annie knew some people thought, unkindly, that this was because the Irish were too lazy, or too worn out after a Saturday night's carousing to get up any earlier on a Sunday morning but the truth was that many of the Irish in Manhattan worked in domestic service and were unable to leave for church until they had prepared and cleared away breakfast for their employers. There were even families, she had heard, who warned their maids that if they left the house to go to church on Sunday morning they would be denied the traditional Sunday evening off in return. Thankfully, in her own case, Mrs Cavendish was herself a practising Catholic and quite happy for her staff to attend a service of their choosing – as long as, of course, they were back in time to serve lunch.

This waitress, on the other hand, judging by her large brown eyes and golden complexion, belonged to one of the many Italian families who attended the nine o'clock service at St James and could still be found chattering outside afterwards when the Irish Catholics arrived two hours later. Often, Annie found herself walking more slowly as she passed them, thrilled by the exuberant language and their exotic – to her eyes anyway – gesticulations. Sure, what was the point, she would think afterwards as she looked around at her fellow countrymen, heads bent over prayerbooks they had carried across the Atlantic, what was the point of coming all this way only to meet the same people you would at home? She herself longed to speak to new people. And maybe now she had been offered an opportunity.

'You should come with us!'

The waitress looked at her, a tentative smile on her pretty face.

'Oh, I don't think so. It's an Irish dance, isn't it? Or maybe I was mistaken...?'

'Ah, don't worry about that.'

Annie placed her knife and fork neatly back on her empty plate.

'It's the Kerryman's Association that organises it but they're not going to turn you away at the door, they'd be delighted to see a new face. Are you free on Sunday?'

'We close here at six, but I'm not sure—'

'Oh go on,' Annie urged, excited by the idea of having someone new to spend the evening with, particularly in the very likely event of Noreen being whisked away by an admirer as soon as they got in the door.

'We'll meet you outside the dance hall at seven, it's only two blocks away from here. We'll have a fine night, won't we, Noreen?'

'Elena!'

The call came from across the restaurant and Annie looked up to see a short stocky man poke his head through the serving hatch and unleash a rapid stream of Italian, followed by a curt 'I'm sorry if she is bothering you' in heavily accented English.

'Good heavens no, she's not—'

Half rising from her seat, Annie was about to give the man a reassuring smile when Noreen let out a piercing scream and Annie turned to see her clutching her arm, underneath which a dark pool of steaming coffee was flowing over the table.

'Oh no...'

Hands shaking, Elena put the now empty coffee pot down and began to dab at Noreen's arm with the dirty cloth she used to wipe down the tables, but Annie shooed her away.

'It's all right, lovey, it was an accident but we need to get water on this, quickly. Is there a sink over here?'

Still talking, she led a white-faced Noreen out of her seat and towards the kitchen, Elena flapping in their wake.

'Maybe butter? My nonna says—'

'No, running water,' Annie insisted firmly, pushing open the double doors that separated the working area of the kitchen from the public space. Inside, all was bustle but she quickly spotted a large industrial sink on one wall and led her friend towards it, then opened the cold tap and shoved her arm under the flow.

'You'll be all right now, Noreen love, just hold it there for a minute.'

Her voice came out firmer than she intended, she had never known her friend to be silent for this long and her passivity was far more worrying than her initial scream had been. But after a moment Noreen shuddered, then looked up at Annie with relief.

'I think it's working. It's cooling down now.'

'Just keep it there. That's right.'

Noreen's breathing slowed and, when small darts of colour appeared on her cheeks, Annie sent out a silent prayer of thanks to her aunt Kathleen, many thousands of miles away across the Atlantic, who had taught the girls of the parish how to deal with common childhood illnesses and much more besides. Of course, if they had been at home they would have had to rush Noreen down to the sea to douse her arm. In America, Annie mused, even nasty accidents were easier to deal with when there was running water in almost every room.

Finally satisfied that her friend was not too badly injured, she took a step backwards and, for the first time, allowed herself a proper look around the restaurant kitchen. Their dash towards the sink had earned them a few curious glances, but it was now approaching dinner time and it was clear the white-coated cooks were far too busy to bother about two Irish maids. And then came another scream, although this time far more muted than Noreen's had been. Startled, Annie turned and looked towards the far side of the kitchen where the stocky man was clutching Elena's arm. For a moment Annie assumed he was comforting the young woman but then the waitress yelped again and Annie realised to her horror that he was brutally twisting the soft skin. Annie didn't speak Italian but she didn't need to understand the words to register the anger in the man's voice and worse than that, the derision.

'Leave her alone!'

Noreen started, then followed her gaze and added her own words of support.

'It was an accident, I'm fine—'

But the man ignored them and as the other staff raised their heads to stare, not at their boss but at the two Irishwomen, Annie realised with a jolt that it was their reaction, rather than his behaviour, that was attracting attention. Annie Thornton suddenly felt very foreign in that loud, hot space and very, very small.

'Come on.'

Turning off the tap she grabbed a towel from a near-by hook and patted Noreen's arm dry. Across the kitchen the man gave one final, vicious twist then dropped Elena's arm and marched through the double doors that led to the restaurant, leaving them swinging in his wake. There was a moment's silence and then the hum of a busy kitchen rose again. Annie and Noreen made their way across the floor, heads down, and reached Elena who was standing by the wall, white-faced but dry-eyed, cradling her injured arm. Annie hesitated, then reached out and touched her gently on the shoulder.

'Are you all right, my darling? There was no need for that, it was an accident, and Noreen is fine.'

The girl looked at her blankly.

'I'm so sorry about your arm.'

This time it was Noreen who attempted a smile.

'Don't be worrying yourself, girl, I've done way worse than that myself. I can hardly feel it now, look...'

She extended her forearm which, Annie was pleased to see, had now calmed down from the initial roaring red to a light pink colour. But Elena didn't move, just kept staring straight ahead and Annie had to strain to hear her response.

'I'm very clumsy, my father always said it. He got me this job, he'll be so angry when he hears what happened today...'

Annie smiled.

'Ah now, Noreen here is tough as old boots, she'll be grand. I'm more worried about you, pet, there's no way anyone should treat you like that. Is there an owner, someone you can talk to?'

Elena finally looked up at her but shook her head dejectedly.

'That man is Lorenzo, he owns this restaurant. My father, he works for him too and begged him to give me this job, I can't tell him anything...'

For a moment her eyes filled with tears, and then she blinked them away.

'I'm happy you are not hurt. I must go back to work now.'

She turned in the direction of the double doors but before she could disappear Annie reached out and grabbed the back of her apron.

'Will you come to the dance with us on Sunday?'

The girl shook her head.

'My father – I don't think—'

'Oh go on!'

Annie couldn't quite understand why, but it suddenly felt vitally important that she see the girl again and ensure she was all right.

'Forget about your father, come with us!'

Noreen shot Annie a surprised look, unused to such directness from her usually sensible friend, but Annie was staring at Elena now.

'I'd love to see you there. Seven o'clock. I'll be watching out for you.'

The Italian girl held her gaze for a moment and then without another word turned and walked away.

Chapter Twelve

BALLYDRYNAWN

2022

'Will they be having fish, do you think? Because this is a lovely Picpoul. Or if you don't know maybe you'd better stick to a red, I've a nice light Italian here. Unless you think it's a Sunday roast, now for that you'd need something a bit more substantial...'

Emer blinked. Having decided she couldn't turn up at the Lynch home empty-handed she had stopped off at the Spar in Ballydrynawn to pick up a bottle of wine but hadn't expected the man behind the counter to be a) apparently a qualified sommelier and b) the nosiest man in the county – which in this part of Ireland was saying quite a lot. Her first mistake had been to admit she was buying the wine because she had been invited to lunch, enabling the man to deduce that the invitation must be a local one as it was already half past twelve. He then almost tied himself in knots trying to figure out who had invited her, without asking directly – 'Will you need a chiller bag for the car or is it only out the road you're going?' 'Mary Fahy was looking for something to go with a leg of lamb yesterday, but she didn't mention they were having visitors...'

It was only after promising she'd return to let him know how the Picpoul tasted that Emer was finally allowed to escape, clutching a paper bag containing two more bottles of wine than she had actually wanted to buy and with the words 'and sure won't you drink them yourself if it comes to it!' following her out the door.

Maura would love him, she thought as she steered the car out of the village, but as Ballydrynawn receded in the rear-view mirror her nerves began to jangle. It was going to take a lot more than a glass of nice wine to soften up Rob's mother. But just as she was toying with the idea of pleading a Covid scare and turning the car around, she caught sight of a van on the road just ahead, its roof rack laden with multicoloured surfboards, and became aware of a not unpleasant fizzing in her solar plexus at the thought of seeing Rob again. It was a long time since Emer had flirted with anyone – or been flirted with, for that matter. She'd been on a few dates in LA over the years and the last guy she'd been seeing had actually hinted that he'd give a relationship a shot until lockdown had struck and it became clear that whatever bond the two of them shared wouldn't withstand the dead hand of Zoom cocktails. Emer had no expectations of anything long term with Rob, of course, he was as deeply rooted in the Kerry countryside as the bushes that were at this very moment separating her car from the Atlantic Ocean, while she herself was fully committed to going back to the States at the end of the summer. But if the flirting did turn into something a little more tangible, well then she'd be happy to go with the flow. And if it didn't, she'd still have the surfing.

The wooden gates were easier to find in daylight but just as imposing and when Emer reached them she texted Rob to let him know she was outside. As they slid open, however, it was Siobhán, not her son, who was standing in the driveway and Emer felt her good mood pop like a balloon. Then her phone buzzed and she looked down to see a text from 'Hot Surfer Dude' flash up on the home screen.

Knee deep in prawns back here, not a euphemism, see you in 5. Rx

The Rx made her blush, as did the reminder of how she had saved his name in her phone, and Emer was still grinning as Siobhán guided her across the driveway and into a space between the red van and a gorgeous Mercedes convertible. Mindful of the mention of prawns, she left two bottles of red rattling around the footwell of the Focus, grabbed the white and climbed out of the car.

'Emer, you came.'

Siobhán's tone made it clear this was not, in fact, a cause for celebration. Emer tugged down the skirt of the only summer dress she'd brought down to Kerry, which she'd worn out of deference to the lunch invitation and paired with white, low-heeled sandals. Siobhán, who was wearing jeans and a rather tatty fleece, gave her footwear a dubious look before continuing in a slightly brighter tone.

'I've asked Alison to join us too – seeing as Robert is so keen on company today I figured the more the merrier!'

'Great!'

Unable to think of anything else to say, Emer handed over the wine which Siobhán studied with a slight eyebrow raise.

'I see you met Gerry.'

'The guy in the shop?'

'The very man. He bought a case of this last month and he's been pressing it on everyone who comes through the door but I have to admit, it is delicious. Did he make you tell him where you were going?'

Emer permitted herself a small smile.

'He shone a light in my face all right but I managed to get away before he produced the thumbscrews.'

She could have sworn she saw an answering grin flicker across the older woman's face but it had disappeared by the time she had led her through the sliding glass door and into the kitchen where Rob was standing at the sink, attacking a bucket of shellfish.

'Who's that you're talking about?'

Siobhán placed Emer's wine into a fridge which was built into the kitchen island – another morsel of information which Emer filed away for Maura – then looked across at her son.

'Gerry from the Spar, he was mad to find out who was feeding the summer visitor. He's a divil that fella, if there are no customers he'll stand out in the road looking for news. He'll be too busy in July and August to do much chatting, that's when all the holiday homes will be booked solid but right now his tongue is hanging out for anything strange.'

'He knows his vino though!'

Rob threw the comment over his shoulder.

'And he knows his market. Some of the summer crowd are real wine snobs.'

'They are that.' Siobhán sniffed. 'How are you getting on over there?'

Rob returned to his shelling.

'Grand. I'll stick the veg on shortly and we'll be ready to eat in around a half an hour, does that sound OK?'

From across the room, Emer nodded.

'Sounds great. Can I give you a hand with anything?'

'Oh no.'

Siobhán jumped in before her son had a chance to answer.

'Gordon Ramsay here gets very stressed if he's not left alone in the kitchen. I'll tell you what...'

She took another pointed look at Emer's footwear.

'Why don't we go for a walk? I'll show you around the grounds – if you're interested that is – and you can fill me in on what Maura has been up to.'

The prospect of being alone with Rob's mother was, not to put too fine a point on it, terrifying, but she had issued a command, not a request, and Emer answered as brightly as she could.

'That would be lovely. It's an amazing house, we came down to Kerry every summer when I was a kid but I've never seen anything like this.'

'You're saying all the right things anyway!'

Rob heaved the massive bucket of shells out of the sink and began to scrub his hands.

'The quickest way to her heart is to say nice things about this place. You'd choose the house over me any time, wouldn't you, Mother?'

Siobhán pretended to think for a moment.

'Ah, I think I'd miss the catering. Come on so, Emer, we'll go this way.'

Emer followed Siobhán through a vast, flag-stoned hall and out the front door of the house which was wooden and painted in a tasteful blueish grey. It was strange, she thought, that the house had been laid out in such a way that encouraged visitors to enter through the kitchen rather than this beautifully designed front entrance but that architectural quirk was soon forgotten about as Siobhán led her into a garden that could best be described as a wild meadow.

'We're cultivating it for the bees.'

Siobhán reached down and brushed some pollen from her jean-clad shins, while Emer tugged down her summer frock and tried to ignore a nettle sting.

'Rob used to make his pocket money cutting this but letting it go wild is better for the environment and I have to say I kind of like it. It doesn't make sense, trying to put manners on the land around here.'

Siobhán led Emer across the meadow, stopping when they reached what looked like the remains of an old stone wall.

'This was once part of the outbuildings of the old house. Thankfully we were also able to preserve some of the original structure – can you see it?'

Emer turned her head. They had walked quite a distance from the house now and she could indeed see that part of the gable end of the vast mansion was far older than the rest of the structure.

'Oh, that's lovely.'

Siobhán answered with a little more enthusiasm than before.

'It is, isn't it? My own father built a bungalow on the site of the family farmhouse, but kept one of the original walls and when I knocked the bungalow down to build this place, I made sure the architect kept it too. It's nice to have a link to the past, I think. My mother didn't live long enough to see it, sadly, but Dad loves "the new house", which is what we still call this place even though I had it built fifteen years ago.'

They turned and began to walk again. Emer could hear the sea now and there was salt on the fresh afternoon breeze but as far she could work out Siobhán seemed to be walking parallel to, rather than directly towards the coast. She had fallen silent too, since the mention of her parents, and Emer cast around for a way to move the conversation on.

'Did you say Alison was coming for lunch too? Have you seen her this morning?'

Siobhán nodded.

'I did indeed, she called in earlier on her way for a swim. She's grand. Sure you know what you young ones are like, there's no hangover a bottle of Coke and a dip in the sea won't fix. So tell me, Emer...'

They seemed to be heading uphill now and Emer felt her lungs starting to work a little harder, although Siobhán didn't seem in the slightest bit out of breath as she continued.

'I haven't seen your mam in years but do tell her I said hello, will you? She was great fun in school, got into her fair share of trouble too, as far as I remember! What line of work did she go into in the end?'

Emer grinned.

'Teaching, actually. English and Irish.'

'No way!'

Siobhán's smile was genuine and Emer realised she'd

actually like this woman, if she wasn't utterly terrified of her.

'Maura Delaney teaching. Well – she's probably brilliant at it, she'd know all the tricks!'

Emer felt a squelch as she stepped into a patch of soggy grass but given the sudden uplift in the conversation tried not to let her discomfort show.

'She didn't let us away with much anyway.'

Siobhán, who was wearing hiking boots, was striding comfortably alongside her.

'And are there many of you at home?'

'Just two, me and my brother Niall. Well, neither of us are at home actually, Niall is in Australia and I've been in LA for nearly ten years.'

'Oh really?' Siobhán slowed her pace a little. 'When Rob said you were around for the summer, I was wondering if you were thinking of making a permanent move down here.'

'Oh God no!'

Emer gave Siobhán a quick summary of her life in LA and her decision to return for a break, taking care to leave out the whole breakdown bit and paint instead a picture of a weary professional in need of a change of scene.

Siobhán gave an approving nod.

'A director? That sounds fascinating. Not easy either, I imagine, to keep a freelance job going, particularly these last few years.'

'No, but I love it.'

Her sandals, covered in mud and grass stains, were probably beyond repair but Emer decided it was a small price to pay for what was at last approaching a friendly conversation.

'I've been over there for ten years. I could have joined a studio, I suppose, but I like being my own boss. It's relentless, but I can't imagine doing anything else.'

'Good to hear!'

The path took a steep rise suddenly and Siobhán walked swiftly ahead of Emer for a couple of steps before turning to watch her approach.

'Now!'

'Oh my gosh.'

'Quite something, isn't it? I like to see people's reactions when they see it for the first time. Although I have to say even those of us who live here never really get used to it, it changes every day.'

'I can imagine...'

Emer walked forward until she neared the edge of the cliff then looked out onto the foaming water below. It was a dull, overcast afternoon and the Atlantic was a whirlpool, grey and foreboding, yet still beautiful in all its threatening power. Despite its ferocity, the waves that made it as far as the shore were small and delicate, their power sapped by a rocky shelf that ran from the beach into the water.

Siobhán indicated the shoreline with one long finger, the nails square-cut and unvarnished.

'Useless for surfing, as my son will no doubt tell you. He has to travel beyond the headland to get decent waves. But it's beautiful for swimming and very safe because it's so sheltered. Saved my sanity during lockdown, I can tell you.'

She pointed again and Emer noticed, for the first time, that a set of metal steps had been hung on the side of the cliff.

'My dad had these built when he was a kid; before then

they just scrambled down, I think! But it's great to have the access. I swim every day when I'm down here. I had to laugh when I heard people talk about taking up "sea swimming" during lockdown. Or "wild swimming", would you ever? Swimming, we always called it.'

'It's stunning.'

'It is.'

Siobhán looked at her watch.

'We'd best be making tracks, or the chef will be getting his shellfish in a twist. But seeing as you said you came down here as a child...'

Taking a couple of steps back from the edge for safety, they walked along the side of the cliff then came to a line of thick hedgerow, which Emer assumed marked the end of Siobhán's property. But her hostess kept walking, moving along the line of the hedge before stopping to push some branches aside.

'Through here – mind your eyes now, I could do with getting the shears out and doing a bit of pruning.'

Siobhán walked forward – then disappeared.

Emer's heart sank. She had thought she was making real headway with Rob's mom, they had been having a genuinely decent conversation there for a minute, or so she had thought anyway, but now it looked like the woman was playing some sort of practical joke on her. But just as she was considering giving up and going home, she walked closer to the hedge and noticed for the first time that it had been trained around a metal fence into which was set a sturdy wooden door, camouflaged in green paint. Emer opened it and then many things became clear.

She had never approached it from this angle before and

the long walk around the garden had caused her to lose her sense of direction anyway but there it was, right in front of her. The Fairy Tree. And of course, Emer thought as she shut the gate behind her and saw the way the clever construction caused it to melt back into the leaves, of course it must have been Siobhán she saw up here on her first day. Rob's mom hadn't jumped into the sea and she certainly hadn't evaporated into thin air, she had simply exited through a perfectly sensible, albeit beautifully constructed, door that led right back into her own garden.

It was difficult to reconcile the upset figure she had seen that day with the woman who stood before her now, smiling and utterly composed.

'What do you think of our Fairy Tree?'

Emer walked over to the nearest branch and took a leaf between her fingers.

'I've seen it before, actually! My mother used to bring me and my brother up here, when we were little.'

It would be best, she decided, not to mention her more recent visit. Siobhán nodded.

'I thought she might have. It's a bit of a scramble up here from the main road, but worth it!'

A sudden thought crossed Emer's mind.

'This is all your land, isn't it? My dad said the locals all had right of way up here – God, I hope we weren't trespassing all those years ago?'

Or indeed last week, she thought, but didn't say. Siobhán, however, just shook her head.

'No, your dad was spot on. We're on Lynch land, all right, technically speaking at least, but this tree has been growing here since before my father's father was born and it would have been considered terrible bad luck to fence it off. My dad always said it belonged to the parish, not to people who were lucky enough to have their names on a bit of paper. He built the fence over there a good few years ago to give us a bit of privacy and over the years I added the hedges and strengthened the door, but I was always careful to leave the tree itself on this bit of open land. Dad would never forgive me otherwise. It has made things a bit difficult – you'll have noticed you have to access our house by the back roads?'

Emer nodded.

'Yeah, I was wondering about that, it is a bit of a tricky drive up from the village.'

Siobhán gave a resigned shrug.

'Well we actually own all of the land right down as far as the main road and it would have been easier, obviously, to have a road to the house from here but that would have meant restricting public access to the tree or maybe even cutting it down altogether, and I had no intention of doing that. The architect thought I was mad, he was a lovely man but pure Dub, hadn't a notion why I'd want to make our lives difficult for what he thought of as some mad country tradition. But Dad would never have forgiven me if I'd cut down the tree and I wouldn't have been able to live with myself either. And besides...'

Siobhán gave Emer a sideways glance.

'You wouldn't want to go messing with the fairies, now, would you?'

Emer laughed, but Siobhán's face remained entirely serious.

'You don't – you don't actually believe in it though, do you? I mean – that it grants wishes and everything?'

'And you are telling me you don't?'

As Siobhán fell silent again, Emer could feel all of the ground she had gained over the course of their conversation slip away. And then the older woman's face creased into a wide grin.

'God, you're very easy to tease, Emer. No, I don't believe in fairies. Well, not little creatures with wings dancing around the place anyway. But this tree was here long before you or I and it has given the people of Ballydrynawn great comfort over the years. And I think it would be very arrogant of me to mess with that, or to assume it's all nonsense, just because I can't get a Tesco delivery when I need one.'

Emer was moved, both by the sincerity in the other woman's voice and the fact that she didn't seem to have insulted her by mistake.

'I totally get that.'

'My parents were unusual in their own way,' Siobhán continued. 'My dad, Harry, he didn't believe in God, and that would have been a big deal around here when I was growing up. Mom brought us to mass and insisted we were baptised and all that sort of thing, and he never stood in her way. But Dad never went to church himself, or talked about anything spiritual. At the same time though, he'd never hear a word said against this tree, nor the people who believed in it. He always said they had the right to their beliefs and we had no business questioning them. His own mother had great faith in it too and made him swear he'd never tear it down, and he had me make the same promise. And to be honest with you, Emer, I've grown very fond of it over the years. You remember the first Covid lockdown, early summer 2020? I'm not sure what it was like for ye over in the States but my God it was dreadful here, and leaving wishes on a fairy tree didn't seem particularly strange in a world where you couldn't go more than two kilometres from your own front door. My poor dad was in the nursing home by then and we couldn't visit, so I used to come up here and just think about him. It was the only place I could really feel close to him.'

There were tears in Siobhán's eyes now and Emer gave her a moment before responding.

'It must have been really tough.'

'It really was. He hasn't been the same man since either. I mean I know he's nearly a hundred but he was flying it till all that happened. Anyway.'

Siobhán gave herself a small shake.

'That's enough Lynch family history for the moment. You can leave a note here yourself today though, if you have a piece of paper!'

Emer felt in the pocket of her hoodie, then shook her head.

'Not even a sweet wrapper.'

'That's a shame. You wouldn't know what the fairies might have in store for you this summer.'

She gave a brief half wink, that made her look very like her son.

'Come on so, let's go back or the chef will disown me.'

Right on cue came a beep from her fleece pocket. Siobhán withdrew her phone and read the message, then glanced at Emer.

'Rob wants us back all right. And he says Alison has landed in and wants to talk to all of us, she wants you there as well. Not sure what that's all about but we'd better find out!'

'Grand so.'

They turned and Emer followed Siobhán back through the gate which she now saw was opened by means of a very non-magical security keypad. That didn't mean the whole mystery was solved though. Siobhán's story about visiting the tree during lockdown made perfect sense and it made sense too that not being able to visit her dad would have made her emotional but that was all in the past now, people were moving freely again. There was no reason, surely, for her to have been so upset when Emer saw her up here the other day? And it *had* been Siobhán she had seen, Emer was certain of it, the figure had been too tall to be Alison, too slight to be Rob and probably only people who lived in the house would know the code to the gate.

It was a puzzle all right but at least, she thought, as they retraced their steps back past the cliffs and towards the meadow, at least she seemed to have made some sort of headway with Siobhán, who was chatting away quite freely about the weather and a forthcoming trip to Dublin. It wasn't like they needed to be best friends or anything but Emer was harbouring a hope that she might be seeing a bit of Rob over the summer and it would be easier if she was on speaking terms with the woman who shared his home. They were approaching the house again now, it really was the most idyllic location, Emer realised, that view, that access to the sea, surf...

'Rob is so lucky.'

She was thinking aloud, really, rather than addressing Siobhán, but the other woman gave her a sharp look.

'I'm sorry?'

'Oh, I was just thinking how beautiful it is around here, how lucky Rob is to have this amazing house.'

'Well it's my house actually.'

Emer found herself suddenly flustered.

'Oh I know, but to grow up around here, to be able to hang out on the beach all day, it's a dream come true, isn't it?'

'Well I'd hardly call it hanging out.'

All of the friendliness had disappeared from Siobhán's voice now.

'Rob works damn hard on Breaking Waves, it's not some vanity project, if that's what you think. He built it up from scratch.'

Emer was bright red now.

'Oh God no, I didn't mean—'

'I'm not sure what you did mean actually. But here…'

They had reached the house again and Siobhán pushed open the front door, calling over her shoulder as she walked.

'Wipe those shoes, will you? Not what I'd wear on a country walk, to be honest with you, but I supposed you're not used to our ways down here.'

Unable to think of any response that wouldn't further inflame the situation, Emer miserably followed her inside.

Chapter Thirteen

NEW YORK

1926

'You look nice, Annie!'
For a second, Annie wondered if she had imagined the words, but as she placed the tea tray on the small side table Miss Cavendish's face broke out into a wide, slightly vacant smile.

'I love the lace collar on your blouse, did you bring that with you from Ireland?'

'I did, miss. My mother made it for me.'

Muther. Annie had never thought of herself as having an 'accent' before she came to America. If anything, she and her brothers and sisters, all of whom had finished primary school, had been considered 'nicely spoken' by their Ballydrynawn neighbours, and Eve in particular was often called on for a recitation when they had visitors. It was also the case that the nuns who had secured her position here on Fifth Avenue prided themselves on only providing 'English-speaking girls'. But a full two years after coming to America Annie knew that some native New Yorkers considered the Irish way of speaking to be rough and unintelligent, so she had learned to soften the edges of her words and let them run into each other the way they did over here, to be better understood.

'Well I think it's very pretty.'

Miss Cavendish – her name was Jemima, although Annie would never dream of using it – sat forward on the peach-patterned love seat and watched as Annie poured her tea. Instead of adding milk, however, the younger woman pulled a small glass bottle from the inside pocket of her tweed jacket, removed the cork with her neat white teeth and poured a stream of clear liquid into the tea before replacing the bottle in her pocket again. She sipped from the cup, sighed then looked up at Annie from under her arched, over-plucked brows.

'Oh, don't look so disapproving, Annie. I was at a function last night and I have such a headache today.'

Annie kept her voice level.

'I could ask Mrs O'Toole for headache powders, miss.'

'There's no need.'

The other woman glanced at her 'tea'.

'This is all the medicine I need.'

She took another sip then replaced the cup on the table, colour rising in her cheeks.

'That's better. So, Annie, where are you going all dressed up like that?'

Annie looked around the room for a coat of dust, or an ornament out of place that would give her an excuse to move away from this overly personal question but the room was entirely in order, every item exactly as it should have been, except for the young woman who was so clearly in the mood to be entertained. Miss Jemima was twenty-one, not much younger than Annie herself but right now the two looked as if they could be from different generations as well as different continents. Today, the Cavendishes' only daughter was wearing a three-quarter length skirt in moss-green tweed which, given the way she was sprawled on the sofa, showed most of her legs from the knees down. It was accompanied by a short, matching jacket, a black and white striped blouse and a navy velvet ribbon arranged around her slender neck to mimic a man's necktie. If Annie herself wore that outfit at home she'd be read off the altar, she thought, although the short skirt would certainly make it easier for her to run up and down the kitchen stairs – and then she almost giggled at the thought of cleaning out the grate or clearing away the breakfast things in an outfit that probably cost more than her month's wages.

Miss Cavendish saw the glimmer of a smile, and pounced. 'Oh of course, it's your free evening, isn't it?'

She was just making conversation, Annie decided, noting the slurring of the T on the end of the final word, which indicated that the glass bottle had already made more than one appearance that afternoon. Annie's parents had neither the money nor the inclination to be regular drinkers, but twice a year her father would meet his brothers at the fair in town and would come home hours later smiling and garrulous, with a doughy softness to his features that she always found unsettling. Pádraig would sit for a while by the fire then, trying to draw the others into rambling conversation, his eyes growing redder and losing focus until a single cough from her mother and a 'that's enough now, Pat' would send him ambling to the bedroom. The difference was, of course, that Pádraig's indulgence was entirely his own business while Miss Cavendish was in fact breaking the New York law. There was no cough, however, that would silence her.

Annie bent forward and lifted the tray again, feeling pain swell in the balls of her feet. They never hurt while she was running around, she found, only when she sat down to a meal, or in bed at night, as if she had to be at rest before her body gave the nerve endings permission to complain. She was indeed due to finish work shortly, Miss Cavendish was the only member of the family at home and once she had cleared away her tea Annie would be free to meet Noreen at the local church hall. But her young employer was still waiting for an answer.

'I'll be going to a dance later, miss. With a friend from home.'

'Well how lovely!'

Miss Cavendish took another sip from her 'tea' then replaced it on the ornate mahogany side table.

Annie knew that the heavy furniture, plush sofas and heavily decorated cushions in the lady's drawing room were supposed to be the height of sophistication, but Miss Cavendish didn't look sophisticated right now. In fact, as she pulled herself forward onto the edge of the patterned sofa again she looked, Annie thought, rather like her own grandmother on Sunday mornings when the family returned from early mass. Hungry for gossip and entertainment.

'Do you like to dance, Annie?'

'I can't say I care for it, miss.'

Distracted by the unusual turn the afternoon had taken Annie spoke without thinking but, instead of being annoyed at her impertinence, Miss Cavendish let out a peal of laughter.

'Oh, well maybe you're just going to the wrong dances! Have you heard any jazz?'

'Not really, miss.'

Annie had heard OF jazz, of course, and had once stopped on the way home from mass to listen to a group of street musicians, becoming so entranced by their playing that she had been almost late for the lunch service and earned from Mrs O'Toole what the housekeeper liked to call a 'stern word'.

But she had never been to an event where jazz was actually performed, or where the flappers she read about in the household's cast-off newspapers gathered to dance – and, if she was reading the articles correctly, get up to a lot more besides. No, the music at that evening's social, just like every other Irish dance she had been to in New York, would be provided by accordions, fiddles and whistles, making it practically indistinguishable from the hops she'd be going to if she had stayed at home. Some of her reluctance must have shown on her face because Miss Cavendish laughed again.

'Come on now, you look like you're being led to the gallows, Annie. It'll be nice, surely, meeting up with your friend? Oh please...'

She had finally noticed the awkward angle at which Annie was standing and, leaping up from her seat, took the tray out of her hands.

'You'll hurt your back with that heavy thing, let me help you!'

'I...'

Annie watched dumbly as the young woman put the tray back down on the table, then shot the door a quick glance, fearful of what Mrs O'Toole would see if she walked in to find one of the family helping with housework. But the door remained shut tight and Miss Cavendish looked so genuinely interested in what she had to say that Annie felt it would be rude not to answer.

'It'll be a nice evening, I suppose. It's just sometimes I wonder why we bother, you know, coming all the way to America just to dance with lads from the neighbouring parish.'

Miss Cavendish nodded, thoughtfully.

'Why, you're right! I never thought of it like that before. And will you have a meal?'

'Not at the dance, but I'm meeting my friend Noreen first and I'll have dinner with her cousin's family, in the East Village.'

Miss Cavendish's smile widened and she patted the sofa cushion once more.

'How interesting! Do sit down and tell me more, I promise not to keep you long.'

It was as if the sore and tired feet made their decision for her and Annie suddenly found herself perched on the edge of the peach sofa. The woman was lonely, she realised, and found herself softening.

'Well, there could be ten people at Bridget's house, or twenty even, but she just makes a big pot of stew and that feeds everyone.'

'Twenty people! Why, it'll be a real dinner party.'

'Not quite a party, no.'

Annie paused, thinking of Noreen's cousin's crowded

kitchen, where guests would be seated at the scrubbed table and family would have to perch anywhere they could, on wooden stools or even on the floor, nothing at all like the Cavendishes' candlelit dinner parties, where the guests attacked five courses or more with silver cutlery, patting the juices from their mouths with napkins made of Irish linen that Annie would have to launder by hand the next day. But it was refreshing to be asked questions by a member of the gentry and Miss Jemima did seem to be genuinely interested in what she had to say, so she decided to keep talking.

'It'll be a nice occasion, with lots of friends calling around.'

'And will she have help, your friend? To cook the meal and serve it?'

'Oh, we'll all pitch in. It'll be like the Bible story, only with mutton and carrots instead of loaves and fishes!'

'How marvellous!'

Miss Cavendish took another drink of tea and her breath, when she exhaled afterwards, made Annie's eyes water.

'Please do go on.'

'Well, sometimes there will be a song or two, or a tune, if anyone has brought an instrument.'

Annie was a good storyteller, she was known for it. At school she had always been the pupil chosen to read her essays out in class, and at home she could set her parents and siblings into fits of laughter, telling them about someone she met along the road, adding in voices or exaggerating dramas, never exaggerating maliciously but just for the sheer joy of eliciting a smile. These days she mostly poured that energy into her letters back home, imagining as she wrote the joy on her family's faces when they heard her news and realised how well New York was treating her. But despite the pleasure she got from writing Annie had missed the simple act of face-to-face storytelling, of sitting with her mother, or her sister, or with May and just chatting, letting the words flow. She had Noreen, of course, but she was more usually the audience than the entertainer in that relationship. And so she began to tell Miss Cavendish, or Jemima as the woman now asked to be called, more about the Irish in New York, and about Bridget and her eleven children and how they were all called on to work in the family store.

'You're a tonic, Annie!'

Miss Jemima was nodding furiously now, a patch of pink glowing at the end of her nose.

'You should write all of this down, you know, you're a natural! Oh, how they'd love you out in Harbour View.'

Annie must have looked quizzical because the woman smiled before replying.

'It's our summer cottage, you know, out on the coast.'

Annie had of course heard of Harbour View. Mrs O'Toole had told her all about the Cavendishes' second home, where Mrs Cavendish and her daughter escaped from the New York heat for the summer months, leaving Mr Cavendish behind – to pay the bills, as the housekeeper waspishly remarked. She also knew that the word 'cottage' was a misnomer, if not an affectation, and Harbour View was almost twice the size of the city chateau, with thirty bedrooms, a ballroom with its own stage, private access to the beach and a well-maintained jetty. But Annie couldn't imagine why anyone would 'love' her out there. Harbour View had its own staff and she and Mrs O'Toole were expected to stay behind in New York while the others were on holidays, taking the opportunity to clean the Chateau from top to bottom. But Miss Jemima's eyes were shining now and the bottle, Annie noticed when she withdrew it from her pocket again, was almost empty.

'It's so beautiful, Annie, so much fun. People just come and go, we have parties, and grand balls – honestly, all sorts of people call to see us. They'd love to hear your stories.'

Annie, caught between offence and amusement, stifled a snort. What was the woman suggesting, exactly? That she come and work in the place, or better still, that she act as Cinderella, casting off her rags every evening to entertain at the ball? Was it a court jester she thought she was? But Miss Cavendish didn't notice her change in mood, instead she hauled herself into an upright sitting position, and closed one eye in an attempt to focus.

'I'd love you to see Harbour View, Annie, it's so pretty! My grandfather built it for my grandmother and my father owns it now but he doesn't appreciate it, he's too busy in the city making money.'

She almost spat out the final two words and Annie had to bite her lip to stop herself from smiling, as she wondered how Miss Jemima would cope without the money she appeared to hold in such disdain.

'Maybe you could travel there as my maid! My parents won't mind, they could easily get someone to replace you in the city.'

'It would be easy replace me right enough.'

Despite her inebriation, Miss Jemima couldn't miss the edge to Annie's words.

'I'm so sorry, my dear. I didn't mean to offend you, I just

got carried away. And you are just waiting to go on your lovely evening off – here!'

She took a sudden leap from the sofa, so quickly Annie almost fell across into the space she vacated.

'Come here for a moment, will you?'

Unsettled by the sudden change in the conversation Annie rose and moved across to where the other woman was now standing in the middle of the floor. Muttering to herself, Miss Jemima fiddled with the ribbon around her neck then smiled as it fell loose into her hand.

'Now! This will set your blouse off beautifully.'

Before Annie knew what was happening the young woman had reached up and fastened the thin strip of material around her neck. It was as if the movement had been broken into a series of distinct sensations, the brush of velvet against her neck, the scent of lemon soap from her fingers, the light tickle of those fingers on her skin... and then Miss Cavendish stood back, a look of satisfaction on her face.

'There, you see? Just beautiful.'

She beckoned to Annie to follow her, and the two walked to the mirror on the far side of the room, a large, gold-framed affair set atop an ornate black fireplace. Annie had torn several soft dusters trying to extract the dust from that fire surround, but those dusters seemed very far away now as she stared into the mirror, her cheeks flushed. The navy ribbon had changed her somehow, made her look older, or more sophisticated. More American. Still standing behind her, Miss Cavendish gave her a light pat on the shoulder.

'There! I knew it would suit you. Now, can I ask you to

please forgive my rudeness, Annie, and go and have a lovely evening?'

She turned and retrieved the tray.

'I'll bring this down to the kitchen myself, let you get away.'

'Oh no, you can't! Mrs O'Toole—'

'Don't you give Betty O'Toole a second thought, Annie, she's known me since I was a baby. She thinks I'm completely insane, which means I can get away with anything, and she won't hold it against you, I promise. Go on! And have a lovely evening.'

And before she could be quite sure what had happened, or why, Annie Thornton found herself being ushered out of that stuffy drawing room, the scent of the not-quite-tea still in her nostrils, and standing at the top of Fifth Avenue, ready to head into a New York evening.

'She's clearly not coming, Annie, and I have far better things to be doing with my time than be standing around here waiting for her!'

Noreen wound a Titian strand around her finger.

'I didn't go to all the trouble of pinning my hair last night just to have it destroyed by this breeze.'

Annie, whose own hair had been whipped into unmanageable fuzz both from the heat of the day and the fact that she hadn't sat down in more than twelve hours, bit back a retort. Noreen was right, of course, they had told Elena what time the dance started and it was twenty to eight now. If they went into the dance hall without her then the young Italian woman would have no one but herself to blame.

It was just that Annie had really hoped to see her today. Turning her back on the dance hall, she narrowed her eyes and took another look down the street. They were just minutes from Broadway and, through a gap in the surrounding buildings, the bustle of a New York evening was distinctly audible, the clopping of horses, the shouting of paper boys, the stuttering of the occasional motor car. The dance hall itself, however, was situated on a much quieter side road, where even the trees were brown, dusty and down-at-heel. A steady stream of people was coming towards them them now, couples walking arm in arm, groups of women giggling as they approached, the odd single man trying to pretend he didn't really care where he was going or who he would meet there. But no matter how hard she looked, Annie couldn't see Elena's dark curls. She craned her neck, ignoring Noreen's sigh. She had been thinking about the Italian woman ever since that horrible encounter in the restaurant and was anxious to make sure she was fully recovered. In truth, she was simply anxious to be in her company again although Annie knew if Noreen questioned her, she would not have been able to explain why.

'Come on, Annie! It's ten of eight, the fun will be half over if we don't go inside!'

Noreen was looking downright annoyed now and Annie knew, no matter how much she craved a little solitude, she couldn't let her friend down. Taking note of the 'ten of eight' – Noreen had been right quick to pick up the American way of speaking – she gave one last look down the dusty street but it was empty now apart from two young men who were squabbling happily about the result of a football game and definitely not concealing any young Italian women behind their stiff Sunday suits and flat caps. Elena wasn't coming, Annie accepted, and wondered why she felt so miserable as she followed Noreen inside.

'Will you take a drink?'

Having handed over their money to a sweating man at the door who had addressed his 'good evening, ladies' directly to her bosom, Noreen skipped down the two steps that led to the dance floor and turned to Annie, her good humour fully restored.

'I'll get us some lemonade, shall I?'

Not bothering to wait for an answer, Noreen strode across the hall towards the 'bar' – in reality a long trestle table set up at the far side of the room. Annie had no real interest in the lemonade, she knew from experience that it would be warm and sticky and would make little to no difference to her thirst, but, given the din, even if she had refused the offer there was little chance of Noreen hearing her. The dance floor itself was almost empty, populated only by two older couples and a pair of women who were giggling their way through a practice waltz, but the area around it was thick with people, the crowd three or even four deep in places, the men laughing and talking among themselves and the women looking around with open curiosity to see who was out for the evening.

The musicians were already in flying form, led by a concertina player whose head was bent low over his instrument, his arms a blur of activity. Two toe-tapping whistle players kept time and, as Annie looked on, an older man slid a well-polished fiddle from a piece of sacking and joined in seamlessly with the tune. It was, without doubt, going to be a lively evening. Most of the Irish in New York were young people like herself, hard workers who were literally building and cleaning the city they now called home, and they worked just as hard when it came to enjoying their nights off. Annie wasn't fond of dancing but she usually enjoyed watching the fun and chatting to a couple of people she recognised. Tonight, however, she couldn't help but feel on the outside of the merriment.

She took a step sideways, then found a precious piece of bare wall and wedged herself against it, taking care not to catch anyone's eye. Annie was physically tired from her long day's work, but that was to be expected. This evening she also felt mentally drained, as if the earlier conversation with Miss Cavendish had exhausted all her reserves of sociability and it felt utterly daunting to have to make polite conversation with strangers all over again. With a dramatic flourish, the accordion player finished his tune and Annie joined in with the applause as he mopped his forehead with a handkerchief, then addressed a few words to the fiddle player, who was taking the opportunity to put resin on his bow. The older man looked a little like her uncle Danny, Annie mused, and saved the thought for her next letter. It was just the sort of detail that Eve and her mother liked to hear.

'There you are!'

Noreen pushed her way through the crowd towards her, followed closely by a tall, thin man with a long nose who was wearing heavy work trousers and a wide, somewhat vacant smile. Sweat was running down the side of his face and Annie, with a sudden lurch in her stomach, watched as a bead of it dropped into one of the glasses of lemonade he was holding in his large hands. Noreen, meanwhile, was smiling as broadly as if she had won him in a raffle.

'Pat here offered to buy us lemonades, wasn't that nice of him!'

Pat's face turned an even darker shade of puce.

'Not a bother sure, two lovely young ladies like yourselves. And while I'm at it...'

After handing the drinks to the women – his fingers had been right inside the glasses, Annie noticed with a wince – he took a quick look around the room and then opened his jacket to reveal a bulging inside pocket. Withdrawing a small glass bottle – not dissimilar to the one she had seen earlier at the Chateau, Annie thought wryly – the man gave Noreen an exaggerated wink.

'I could make them dangerous for you if you like?'

'Is that – moonshine?'

Noreen opened her eyes wide.

'I couldn't possibly agree to anything illegal now, Patrick...'

The man blinked at her and then noticed the twinkle in her eyes.

'Would you get away out of that? Hold out your glass now like a good girl.'

The good girl accepted a healthy slug of the clear liquid into her lemonade and then looked over at Annie.

'Go on, Annie, it's very refreshing.'

As Noreen waved the glass in front of Annie's face the bitter scent caught the back of her throat, making her cough. She had no interest in the drink, having seen quite enough liquor already earlier that afternoon and had no desire to end up like Miss Jemima, meandering her way through aimless sentences. Besides, there was no telling where the alcohol had been brewed, or from what source. 'Bathtub gin', they called it over here, but from what Annie had heard, you'd be doing well if it had only come from a nice clean bathtub. She shook her head, softening the refusal with a smile.

'No thanks, I've a bit of a headache. But you go ahead.'

'Please yourself.'

Noreen tossed her head and gave her new friend another bright, beaming smile.

'All the more for us, Pat, isn't that right?'

Pat replenished his own glass with a hand, Annie noticed, that was not quite steady, then replaced the bottle in his pocket.

'Would Madam care for this dance?'

'Madam would, surely! You'll mind the drinks, Annie?'

Without waiting for a response, Noreen handed them over then followed her new friend onto the dance floor. Her hands now struggling to contain three glasses, Annie looked around helplessly for a moment then spotted a table underneath a window which, despite the heat, remained tight shut against the evening air. She walked across and deposited the glasses on top before realising, too late, that she couldn't remember which one was her own. Then again, she thought glumly as her face grew even hotter, doctored or not she didn't feel like drinking the lukewarm liquid anyway – and why in the name of God didn't somebody open that window?

Annie turned to face the room again, feeling sweat trickle down between her shoulder blades. The band had struck up a bright polka which Noreen was executing with great style although Pat, judging by the look of disappointment on his face, would have much preferred a slower number. Annie smothered a smile and then winced as a man stumbled into her, mashing his heel into her toe. Muttering an apology, he moved away but not before knocking one of the glasses of lemonade to the floor. Fearful it would shatter under someone's foot, Annie bent to pick it up and felt the sudden throb of a headache in her temple. She could just leave, she thought suddenly, she could just turn around now and go. All Noreen had really wanted was someone to arrive at the dance with, to avoid walking in the door alone. She had Pat to keep her company now and even if she tired of him Annie knew from experience that others would queue up to take his place.

'Will you dance?'

The hot alcoholic breath on her cheek made her wince and Annie shook her head even before taking a proper look at the small dark-haired man who had materialised by her side.

'No, thank you.'

The man peered up at her, as if assuming she had not heard him correctly.

'I asked if you'd like to dance?'

'And I said no!'

But her words coincided with a sudden lull in the music and came out louder and sharper than Annie had intended, causing a few people around them to turn and stare.

'Sure what's the point in you coming out at all if you're going to be so sour about it,' the man muttered, before stalking away across the floor. As heads turned in her direction, Annie felt her cheeks grow even hotter. Oh, this was surely a miserable way to spend an evening! All she wanted now was to be out in the open or better still back at the Cavendishes', in her cool bed on the top floor of the house, where she was guaranteed a breeze from the open window, even on a sticky evening such as this one.

Straightening her shoulders, Annie cast an acidic look at the doctored glasses of lemonade which were still arrayed on the table beside her. Blast it anyway, why shouldn't she leave? Why did everything have to be about what Noreen wanted? It was Annie's night off, surely she had the right to spend it as she saw fit? Maybe, if she left now, she'd even have time to walk all the way to the water after all.

She turned her back on the glasses, and on the dark-haired man who was still sending baleful looks in her direction, and began to push her way out of the crowd, which seemed to have tripled in size in the short time since she'd arrived at the hall. She stepped on a foot, muttered an apology but kept moving, she needed to get to the door, to get some air, she needed a little time to herself...

And then a heavy-set, middle-aged woman stepped aside and Annie saw, across the hall, a pair of brown eyes. Large and serious, those eyes raked the room and for one terrifying second Annie thought she would not see her, that Elena would leave again without finding her – and then the crowd moved again and Elena's gaze found hers. Within seconds she was by her side.

'I didn't think you'd come!' 'I wasn't sure if I should come...'

As their words flowed over each other, the warmth in their smiles banished any confusion. After a moment, Elena looked around the room.

'This music is a lot of fun.'

'Do you think so?'

As they walked back towards the dance floor – no longer overcrowded and stuffy, but a place of pure magic – Annie paused to listen to the sweep of the fiddle, the whistle urging on the tune.

'It is, I suppose. They are good musicians anyway. Would you have anything like this now, back in Italy?'

'I don't know.'

They found a space on a bench and sat down, they were so close to the musicians they had to huddle together to hear each other but for some reason their proximity didn't feel in any way strange or awkward. The hall was even more crowded than it had been earlier but it felt as if the two of them were in a bubble, Annie thought, protected and utterly content.

'I was only seven when we moved over here. There might have been dances but I'm not sure. We didn't have much money – it was always my father's dream to come to America.'

They were sitting so close together now that Annie could feel strands of Elena's silky black hair brush against her cheek.

'And are they glad they came over, your parents, are they happy here?'

Elena paused for a moment before answering.

'You know, I never really thought about that? My mother, I think she would be happier back in Italy. She complains sometimes about the dirt in the city and writes long letters to her sisters that she never lets us read. But my father works hard, and I think that makes him happy.'

'And does he like working at the restaurant?'

Annie was aware she was sounding inquisitive but couldn't bring herself to stem the flow of questions. It was just so unusual to meet someone from another background, with a fresh story to tell. Other than her employers and their friends, she could still count on the fingers of one hand the number of conversations she had had with people who weren't Irish, or of Irish heritage. There was Karla and Stefie, of course, but their English was still so basic, particularly Stefie's, that conversation was limited to what they were planning on doing that day. But now here she was, sitting beside an Italian woman with a life and a language she knew nothing about, and just speaking to her and listening to her was so new and exciting that Annie felt as enthusiastic about New York as she had the first day her ship had docked. Besides, she realised suddenly as the music dipped again, she really liked hearing Elena laugh.

'My papa?'

The Italian girl looked around the room before answering, and Annie found the simple parish dance grow almost exotic under the stranger's cool gaze.

'He would like to own his own restaurant someday, but I'm not sure if that would be possible...'

Her voice tailed off as she touched the sleeve of her blouse and Annie had to do everything in her power to prevent herself from gently lifting the material to see if the bruises had faded. She reached for another question as a distraction.

'And do Italian families spend a lot of time together, the way the Irish do?'

'Yes, we do.'

There was a pause as they both looked around the room again. A Paul Jones dance was in full swing and Annie could see Noreen in the thick of it, delight on the face of every partner lucky enough to enter her orbit. Pat, meanwhile, was nowhere to be seen, but that wasn't surprising. It wasn't Noreen's way to spend an entire evening with one consort, much less to agree to meet him another evening. She had no intention of marrying yet, she told Annie regularly. She liked men's company and liked having fun but had ambitions far beyond marriage in New York City and renting a room from her cousin on the Lower East Side. She didn't make false promises either; she danced with men but never allowed them to walk her home but that didn't stop them queuing to be the next to take her for a turn around the floor.

Noreen was beautiful, and that wasn't Annie's opinion as a friend, it was a simple fact. She had been the most beautiful woman on board the ship coming over from Ireland and she was always the most beautiful woman at any social they attended. Even on a night like tonight, when everyone else, man and woman alike, was red-faced and sweating, Noreen's face remained pale, her hair pinned back and smooth, her green eyes managing somehow to be both full of mischief yet at the same time perfectly sober and restrained, gliding around the floor as if there was a window open somewhere with cool air directed only on her. Elena, on the other hand, looked just as overheated as Annie did herself, her hair had escaped its low bun and was curling against her face in damp waves. But she was beautiful too, Annie thought suddenly, as beautiful as Noreen in her own way. And then she realised she was staring and cast around quickly for something else to say.

'So your parents were married back in Italy?'

Elena nodded.

'Yes. Their own parents introduced them, my mother had just turned seventeen. Do they do that in Ireland? Do parents organise marriages?'

'Sometimes.'

Annie shrugged, and then fell silent, well aware of just how lucky she had been in that regard. Some of the older people in Ballydrynawn still talked about 'making a match', and she knew her late grandmother had been very much in favour of the practice, but her parents had met at a fair and fallen in love, and had always been determined to allow their own children the same freedom.

'Yes, sometimes in Ireland people like to make matches. But my parents were happy for me to find my own way in the world.'

Elena gave a slight smile.

'You're lucky.'

Her voice was so soft, and the look on her face so wistful it was all that Annie could do not to reach out and touch her hand.

'Why do you say that? Are you—'

And then the younger woman leapt to her feet, not waiting for Annie to finish her question.

'I'd like to dance!'

Annie took a moment to gather her skirts before looking up at her new friend.

'But we haven't been asked!'

'Let's not worry about that!'

Elena nodded in the direction of the dance floor.

'Girls can dance together in America, look!'

Annie followed her gaze to where two middle-aged women were escorting each other on a sedate waltz around the edge of the dance floor, watched on by their husbands who seemed more interested in their 'lemonade' than their one-two-threes.

'I don't know…'

But Elena's eyes were twinkling with mischief now.

'This is a new world, isn't it? Let's not wait to be asked any more.'

She grabbed Annie's hand and tugged her towards the floor. For a moment, Annie felt as if all of the eyes in the room were on them as they stood facing each other, Elena's body swaying gently as if allowing the rhythm of the music to seep into her. Then she placed her hand around Annie's waist and drew her closer.

'You hold me here – see?'

She moved Annie's hand until it was resting on her hip.

'Now you lead.'

It was such a small hand, yet its touch seemed to burn through the waistband of her dress and Annie was afraid to move – surely they would all be staring at them now? And then as the notes from the fiddle soared she allowed herself to relax in Elena's grasp. It was true, women did dance together sometimes, even back in Ireland, older women usually, widows or those whose husbands felt their duty to the dance floor ended as soon as they produced a wedding ring. And some traditional Irish dances saw the ladies stand in one line and the men in another so no, this was not the first woman's hand Annie had ever held. But it had never felt quite like this before. Elena smiled and Annie pushed herself away from the edge of the floor, moving tentatively at first and then more firmly as her feet found their rhythm. No, this was nothing like she had ever felt before. Maybe it was just the feeling of being in control? Annie had never really enjoyed dancing, the sensation of being hauled around the floor, totally at her partner's mercy. Some men even tried to spin her away from them, bending her to their will like a doll, or a small child. Tonight, however, she was leading Elena who felt soft and accommodating in her arms and it was as if the whole business was making sense to her for the first time. Elena looked up then and Annie caught a soft scent of lilac from her dark hair.

'Are we doing it right, do you think?'

'Sure we are,' said Annie as they continued to move around the wooden floor, perfectly in time, Elena's small hand solid and reassuring in her larger one. One two three, one two three – it was only when Elena giggled that Annie realised she was counting out loud.

'You're a good dancer, Annie, don't worry! Gently now, that's right. It's a beautiful night, I'm so glad I came.'

'Me too,' is what Annie wanted to say but Elena was holding her gaze now and no words came and none were needed—

And then a shout pierced the room, a bellow so deafening that even the musicians faltered and Annie and Elena found themselves slowing and then standing in a confused muddle with the other dancers as they heard the word again.

'Elena!'

There was a ripple in the crowd and as people began to move aside Annie saw him, charging towards them, the stocky manager from the restaurant and another older man by his side. She could hear harsh words too, a violent stream of Italian, and she didn't need to speak the language to understand the tone. Elena cringed and all Annie wanted to do was hold her tight, protect her... but without warning the girl stepped away. A couple of steps later and the younger man had grabbed Elena's arm. Annie opened her mouth to protest but the Italian woman gave an almost imperceptible shake of her head. Both men were shouting now and as their voices continued to rise Annie felt a murmur of objection ripple through the Irish around her. Maybe somebody could help them? But although many of the men were sighing and shaking their heads, none caught her eye and no one moved forward. This was a foreign argument, foreign people, an Irishman would have no right to intervene. Elena was being pulled through the crowd now and Annie tried to follow but the music struck up again, a polka this time, and dancers spilled onto the floor, eager to capture the evening's earlier good humour.

'Excuse me – let me through – please...'

But by the time Annie had fought her way to the outside Elena had disappeared.

Chapter Fourteen

BALLYDRYNAWN

2022

'So it all began when I started doing this project – I guess you'd call it a family tree? I'm sorry—'

Alison stopped, then gulped water and replaced her glass on the table, making space for it among the mess of plates and glasses. Lunch had been just as delicious as Rob had promised, the prawns followed by monkfish skewers, all sourced from Dingle earlier that day and washed down with the now crisply cold Picpoul – 'we'll have to give our compliments to Gerry', Siobhán had commented drily. But now the main course was finished, and the fish cleared away and there was nothing stopping the young American woman from telling her story. Nothing, it seemed, apart from her own nerves.

'Take your time, Alison.'

Siobhán stood up from the table.

'I'm going to have a coffee, would you like one? A latte, maybe?'

The American gave her a grateful smile.

'That would be great!'

'Make sure she doesn't give you that oat milk stuff!'

Rob looked across at his mother, his eyes twinkling.

'I don't know what's wrong with a good Kerry cow myself.'

'You're more of an old man than your grandfather,' his mother retorted, making her way to a countertop coffee machine and busying herself with a series of complicated-looking levers.

'Wouldn't do you any harm to start eating a little healthier either.'

'I'm not starting today anyway.'

Rob waved the wine bottle at his guests but Alison just winced and Emer, mindful of her car parked outside, turned it down too although with some regret – she was sitting next to Rob on a low wooden bench and very conscious of how close his leg was to hers. That pleasant train of thought was derailed when Siobhán returned with two coffees and placed one in front of Alison who took a sip before beginning her story again.

'It was during lockdown.'

The caffeine brought a little warmth back to her cheeks.

'It's kind of a long story. You see, I grew up in California but not, like, California you see on TV. Have you heard of San Luis Obispo?'

Rob shook his head but, from their opposite sides of the table, Siobhán and Emer nodded, both familiar with the picturesque town on the edge of California's wine region.

Alison gave a wry smile.

'Well our town is physically near there but a million miles away in every other way, if you follow me. Definitely not on the tourist trail. And things were pretty tough when

I was growing up – my mom died when I was nine years old.'

The other three muttered condolences which Alison accepted with a small smile.

'My dad raised me and my little brother Felix and that wasn't easy, you know? I mean, he was a good father but he had to work, like really long hours. So we just looked out for ourselves. I did OK in school but there was no one to push me, no one to check if I had done my homework or anything so after a while I guess I just stopped trying. I left school before graduation, got a job in a bar – my dad tried to talk me out of it but he didn't try too hard, it was good to have extra money coming in. I got really lucky though. The owner was a decent guy, and when he heard my story I guess he thought I needed a bit of guidance so he paid for me to go to night school to learn about the business end of things. They treated me like an adult there, I liked it a lot more than normal school.'

She paused to take another sip of coffee before continuing.

'So one of the subjects I took was history and I really got into it. The teacher made it come alive, and he could see I was interested so he started to encourage me to do all these extra projects, learn how to research stuff on my own. And then Covid happened and all our classes moved to Zoom anyway, and the bar was shut most of the time, of course, so that's when I started looking into a family tree. It was just a way to fill the time really. My dad was from California, my grandma and grandpa on his side lived right down the street when we were growing up so there was no mystery there but all I knew about my mom was that her family were originally from Mexico. So I decided to do a bit of digging. My mom's mom lived with us for a while when I was a baby but she didn't really get on with my dad so after Mom passed away she went home and she died herself a few years later. We were still storing lots of her stuff in the basement though and none of my uncles or aunts wanted to pay to have it shipped back, so I decided to go through it, see if there was anything interesting. And man, it was incredible, the stuff I found. I guess my *abuela* was what you'd called a hoarder, she had kept everything. Newspapers, toys belonging to my mom and a whole bunch of documents. Then I found this photograph, and scribbled on the back was the word Papa and a name, and that was the first time I'd heard it. John Lynch, from County Kerry. My great-grandfather. There was another word on there too but I couldn't read it, Bailey – baily...'

'Baile Uí Dhroighneáin.'

Emer, much to her mother's displeasure, hadn't spoken a word of Irish since leaving school almost twenty years ago and empathised with the quizzical expression on Alison's face. But Rob jumped in with an explanation.

'Comes from the whitethorn tree, or the Thornton family, I'm not sure which. Bal-ya ee Grynawn. It got converted into Ballydrynawn somewhere along the way.'

Alison nodded.

'That's it. I Googled it and it led me here. And I know what you're thinking, there must be, like, a million John Lynches out there but I was intrigued, you know? How did this Irish guy end up in basically the boonies of California in the 1930s, how the heck did he meet my great-grandmother, how had I never heard of him before? They never married, I knew that much, because my great-grandmother kept her maiden name and that must have been a big deal back in those days too.'

She paused as if waiting to be interrupted but none of the others spoke so after a moment she began to speak again.

'I didn't have much else to do so I just kept on looking. You can find the most amazing things online. I found ships' logs, details of sailings from Ireland to the States, a whole bunch of John Lynches, obviously – but only one guy from here. He was listed as a single man, a farmer, aged twenty-seven. It was like a puzzle, you know? I looked this place up on Google Earth, it might as well have been Middle Earth!'

She attempted a weak smile but Emer was the only one who returned it.

'And then my dad passed away.'

She sounded so miserable, Emer couldn't stop herself from reaching across the table and giving her hand a quick squeeze.

'Oh, Alison, I'm so sorry.'

'Thank you. He got Covid, in the first wave. He hated hospitals, he wouldn't even call a doctor until it was too late. Turned out his heart wasn't in great shape to begin with. It was horrendous. I wasn't able to be with him in the end. The nurse let me FaceTime—'

The word disappeared in a sob and Rob rose from the table, returning after a moment with some kitchen paper which he pressed into her hand. His mother glanced at him, but said nothing. Alison blew her nose and then, after a moment, took up her story again.

'It was brutal, losing him like that. He did leave us a little money though, which surprised me; he had paid off his mortgage and put a little aside. And my brother is married now so we sold the house and he used his share to buy his own place and as soon as they started letting people travel again I just jumped on a plane. I had to get out of there, you know? It was coming up to Christmas and I couldn't bear the thought of being on my own.'

Alison was staring at the table now as if unable to catch anyone's eye.

'I had no plan, not really. I just needed a fresh start and coming here seemed like the right thing to do. It was like a dream to me, this little village on the far side of the world which might be where my ancestors came from. So I flew to Dublin, stayed in a hostel until Christmas was over and got the bus down here.'

She paused, then directed the next part of the story towards Emer.

'In a way the whole pandemic thing was a help – things were starting to open up but it wasn't really back to normal, everyone was wearing masks, that sort of thing. Nobody was asking too many questions. I stayed in a B and B in the village the first few nights – Lynch's B and B. It didn't take me long to figure out half the village was called Lynch, and there's about six Johns or Seáns in every family too so for a while I figured this would be as far as I'd get. I was going to give myself a week or two, just to look around, and then I was going to head off again. And then Rob had a party up here.'

Siobhán gave Rob a quizzical look but he simply nodded, his face open and unguarded.

'Yeah, that's right. God, you forget how mad it was back then, having to carry around Covid certs and all that, even Christmas week. The restaurants and bars were open but you had to book a table and they shut at eight. That's why I invited a crowd back here, just Paudie, Cian, the usual crowd. You were working in Dublin, Mom – I can't even remember who brought you up, Alison, was it Paudie?'

Alison flushed.

'Yeah. I met him in the chipper and he asked me along. He seemed pretty decent, clearly I'm a shit judge of character. But he said there was a party and I could come and I was like, why not? He had a wedding ring, I guess I believed in all that "Ireland of the welcomes" bit.'

There was a bitter tone to her voice now and Rob raised his eyebrows.

'Ah here, Paudie's an eejit but there's no real harm in him. But yeah, I remember, it was mellow enough. We'd a fire going in the pit, few drinks, nothing major. It was just good to see people again, even if we all had to stay outside.'

'Yeah.'

Alison flushed even deeper.

'I kind of came into the house though. I know I wasn't supposed to.'

'Did you now.'

Siobhán fixed her glasses a little higher on her nose.

'I'm not exactly sure where you are going with this, Alison. Your granddaddy may well have been a Lynch from Ballydrynawn, but sure you've said it yourself, you could be related to half the parish, or no one at all. But now you're telling me you came in here in the middle of a pandemic and walked around my house! Christ almighty, I wasn't allowed to visit my own father without a plastic apron and you were just wandering around...'

The look she shot her son now made it very clear that

she didn't consider him and his 'mellow gathering' immune from criticism either.

'I'm sorry!'

Alison buried her head in her hands for a moment. When she emerged, she looked bleak, but resigned to finishing her story no matter what the reaction.

'I'm so sorry. I just came in to use the bathroom and it's such an amazing house, I'd never seen anything like it, so I took a look around. And then I saw the photo and I knew I had the right John Lynch.'

'What photo?'

Siobhán's voice could have chilled Gerry's white wine without any need for a fancy refrigeration cabinet.

'Alison, I'm not short of a few bob, everyone knows that. And if you think I haven't had my share of begging letters and people turning up here looking for money, you'd be sorely mistaken. So if you've come over here with some notion that you're related to us then you'd want to think again very quickly—'

'Does this look familiar?'

Alison had hung her backpack on the back of the chair when the meal started. She reached into it now and took out her phone.

'What I saw in your sitting room – I couldn't believe it. I stupidly hadn't brought my own copy with me, I was too afraid of it getting damaged so I called my brother, asked him to make me a copy. It took him ages to get around to it, half of my stuff is in storage or in boxes in his basement. But he finally sent me this last week.'

She unlocked her screen, fiddled for a moment then passed it to Siobhán who took it without a word. After a moment, the older woman rose and, still moving in complete silence, left the room. The other three looked at each other then followed her out, Emer not sure if she was welcome but too engrossed in the drama to risk being left behind. She was, in fact, starting to feel like she was in one of those TV Christmas movies, where the Big City Girl goes back to the Small Town and discovers all sorts of shenanigans. And Emer really loved those films.

In single file they walked, first through the entrance hall then up the stairs. Siobhán, marching at a serious clip, led them across the landing, down a short corridor then through a door which closed noiselessly behind them to reveal a vast, brightly lit space.

'Cool.'

Emer managed to keep her reaction under her breath, but only just. It was like being on board ship, that was her first thought. It wasn't usual in Irish houses to have a sitting room on the second floor but whatever Siobhán had paid her 'Dub' architect it had been worth it, because she had ended up with one of the most beautiful living spaces Emer had ever seen. One wall of the room was made entirely of glass, the room angled in such a way that the garden below was barely visible, the view consisting almost entirely of sky and the sea. Today, the sunshine meant both were contrasting shades of blue and Emer wanted nothing more than to sink into one of the artfully placed armchairs and drink it all in. There was no television in the room, no screen of any description as far as she could see and why would there be when you had all of this to look at? Above her head a seagull wheeled and a single cloud drifted lazily towards them, changing the light by subtle degrees as it crossed the sun. The others, however, had completely ignored the stunning vista and crossed instead to a sideboard on the far wall, an old-fashioned piece of furniture, not at all in keeping with the rest of the decor. A row of photos stood on top of it and Siobhán lifted one up, squinted at it then handed it to Alison.

'This is the photo you saw?'

Alison nodded.

'Yeah.'

Siobhán was still carrying Alison's phone and handed it now to her son.

'Have a look.'

Her voice, for the first time ever, sounded uncertain. Rob squinted at the small screen, then exhaled.

'I see what you mean.'

Unable to contain her curiosity, Emer walked over and looked over his shoulder and then she, too, saw why Siobhán appeared so shaken. The photo on the sideboard, neatly framed in brass, was of a young man, probably in his mid to late twenties, with a long face and narrow, rather beaky nose. It wasn't an attractive face and his expression was almost sullen as he glared rather than stared into the camera lens but Emer imagined she could see something of Rob in the broad shoulders and shock of curling hair. The photo on the phone, although faded and badly creased, was undoubtedly a copy of the same one.

Alison looked from mother to son.

'That's what I've been trying to tell you. This...'

She gestured at the phone in Rob's hands.

'That's the picture my *abuela* had of her father. And it's him, isn't it? The same guy. The minute I saw it here I knew,

I just needed my brother to send it over so you wouldn't think I was a complete nutcase. It is him, though. My great-grandfather was your John Lynch. He must have gone to America and had another family over there. I'm sorry but it's the only explanation I can come up with. I think we're – I guess you'd call us cousins?'

If this was an afternoon movie, Emer thought wryly, this moment would make one hell of a commercial break.

Chapter Fifteen

NEW YORK

1926

'Annie, can you set out a tray? Miss Jemima has invited a number of guests to afternoon tea.'

'Which cups will I use, ma'am?'

'Oh heavens, it doesn't matter.'

Mrs O'Toole sounded tired, Annie thought, and looked it too. There were twelve people expected for dinner that evening and the housekeeper had been up since dawn planning the menu, and while Miss Jemima wouldn't have given a second thought to her spur of the moment invitation, the addition of extra guests in the middle of the day would stretch the kitchen to its limits. Mrs O'Toole would have to prepare the food herself, for a start. Mabel the cook had resigned less than a month previously and although her replacement, a sad-eyed Frenchman named Alphonse, had arrived at the Chateau laden down with references from his previous employer, those noble pieces of paper had failed to mention that Alphonse considered some elements of food preparation beneath him, namely the baking of bread, the preparation of cold lunches or anything, as Mrs O'Toole caustically observed, that didn't look as if it belonged in a gallery and not on a nice sturdy dinner plate.

Mrs Cavendish had been delighted with Alphonse, however; indeed Annie had overheard her telling her daughter that all of the 'significant' New York families had French chefs this year, so Mrs O'Toole had been forced to quite literally roll up her own sleeves and return to the baking and plain cooking she had specialised in before her elevation to the housekeeper's position. And although she had complained to Mrs Cavendish that if she was back making porridge and buttering bread, she wouldn't have time to devote to the actual running of the Chateau, her employer had informed her with a smile that she herself would take over some of the housekeeping duties, if that was what was needed to accommodate Alphonse.

The end result of all of this disruption was that Alphonse was producing on average one – admittedly delicious – dinner a day while Mrs O'Toole and the rest of the kitchen staff toiled over the other meals, often working with the wrong ingredients because Mrs Cavendish hadn't quite got to grips with how to order groceries, and when.

As Mrs O'Toole, sighing deeply, pulled a bag of flour from the larder and wondered out loud how to make the last of the buttermilk stretch for a fresh batch of scones, Annie filled the kettle and placed it on the range before making her way to the large cupboard – she had finally learned not to call it a 'press' – at the far end of the kitchen. She paused for a moment before selecting her favourite set of crockery, white, with a delicate pattern of red roses so realistic, she sometimes imagined she could smell a flowery perfume rising along with the steam as she poured the tea.

She loaded her tray then walked carefully back through the kitchen, taking care not to slip on the flagstones, which were greasy underfoot thanks to Alphonse's rather sloppy basting of the pair of geese he was roasting in the range. Karla and Stefie were peeling carrots and potatoes, Karla with a rather sullen expression on her face as she had hoped to begin training as a cook herself until Mrs O'Toole's sudden demotion left her back at the sink where she started. In fact most of the staff, Annie noticed, seemed out of sorts today, their humour not helped by having to work in a warm, damp, steamy room. Annie often wondered why the men who had built this stunning house, where some of the windows were made from stained glass and could be considered works of art in their own right, had neglected to provide anything like adequate ventilation in what was by far the busiest room in the entire Chateau, as if they had simply run out of interest by the time they reached the basement level. But at least, she thought now as she waited by the range for the kettle to boil, at least the frantic nature of the day's work meant that nobody had noticed her own glum mood.

It was almost a week now since the dance at the parish social and Annie had not been able to get Elena out of her head. The Italian woman was the first person she thought of in the morning and the last on her mind before she fell asleep at night or, more frequently than not, lay awake in the darkness. It didn't matter how weary she was from the day's work, how heavy her limbs, every time Annie closed her eyes worry about Elena would churn within her and deny her rest. There was no rhyme or reason to her feelings, it simply didn't make sense to feel so intensely about a woman she barely knew, it was just—

'ANNIE!'

'I'm sorry!'

She had done it again, lapsed into a daydream so deep she hadn't been aware of Mrs O'Toole's shout or indeed of the piercing whistle of the kettle which was now adding to the din and the warmth of the already chaotic kitchen. Flustered and upset, Annie turned towards the noise but the hem of her sleeve caught on the chair behind her, jerking the tray and sending one of those beautiful cups crashing onto the flagstones.

'Oh no...'

It was just a cup, that was all, a very beautiful cup but a cup nonetheless, but for some reason the sight of that beautiful, delicate thing smashed to pieces brought tears to her eyes. Annie dropped to her knees and began to collect the white slivers but she was sobbing now, in a way she hadn't done since she had come to New York or even that day on the boat when she left Ireland behind. Such was her distress that Mrs O'Toole didn't even reprimand her, just barked an order to get the area cleaned up as quickly as possible. Annie did as she was told, but the tears simply would not stop and by the time she rose to her feet again her shoulders were heaving and even Alphonse paused in his carving of carrots into floral shapes to stare at her as if she was something that did not belong in his domain.

'Are you quite well, Annie?'

Mrs O'Toole walked over then and grasped her, not unkindly, by the arm.

'Are you ill, child?'

Not ill, no. But Annie had come to a decision. She needed to find Elena, to discover what had happened to her after the dance. She would go back to the restaurant on her next free evening. Only by doing so would her mind be at ease; only then could she forget about the whole matter and begin her contented life again.

There was a menu pinned to the door of the restaurant and Annie scrutinised it for a moment, buying time to compose herself. Then her gaze drifted from the descriptions of minestrone soup and roast beef dinners and she found herself staring at her reflection in the glass, her face pale to the point of illness. She had put on a clean blouse before leaving the house that evening but its collar was yellowing and fraying around the edges – maybe she should have waited until she had found something new to wear? But now she was being ridiculous. Giving her hair a final pat, Annie stepped back from the door with a scowl. New blouses, whatever next? She was here to meet a friend, that was all, there was no need to get so het up about it. She was just going to assure herself that Elena was not in any danger and then she would be on her way again.

It was less than an hour before closing time and the restaurant was quiet with just a couple of tables near the door occupied by men in labouring clothes who were working their way stolidly through the roast beef special. Annie kept her head down as she walked past them, not wanted to draw attention to herself, and slid onto a vacant bench near the wall. Then a shadow fell over her and she looked up to see Elena standing there, notebook in hand.

'Can I take your order?'

Annie was suddenly unable to remember a word from the menu in the window.

'Elena! I had hoped you'd be working today. It's lovely to see you!'

The waitress gave a quick, darting look in the direction of the kitchen before putting the question again.

'What can I get you? Today's special is beef, or we have minestrone soup.'

Flustered, Annie threw the menu a brief glance.

'Well, yes then, beef please. Or no – soup. Soup would be lovely. But how are you, Elena?'

She tried to put as much compassion as she could into the question, but the girl had already turned and was walking away.

Bewildered and not a little hurt Annie pulled a twist of sugar from the bowl in front of her and began to roll it between her fingers, scarcely noticing when it tore and spilled its contents across the table. Elena was like a different person today, she thought, wan and defensive, nothing at all like the warm woman she had held in her arms during that fleeting but surprisingly tender waltz. Maybe she shouldn't have come here at all today, maybe she was only going to cause the woman more bother – but even as those thoughts swirled in her head Elena returned and placed in front of her a bowl of steaming liquid.

'Your soup, ma'am.'

She turned to leave but Annie reached out and grabbed her by the sleeve.

'Can we talk, Elena? If not here, then maybe after you are finished for the day?'

There was no mistaking now the look of terror that came over the girl's face as she glanced not at Annie but over her shoulder to where other members of staff were cleaning tables. She waited, almost motionless for a moment, before speaking in a whisper.

'I finish at seven.'

Then she jerked her arm out of Annie's grasp and scuttled away.

The soup could have been made from cooked straw for all Annie could taste of it and it burned her mouth as she swallowed it down, anxious to leave the restaurant as soon as possible yet afraid that if she left a full bowl behind her, with the implication that she hadn't enjoyed the food, she might somehow get Elena into even more trouble. Because Elena *was* in trouble, there was no denying that now, no ignoring the look of terror in her eyes or the tension she was carrying in her slender body. And there was also no ignoring the fact that Annie cared very deeply about what kind of trouble she was in.

She had almost an hour to wait before Elena would be free to meet, so after leaving money for her meal and a generous tip she hoped Elena would receive, Annie left the restaurant and walked blindly for a couple of blocks before spotting the entrance to a small city park. There was a bench just inside the gate and she sank onto it, near a young mother who was watching two small boys toss a ball around, utterly unaffected by the evening heat. Emmet and James would have joined in with their game, Annie knew, and the sudden thought of home reminded her she was carrying a letter from her mother in her skirt pocket. She had read it already, of course, had devoured it over breakfast, but anxious for distraction she pulled it out and smoothed it with her fingers before beginning to read it again.

And oh, what a comfort it was! Within seconds Annie was lost in news of home, her mother's precise script outlining mundane but delightful details about the birth of a lamb, the death of the schoolmaster's mother, a gentle observation that Eve might find it easier to manage their household in her absence. Her father, Pádraig, had included a note too, telling Annie of the many changes that were taking place 'above in Dublin', where Colm O'Flaherty was now a minister in the new government and had been quoted in the *Cork Examiner* as saying his main priority was to repair the roads between Tralee and Dingle. Deputy O'Flaherty, Annie thought with a smile, it suited him. Her father's few words ended with a prayer, as they always did, asking God to keep her safe in America and advising her not to speak to anyone strange. Pádraig always spoke of America, Annie thought, as if it were a town no bigger than Dingle – and then she stopped and angled the letter away from her, noticing for the first time a third block of handwriting, running lengthways across the bottom of the second page. May was not a frequent letter writer – now rearing two children on her own as well as running the farm it wasn't surprising that she found it hard to find time to put pen to paper and besides, she had never been one for books even back when they were in school. But she must have called over to the house while Eileen was finishing her own letter, Annie surmised, and it was easy to imagine her mother persuading her friend to add a note of her own. Her theory was proven correct as she began to read the untidy, looping handwriting, squinting as the New York sun beat down on the pages.

Dear Annie, I had a fine crop of rhubarb this month and called to ur mthr this evening to see wld she like them and she advised me she was writing to you and invited me to add a line. Poor Mrs Lynch died six weeks ago, we were all sad but she was in terrible pain the last few weeks God love her and it was an ease to her in the end. The rest of us are well TG. Muireann is talking away, you can't keep her quiet and Harry is a lovely sturdy little boy running around u wld not know him Id say. People ask me is it hard rearing them without a man and I tell them it is but I am going to be honest with you now my dear friend and tell you life is very good and quite and happy with us. I have a little kitchen garden now and it is doing right well. Billy Madden looks after the cattle for me and I have an arrangement to pay him and it suits us right well. Billy has asked me several times if I think Seánie is dead and I tell him that I do not know. But I do not want Billy Madden to have any false hope of me. Eileen tells me she will seal this letter now and only you will read it so I can tell you here and now that I do not wish my husband to be dead but I do not want him to return to me either, nor do I want any other man. My life is simple now and it is an ease to me. I am happy on my own and will be same DV as long as God spares me.

God Bless you Annie over there in America. I can't picture you in America but I know you are happy and will make a huge success of ur life as you always did.

Urs May

I am happy on my own and will be same please God.
Please God.

Annie folded the letter and placed it back in her pocket. Two healthy children, an income from the cattle and a kitchen garden, it was a life of happiness that once seemed beyond May's reach and she could not wish for more for her friend.

But at the same time, she realised as she rose from the bench, it was not a life she had ever wanted for herself. Calling over to the same neighbours every evening, rearing children who would go to the same school as you did yourself – Annie was happy for May, beyond happy, but reading those few lines proved to her once again how right she had been to come to America, how happy she was here, in a place where nobody knew you and you could lead a different life. A place where you could meet people like Elena? The thought shot across her mind and she did not know what to do with it so she shut it away and strode out of the park, anxious now to see what the evening would bring.

The restaurant was closed by the time she got back but just as Annie was starting to fear she had missed Elena altogether she heard a scraping sound coming from the side of the building and rounded the corner to find a narrow, foul-smelling alleyway where a burly man in a white apron was emptying a bucket of rotten food into a large metal bin. He looked up at her but said nothing, just spat on the ground before making his way back into the building through a heavy metal door, which swung shut behind him then opened again almost immediately to reveal a head of thick dark curls.

'Elena!'

Annie's voice sounded strange, almost croaky, and she wasn't sure if the girl had heard but as she opened her mouth to speak again Elena looked at her, shook her head and hissed.

'You can't be here!'

Annie was at the top of the alleyway now and hesitated, one foot still on the main street.

'Can't we just talk for a moment?'

The girl glanced from side to side as if hoping to make her escape but there was no way of exiting the alleyway without passing Annie, so she lowered her head and walked quickly towards her, not pausing as she passed by but muttering under her breath.

'Walk behind me. You can't let them see us together.'

Unsure of who 'they' were, but alarmed by the panic in the young woman's voice Annie didn't question her, just followed her at a distance down the main street and around the corner until she found herself back at the park again. Once inside Elena didn't slow her pace, just kept walking, head bent, until she reached a fountain on the far east side. The fountain was a small, ugly structure, little more than a stone basin, and as its water had been turned off it was dirty too, its base filled with cigarette butts and dried leaves but Elena ignored the mess and sat down on the edge, then looked straight at Annie for the first time.

'You shouldn't have come.'

Annie sat down beside the Italian woman who turned to her with a frown.

'Why did you come back? You must have known it would cause trouble for me.'

The flatness of her tone made Annie flinch but she kept her voice as light as she could.

'After the dance – I was worried about you, I just wanted to see if you were all right.'

'There will be trouble if they see me talking to you.'

Despite her fondness for the girl, Annie found herself growing irritated. Why was Elena being so mysterious? Why was their friendship the cause of such strife? All she had done was invite her to a dance. Certainly there had been many times over the past week when Annie's mind had slipped back to the night of the social and her heart had given a strange kind of double beat as she remembered how happy she had felt in Elena's company; indeed sometimes she even permitted herself a curious but undeniably satisfying daydream about what it would be like to take the woman in her arms again. But Elena was not privy to those thoughts and neither was her father. As far as he was concerned they were just friends, and Annie simply couldn't understand why he would deprive his daughter of the simple companionship of another young woman. Unless it was the case that Elena herself didn't want that companionship?

And then Elena looked up briefly before dipping her head again but not before Annie noticed the ring of purple around her left eye and the swollen and bruised cheekbone.

'Dear Lord!'

Annie stretched out her hand and Elena did not move away as she gently touched the precious, battered face.

'Who did this to you? Your father?'

Elena shook her head. It was clear the action caused her further pain and Annie felt tears spring into her own eyes at the sight of it.

'No! My father would not do this.'

They stared at each other for a second and then Annie saw, as clear as if he was standing in front of her, the shorter of the two men who had dragged her from the parish hall, the same man who had been so brutal to the little waitress on their first meeting at the restaurant.

'That man you called Lorenzo – he did this?'

'My father, my mother – we all work for him. He paid the fare for us all to come to America, we owe him a great deal.'

Annie bit her lip. She herself had been lucky enough to be able to save up and afford her own fare to the United States, and an agency affiliated with the church had organised her position with the Cavendishes, who had proved themselves to be decent people. But she had heard terrible stories of girls brought to America and then used almost as slaves, with bed and meagre board the only reward for their labour and no prospect of them ever earning money of their own or of getting away. It was clear from the look of despair on Elena's face that this was not just an Irish problem.

'Lorenzo's family owns the house we live in. If it was not for them, we would have nowhere to live, we would be on the streets. We can't afford to go back to Italy, we would be destitute. We have no choice in any of this.'

'But this is America!'

Not caring who saw them now, Annie clasped the young woman's hand in hers.

'This is America, you don't have to live like this! Your father can get a new job, or you can – there's no need for this, Elena! We were just at a dance, that night, a parish dance, that man had no right to pull you away. And he certainly had no right to do – to hurt you like that.'

And then her words deserted her because heat from Elena's hand seemed to be flowing into hers and was causing a curious darting feeling deep inside, a sensation that was both utterly new yet alarmingly familiar, a candle wick responding to the strike of a match. Annie had felt flickers of that flame before, late at night while thinking of Elena and one morning when she woke, dazed and dry-mouthed from a dream where they were dancing alone. But now the flame caught and burned inside her, growing in intensity until she felt a sudden urge to pull the Italian woman towards her, to take her in her arms...

The sight of tears on Elena's face brought Annie back to her senses and she forced herself to release her hand before continuing.

'They can't stop us being friends. We could go for a walk sometimes, in the evenings, after you finish. Do you get any time to yourself?'

Elena wiped her eyes.

'I give English lessons on Thursday afternoons to a family from my father's home village. I go to their house at four but I never stay much longer than an hour. I could tell him, I suppose, that they need me for longer.'

Annie grasped the thought as a lifeline.

'Thursday is my half day.'

'I know.'

Elena blushed.

'You first came to the restaurant on a Thursday. I remember. I remember everything about that day.'

'So do I,' Annie replied, and she wanted very much to hold Elena's hand again but didn't have the courage. And she wasn't able to find any words either, even though there was so much she wanted to say. It was Elena who finally broke the silence.

'Thursday afternoons, then? We can meet here maybe?'

'I would like that very much. But your father? What will you do if he finds out?'

The smaller woman shrugged and for the first time Annie heard a note of steel in her soft voice.

'I will manage my father. But I have to leave now or I will be in trouble, they expected me home a half hour ago.'

It was growing chilly but Annie didn't feel the cold as they left the park, warmth from the encounter glowing inside her. When they reached the gate they paused and then Elena pulled her into a light embrace, her lips brushing against Annie's cheek, a butterfly kiss that seemed to burn away several layers of skin.

'Until next week, Annie.'

As Annie watched the Italian woman walk away she felt a sudden lurch deep inside, for all the world like the moment back in Cobh when the ship's horn had sounded and the vessel began to pull away from shore. She was heading to another world again, only this time there was no guard rail to cling to, no Noreen to tell her what to do. But Annie knew, despite her fear, that she wanted very much to go on this journey.

She was so dazed by the encounter that she barely noticed the walk back to the Chateau, but when she let herself into the kitchen realised it must have been much later than she thought because the room had finally fallen quiet. Mrs O'Toole, who had been sitting, head nodding, in the chair nearest the fire looked up with a start.

'Annie! Did you have a pleasant evening?'

'I did, ma'am. I thought you'd be away to bed by now.'

'I wish I was.'

The older woman yawned.

'But they' – she rolled her eyes in the direction of the ceiling – 'had a late dinner this evening and I haven't sent the coffee up yet. I've the kettle on and I was just about to call Karla to ask her to serve it.'

'Oh, don't bother her.'

Such was her good humour at seeing Elena, Annie didn't mind working on what was supposed to be her free evening, and made her way to the cupboard to prepare the tea tray. She opened the wooden door and then let out a gasp.

'You've fixed it!'

In front of her sat a complete set of four rose-covered cups, each one whole and undamaged.

Mrs O'Toole gave an amused snort.

'There's boxes of those cups above in the attic, Annie, I told you not to distress yourself. Sure the family won't know any difference.'

'I see…'

As the housekeeper prepared to leave for bed, Annie bustled around the kitchen preparing coffee, and a small pot of camomile tea for Mrs Cavendish who never drank anything stronger. She poured the boiling water, let it sit for a moment and then carried the pot to the pail in the corner that was used for kitchen refuse. The meaning of Mrs O'Toole's amusement became clear as she opened the pail and saw three, perfect, unbroken rose-covered cups glinting from under a mess of spent tea leaves and potato peelings. Mrs O'Toole paused on her way to the door.

'The other cups were looking a little worn, when I got the

new one down from the attic it was as easy just to replace all four. Good night, Annie, you make sure you get some rest when you're done here.'

For a moment Annie considered taking one of the cups from the bin, washing it and keeping it in her room for her own use. Millie would empty that bin in the morning and no one would be any the wiser. But for some reason it would have felt dishonest to do so, so she took one last look at the discarded perfection then replaced the bin lid and finished preparing the tea.

Chapter Sixteen

WEST KERRY

14 June 2022

The sea lapped against her waist, cold water seeping through the thick wetsuit before being warmed by the heat of her body. Emer took a quick look over her shoulder then grabbed her board by its edges and pulled herself on. Now lying flat against its rigid surface, she felt the water swell behind her and began to paddle with her arms. It was the same front crawl motion she had learned as a seven-year-old in her local pool, her father occasionally looking up from his crossword to shout encouragement, but there was no shallow end here, no lifeguard – the thought made doubt swell for a moment along with the water – and then Rob's voice rose above the wind.

'This one's yours!'

And why wouldn't it be? Emer thought suddenly as the board picked up speed and she lifted her head to watch the shore rush towards her. It was ten o'clock on a Monday morning, and given how odd life was at the moment, surely lying on a piece of rigid foam in the freezing cold Atlantic Ocean was just one more strange thing to add to the litany.

Although she had tried not to let it show, the news that her great-grandfather may well have sired a second family in America had clearly knocked the stuffing out of Siobhán the previous afternoon and she had retired to her room soon after seeing the photograph, claiming she had lost her passport and needed to find it. Emer would have loved a few minutes alone with Rob, just to get his take on the whole bizarre situation, but Alison had asked her for a lift to Ballydrynawn and Emer had agreed, feeling that putting a bit of space between the Lynches and their lodger was probably the biggest favour she could do for all of them. Alison had been in a hurry, leaving Emer with barely enough time to thank Rob and make a hasty promise to go surfing the following morning before hitting the road.

So now here she was, vac-packed into a borrowed wetsuit, trying not to think of how many strangers had surfed in it before her – or, God forbid, weed in it – and waiting for the right moment to try and stand up in the middle of the freezing cold ocean.

The board continued to pick up speed and she pressed down on it, then moved into plank position, sending a quick thanks across the ocean to Yoga with Adrienne for all those lockdown yoga videos which had left her with enough strength and flexibility to support herself on her arms for long enough to move her leg forward into position. Now her foot was stable at the centre of the board, now it was taking her weight, now her second foot too was in position, now she was standing, now she was wobbling – but wait, now she was finding her balance, now she was steady and now she was flying, spray in her face, shooting forwards towards the shore. It was only when Emer felt sand scrape the bottom of her board that she realised that the ride was over and that, rather hilariously, she didn't actually know what to do next because she had usually fallen off well before this stage. She wobbled in place for a moment, wondering if the sea was too shallow for her to jump in, and then Rob surfed in on the following wave.

'Woo hoo!'

He leaped off his board and extended his hand for a high five.

'I told ya you were a natural!'

And somehow, although she wasn't quite sure how it happened, somewhere between her stepping off her board and landing in the sea that high five turned into a hug. They held the embrace for a moment, boards bobbing at their feet like neglected pets before Emer pulled away.

'So is this standard then, with all private lessons?'

Rob's eyes opened wide.

'Would you feck off, I'll be drummed out of the surfing association.'

'There's a surfing association?'

Rob tossed his head in mock indignation.

'I'm a highly qualified professional, I'll have you know.'

'Oh I believe that all right.'

Emer's hair was plastered against her head and both she and her wetsuit smelled mildly of disinfectant, but she didn't give a damn, and judging by the way Rob was looking at her he didn't either.

'But what are you like as a surfer?'

She held his gaze for a moment, then took a step backwards.

'Come on, we're missing some great waves.'

Emer didn't feel the cold this time as he followed her, laughing, back into the ocean.

It was more than an hour later when Emer stepped off the board again and this time found that her legs were still wobbling, even though she was now back on hard sand. She stood for a moment, arching her back to relieve the tightening muscles, then looked out to sea, and further again to the mountains that guarded the east side of the bay. It had been a grey morning but the cloud cover was thinning out now and every so often a ray of sun broke through, picking out smears of emerald and moss on the slopes, light that disappeared within seconds but held the promise of return.

She was tired but that wasn't the only reason she was finishing her session – the wind had picked up in the last ten minutes and the waves were larger, stronger, less friendly than before. She looked further out to sea where Rob was lying flat on his board just ahead of a rising mass of grey water. He paddled once, then twice, then bunny-hopped into position, a light, fluid, gravity-defying jump that didn't require any plank or yoga-inspired contortions and left him rock solid on his board. He and the wave surged forward, and then some subtle movement saw him tip the board downwards and now he was zig-zagging across the face of the wave, moving diagonally to the shore, even holding out a hand to touch the wall of water, utterly sure-footed and in control.

'Yer man showing off again, is he?'

Emer jumped, then turned to see Paudie and Cian stride down the beach towards her. Both men were carrying surfboards but as they drew closer she could see the crafts were as different as their owners. Paudie's was a long, broad, cream-coloured affair, almost as large as a paddleboard, while Cian's board was shorter than her own, bright white with a red stripe down the middle and three short fins at the back. Emer swallowed back a surge of disappointment – she might have finished surfing for the day but she had hoped there'd be time to see if that hug was going to lead anywhere and she didn't fancy having Paudie and Cian as an audience if it did. But she didn't own the beach so plastered a smile on her face as they approached.

'He won't be much longer I'd say, there's a class at eleven thirty.'

Cian gave a quick glance at the rapidly clearing sky.

'Nice morning for it anyway.'

'Gorgeous. Are ye heading in yourselves?'

'Yep.'

Paudie raised a fist to his mouth, making only half an attempt to disguise a belch.

'I'd a feed of pints last night, so this will either kill me or cure me.'

Of course, it was the June bank holiday weekend. Emer herself had reached that happy stage of a vacation where she was hard pressed to remember what day of the week it was, but obviously a teacher and a bank worker would be revelling in the extra free day.

'How did you get on yourself?'

Cian looked at Emer, then nodded towards the ocean.

'Ah, it was fabulous. Loved it.'

'Well, Rob's a good teacher.'

'Speak of the divil!'

Paudie raised his hand in greeting and all three watched as Rob surfed in on a final wave then hopped off his board and tucked it under his arm before walking towards them. There followed a couple of minutes of high-level banter, mixed with surfing terminology Emer only half understood before Rob noticed she was shivering.

'Sorry, Emer – you must be dying to get changed. Here's the key to the van.'

He fished around the neck of his wetsuit and withdrew a car key from a hidden pocket.

And would you mind bringing me down my bag when you're coming back? I need to check my phone before the lesson.'

Rob handed over the key with a smile and Emer pretended not to notice a wry glance from Paudie as she made her way back up the beach. When she returned, fully dressed in tracksuit and a warm fleece – it was June in Ireland, after all – and carrying Rob's gym bag, the three men were still discussing conditions. Judging by the look of amusement on Cian and Rob's faces, they were taking great pleasure in slagging the hungover Paudie as well, but he didn't seem to enjoy being on the business end of the banter and as Emer drew closer she saw him give Rob a sidelong glance.

'I hear ye had drama up at the house last night.'

Rob's smile disappeared.

'We did, I suppose. Where did you hear that?'

Paudie snorted.

'Sure your mom was straight on the phone to mine after, you know what those two are like when they get going.'

And your 'mom' clearly didn't think she needed to keep the news to herself, Emer thought. Rob remained silent while Paudie filled Cian in on the previous day's events, or what he had learned of them at least, then gave a brief, dismissive shrug.

'Sure ye know the whole story now. I'd better get changed—'

But Paudie had no intention of letting sleeping gossip lie.

'Well if you call that the whole story, like...'

'What do you mean?'

Rob's voice was calm, almost pleasant, but Emer could see how tightly he was gripping the board, his knuckles standing out bright white against his tanned hand.

Paudie, however, was clearly enjoying himself.

'Well, Alison is saying she's known about this photo since New Year's, yeah? She was just waiting for her brother to send her a copy or something? I don't know, I suppose I just find it a bit odd that she'd keep something like that to herself for so long. She's been in Ireland for six months but only now decides to say, oh guess what, we're related?'

'I dunno.' Rob shrugged, making what looked like a supreme effort to appear indifferent. 'No point in talking to us when she was only half certain, like.'

'Huh.'

Paudie was making no pretence at hiding his scepticism. 'She was waiting to find out the lie of the land, you mean.'

Beside him Cian was hopping from foot to foot, clearly anxious to get into the water, but Paudie had settled into the conversation as easily as if he was still standing at the bar.

'Come on, you must be thinking the same thing, Roberto. Your mom's loaded. Doesn't mean fuck all to us, never did, you were a gobshite when you arrived in Ballydrynawn and you were still a gobshite when we found out your mother is basically Bill Gates in a dress, but not everyone is as laid-back as us, you know!'

The expression on Rob's face was stretching the definition of a smile as Paudie continued.

'But a returned Yank, now that's a different story. I mean, it's not like she rocked up and decided she was a cousin to me or to Cian here, is it?'

He turned to Cian.

'Your family has been in the village since the dawn of time too, Ciano, they even called the bloody place after ye but Alison didn't find you on any family tree.'

Cian nodded uncomfortably as Paudie continued.

'Alison could have decided that Séamus in the pub was her uncle, or Dinny Lynch at the garage even. But instead she reckons your mom is her long-lost relative and, what a coincidence, just happens to have a photo that proves the whole thing. Oh yeah, and by the way, I hear she's saying I invited her up to the house that night, the night of the party? 'Cause that's just not true, man, and the missus will go through me for a shortcut if she hears about it. The way I remember it she was hassling half the village for a lift and I just happened to be the one who gave in to her.'

Rob looked genuinely impatient now.

'So what are you suggesting? That Alison is making it up?'

Paudie shrugged.

'Well it's not beyond the bounds, is it? She could have taken a copy of the picture in your house at any stage, got it printed up then or something. I don't know, I'm not a detective! It just all sounds a bit funny to me and I hope your mother gives it a week or two before she starts redrawing the will, that's all.'

'That's enough, man.'

Cian's face was flushed as he turned to his friend.

'You always have to go too far.'

He shook his head, then looked at Rob.

'This fella is still half jarred. Let's get into the water and cool off, OK?'

He turned and headed into the sea, throwing the board in front of him and paddling so smoothly he was out beyond the waves in moments. Paudie picked up his own board then turned to Rob, his spare hand open in a conciliatory gesture.

'I might have hit a nerve there, I forgot Cian is soft on her. Look, don't mind me. I wasn't trying to interfere or anything. But I'm fond of your ma, you know? And you, ya bollocks, and I just want to make sure ye're not taken for a ride. No hard feelings, OK?'

Without waiting for Rob to respond he followed his friend into the water.

Emer waited till they were out of earshot, then looked at Rob.

'Are you OK?'

He nodded, but his mouth was set in a tight scowl.

'Yeah. Paudie is all talk, he always was. You're not seeing the best of him this week at all, he can be decent at the back of it and he probably is genuinely trying to look out for us. But he's as subtle as brick, the same fella.'

'Surfs like one too!'

They both turned to see the bank official take a dramatic nosedive off his board into the ocean.

'He deserved that.'

Somewhat mollified, Rob unpeeled his wetsuit from his shoulders then rifled around in his bag before extracting his phone.

'I'm going to have to make tracks, the next group will be here any minute.'

They headed back up the beach together, Rob scrolling through his texts as he walked.

'Huh.'

He stopped, stared at the phone for a moment then handed it to her.

'What do you make of this then?'

The message was from 'Mom', and Emer hesitated before reading it, but Rob shrugged.

'Have a look sure. You might as well – if she's keeping Paudie Kelleher's mother in the loop she might as well broadcast the whole thing on Radio Kerry anyway!'

'Fair enough.'

Emer was amused but not particularly surprised to see that the text was perfectly punctuated.

I just took these down out of the attic. I knew they were up there but I had never really looked at them before. I'm heading to Dublin now for a couple of days but let's talk when I get back, ok? Mx

When she opened the accompanying photograph, however, her amusement disappeared. The envelope in the picture was brown with age and the stamp had been removed but otherwise it looked perfectly preserved, while the exquisite copperplate handwriting on the front was still fully legible.

Mrs John Lynch, Ballydrynawn, Co. Kerry

Emer looked up at Rob.

'Is that your great-grandmother?'

'I guess so. Take a look at the next photo now.'

The second image showed the reverse of the envelope, the writing just as clear.

Sender John Lynch, St Louis Obispo, California

Emer took a long look at the screen before handing the phone back to Rob.

'So it was him. Alison's relative, he did come from here.'

'Looks that way, doesn't it?'

They had reached the red van now and Rob balanced his board carefully on the ground before sliding open the door, grabbing a Breaking Waves fleece and pulling it on.

'I'm sorry for dragging you into the drama.'

'Don't worry about it. But look, you have a class. I'll head off.'

But she didn't move. Rob gave a half smile.

'Leaving the soap opera aside for a minute, did you enjoy the surfing?'

'God yeah. It's the best thing in the world.'

Rob's mouth twitched.

'One of them, anyway. But that's good to hear, I want to make sure you enjoy your summer, like.'

'No complaints so far.'

'I'm glad to hear it.'

There was a pause, and then a look crossed Rob's face as if he had just come to a decision and he bent forward and brushed his lips against Emer's. And it wasn't just a surfboard, she discovered, that could make your legs feel unsteady. When he stepped away again he was smiling.

'I've been wanting to do that for a while.'

'I've been wanting you to do it.'

And now it was Emer's turn to pull Rob into a sea-salt kiss, her tongue flicking at the edge of his lips before going deeper, probing and teasing. After several minutes he groaned, and pushed her gently away.

'Christ, woman, I've to get ready for a lesson. Can we get back to this later?'

It was Emer who was smiling now.

'We've plenty of time.'

'We do. Actually...'

Rob reached across and took her hand.

'Siobhán is heading to Dublin tonight, she'll be gone for the rest of the week. Would you like to come up for dinner? I'll leave the family skeletons off the menu.'

'Sounds good!'

But something in her face must have bothered him.

'Is that all right? Because I thought...'

'Oh it's all right.'

Emer swallowed.

'It's great. It's just – there's something I need to say. Before anything else happens.'

'Ah.'

Rob released her hand and leaned back against the side of the van, his face blank.

'You have a boyfriend back in the States.'

'God no!'

The words came out at a higher pitch than Emer had intended.

'The opposite – I mean, I'm totally single.'

Rob's expression softened a little.

'Well, then?'

'It's just...'

Her heart was racing now, and not just from the kiss. It would be so much easier just to go with the flow, Emer thought ruefully, and she certainly wanted to. But it wouldn't be fair on Rob not to tell him what was on her mind.

'It's just, I really didn't come back to Ireland for this.'

'For this?'

'I wasn't looking for... you know.'

Rob gave a resigned sigh.

'Look, Emer, if you're not interested, it's grand. Maybe I read the signs wrong, it happens to the best of us.'

'No! I mean, I'm totally interested!'

He held her gaze for a moment, then smiled.

'Well that makes two of us so.'

He was holding her hand again, his thumb tracing a pattern on her palm.

'So if you're interested, and I'm interested, then what's the problem?'

'I'm very interested in – this. But I didn't come to Ireland for...'

The tracing was very distracting and Emer felt herself shiver.

'For a relationship. Or anything.'

She muttered the words and Rob placed one finger under her chin, tipped it upwards and looked at her.

'So let me get this straight.'

'Mm-hmm.'

'You didn't come to Kerry for a relationship, or anything.'

'Nope.'

Another butterfly kiss made her head spin.

'But you are happy to do this.'

'Yeah.'

'And this...'

'Mmhmmm.'

'And at the end of the summer...'

He was holding her now, his voice rumbling through her.

'You'll just feck off back to America.'

'I suppose...'

The next kiss was much longer and afterwards, it took Emer a moment to formulate her answer.

'Well yeah. I'll just feck off back to America.'

'Having blatantly used me.'

'Yeah.'

'With no strings attached.'

Rob's grin was so wide now, Emer began to giggle.

'Other than the odd surfing lesson, yeah. And I was wondering, you know. If that was a problem.'

'Is it a problem, that a gorgeous woman moves in down the road and says she wants to have a fling' – he rolled the word around his mouth and Emer wondered why she had never realised how sexy the Kerry accent was before – 'she wants to have a fling with me, no strings attached and she's wondering would that be all right?'

'That's about the size of it, yeah.'

There were long, kiss-filled pauses between the questions now.

'Emer?'
'Yeah?'
'That's no problem at all.'

Chapter Seventeen

NEW YORK

1926

It was never easy for Annie and Elena to find time to meet. Elena's father forbade her to attend any more dances, making sure she was kept busy in the restaurant late on Saturday and Sunday nights, always finding her another chore to do, a burned pot to scrub, tomorrow's meals to prepare. Her father was not a bad man, Elena insisted, but he truly believed what Lorenzo told him, that New York was a dangerous place for girls, that she needed to be protected, hidden away. Believed, too, that only Lorenzo could protect their family and keep them off the streets. There was no more dancing, then, but they still had Thursday afternoons. Elena was giving English lessons to a family newly arrived from Italy, they were from the same village as her father so he couldn't refuse the request and she left the restaurant at four every Thursday, not returning until after seven. What she didn't tell him was that she spent barely an hour with the children before telling their mother she had to return to work. That left an hour and a half, sometimes more if she hurried, to spend with Annie. It was a morsel of time. But it was golden for them.

One afternoon they returned to their favourite spot in the city's largest park, an overgrown corner near the least fashionable entrance where the grass was too long for ball games and there was no fountain, nor even a bench to attract passers-by. As they wandered through the rusting metal gate Elena linked her arm through Annie's, and the Irishwoman felt a sensation not entirely dissimilar to pain dart through her. This was what she lived for now, these Thursday afternoons, these bites of pure happiness. But she didn't let any emotion show on her face, not even when Elena, laughing about something one of her pupils had said to her, pulled her in even closer and squeezed her hand. The sensation, the not-quite pain travelled all the way to her toes this time and Annie had to struggle hard not to acknowledge it, to keep her gait steady and her expression calm. But she could not afford to let her face betray her, could never tell Elena how she felt because she did not have the words to explain and besides, she was terrified that if she did try to express her feelings she would shatter the fragile, mysterious beauty that had blossomed between them. Better to be in agony, Annie decided, than to lose the chance of seeing Elena at all.

It was another warm, muggy day, the type of weather that made Mrs O'Toole flap her hands in front of her face and declare herself weary of 'this dratted country', with its lack of honest Irish rain. But to Annie and Elena the weather was a blessing, it opened the city up to them, made its parks and public spaces their sitting room. As they settled on the blanket she had brought from home,

Annie made Elena laugh by telling her about the weather back in Ireland and how even on a fine day you had to keep half an eye outside at all times in case the washing on the hedge would be drenched when it was almost dry. They loved hearing about each other's home countries and although Elena had been much younger than Annie when she left Italy she could recall enough about the fishing boats and the old, black-clad women and the quayside to make Annie feel they had more in common than they had initially realised.

'And tell me again about the Fairy Tree?'

Elena was sitting cross-legged on the blanket, her skirt folded neatly under her legs. It was a very small blanket, and so they had to sit quite close together, their arms brushing against each other as they chatted.

Annie looked down at the small dear face and smiled.

'You're not making fun of me now?'

Elena returned a look of such intensity it made her head swim.

'I'd never make fun of you, Annie. Tell me again. Tell me a story.'

And somehow, and Annie didn't know how it happened, but somehow Elena was now resting her head on her shoulder. But girls sat like that sometimes, didn't they? Surely she and May had sat like this once upon a time – but Annie couldn't remember – she couldn't remember anything now, there was nothing else in the world but this park and the rug and Elena's head nestled into the curve where Annie's neck met her shoulder, as if the space had been created for that very purpose. And if Elena wanted a story she should have one, so Annie began to speak about the Fairy Tree and the faith the people of Ballydrynawn had in its powers.

'And do you believe in it?'

Annie shrugged, the action causing Elena to curl even closer into her. Her skin tingled inside her light summer blouse, it was as if her nerves were too close to the surface, and it was almost too much to bear, being this close to Elena because somehow it was suddenly not close enough at all. She paused for a moment to catch her breath before continuing.

'I don't know. My head tells me its just a piseog – a story,' Annie clarified as Elena turned, a look of amused puzzlement on her face.

'A story to keep children happy. But there's no doubt others believe in the tree. My friend May does, for sure.'

Annie stopped speaking then, she had already told Elena a little about May, and her marriage, and Seánie's subsequent disappearance, but she didn't want the memory of him or even his name to cloud this perfect summer evening.

'Well, you made a wish to travel! And that worked, didn't it?'

Elena giggled, then sat up and opened the brown paper bag she had brought with her from the restaurant. She had selected cannoli today – Annie had squealed when she described it and pretended to be horrified at the thought of sweet cheese wrapped in pastry but truth be told, she would have eaten frogs' legs if Elena had suggested it. Elena broke the flaky cylinder in two and handed one half to her.

'You wished to travel across the sea and here you are!'

'Here I am.'

Her shoulder felt lonely without Elena nestled there.
The pastry tasted delicious but there was no cake, Annie
thought, no treat that would compare with the feeling of
Elena's skin on hers. And then Elena reached out one long
brown fingertip and stole a crumb of cheese from the corner
of Annie's mouth. The two women stared at each other for
a long time before Elena spoke again.

'Did you wish for love at the Fairy Tree?'

'Yes.'

Annie's voice was low, and unsteady.

'But I wasn't sure – I didn't think I would ever find it.'

I love you.

She started, sure for a second she had spoken the words
out loud but Elena was finishing her cake now and certainly
didn't look as if she had heard anything amiss. But the
words, now they had finally arrived in her mind, were so
simple and so obvious that Annie had to hide a smile. She
loved Elena. Loved her, adored her, not the kind of love she
had for May or Noreen but the other kind, that type of love
her parents had for each other or that May would have had
for that fool Seánie Lynch if he had been in any way worthy
of it. Annie loved Elena – and it was utterly wrong for her
to feel this way.

Annie's stomach gave a sudden, nauseating twist. Women
should not experience such emotions, not for each other, it
was not possible. There must be something wrong inside
her, something deformed. She had never heard of girls
having such feelings but there had been a man once, a
dreadful man, a teacher in the secondary school back home
about whom terrible stories were told. Annie had asked an
older cousin once why the boys were so afraid of him and

when she heard the details she thought she would get sick, it was such an evil thing to think about. Surely the idea of two women together was just as perverse, and Elena was so beautiful and pure and precious, it felt like a sin to even think such things in her company.

And then Annie noticed that Elena's face had darkened and she pushed her own fears aside for a moment and turned to her.

'What is the matter?'

'If I had a magic tree…'

Elena took a deep, shuddering breath.

'If I had a tree I would wish for a woman for Lorenzo.'

The name was like a clap of thunder in the golden afternoon. Annie fought to keep her own voice steady.

'Is he bothering you?'

'He wants to marry me.'

'Oh, Elena.'

And now she couldn't help herself, couldn't stop herself from taking Elena's hand and clutching it tightly.

'You can't – you can't possibly think of doing that?'

'He has made my parents very frightened.'

Elena was staring at the ground now.

'He has told them there are other families looking for jobs, for homes. Other families with more workers, better workers. He says my mother is old and fat and can't move around quickly enough and that my father's food is bland, that he has forgotten how to cook properly. There is a family of six, he says, that could move into our house straight away, they would all be better workers. Unless I become his wife, and then my parents will be his family and they would be protected forever.'

'And would your parents force you to marry him? Have they said this?'

Elena shook her head.

'They would not force me, no, at least I don't think so. But my mama is crying all the time now and my father works later and later into the night and he scolds my brother, tells him he is useless and—'

'Come away with me.'

The words leapt straight to Annie's lips, the thought not fully formed before she voiced it.

Elena stared at her and pulled her hand away.

'What do you mean?'

'Not now, not straight away. But soon. I'm saving money...'

Annie's words were tumbling over each other now, excitement for her idea growing by the second.

'The Cavendishes are good to me, they provide my uniform, they don't take money for board, they are decent people. And I was sending money home to my family for a while but my brothers and sisters are working now and my mother has told me not to send any more, to keep it for myself. I always dreamed of travelling across America – you could come with me!'

She was sitting bolt upright now, her earlier shame pushed aside for the moment, nothing on her mind but protecting Elena, getting her away from Lorenzo.

'Noreen is leaving for Los Angeles soon, she has the chance of a job out there. We could start there, or go further again even. Not Chicago, not somewhere with Irish people or Italian people. Somewhere small, where they will need women to work in restaurants. We could rent a little

apartment maybe. And we could plant a little garden and...
and get – a cat!'

They were both laughing now, and Annie could almost
see it, a small tabby cat winding around their ankles as they
prepared a meal at the end of the working day. A small
home just for them. And it would be agonising, she knew,
to live that close to Elena but so much less painful than the
alternative, to lose her altogether.

I love you, I love you.

It took every bit of willpower she had to stop herself
from saying the words out loud.

It was almost seven thirty when they left the park, Elena so
afraid of being late home that they had barely time for more
than a rushed goodbye at the gate before she scurried off,
retying her bonnet as she ran. But Annie was in no such hurry
and kept a steady pace as she strolled along the familiar
streets, excitement from the afternoon still churning inside
her. She waited for an automobile to pass then crossed the
street, proud of how she was no longer afraid of the noisy
machines, how she could judge their movement and speed
just as she had once judged the approach of JJ's old mare
back home. The familiar exterior of the Cavendish home
came into view as she reached the top of Fifth Avenue and
Annie picked up her pace as she rounded the building and
headed down the small lane that led to the tradesmen's
entrance. In her haste she dropped the little latch key that
opened the side gate and she got to her knees to pick it
up. But when she tried to stand again there was something
preventing her. There was pressure on her from above – she

fought to turn around but there was an arm around her waist now and she was being dragged from the gate, further into the dim alleyway. She felt hot, rancid breath on her cheek, and then a voice she had never forgotten.

'I have you now, you little bitch.'

Seánie Lynch had been drinking but only enough to make him angry because his grip on her waist was strong and sure. Annie twisted, but merely succeeded in hurting herself as he bent closer and hissed into her ear again.

'Did you really think you'd get away with it, huh?'

She made one last desperate attempt to pull away and then felt at her waist the thin point of cold steel.

'Hold your whisht now, don't even think about making a fuss.'

Her legs obeyed him even if her mind didn't want her to and Annie fell limp into his arms. Seánie dropped her to the ground and propped her against the wall, then sat down beside her and pointed the knife at her throat.

'Did you think you'd never see me again? You thought your money was enough to send me away for good?'

'No—'

But Annie's breathing was too shallow to allow her to speak and she forced herself to slow it down, trying to untangle her thoughts at the same time. Had she thought she would never see him again? She had hoped she had done enough, certainly, to ensure May's freedom. But had never imagined it might compromise her own.

Memories flooded her mind, memories she hadn't allowed herself to revisit for almost two years. Memories of too many nights when she had met May walking the roads, her baby clutched to her breast, afraid to go home even on the coldest of nights because it was easier to freeze in a field than go back and face her husband's temper. One night May had left it too late to run and by the time Annie found her she was bleeding from a cut lip, one eye bruised almost shut. There was nothing she could do, May had sobbed over and over again. She was a married woman, there was nowhere else she could go. She had even visited the Fairy Tree, she told Annie hopelessly, and begged it for mercy but God had joined herself and Seánie together and it was too late for anyone to help her now.

Annie didn't believe in fairies, not really. But she believed May deserved a better life than this and her mother's words from the evening of the wedding had floated back to her.

'Sometimes you make your own luck in this world.'

Annie had been saving for America, but she hadn't booked her passage yet, and so she sent word to Colm O'Flaherty that she wanted to see him. It had taken several weeks but finally they met one afternoon in a house on the outskirts of the village, where a woman ushered her into the kitchen and then refused to meet her eye. Colm had batted away her request at first, telling Annie it was not his role to interfere between a man and his wife, but then Annie had explained in detail the hell her friend was living through. Surely Colm, of all people, understood what it felt like to be a prisoner in your own home, to feel trapped, to know that no matter what you said or did you could never be right and certainly never be free? It was a crude analogy but must have been effective because after a moment O'Flaherty had given a quick, sharp nod and asked how he could help.

The plan had been a simple one. O'Flaherty would tell Seánie he needed a hiding place for the night, knowing that such a request would appeal to the man's vanity and knowing, too, that providing a safe house would be a way for Lynch to feel himself a hero without actually getting his hands dirty. Colm would then contact Seánie a few days later and tell him that he was in deep trouble for what he had done, that he'd have to leave Ballydrynawn, but that money had been put aside to help him go. Annie had bargained on Seánie being too much of a coward to ask too many questions, and so it had transpired. She had given Colm enough money to buy Seánie a passage to Australia and told him the rest was a donation to his cause – she didn't ask for any details. The plan had taken most of her savings, and delayed her own departure for America by more than six months. But none of that had mattered as long as May was safe.

Except Seánie Lynch had never done a damn thing he said he would, not even when supposedly fleeing for his life. He must have come to America instead of Australia, and now he was here.

The knife jabbed into her side again as Seánie answered her unasked question.

'There's a bar down in Brooklyn, a lot of lads from home drink there. One of O'Flaherty's men was in a few weeks ago, when he had enough drink taken he laughed in my face and told me everything that happened back home. That there was never anyone after me. You bitches cooked it up between ye, made a fool of me.'

With his free hand he slapped her across the face, a swift and brutal blow, and as Annie's head slammed back against the wall she realised that feeling foolish was the thing he resented most of all.

'I've a right to kill you now.'

The back of her head was throbbing and there was a thick, heavy feeling in her skull which made it difficult to think, let alone talk. Seánie's breath was sour in her face.

'What do you reckon, hah? Just one more little Irish tart found with her throat slit in a back alley.'

She would never see Elena again, Annie thought dully but her tongue was too thick in her mouth and she could not see, could not speak. And then Seánie took a step back and his voice grew thoughtful.

'But maybe you are of more use to me alive.'

Annie opened her eyes, blinked, tried to focus. Seánie was staring at her now.

'This is a nice place you've washed up in. I'd say you've a pile of money saved by now. And I'm sure the Cavendish family are dripping with jewels, stuff they mightn't miss even.'

Annie tried to shake her head but the movement made her so dizzy she forced herself to form the words instead.

'I'm only a maid. I have nothing for you.'

'You're a liar!'

Another slap came but a lighter one this time, she would be no use to him unconscious, Annie realised.

'Get me money and you'll never hear from me again.'

It was tempting. Annie had never felt so sick before, so alone and so frightened, and it was so tempting to get up, right now, and to go into the Chateau and find the money she had hidden in her bedroom and yes, maybe some ornaments from the drawing room too, because the truth was the Cavendishes had so much they would not miss a silver candlestick or even some minor pieces of jewellery, certainly not for a week or two. The image of the rose teacups, their discarded perfection, swam in front of her. Maybe if she helped him, maybe Seánie would leave her alone, for good this time.

But then Annie thought of Elena, and the feeling of Elena's hand in hers. The plans they had started so tentatively to make, the journey across the country, their small home. The evening meal, the kitten at their feet. None of it could happen if she spent the money she had saved and if the Cavendishes discovered she was a thief they would sack her and she would have no chance of earning any more. And besides, the Cavendishes had been so good to her, they didn't deserve to be cheated.

The ground beneath her skirt was damp and the cold seeping through to her skin brought her to her senses. But as her mind scrambled to come to a decision, Annie took care not to speak too quickly, to make Seánie think she was still terrified.

'I'll bring you the money, but I have it saved in a bank. It'll take me three weeks to get it together.'

'Three weeks? You're lying.'

Annie shook her head.

'I have it saved in a bank account, the Cavendishes helped me open one. It takes three weeks to reclaim it.'

She had no clue if she was telling the truth but given Seánie's ragged appearance and old clothes she trusted he knew even less about the American banking system than she did. Her faith was rewarded when he sat back with a grunt.

'Three weeks, that's all I'll give you. I'll meet you back here.'

She shivered, then forced herself to look at him.

'I'll get you your money.'

'Make sure you do.'

And with a final slap, more of a tap this time, just a reminder of the pain he could cause her, Seánie climbed to his feet and lumbered away down the dark alleyway. Annie gave a sudden, violent shudder. She had tried so hard to get rid of Seánie Lynch, to pay for May's freedom. But this time it was she who would have to run.

Chapter Eighteen

NEW YORK

1926

Annie didn't know how long she spent sitting on the ground after Seánie left but when she finally stood up, stiff, sore and shaken, she was, at least, in possession of a plan. All she needed now, she thought to herself grimly as she let herself inside the Chateau then tiptoed up the back stairs, careful to avoid any creak that might wake the ever-vigilant Mrs O'Toole, was one piece of luck. And there mightn't be a Fairy Tree here in New York City but surely, given everything that had happened to her this evening, surely a small piece of luck was the least she deserved.

And that good fortune did present itself the very next afternoon when Annie answered a bell from the second-floor drawing room and entered to find young Miss Jemima alone and in the mood for conversation. Annie's back was still aching from her late night, and she had carried a heavy pot of coffee for two all the way upstairs even though nobody had told her that only one was needed, but she kept a bright smile on her face as she placed the tray gently on the table in front of Miss Jemima then straightened the cups carefully before stepping away.

'Have you been to any more dances, Annie?'

For a second, Annie wondered if the small glass bottle had been put to use again but no, although Miss Jemima was smiling at her, her eyes were clear and there was no tell-tale scent of hard liquor. Just a lonely woman, in the mood for conversation. Exactly the opening Annie had been hoping for.

'Not for a while, ma'am, no.'

The younger woman pouted.

'Oh, that's a shame. Tell me, what else do you like to do on your free evenings?'

An idea started to form in Annie's mind and she forced herself not to sound too eager as she answered.

'I like to walk down to the sea, ma'am, on these fine evenings. It makes me think of home.'

Annie paused, thinking of how happy she was in New York, how much she loved the city and its sounds and its smells and how saying any different felt like a betrayal – then the memory of Seánie hit her like a thump and she continued with as much emotion as she could manage.

'Your parents are very good employers, Miss Cavendish. But I must admit to feeling far from home, sometimes.'

Miss Jemima took a sip of her coffee and settled back on the sofa.

'And where exactly are you from in Ireland?'

There it was, the chance she had been waiting for. Annie blinked a couple of times before answering.

'I'm from County Kerry, Miss Cavendish, near the ocean.

I like to feel the sea breeze on my face, it reminds me of home.'

And then I come back here to my indoor plumbing and my electric light, she thought to herself but kept her face sombre, waiting to see if her hint had been sufficient. The next thing Miss Jemima said made her wonder if there were in fact fairies hiding in the cracks of the New York pavements after all.

'But we have a house by the sea too, Annie! Didn't I tell you about Harbour View?'

'You did, ma'am.'

The younger woman sat up straighter, a splash of coffee falling on her sleeve.

'I'm going there next week. In fact, I'll be there most of the summer. It's so beautiful – so much cooler than the city, none of that nasty dust. You must come, Annie! It will help you feel much less homesick, I'm sure.'

'Well, miss.'

Annie kept her eyes downcast, to avoid looking too victorious.

'If it pleases you – it does sound very pleasant.'

'It pleases me!'

Miss Jemima waved her butter knife, causing a shower of crumbs to fall on the Japanese rug which was the hardest in the house to clean.

'So that is exactly what we shall do!'

The eyes in the portraits were definitely following her now, Annie thought after she had taken leave of her young employer and scurried down the corridor, empty delph rattling on her tray. They knew she had manipulated the kind-hearted – and, God bless her, possibly soft-hearted

– Miss Jemima for her own means. And Lord, she would miss this house, she had the measure of it now and she and Mrs O'Toole were a good, efficient team. She would miss the lamps glowing gently through the night, the shouts of the early morning delivery boys that were better than any alarm clock, afternoon strolls with Noreen, visiting the stores on the Lower East Side and choosing trinkets to send back to her brothers.

But Elena needed her, just as much as May had needed her, so Annie put her own comfort and the eyes of the ancestral Cavendishes firmly behind her and descended the kitchen stairs. Moving to Harbour View would remove her from Seánie's orbit and give her time to save for the future, a future she fervently hoped would include Elena. Sometimes you had to make your own luck indeed.

In the end it took less than two weeks for all of the plans to be put in place. Jemima was her parents' pet and once she set her mind to taking Annie with her to Harbour View, no one, not even a visibly irritated Mrs O'Toole, was able to stand in her way. Annie hadn't enjoyed telling the housekeeper that she was leaving, she had grown very fond of Mrs O'Toole and knew the older woman would be greatly inconvenienced by losing her best worker for the summer, and not a little hurt by her enthusiastic acceptance of her new position. But fear of Seánie drove Annie onwards, it was imperative she remove herself from the city before he came looking for her again.

She still had to break the news to Elena, however. On her final night at the Chateau, although Mrs O'Toole had prepared her favourite meal of light fish and boiled potatoes, Annie bolted the meal and then, ignoring the look of betrayal on the older woman's face, cleaned the dishes in as slapdash a manner as she could get away with before heading for the door. She hadn't dared visit the restaurant since Seánie had made his reappearance, hadn't even sent Elena a note for fear he or his cronies might be following her. But she couldn't leave the city without saying goodbye.

Terrified she was being followed, Annie took as circuitous a route as she could manage through the New York city streets and by the time she reached the restaurant it was shuttered and dark. The side alley was deserted too, the cloud of flies around the bin evidence that the restaurant had been cleared for the evening and Annie began to worry she had missed her chance. But then the large metal door to the side of the building swung open and Elena emerged, a pail of slops swinging from one hand. As Annie loomed out of the darkness she gasped, then pressed her free hand to her chest.

'What are you doing here?'

Annie stepped forwards, trying to muster a smile.

'I hoped we might talk for a little while.'

But Elena, now her shock had faded, was staring at her with something approaching anger.

'You didn't come last Thursday, or the Thursday before.'

Annie dipped her head in apology.

'I'm sorry, I—'

The younger woman placed the bucket on the ground and folded her arms across her chest.

'I went to the park both days, I sat for an hour waiting for you.'

'I'm sorry—'

'If you didn't want to see me again you should have sent word. I thought we were friends, Annie!'

And suddenly all thoughts of Harbour View and even of Seánie Lynch disappeared as Annie took in the look of disappointment and acute embarrassment on the young woman's face. Elena had missed her, she'd thought Annie didn't want to see her! It was all Annie could do to stop herself from rushing forward and pulling the young woman into her arms. But she couldn't do that, of course, so instead she took one tentative step towards her.

'I'm sorry. If you could come walking with me now, just for a short while, then I promise I can explain.'

Elena shook her head.

'I am working late tonight.'

'Is Lorenzo – is he inside?'

'No, just two of the cooks. There is a big party here tomorrow, a wedding, we are preparing food. My father gave me permission to stay.'

'Then maybe you could tell them you have to go home for something, but that you'll return? Please, Elena, I wouldn't ask you if it wasn't important!'

Elena looked at her for a moment then gave a brief, taut nod.

'I can't stay long.'

It was unusually cool that evening and grey clouds were massing overhead as they headed towards what Annie now thought of as 'their' park. By the time they reached the familiar rusting gate large drops of rain had begun to fall and the women scurried towards a small copse to seek shelter from the downpour. By day children sometimes played hide and seek in here but this evening the small cluster of trees was deserted and they pushed their way through the branches until they came to a small, dusty but very private clearing. Annie removed her shawl and placed it on the ground and after a moment Elena sat beside her, although she took care to leave as large a gap as possible between them.

'Elena, I have to tell you something.'

Elena folded her arms tightly.

'You don't want to be friends with me any more.'

The words, like a slap, sent blood rushing to Annie's cheeks.

'Elena! My God no! How could you think such a thing?'

But she was resolute.

'What else am I to think? I waited for you and you never came, Annie. You left me sitting alone. And now you appear out of nowhere, looking upset – just tell me, tell me you have tired of me and I will leave, and you will never have to see me again.'

Her composure slipped on the final word and Annie felt her heart give a sudden, startled thump. Could it possibly be that her feelings towards Elena were, in fact, reciprocated? Those terrifying emotions she had been afraid to admit, even to herself?

In that instant, in the dusty clearing with the trees overhead throwing dappled shadows on their faces, Annie Thornton came to a decision and reached over to take the hand of the woman she adored more than anyone else in the world. It was the most frightening thing she had ever done, more frightening than leaving Ireland, more terrifying than confronting Seánie Lynch even, because if she was wrong, if she had misjudged this situation then surely Elena would run away and never speak to her again. But Annie was leaving the city tomorrow and did not have the luxury of time. Summoning all of her courage she pressed her lips against Elena's, a gossamer touch, then sat back on the shawl again. Her first feeling was one of panic – she had made a terrible mistake, Elena would hate her, she would run – and then the other woman's dear, beautiful face widened into a smile. Now it was Elena who was leaning forward, now it was Elena who was kissing Annie in a way that banished any further doubt. And it was wonderful to hold Elena in her arms, wonderful to feel her lips respond to hers, but the best thing of all, Annie thought as their kisses grew more urgent, the best thing of all was the knowledge that she had not been wrong after all.

After several long, delicious moments Elena tipped her head back and looked at her.

'I wanted to do that for so long, Annie, but I was sure you would hate me.'

'Hate you? Oh, Elena – is this how hate feels?'

You could smile and kiss at the same time, Annie discovered, which was a very beautiful thing to learn. Elena felt exactly as she imagined she would, the creamy skin on her neck and cheeks like satin, but then those cheeks flushed and Elena pulled away again.

'I thought there was something wrong with me. I didn't know that two women...'

She took a deep breath before continuing.

'There were two customers in the restaurant one day, two men. I heard one of the waiters discuss them afterwards, they said they had been holding hands under the table and they should be arrested, that it was disgusting behaviour. And so I thought if it was wrong for them then surely it is wrong for you and me?'

Annie shook her head.

'I don't know. I don't even know if there is anyone else in the world like us. Maybe we just found each other. But this doesn't feel like a bad thing.'

Elena gave her a sideways glance.

'Have you spoken to anyone else about this?'

'Oh God no!'

Annie had, in fact, briefly considered telling Noreen about her feelings towards Elena. Her friend was so breezy, so willing to embrace everything that this New World had to offer she thought there was a possibility she might understand. But in the end she hadn't been able to come up with the right words to start the conversation, even. How could she describe a feeling that simply could not exist? She looked at Elena now, desperate to find some way of alleviating her anxiety.

'If I could, I would run down Fifth Avenue shouting about you!'

Despite herself, the Italian woman gave a small smile.

'People would think you were a crazy woman, then.'

'I wouldn't care!'

Annie sat up straighter.

'I would take you to the grandest shops on Fifth Avenue and I would buy you jewellery and I would tell the world that you are my beautiful Elena.'

They gazed at each other for a moment before a rustle in the trees made them leap apart. Annie's heart thudded in her chest – Seánie? Lorenzo? Oh dear God they would have her killed – and then she looked down to see a small, wet nose appear through the undergrowth. The dog gave them a disinterested look, and watered a branch before turning and leaving again, the voice of his owner barely audible from outside. Shaken, Elena began to pick at the tassels on the edge of the shawl with her long, thin fingers, scarred with burns and callouses from the restaurant.

'Do you think there are other people like us in the world? Women who love… other women?'

Annie shook her head, waiting a moment to make sure they were entirely alone before answering in a low whisper.

'I don't know. Maybe not. Maybe it's just us, maybe it has nothing to do with being women even. Maybe we are just two souls who found each other. If there was a Fairy Tree here in New York, Elena, I would wish for you, always.'

Elena smiled.

'There is no need to wish for me, Annie. I am right here.'

Oh Lord. Annie felt her heart sink, she had been so carried away by the events of the evening she had forgotten her reason for visiting Elena today.

'My love, there is something I have to tell you.'

Elena gazed at her in silence while Annie told her the story as quickly and as plainly as she could, how Seánie had come back and how she needed to escape from him, how she planned to leave the city for the summer to save some money and start again. Elena's fidgeting grew more pronounced as the story came to an end.

'You will forget about me, out there on the coast.'

'Never. But I have to do this, just for a short time, I promise you.'

There were tears in the other woman's eyes now.

'I did not see you for two weeks and it was horrible, now you say it could be three months, maybe more? I'm scared, Annie. Lorenzo is growing more persistent, I'm not sure if I can continue to refuse him.'

'It will just be for a few weeks, I promise.'

Annie was on her knees now, holding Elena's hand so tightly it was as if she was trying to press determination into her.

'Just hold on for a few weeks, I will come back for you. Will you wait? And then we can go away together. I promise, Elena. My love. I promise you.'

My love. The words hung in the air between them and then there was nothing uncertain about their kisses any more.

PART TWO

Chapter Nineteen

WEST KERRY

July 2022

'Have you any plans for the day?'
Rob returned from the shower, a towel wrapped around his waist. It was Sunday morning, which meant he had no classes and, following a very enjoyable lie-in, Emer had in fact been wondering how to spend the coming hours and, more to the point, if it was about time she did some formal sightseeing. In the two months since she'd last seen them, her parents had been flooding her WhatsApp with photos from LA and Australia, while she had little to offer them in return other than a few snaps from the local beach and one of a session in the Hitching Post with Cian staring moodily at Alison, and Rob a mere blur in the corner.

Those two months, however, had also seen Emer having more fun than she could ever remember having before.

Pulling herself up on the pillows, she accepted Rob's offer of a cup of coffee then yawned expansively as he headed out to the kitchen. It turned out that she was quite good at doing nothing, now she'd had a bit of practice. Her days had fallen into an easy pattern; Emer would surf in the morning, laze around the Tigín in the afternoon and then, although they never seemed to plan anything, spend every evening with Rob. They'd hang out at his house, if Siobhán was away, or at the Tigín, or even down in the Hitching Post with the others, listening to music or simply shooting the breeze. And the banter! Emer hadn't realised how much she had missed aimless Irish chatter until Paudie came to the bar straight from work one Friday and Rob handed him a fiver to go with his 'first communion suit'. Other nights she'd simply sit and listen to Cian's woes. Cian was having a difficult summer, his father was unwell and he was running the family guesthouse single-handedly and worrying about how he'd manage once school started again. And although he'd never admit it, Emer also knew that Cian's low mood was exacerbated by the fact that Alison was spending most of her spare time back in Tralee with a group of American backpackers she'd met on the beach. She and Siobhán hadn't discussed her ancestors since that fraught lunchtime, and in fact Rob's mother had spent most of the subsequent weeks travelling, but it was clear the American was unsettled and Cian feared she was getting ready to go back the States again.

For Emer herself the long summer days were as near to perfect as she could ever have hoped for. Their 'fling', as Rob insisted on calling it, was transient, of course, she was already getting emails from clients back in the States wondering when she'd be free for work again. But she was enjoying taking each day as it came, and the nights were even better. So yes, she thought as Rob reappeared, carrying a tray of coffee and Spar-fresh croissants, she probably should go out and take a few photos for her parents to prove what a great time she was having. But she couldn't bring a camera with her on the surfboard and, she mused as his towel slipped slightly, there was little else she'd been doing that was suitable to be photographed.

Rob saw her giggle but didn't ask why. Instead, he placed the tray on her knees then lowered himself down beside her.

'I was actually thinking of going to see my granddad today, would you like to come?'

'Your granddad? Right...'

Emer withdrew her thoughts from towels and Rob's fine little arm hairs, toasted golden by the sun.

'Yeah, he'd love to meet you. It won't take long, it's just that he gets really bored in that place and he'd love to see a new face. We'll stay for an hour, max, and we can head off then, maybe go back west for the day, have lunch somewhere nice? Besides...'

Rob's eyes flickered around his bedroom which looked exactly what it was, a room that neither of them had left for more than twelve hours.

'Mom's due back from the States this afternoon, she'll probably want the house to herself for a bit.'

'I'm sure she will.'

Emer hadn't meant to say the quiet bit out loud and Rob looked at her sharply.

'What do you mean?'

She took a sip of coffee.

'Nothing.'

'Ah come on.'

Rob was staring at her now.

'Is there something I don't know?'

Emer leaned back against the pillows and sighed.

'It's just... look, don't get me wrong, I think Siobhán is amazing. But she's not exactly my number one fan, is she? Which is fine, I mean totally her call, and it's not like you and I are actually going out or anything. Come the end of the summer I'll probably never see her again, but I just don't think she'll be weeping at the airport, do you?'

A flicker of something crossed Rob's face and Emer winced, wondering if she had sounded too critical. But when he spoke again his tone was pensive, rather than offended.

'Siobhán has nothing against you, Emer. Not personally, anyway.'

He paused for a moment before continuing.

'You know I told you that I don't have any contact with my father?'

Emer nodded, at a complete loss now as to where the conversation was going.

'Well, not many people know this but Mom was actually married to him, back in the States.'

'Ah. And I'm guessing it didn't end well?'

Rob shook his head.

'Nope. He started spending money like it was going out of fashion, her money obviously. She managed to get rid of him when I was only a baby but he got himself a fine lawyer and a big settlement. Granddad said she could have fought it but she wanted to make sure he had no claim on me so she paid him off, basically. He had no interest in me anyway.'

It was as if, Emer thought, he was telling a story about someone else entirely and for the first time she saw his mother in him. In response, she too kept her tone light.

'So you haven't see him since?'

'Just the once.'

Rob turned his cup round and round in his hands before answering.

'He turned up here when I was three or four. I don't remember much about it. It was the old house, long before this place was built so there were no electronic gates or anything. I was playing out in the yard, I had this little red tractor and I just remember I was running it along the ground when this fella came up to me and asked me about it. The sun was in my eyes, I was kind of squinting at him, you know? And he put his hand in his pocket and took out a little car, a Dinky toy, and handed it to me. It was red too. The next thing I remember is my granddad shouting and that's it really.'

'That's it?'

Rob shrugged.

'Of course he was only back looking for money but they got rid of him, and that was the last any of us saw of him.'

Emer decided she was absolutely definitely not thinking about three-year-old Rob and absolutely definitely not getting sentimental about his story. But...

'Did you keep the toy?'

Rob gave a surprised laugh.

'Do you know, I haven't a clue? I'd say it's around here all right. I never thought to look for it. But look, I don't want to bore you with more family history!'

You could never be boring, Emer thought but didn't say, as he continued.

'The point I'm trying to make is that Mom is super sensitive about relationships and that sort of nonsense, she has it drummed into me to make sure I'm very careful about

who I get in involved with. So if she seems a bit standoffish
to begin with, it's nothing personal, she's just looking out
for me. But sure that's not an issue with us anyway, we're
not in this for the long haul.'

'Mmn.'

'Enough of that now!'

A drop of Emer's coffee slopped onto the tray as Rob
moved closer.

'Will you come up and see the oul lad? Just for an hour, I
promise you. And then we can head off somewhere for the
day. Killarney, Dingle, wherever you like.'

'Sounds great!'

But Emer didn't feel great, in fact she felt a bit flat, all of
a sudden. Too much coffee on an empty stomach, probably,
but even when she tore off a piece of croissant and ate it, it
didn't make much of a difference.

Chapter Twenty

NEW YORK

1926

'Annie, could you drop by my salon later? When you've finished your work.'

Miss Jemima narrowed her eyes through a stream of cigarette smoke and smiled. Her 'salong'. Annie didn't have the benefit of her employer's expensive education but one of the French kitchen maids here at Harbour View had been trying to teach her a few words of the language and she was fairly sure the word was not designed to be pronounced that way. She wasn't going to correct Miss Jemima though and gave instead a small, neat curtsy.

'Certainly, ma'am. It could be late, mind you, we're serving several courses this evening.'

And you and your friends will be sitting around the dinner table for hours after you've finished eating, she thought, but again didn't say anything, just backed silently out of the room.

The hall door stood open, as it usually did at this time of the afternoon, and Annie walked towards it, intent on stealing a breath of fresh air before she headed back to the kitchen. In front of her a gravel driveway linked the main residence with its velvet gardens, coloured a rich deep green by daily watering despite the summer's heat, and beyond them again a light blue sea sparkled. Harbour View was no more than sixty miles from the Cavendishes' Manhattan home, but so different, Annie thought, it might as well have been on the far side of the country. The New York house had been large, at least for a family of four, and opulently decorated, but the Cavendishes' summer mansion was another matter entirely with four distinct wings, twenty-seven guest bedrooms, a ballroom with a stage that could accommodate a full-size orchestra, and no fewer than four dining rooms, the largest of which could accommodate up to fifty people at a sit-down dinner, and often did.

To Annie, however, the residence was like a painting in a gallery – it was undeniably beautiful but she felt utterly distanced from it. Her heart and soul were still back in New York City and she would have traded a year of Harbour View's gleaming sands and fresh breezes for an hour in a sun-scorched Manhattan park with Elena by her side. She had in fact planned on being back in the city by now but as summer had slipped into fall, Miss Jemima's parties seemed to be growing in number rather than decreasing and the young woman, although still unfailingly cheerful, could be surprisingly firm when it came to her staff. Annie was needed at Harbour View and so on the coast she would stay until Miss Jemima decided otherwise. The truth was, Annie knew the longer she stayed out here the better, the more chance there was that Seánie would think she had escaped his clutches and would move on to some other victim, and given that there was little to do out here other than work and sleep her small pile of savings was growing by the day. But that truth didn't make the distance from Elena any easier to bear.

From deep in the house a bell clanged but Annie chose to ignore it and instead closed her eyes, inhaling another lungful of salt air. Having grown up beside the sea, she had thought that Harbour View's location on the coast would help her feel more cheerful but in all the weeks since her arrival she had only actually made it down to the sea on two occasions. On the first, she had been too intimidated by the sight of Miss Jemima and her guests sprawled on the sand on multicoloured towels to dare approach the water – although she had allowed herself a small smile when she saw a friend of Miss Jemima's trip across the hot sand in a skintight one-piece bathing costume, and imagined how her mother would react, or even May, if she wrote home and told them she was going to adopt similar attire. Meanwhile the second time, even though she had been on her half-afternoon off, she had barely felt the first scrapings of sand under her boots before Miss Jemima's light, charming voice could be heard from the house asking if Annie could just spare a moment to help her find her blue ge-own, the one with the sequins on the neckline because she was sure she had seen her hanging it up only the day before...? Miss Jemima Cavendish was very fond of calling Harbour View 'a house of welcomes'. Her father had spent a sizable chunk of his vast fortune on the elaborate building and his daughter seemed determined to get full value from that investment. In fact there hadn't been a night since Annie had arrived that hadn't involved elaborate meals, professional entertainment and usually a number of overnight guests who created a gruelling amount of housework.

But none of it mattered, Annie thought as she finally turned her back on the ocean and began to trudge back towards the kitchen stairs. None of it was important, not really – not her homesickness for the Chateau, nor Miss Jemima's endless, smiling demands, not the broken sleep nor even the ache that occupied a permanent position in her lower back under the greatly increased workload. The Italian woman was the first person she thought of when she woke every morning and the memory of her kiss was the last thing she felt before she fell asleep. Saving money and saving Elena was all that mattered to her now.

The heat from the kitchen rose to meet her as she descended the stairs then pushed open the heavy green baize door. Harbour View had been designed by the same architect who worked on the Cavendishes' New York home and although the coastal property was much larger, certain aspects of the design remained the same, including the basement kitchen whose mean, narrow windows were unable to admit much fresh air and trapped the heat to an almost unbearable degree. Without having to be asked, Annie walked towards the sink and began to address herself to the mound of potatoes that had been left there for her to peel. Florence, Harbour View's cook/manager, was younger and less experienced than Mrs O'Toole and her lack of organisational skills created more work for everyone on the staff but Annie didn't really care. It was easier, she found, to be busy, it helped block out her worries.

Drop by my salon later.

Annie had no idea what Miss Jemima wanted from her but she would follow her orders faithfully because, right at this moment, there was nothing else she could do.

★

It was, as Annie had suspected, well after ten o'clock by the time the last of the guests had finished dinner. As the party drifted outside, wisps of cigarette smoke curling in the dusk, Annie and one of the French girls set about restoring what was known as the blue dining room, the second smallest of the four, to its usual state of highly polished perfection. But while Monique was then permitted to disappear along with the last of the dirty glasses, Annie had to follow Miss Jemima's instruction. She thought about fetching a fresh blouse but that would involve traipsing up four flights of stairs and she greatly feared that if she saw her duck-down pillow she would be unable to resist it, so she simply fixed her hair, then walked out through the double doors that connected the room with the garden.

There had only been ten people at dinner that evening but Annie had heard the rumble of cars arriving while she was serving. The earlier arrivals were in full evening dress but many of the newcomers were in more casual attire, the men in open-necked shirts with brightly coloured pullovers draped over their shoulders, the women in tight skirts that stopped just below their knees.

'The Moderns', was what Mrs O'Toole had called women like these. Annie liked to listen to the female guests as she served dinner, noting with some amusement how loudly they spoke about their ambitions, their jobs, how confidently they discussed their demands to vote and work and live on equal footing with men. They exhaled views on 'women's freedom' along with their cigarette smoke and although it was interesting, Annie sometimes thought to herself, their desire for sisterly solidarity never extended to helping her clear away the dirty plates at the end of the evening.

It was a warm night and Annie slowed her steps as she wandered further out into the garden, keeping her gaze low and level, although noting as she often did that New York's ban on alcohol seemed to matter less and less the nearer you got to the coast. In fact there were mornings since she had come to Harbour View that she'd found herself in full sympathy with the prohibitionists as she stepped around snoring bodies, still sleeping where they had fallen the night before. There had been a time when the antics of the guests might have amused her but now their silliness just added to her weariness. One young man, his white jacket streaked with grass stains, had set himself up as a barman tonight and was standing in the drawing room, dispensing cocktails through the open window while laughing uproariously at his own jokes. He was, Annie noticed grimly, pouring more drink onto the floor than he was serving and a real barman would have been fired for such sloppy work.

A woman in a grey silk evening gown, cut on the bias and clinging to her hips in a way that indicated she wore very little underneath it, had brought a full dinner plate out into the garden and was sitting on the ground, picking at the rare roast beef and creamed spinach with long, quivering fingers. A sliver of meat fell onto her lap and she stared at it quizzically for a moment before proclaiming, to no one in particular, that it would probably stain. The sight reminded Annie that the group would probably come looking for more food before the end of the evening, and she mentally ran through the contents of the kitchen, wondering what could be recycled as a late-night snack. It was not amusing, Miss Jemima had once told her, to be 'too predictable' or to plan menus, it was much more exciting when guests arrived without warning for spontaneous fun – all very well if you weren't the person having to spontaneously turn eight eggs into an omelette for twenty-three.

'Oh, Annie! Over here!'

Miss Jemima's voice was coming from the centre of the garden – the 'near garden' as it was known – and Annie picked her way across the grass towards it. When her employer had mentioned a 'salon' the word had called to mind a smoky drawing room, intelligent conversation, energetic debate – but this was just another party, Annie now realised, being held right out here in the open. There was garden furniture at Harbour View, of course, and beach furniture too, deeply padded beds designed to be carried right to the edge of the sea, as well as perfectly serviceable, brightly striped deckchairs, into which older members of the household often sank and had to be helped out of again.

Tonight, however, the company had dragged furniture from the main house out onto the grass, paying little heed to its age, design or value. Here was a plush dining chair, there a footstool, its velvet cushion already stained by mud and, in the corner of the lawn, Annie saw an entire sofa had been pushed out through a set of French windows and was being used as a horse by a red-faced young man, who was braying about the odds he had been given just a day before. She would have to get up even earlier tomorrow, she thought with a shudder, to make the garden in any way presentable before breakfast... But even as she was mentally ticking off the hours of sleep she was going to lose because of all this merrymaking she heard her name being called again and looked up to see Miss Cavendish stretched out on the red velvet chaise longue from her private sitting rom. The sofa would be destroyed if it rained, Annie thought, and then just as quickly realised this did not matter a jot. Just like the bone china back in New York, it would be as easy to buy a new item as repair the old and the fear that this principle might apply to servants as well as possessions made her hurry towards her employer.

Miss Jemima was also dressed in red velvet this evening, the train of her dress blending in so perfectly with the upholstery that, from a distance, only her long white arms were visible in the darkness. She held a triangular glass in one hand and a cigarette holder in the other and raised each one to her lips in turn with such metronomic regularity that Annie feared she might mistake one for the other before the end of the evening.

She turned to laugh huskily into the face of a young man who had perched himself on the back of her throne and, as Annie watched him make a murmuring response she suddenly – despite her exhaustion – found herself perceiving a certain beauty in the evening. Laughter was floating around the garden like a gift from one partygoer to another and the tips of their cigarettes were fireflies in the darkness. There had been no band tonight, not a formal one anyway, but somewhere between the garden and the sea a lone saxophonist had begun to play a slow, sensual air and as the notes reached her Annie felt a sudden desperate tug of longing to be one of these people, carefree and beautiful, not missing anyone at all because all of the joy in the world was right here.

'Annie! Thank you so much for joining us!'

Miss Jemima's smile was broad and Annie took a worried look at the contents of the glass in her hand. But although the young woman's eyes glittered, her voice was reasonably steady and her smile of welcome appeared genuine.

'Do sit down for a moment.'

Miss Cavendish extended one long white foot and poked the young man gently in the thigh.

'Get up, Charles, and let Annie join us.'

Join them? None of this made any sense but the young man did as he was told and Annie accepted the vacated seat, too nervous to argue but feeling lumpen, sweaty and utterly out of place, an old housefly amid fireflies. The young man returned after a moment and pushed a glass into her hand which Annie felt too intimidated to refuse, but when she sipped at the drink cautiously she was relieved to find the taste of the liquor almost completely masked by sweet lemonade.

'It's gin fizz!'

A girl loomed out of the darkness and perched on the side of the sofa. She had red hair, the same colour and length as Noreen's but that was where the comparison ended because this woman's face was long, and solemn, with a rash of freckles across her large nose.

'Do you like it?'

'It's very nice, ma'am,' Annie answered uncertainly, wishing desperately that Noreen could be here instead of her. How her friend would have loved this evening! She would not be lost for words, would engage everyone around them in conversation, smile at their answers and egg them on. It wouldn't matter what she was wearing either, because even in her shop worker's skirt and blouse Noreen would be the most beautiful woman here and every man would be crowding around to refill her glass or light up a fresh cigarette.

But Noreen was not here and now the girl was speaking again and Annie had to lean towards her to hear her properly.

'I said, I've heard they have fairies in Ireland! Real ones!'

A short man with a shock of blond hair overheard them as he walked past and groaned, but the girl shushed him and turned back to Annie, her blue eyes wide and rather vacant.

'It's true, isn't it, Annie? And if you catch them they have to give you a pot of gold! Maybe that's where Jem's father made all his money after all.'

She released a peal of laughter and Annie caught, on the end of her breath, a tang of onions, onions she herself had spent all afternoon chopping. The thought gave her courage to reply.

'That's not really what it's like in Ireland.'

'Oh it is, it is!'

The redhead waved her glass around.

'I've heard all about them, the leprechauns, they're angry little men, little fairy men with beards and green hats. Maybe I'll go to Ireland and catch one and then I won't have to listen to my father going on and on about saving money any more—'

'Lily, don't be a tease.'

The voice was rich, and deep, and Annie squinted into the darkness as the man approached. At least she assumed it was a man, as he was wearing trousers, but then she saw it was in fact a woman, a tall woman with a long elegant neck whose dark hair was shingled close to her head. The trousers were brown tweed, cinched at the waist with a leather belt, and above them she sported a white man's shirt, open at the neck and lined with a gold cravat.

Lily rolled her eyes and heaved herself up from the sofa.

'I was only having fun, Meg. Or have you taken against fun these days too?'

As the redhead stumbled away into the night the newcomer approached and gave Annie a strangely formal bow.

'Good evening.'

It really was the most delicious voice, Annie thought, rich and creamy and not at all like Miss Jemima's privileged drawl. The sound of it caused a warm feeling inside her.

'There you are, Meg!'

Miss Jemima had rearranged her limbs to make room for all three of them, but Meg perched on the arm anyway, as if mindful of Annie's comfort. And it had been so long since anyone had considered her comfort that Annie felt the headache she had been carrying with her for as long as she could remember finally start to recede. She took another sip of the drink and the newcomer frowned.

'Be careful with that cocktail, do you know who mixed it?'

Jemima's answer contained a hint of scorn.

'Oh it was Henry, don't worry. He's spilling as much as he is pouring this evening.'

'Well that might be a blessing. It's lovely to meet you – Annie, isn't it? I'm Margaret – my friends call me Meg.'

It was a such a cheerful, dependable name that Annie

returned her handshake without nervousness and received in return a warm smile.

'It's good to see you out here enjoying yourself. The food this evening was sublime, but I imagine it took a lot of work to prepare.'

'Thank you. I will pass that message on to Florence, the cook.'

The women smiled at each other for a moment and then Miss Jemima leaned over and tugged at Annie's sleeve.

'Meg here is a journalist, isn't that thrilling! She was looking to speak to people like you for an article and I told her you'd oblige.'

Ah, thought Annie, and felt herself growing tense again. 'People like you'. She should have known she hadn't been invited to this gathering simply to be praised for her cooking. Meg gave Jemima an irritated look.

'Well yes, Annie, it would be lovely if we could have a conversation but the choice is entirely yours, please don't feel under any constraint. But now that Jem has mentioned it I'll tell you a little more, if you like? I'm writing an article about "Bridgets"...'

She paused, as if waiting to see how Annie would react to the word, but it wasn't the first time Annie had heard the nickname commonly used to describe Irish maids like herself and she didn't, in fact, find it particularly offensive. Many of her fellow countrywomen *were* called Bridget, after all, Noreen's cousin among them, and given that Bridgets were usually considered good workers, and highly prized by New York matrons, she saw little problem in being one of their number. She nodded calmly and waited for Meg to continue.

'I had heard, you see, that some of the... that some Irish

girls don't have the best working conditions and I'd like to write about that for my magazine. Now I'm sure you have a wonderful life here with the Cavendishes, Annie' – Meg's gaze flickered towards Miss Jemima for a moment – 'but maybe others in your position are not so lucky. I would so love to interview you, and we won't have to use any names or anything like that, it could be completely anonymous.'

Do you really think I'm going to talk to you about my 'working conditions', Annie thought scornfully, with my employer sitting right beside me? Then someone behind her refilled her drink, and after she had taken another sip she stole a quick glance at Miss Jemima, whose head was now resting on the back of the sofa with her eyes almost completely closed. She could sleep for an hour or more in that position, Annie knew, so maybe there would be little harm in talking to this lovely woman with the gorgeous voice and the kind, intelligent eyes.

A gentle snore from Miss Jemima convinced her.

'You can ask me anything you like, I suppose. As long as the Cavendishes don't mind.'

'How wonderful!'

Meg sat up a little straighter and pulled a leather-backed notebook from her pocket. It had an attachment at the side to store her pen and Annie, distracted at the thought of how much her sister Eve would love it, missed her first question and had to ask her to repeat it.

'I asked, have you been in America long?'

'More than two years, miss.'

'Oh please.'

The woman scribbled in the notebook in a rather ostentatious way before looking up again.

'Do call me Meg, we're all friends here this evening. And you've been working for the Cavendishes all this time?'

'Yes, miss. I came here from the nuns – from the convent, down by the harbour in New York City. The Cavendishes are good employers and they have made me very comfortable.'

'I'm sure they have— Whoops!'

Meg turned a page of her notebook and as she did so, the pen flew out of her hand and landed on the ground. She ducked forward to retrieve it but Annie, long conditioned to picking up after her betters, bent over at the same time. Their hands brushed on the close-cropped grass and as they sat upright again, laughing, a little more of the tension Annie had been holding ever since she had come to Harbour View dissolved. It was the heat, she realised, that made this place so foreign and so freeing. The heat, especially after dark. Back home she often walked the roads at night, had done so many a time with May, particularly during the worst days of her friend's marriage, but back in Kerry they had always worn shawls tightly wrapped around their shoulders, even during summer months, and regularly had to shelter under hedges to avoid the rain. Here in America you could sit out in the dark wearing nothing but a blouse and it was as if the magical foreignness of it all loosened Annie's tongue because she suddenly found herself telling Meg everything she could remember about the voyage over, meeting Noreen, being a maid on Fifth Avenue and falling in love with New York City. She couldn't imagine why the other woman found what she had to say so interesting but the more she talked the more Meg scribbled and before long she found herself telling funny stories too, about dances, and the other maids she met at mass and Noreen's cousin Bridget – a real

Bridget, she informed Meg with a wink – and her legendary
Sunday gatherings that could, in their way, be every bit as
entertaining as nights at Harbour View.

When she finally paused for breath Meg gave her a
thoughtful look.

'Do you ever miss home?'

I miss Elena, is what Annie wanted to say. But this was
not a night for sadness, so she took another sip of her drink
before replying.

'I miss my family, of course I do, but I always had this
longing to travel, to see the world. And when I arrived in
New York – it's a very special place, isn't it? So different to
home but so exciting! The noise, and the people – back home
you are always your father's daughter, do you know what I
mean? Everyone knows your people, everyone expects you
to behave a certain way because your mother did or your
grandmother did. In New York, it's like starting again!'

'It's so wonderful to hear you say that!'

Meg was in danger of tearing through her notepaper,
Annie thought, she was writing so enthusiastically.

'My readers will be fascinated by you. And do you have
a young man back in the city?'

'I...'

It was as if all of the oxygen had been sucked out of
the warm night air and with it all the joy, and now Annie's
throat seemed to swell and close over. She lifted the glass to
her lips but it was empty and what had been in it anyway?
Nothing that was in any way good for her, that was for sure.
There was a thick feeling in her mouth now, she couldn't
speak through it and now she couldn't swallow either and
oh Lord, now she couldn't breathe...

'Don't move. I'll be back in a moment.'

Meg dived into the night, returning within seconds with a brimming glass of water which she pushed into Annie's hands, then raised to her lips when it became clear the Irish girl was incapable of doing so herself.

'Just a sip, that's right. Just one sip, take it easy now.'

It was the tone of her voice, rather than the words themselves that finally broke through Annie's distress and she parted her lips just enough to allow the water to flow over her tongue, its icy coldness shocking her into breathing again.

'That's it, take your time.'

Meg was stroking her shoulder now, and looking at her with concern.

'I'm so sorry, Annie, I've kept you up far too late.'

Do you have a young man back in the city?

For one stark second Annie felt compelled to tell this Meg person everything, to spill out into the velvety darkness the story of Elena and how she loved her. And then, from her side, came a loud snort and Annie and Meg both looked around to see Miss Jemima open her eyes and raise herself slowly into a sitting position again. The noise level in the garden rose suddenly and all three women turned to see the saxophonist emerge from the darkness, accompanied now by a fiddler and a row of uncoordinated, but exuberant dancers.

'Oh, I must have drifted off, please do excuse me!'

Miss Jemima yawned, then forced her blue eyes to open wide.

'How are you two getting along? Didn't I tell you, Meg, that our Annie is a fascinating creature?'

Annie could see Meg bristle at the word but she herself was too exhausted to care. The taller woman hesitated for a moment then sprang to her feet and offered Annie her hand.

'I could stay talking to you all night, my dear, but I have a feeling that you will have to rise much earlier than we will in the morning. Please. Don't let me keep you any longer.'

Annie nodded, then her heart sank as she looked around the garden and took in the frivolous destruction. Meg, following her gaze, gave a brisk nod.

'I'll make sure they take the furniture inside afterwards, we won't leave you to put the house back together on your own, I promise, Annie. Thank you so much for speaking with me, I really appreciate it. And I would love if we could meet again – if that would be agreeable to you?'

Annie nodded, her response blurred by fatigue.

'I'm sure that would be fine – if Miss Jemima permits.'

Meg walked a few paces away and motioned at her to follow.

'Jem won't remember much of this conversation in the morning, Annie, but I will. Will you come to meet me in the city one day, at the newspaper office?'

The city? The thought of bumping into Seánie again terrified Annie but Meg mistook her hesitation for concern about her job and gave her a reassuring pat on the arm.

'You don't have to worry about Jemima or her parents, if that is what is on your mind. My father sends a lot of business Joe Cavendish's way. We'll have a nice lunch, and you'll be home in a couple of hours, I promise.'

It was on the tip of Annie's tongue to say no and then a longing, stronger than the exhaustion even, washed over her. To see the city again, her beloved New York? To hear the traffic, and the shouts of the paper boys, the musicians on the street corners? She even missed the dust and the dirt, it was too clean out here in the country, too lonely, too quiet. Meg worked in a newspaper office, she said, surely there was no way that Seánie could find her there. And to stand on the same piece of ground as Elena – Annie didn't dare envisage visiting the young woman, it was too soon, she hadn't yet saved sufficient money, but the thought of simply breathing the same air as her lover finally made up her mind.

'I would be very happy to meet you again.'

'Well, that's just wonderful.'

Meg reached over and gripped Annie's hand firmly.

'I'll fix it all up with Jem.'

And then Meg pulled Annie forward and brushed her lips against her cheek.

'You take care of yourself, my dear.'

As Annie walked back across the garden, picking her way over sprawled bodies and past inebriated dancers, she found she was not thinking about the work that awaited her the following morning. To her great surprise there had come to that garden an echo of the warmth and companionship she had been missing since she left the city, the sensation of being appreciated and understood in some deep way. For the first time in a long time Annie Thornton was feeling the stirrings of hope.

Chapter Twenty-One

WEST KERRY

2022

'There's a car park around the back – just follow the sign.'

Leaving the main road, Emer took the route Rob indicated and guided the car to the back of the pleasant-looking, single-storey building. The words 'nursing home' had initially made her think of a depressing, grey institution, smelling of over-boiled vegetables but a quick look at St Catherine's made it clear that some of Siobhán's considerable wealth had been employed to make sure her father had the best care possible in his remaining years. The home was surrounded by manicured gardens, themselves dotted with comfortable benches, while in the fields beyond, the baaing of a flock of sheep must, she reckoned, be of great comfort to the rural residents.

As she parked the car in a designated spot, Rob switched off his phone then gave her knee a quick squeeze.

'No need to be nervous, OK? He's dying to meet you. It won't take long.'

Emer nodded.

'Of course. Looking forward to meeting him too. Are you going to tell him about Alison?'

Rob sat back in the passenger seat and sighed.

'I think so. Mom is worried about upsetting him but I don't think it's fair to keep it a secret.'

They climbed out of the car and Emer zapped it shut behind them.

'He is very elderly, I suppose she's worried it would be too much for him to take in.'

Rob pushed his sunglasses on top of his head.

'She is, I suppose, but Harry's not just some old man. You'll see what I mean when you meet him, he's as sharp as a tack, or at least he was until Covid. It was very tough on him being shut up in here, not being able to see us, and it did take a lot out of him but he's still Harry at the back of it. He's the closest thing to a dad I ever had and if Alison really is related to him then it wouldn't feel right to keep it from him.'

The interior of the building was just as attractive as the outside, with a number of very decent paintings hanging on freshly painted cream walls. Only the ramps which led from one area to another and the emergency call buttons on the walls gave any real indication that they weren't, in fact, having lunch in a country house hotel. A smiling woman in a well pressed navy smock buzzed them through the reception area and Rob and Emer followed her through the building to a long conservatory where a number of residents were chatting, knitting or just looking out at the view which today revealed a blue sky dotted with tiny cotton clouds. Given his age, Emer had expected Rob's granddad to be in bed but they found him instead sitting in a wheelchair near the end of the room, a newspaper folded on his knees.

'Ah, there you are, Rob! He's having a good day, he's looking forward to seeing you.'

A second nurse, whose long brown hair had been pulled into a ponytail, bustled over to them and straightened the rug on Harry's knees. The old man looked up at them and gave a wide, welcoming smile.

'I wanted to stay in bed but this one wouldn't let me. Isn't that right, Katya!'

'We can't have you getting lazy now, Harry.'

The nurse's Eastern European accent had, Emer was amused to hear, distinctly Kerry undertones.

'She has the measure of you anyway, Granddad,' said Rob bending down and enveloping the old man in a hug. 'It's good to see you up and about again.'

'Ah, you'd get sick of the bed.'

Harry nodded, then handed his newspaper to the nurse.

'You might give that to one of the old people, please, Katya. I've it read cover to cover and there's nothing in it anyway. But it will give them something to talk about.'

He looked up at Emer, a wicked grin adding even more lines to his incredibly wrinkled face.

'They are some terrible gossips in here but I try to stay out of it. How are you, my darling?'

Instantly charmed, Emer leaned over and shook the proffered hand. Harry's skin was so thin it felt as if his bones might poke through if she held on too tightly and there were several purple bruises on the back of his hand but his grip was sure and he gave her an appreciative look before letting go.

'No wonder he can't shut up about you.'

'Granddad.' Rob gave a warning growl and Emer grinned,

interested to note that you could, in fact, blush under a full surfer's tan. The nurse wagged her finger.

'Now, Harry. You've been waiting all morning for your visitors. Be nice to them. You will take him outside?'

She turned to Rob who nodded hopefully.

'That would be good, if it's OK with you, Granddad?'

The old man shrugged.

'Sure I just do what I'm told.'

Katya fixed the rug again and then, with a warning not to allow her charge to get cold, ushered them towards a set of French doors at the back of the room. As his grandson pushed Harry's chair out into the garden, he beckoned Emer closer.

'Lovely girl, Katya. From Ukraine, God love her. The last few months have been awful hard on her.'

'Oh gosh, I can only imagine.'

Despite the glorious summer Emer hadn't been able to completely avoid the news of the war which had broken out in the spring, but it felt surreal to even think about such misery now on this gorgeous Kerry day with the scent of the new-mown grass doing lazy battle with salt air.

'Has she been in Ireland for long?'

'Oh, ages.'

Harry took a large white handkerchief out of his jacket pocket and gave his nose an expansive blow before continuing.

'She's been here years but she had to bring the mother and the sister over when the war broke out. God love them, they're all sharing her little flat in town, poor Katya tells me she's sleeping on the sofa.'

He gave his grandson a searching look.

'Your mother didn't give any thought to taking in a few refugees?'

Rob parked the wheelchair beside a long wooden bench then sat down beside it, motioning to Emer to join him.

'You'd have to ask her that yourself, Granddad, next time she's over.'

'I will.'

The old man sneezed and wielded the hanky again, but despite the slight cold he appeared, Emer thought, in fantastic fettle, as sharp as a man twenty years younger and clearly having what Katya referred to earlier as 'a good day'. His grandson was obviously thinking along the same lines because he gave her a quick look before turning to Harry again.

'And sure haven't we a tenant in the guesthouse at the moment? An American girl, I think I told you about her?'

'Alice, is it?'

Harry frowned, then shook his head.

'You might have, I suppose. My brain is not what it used to be.'

He directed the last words at Emer with a half smile but she could detect a little frustration underneath the light tone. Rob was not deterred.

'Alison is her name, she's from California. She's been helping me out with the surf school and that.'

A sudden breeze rippled through the garden, and he reached over and touched his grandfather's hand.

'You're not too cold out here?'

'No, no.'

The old man shook the hand away gently.

'You'd go mad stuck in that room all day. Good to get

a bit of air in my lungs, we were long enough inside with that oul virus. There were days I thought I'd never leave the room. And ye waving in at me like eejits!'

Emer grinned as Rob continued.

'It's just this Alison – this girl who is staying with us – she told us a story the other day and I was wondering what you'd make of it?'

'A story, is it?'

'Well...'

Rob inhaled sharply.

'She reckons she might be related to us, Granddad. To your father actually, to Seán Lynch.'

Harry stayed silent for a moment, then shook his head.

'Seán Lynch went to America.'

Rob nodded eagerly.

'That's right. He went to America and... look, this isn't easy, Granddad. But the thing is, this girl, Alison. She thinks she might be his great-granddaughter. She reckons Seán met her great-grandmother and... well. There's no easy way to put it really but she says he had a second family over there, a daughter, her grandmother. I know it's a lot to take in, but have you any clue at all, might she be telling the truth do you think?'

In the minutes that followed, the only sound came from a lone blackbird chirruping overhead. Harry was so quiet, Rob leaned over and tried again.

'Do you think that Seán might have met someone else over there? That that's why he didn't come home?'

'Seán Lynch went to America!'

The shout was so unexpected Emer jumped and she looked across at Harry with concern.

'He went to America!'

There was spittle flying from the old man's mouth now. Rob sprang off the bench and dropped to his knees in front of him.

'I'm sorry, Granddad, I didn't mean—'

'He went to America!'

Harry gave one last bellow and then sagged in the chair, his last words were little more than a whisper.

'Seán Lynch went to America and he never came home. I'm telling you now, he went to America and he never came home.'

And the most frightening thing, Emer thought, was not how ill he looked, but how terrified he suddenly sounded.

Chapter Twenty-Two

NEW YORK

1926

'Come in, Annie! It's wonderful to see you.'
The short hair and thick brows were the same but otherwise Meg looked so different this morning – distracted, and with violet shadows under her eyes – that Annie felt her stomach twist with nerves.

'Do come up and we can talk properly. I trust the journey went well?'

'It did, ma'am.'

But as the elevator doors closed behind her, Annie found herself unable to think of another word to say. Her head was pounding too, but it had been sore even before she reached the city that morning. Miss Jemima had been out very late the night before and was unable to hide her reluctance when Meg called and asked her to 'run' Annie in to meet her. She had already been revving the engine of her small yellow convertible by the time Annie made her way onto the gravelled driveway and sped off while Annie was still shutting her door. With the top of the car folded back, the breeze in their faces had mercifully prevented much by way of conversation and for most of the journey Annie had kept her eyes tight shut, fearing at first she would pass out from the speed of the journey and then, after another few miles, praying she would do so. She had finally been deposited, physically unharmed but very wobbly, on the New York sidewalk and Miss Cavendish had screeched away, barking instructions that she would see her again at two.

This was a part of New York Annie had never visited before and none of it, not the tall grey buildings with their banks of blank windows, nor the stern-faced men who brushed past her, laden down with newspapers and self-importance, was in any way comparable with her beloved Fifth Avenue, so she was already ill at ease as she made her way inside the building and told the sceptical, black-clad receptionist that she had an appointment. And now Miss Meg – Annie still didn't know her second name – was also acting strangely, wooden and uncommunicative and, as the elevator doors slid open and the journalist stepped out onto a long carpeted hallway, it took all her courage to follow.

There was another reception desk inside a set of heavy wooden doors but Meg barely greeted the woman who sat behind it, instead motioning at Annie to follow her into the room. A room? Or a circus – Annie couldn't decide if the noise was most terrifying, a dull roar that every so often erupted into series of yells, or the wall of smoke that caught the back of her throat and threatened to choke her before she took another step. The newspaper office – later, she would learn to call it a 'newsroom' – had been laid out in a series of long tables and as Annie followed Meg through the gap in the middle she could see that each was occupied by four or five men, some in shirtsleeves and waistcoats, others in thick dark suits, all chattering to each other while stubbing out cigarettes in overflowing ashtrays or scribbling in thick yellow notepads. As they approached one man rose to his feet and yelled across at a colleague that he 'needed that copy now, dammit!' although given that he was forced to repeat himself three times above the din it would have been quicker and easier, Annie thought, just to walk across the room. Others were shouting into telephones, and that was the most extraordinary thing about this most extraordinary place because even the opulent Harbour View only had one telephone in the hall. This room appeared to have four or five receivers, dispersed at random on the tables, and as soon as one man had finished yelling and replaced the handset, it immediately jangled again.

Miss Meg was walking more slowly than she had done at Harbour View and Annie noticed she was wearing a narrow, heavy tweed skirt today that sat just below her knees, and a pair of high-heeled slippers. The stately pace of their walk did, however, have the advantage of allowing Annie a proper look around the room and by the time they had reached the halfway mark she saw that there were at least six women here too, seated together at a broad wooden table, their faces almost entirely hidden behind enormous typewriting machines.

Miss Meg's desk, an older and more battered piece of furniture than any other Annie had seen in the room, was in the far corner. There was a typewriting machine on top of it too and as Meg sank into what looked like an abandoned dining chair, she looked at it disdainfully.

'I told them to remove this.'

But her voice was small and seemed more distracted than annoyed as she motioned to Annie to pull up one of a number of stools that had been stacked carelessly against the wall.

'Please – make yourself comfortable.'

The way the stuffing spilled out of the leather upholstery didn't exactly make for comfort but, anxious to please the woman who had been so kind to her the previous week, Annie pulled the stool as close as she could to the edge of the table. Meg opened her mouth to speak but a sudden shout from the centre of the room meant Annie couldn't hear her and Meg was forced to repeat herself.

'I asked, if you had a pleasant journey in from the coast—'

'Go on, you little daisy you!'

Annie jumped, and looked around to see that one of the dark-suited men was standing alone in the centre of the room, a wireless set pressed against his ear.

'Three to one, by jingo, I had a feeling, boys, I told you I had a feeling!'

Annie had learned enough from Miss Jemima's late-night soirées to deduce that his wager on a horse had been successful and as the man continued to yelp with delight the others clustered around him, slapping his back and making jovial suggestions as to how he should spend his new-found fortune. After the worst of the cacophony had subsided, Meg turned to her again.

'I'm really sorry, Annie, let's start over. I asked you here today because I really enjoyed our conversation the other evening and I think you have a fascinating story to tell, both your personal story and that of your countrywomen too.'

My countrywomen? The words made Annie feel as if she

was being squeezed from the inside. Miss Meg wasn't going to ask her about the politics back home, was she? Her father wrote her letters sometimes telling her the fighting was over and there was a new government in charge in Dublin but she tended to let her eyes skim over the details. She hadn't been much interested in armies and wars when she lived at home and, as long as her family was safe, was even less concerned with them now. Her sister had mentioned something about executions in her last letter but these were just fragments of information, nothing Annie could imagine being written about in a magazine.

Meg must have seen the fear on Annie's face because she reached forward and patted her on the hand.

'Don't worry, my dear, I wouldn't ask you to say anything you felt uncomfortable speaking about. I only want to ask you about your own experiences, just as we discussed the other night. I want to find out about your world.'

Annie hesitated, nerves swirling, and then reached into her jacket pocket and withdrew an envelope that, even though it contained only three sheets of paper, felt as if it had been weighing her down ever since she left Harbour View that morning. She handed it to a quizzical Meg, a blush sweeping over her cheeks.

'I... I write letters home, sometimes, telling them what life is like over here. And I thought it might be helpful to write to you in the same way? Just to answer some of your questions, I mean.'

She had barely reached the end of the sentence when they were interrupted again, this time by a tall, heavy-set man with a shock of wheaten hair who ambled over to stand directly in front of them, blocking their view of the rest of the room. Meg shoved the pages into her pocket then looked up at him with undisguised irritation.

'Can I help you, Charles?'

'That was an interesting piece you wrote on the factory workers last week.'

The man rocked back on his heels and stuck his thumbs into his vest pocket. His glasses were smeared, Annie noticed, and there was a smudge of ink on the side of his nose. Meg raised herself up a little higher on her chair, somewhat mollified.

'Well thank you, Charles. It took a lot of work but I'm quite pleased with how it turned out.'

The man sniffed loudly and wetly.

'Pity, of course, that DeVries wrote the same story a week earlier.'

Meg's back stiffened.

'I had it first! The front desk held onto my story for almost two weeks, all because of this stupid decision they made to put all of my articles in the women's pages...'

'Now, Meggie.'

The man extracted one thumb, then used it and a forefinger to wipe his nose. The action smeared the ink further over his face, which Annie managed to derive some satisfaction from, but Meg seemed too annoyed to care.

'I went down to that march that Sunday, and spoke to those women, the survivors of the fire and the relatives of the poor girls that didn't make it. Why, he followed me—'

'There's no point in getting hysterical about it, my dear. You could do worse than to learn from DeVries, he's a good guy. Solid reporter.'

'Solid reporter who used all of my research.'

But Meg had spoken the last words so quietly that only Annie could hear. The fair man, meanwhile, dragged a small notebook out of his vest pocket and dropped it on the desk beside her with a soft thunk.

'Anyway, I was wondering if you could do me a favour, honey. The girls...'

He jerked his head back to where the women continued to pound their typewriters, apparently oblivious to the hubbub around them.

'The girls say they don't have time today. I'm trying to read back my notes from the city council meeting but my mother says I should have been a doctor, my scrawl is so bad. You don't think you could type them up for me? I'd be awful appreciative—'

'Come on, Annie, we're leaving.'

The sound of Meg's chair toppling over as she sprang to her feet was the first loud noise she had made that day.

'Arrogant... narrow-minded... self-important...'

Adjectives streamed from Meg as she stomped through the reception area, so hampered by her tight skirt that she eventually hitched it up above her knees. Annie trotted along beside her, doing her best to keep up while enjoying the receptionist's open-mouthed stare. She wasn't sure if it was daylight or emotion that made tears spring to Meg's eyes as they hit the street, but whichever it was they didn't last long and by the time they had found a crosswalk and marched across the street Meg was visibly more angry than upset.

'They're just impossible, Annie, they really are! I'm

so sorry for bringing you in there. I thought if the other reporters actually saw me carrying out an interview then they couldn't deny how hard I'm working but they don't care, none of them do, all they are bothered about is telling stupid war stories and trying to impress each other. I told them not to leave a typewriter on my desk, I'm not a clerk, I'm a reporter, the same as the rest of them but they just won't listen! Oh, I'm so cross. Let's go for lunch, what time is it? Eleven thirty? Late enough, honestly, I'd have a cocktail too if I didn't have so much work to do.'

She drew up so suddenly Annie almost tripped and then her heart sank as she realised Meg had led her right to a subway station. She was aware of the city's train service, of course, had heard them rumbling underfoot on many occasions but had never been on the underground railway before. Meg sensed her hesitation and stopped ranting for a moment.

'Don't worry. It's just three stops and then we'll be somewhere much more pleasant. Honestly, just hold onto the rail, that's right, walk forward with confidence, and now we are away—'

Before Annie could say another word she was being carried down into the bowels of the earth, daylight and safety receding from her at speed. She gripped the handrail tightly, mortally afraid that if she let go she would pitch forward into nothingness. And then a jet of warm, strangely scented air hit her face and brought with it a sudden rush of how marvellous all of this actually was. She was on a moving staircase – an escalator. Annie Thornton of Ballydrynawn who a couple of years ago had never been further than Tralee was travelling at speed through the centre of this intoxicating, marvellous city with a woman she had only met twice but who she knew, beyond doubt, she would follow anywhere. It all felt frantic and mixed up and terrifying and sure wasn't that exactly the reason she had come to America? By the time Annie reached the bottom, she stepped off the escalator with a confidence that suggested that she had been sailing up and down moving stairs her whole life.

The excitement loosened her tongue too and when she followed Meg on board the train, which departed seconds later at thrilling speed, she settled onto the wooden seat beside the other woman and, in a manner that was quite unlike her, took the reins of the conversation.

'Do you mind my asking why you are so upset, ma'am? Those men you work with – they seem to have really annoyed you.'

Meg now appeared halfway between cross and resigned.

'Oh, I should have known it was a terrible idea to try and speak to you in there. Charles is impossible, they all are. I was hired as a journalist, I did the exact same interview as the rest of them but most of the time they treat me like a glorified typist. It's all the editor's fault, he insists that everything I write goes in the women's pages but they only appear once a month so most of my work, even if I do try to make it relevant, is out of date before it even gets printed.'

Annie glanced at the window, which had been turned into a mirror by the blackness outside. She was wearing her best blouse and a small felt hat and, given Meg's cropped hair and sensible outfit, they didn't look like maid and gentlewoman. If anything, she realised, they looked as if they could be friends and if anyone from home had seen them now they wouldn't have noticed a whit of difference between them. The thought afforded her even more courage and she leaned forward.

'What sort of things do you write then?'

Meg's face brightened.

'Lord, there is just so much to write about in New York, Annie! Especially when it comes to issues that affect women. The factories on the Lower East Side, they are death traps, most of them, you hear the most awful stories but the girls who work there feel like they have no other option. Some of them are supporting entire families on one wage. But the editors...'

She almost spat out the word.

'They want me to write cookery recipes and knitting patterns. You know the sort of thing, there are so many real issues affecting women in this city and they want me to produce eight hundred words on how to get soup stains out of your husband's tie. And then there's the "servant issue"!'

She stole a quick glance at Annie, who didn't bat an eyelid and had, in fact, almost forgotten that she herself belonged to that category.

'That's what they call it, the "servant issue". Article after article on how to manage a household, and where to get the best girls and how to train them. Some of the women even write into the paper with their problems! "My scullery maid wants a second half day, should I release her and find a replacement?" That sort of thing. And that was why— Oh, we're here.'

The train shuddered to a halt and the women disembarked,

Meg continuing the conversation as they made their way across the platform.

'That was why I wanted to talk to you, Annie. I thought it would be refreshing, you know, to hear from someone actually doing the job. And one day I was talking to Jem and she mentioned this really amusing girl she had working for her...'

Annie, concentrating on the upward motion of the moving staircase, decided not to be offended at this description.

'I just thought it would be wonderful to get your point of view. Here we are!'

She hopped off the top step and Annie lunged after her, not connecting with the ground quite as smoothly as she would have liked. She hoped Meg hadn't noticed – but then the signs and sounds around her drove any sense of awkwardness out of her mind. This New York had none of the glamour and splendour of Fifth Avenue, nor was it anything like the grim and grey business district Annie had left behind just minutes before, and it was all the better for it. This New York was a riot of colour and noise, joyful noise that drew the visitor in and made them long to be part of the conversation. The streets were lined with stalls selling everything from fruit to yards of material and sturdy work boots and behind those stalls stood ramshackle buildings, no two the same and many with handwritten signs advertising their wares. Meg took in the delight on Annie's face and smiled properly for the first time that day.

'Welcome to the Village, Annie! I knew you'd love it here.'

The citizens of this place were a rainbow too, Annie noticed, and a stream of exotic voices ebbed and flowed as they walked past. She even thought she heard two women speaking Irish but there was no time to stop and confirm it, Meg was marching at a pace now, her skirt still hitched high, her good humour almost completely restored.

They finally stopped outside a small wooden-fronted building, a handwritten sign proclaiming it to be a 'Tea-Shop and Art Gallery'. Two women, wearing mufflers to protect them from the sharp morning breeze, were sitting at an outside table and called out greetings, but although Meg gave them a friendly wave she didn't stop, just pushed open the rickety wooden door and swept through. Inside, Annie found more colour, more exotic strangeness. The last restaurant she had been in was Elena's, of course, and the thought of her beloved brought with it the usual stab of pain, but there was a comfort to that pain too, it served as a reminder that Elena was lodged in Annie's heart and always would be, no matter how long they were parted. Other than the fact that it served food, however, this place shared no similarities with Elena's family diner. The room was dark and there were no banquettes here, just small tables covered in mismatched oilcloths, some with paper wedged under the legs to keep them steady. The single window was grimier than Annie would have liked and the space was made gloomier still by the dark tapestries on every wall, heavy pieces of woven cloth, some depicting simple country scenes, others abstractly patterned in greens and blues and gold. Meg led them to a table at the top of the room and pulled out a chair.

'Please sit here, Annie, and I'll order for us. I thought some tea? Are you hungry?'

'No, miss.'

Annie felt some of her early nervousness return –

she hadn't brought much money with her to the city, hadn't felt it necessary, and she certainly hadn't envisaged going out socially with the other woman – but Meg, seeming to sense what she meant, shook her head.

'It's my treat, of course, I dragged you all the way into the city after all. Laura does some marvellous scones, you wait here.'

Annie watched as Meg made her way to a small counter at the top of the café, behind which a woman was fiddling with a display case of pastries. As the women embraced and began an animated conversation Annie allowed her gaze to wander around the room. There were only two other occupants, an older woman sighing over a crossword in a newspaper and a man in a dark suit, dressed for all the world like the men in the newspaper office apart from a pink carnation in his buttonhole and – she had to blink to make sure she wasn't seeing things – matching bright pink socks which became clearly visible as he stretched his feet out from under the table.

'Tea and scones it is!'

Meg returned, brandishing a tray on which the cups and saucers were already swimming in spilled liquid. It was all Annie could do to stop herself from jumping up and fetching a cloth but she fought the impulse. Meg could well be only playing at this, pretending to be a servant girl, playing at being a reporter even, who knew? But for this one morning Annie was happy to go along with her and took the proffered cup although she could not resist giving it a quick wipe with her hanky when Meg left to bring back the tray.

'Now!'

Her hostess returned and pushed the plate of scones towards her.

'I wasn't sure if you wanted jam or honey so I ordered both. Laura is a wonderful cook, she's English, she does the most beautiful afternoon tea, you'll have to come back again to try it. Now, I—'

'Why, I didn't think I'd see you this morning!'

Annie looked up to see a woman a few years older than Meg, her eyes bright with delight, bustle across the room.

'I thought you'd be buried in your work until at least dinner time.'

'Oh, Simone!'

The flimsy table rocked as Meg leapt up to greet the new arrival. She was a tiny person, the kind of woman, Annie thought, you'd pass by on the street without really noticing. She had dark hair speckled with grey, drawn back at the neck in a careless bun, sallow skin and plain features and was wearing a mud-brown costume, buckled at the waist, and shoes that could have done with new heels. But Meg seemed overjoyed to see her and was speaking rapidly as she took her seat again.

'It was awful this morning, worse than ever! Those stupid boys...'

'Tell me everything.'

As the woman dropped into the seat beside her Meg did just that, half laughing and half crying as she recounted the tale of their morning. Annie poured the tea, happy to listen as Meg ranted about how rude Charles had been, how impossible it was to have her voice heard 'in that dreadful place'. The scones were nothing on Mrs O'Toole's, of course, but it was refreshing to have a meal served up to her like this and although Meg was in full flow, she was still thoughtful enough to turn around to Annie every so often with a 'didn't he say that?' or 'wasn't it dreadful?' to ensure she wasn't left out of the conversation. Her friend, meanwhile, who introduced herself simply as 'Simone', was one of the most peaceful people Annie had ever met. She listened intently to Meg and nodded in all of the right places, making it clear she had her full sympathy, but there was also an air of calm about her that seemed to transfer to the younger woman and Annie could see Meg's shoulders start to physically relax even as she continued to pour out her woes.

Simone sipped her tea unhurriedly.

'The problem is, I don't think you'd find things any better at another newspaper, Meggie.'

'Oh I know.'

Meg drained her teacup, resigned now rather than furious.

'I can't let them put me off. There's so much I want to say, so much I want to write and I'm not going to let them win. But my word, when I saw the look on Charles's face I really did want to – to...'

As she flailed around for something to say Annie couldn't help interjecting.

'To hit him a clout, miss?'

'Yes! A clout! That's exactly it.'

Simone and Meg dissolved into hearty laughter and, after a moment, Annie joined in. It had been months, she realised, since she had laughed like this and Simone and Meg's easy company reminded her of nights on the town with Noreen or, going further back, evenings spent with her mother and sisters around the fire at home. And she had missed this, she admitted to herself, wiping the tears of mirth from her eyes. Worry about Elena, fear of Seánie – she had been carrying around so much tension this past while it had been a long time since she had been relaxed enough even to smile. The thought made her sad, even in the midst of the merriment and, needing a moment to herself, Annie rose and began to clear away the empty teacups. Meg put out her hand to stop her but Simone appeared to have noticed her change in mood, and interjected.

'Maybe you could ask Laura to put more hot water in the pot, Annie? The rate our Meg is talking she'll need a bucket of tea to wash down all of this annoyance.'

Grateful for the other woman's understanding, Annie made her way across the café floor where Laura smiled as she approached.

'Another round of scones, my love?'

'Just hot water please, for the tea.'

Laura turned and addressed herself to a large iron kettle which was sitting just off the boil on a long low range on the far side of the counter. Her actions gave Annie a moment to steady herself and she was feeling much calmer by the time the woman returned, fresh pot in hand.

'Our Meg seems to have a lot to say for herself this morning.'

Annie was glad the others had warned her that Laura was English because it took her a moment to tune into her accent but the café owner had a friendly way about her as well as a bright curiosity that reminded Annie a little of her grandmother and which made her warm to her immediately. Not wanting to be perceived as a gossip, however, she kept her answer as neutral as possible.

'Well your tea is helping wet her whistle anyway!'

'Irish, are you?'

'That's right.'

Laura pulled a cloth from her belt and began to clean down the counter.

'You going to give one of their talks, then?'

'I'm sorry?'

Annie, who had been about to carry the tray away, looked at the woman in confusion.

'Are you going to be speaking at one of their meetings? Only they'll have to tell me if they want me to close the café on Saturday, I did warn them the last time, I need a bit of notice.'

Annie shook her head.

'I'm really sorry – I don't know what you mean.'

Laura finished sweeping crumbs into her hand then straightened her back, grimacing slightly.

'Well they usually bring the women in here first, you see, when they are giving a talk, to practise what they are going to say. When I saw the three of you chatting I assumed that's what was happening. Winning the vote for women, workers' rights – they've had all sort of discussions in here, those two. I enjoy them too as long as they tell me in advance. So I assumed you were one of their guest speakers!'

Annie shook her head.

'A talk? Ah no. I'm just a maid.'

'You don't want Meg and Simone to hear you saying that sort of thing!'

Laura's eyes were twinkling now.

'No one is "just" anything as far as those two are concerned, particularly not women. Hard to believe but they made me get up and talk one day, all about London and the differences I found working over here. I was that scared when they suggested it to me but do you know what? I quite enjoyed myself in the end!'

She finished her cleaning and gave Annie a broad smile.

'You mark my words, dear, those two will have you up and making banners or even giving a speech if you stay around them for long enough, you see if they don't!'

Still not quite sure what Laura was talking about, Annie thanked her, then lifted the refilled tray and turned towards the main body of the café again. And then from across the room she saw it, a movement as shocking as it was strangely familiar. Simone, reaching forward and tucking a lock of Meg's hair behind her ear. A simple gesture, but one that was somehow so intimate Annie felt her face burn, and she kept her footsteps heavy as she crossed the floor towards them. Simone, however, didn't look the slightest bit put out.

'Thank you so much, Annie! Now, let's have more tea, Meg, and we can plan our revenge.'

The next look that passed between them then was so charged and so raw that Annie had to suppress a sudden shiver. And then as she placed the tray on the table between them, a glowing, glorious notion began to thrum inside her. Maybe she and Elena were not as alone in the world as they had assumed.

Chapter Twenty-Three

WEST KERRY

2022

The pale walls and inoffensive paintings might have made it resemble a hotel but there was no doubting St Catherine's primary role as a medical facility as Emer and Rob pushed Harry's wheelchair back up the ramp and through the French doors. Katya was helping another resident set out a game of Patience, but her bright smile quickly disappeared when she saw their distress. She pressed a call bell and within minutes another nurse had arrived at their side, a tall, wiry man who grabbed the wheelchair from Rob and steered it out of the room, Katya striding alongside him and loosening Harry's scarf as they went. Feeling utterly superfluous, Emer and Rob followed them down a corridor and then waited outside Harry's room as the others tended to him inside.

'Jesus, if I had any idea...'

There were two chairs underneath a wide window and Rob sat down on one then almost immediately hopped up again and began to pace the floor.

'I only wanted to ask him about Alison, I never thought he'd get that upset.'

'He's in the right place.'

Emer was aware, even as she spoke them, how empty the words sounded but felt as if she had to contribute something as Rob continued to walk up and down the wide, brightly lit corridor. Thankfully it was only fifteen minutes later before the door to Harry's room opened again and both nurses emerged. Katya beckoned them over.

'Is he OK?'

Rob sounded frantic but Katya simply nodded, her expression calm and reassuring.

'He's stable now. You can come in, but just for a minute.'

Following Rob into the room, Emer's heart seemed to flip in her chest when she took in how white Harry looked and how tiny in the high hospital bed. Both his thin pale arms lay outside the sheets, a blood pressure cuff clamped to one, a drip feeding into another. An oxygen mask over his face prevented him from speaking but when Rob grasped Harry's hand his eyes opened briefly.

'I'm so sorry, Granddad. That last thing I wanted to do was upset you.'

The old man returned the pressure as best he could, then closed his eyes again.

'Is he going to be all right?'

Raising her finger to her lips, Katya made a few more checks on the various machines then motioned at them to leave the room again. The corridor was deserted but, obviously mindful of her patient's privacy, she kept her voice low.

'He is doing a little better now. But his blood pressure was soaring when you brought him back and his heart rate was erratic, it took us a while to stabilise it. What happened out there?'

Rob gave a helpless half shrug.

'I honestly don't know. I was just asking him a couple of questions about his family, things that happened when he was a boy. I had no idea it would upset him like that.'

He looked like a small boy himself, Emer thought, chastened and worried. Katya tutted sympathetically.

'Don't blame yourself. Harry is a very old man. The cold he had a couple of weeks ago really took it out of him, maybe it was too much to expect to have him up and about today.'

But the look on her face was at odds with what she was saying. Katya exuded competence and there was no way, Emer reckoned, that the nurse would have encouraged her patient to go outside if she really hadn't felt he was up to it.

'You can drop by and visit him tomorrow OK? Just give us a call first.'

As the heavy hospital door closed noiselessly behind her Rob and Emer looked at each other then made their way back through the nursing home and out to the car.

'Are you all right?'

'Not really. But he was in good form to start with, wasn't he? I'm not mad, I really thought he was well up for a chat. He was like his old self, all that bantering with Katya. I had no idea...'

Rob's voice wobbled and Emer shook her head.

'You can't blame yourself. He was grand, they all said he was looking forward to the visit. He's old, that's all. It was all a bit much for him, it happens...'

But her own voice tailed off. She didn't really believe what she was saying, so there was no point in trying to convince Rob. Something had happened to Harry, something bad. The conversation about his father had taken him from relative health to needing emergency care in the space of a couple of sentences, and the truth was neither of them had a notion of why things had turned out that way. Rob stared out of the window for another minute, then turned to her.

'Katya was trying to be nice but she looked a bit freaked out herself.'

'I know.'

Emer sighed.

'But he's in the right place, I know that sounds like a stupid thing to say but he is and they'll take good care of him. And you can come back tomorrow if he's feeling up to it.'

'Yeah.'

'He's a lovely man, I can see why he's so special to you.'

'He really is.'

They sat in silence for another moment, then Rob made a visible effort to gather his thoughts.

'Will we head off so? We're not doing him any good sitting here. Let's stick to the plan, drive back west maybe and get some lunch.'

Delighted to have something concrete to do, Emer started the car. Rob's phone had been turned off for the duration of their visit and, as she exited the nursing home grounds he pulled it from his pocket.

'Paudie texted me the name of a new restaurant a few weeks ago, let's see if can I find it.'

But as the signal kicked in the phone began to emit a series of beeps and Rob frowned.

'Sorry about this, it looks like Mom was looking for me. Wonder what she wants?'

Barely listening to him, Emer kept driving, giving her full attention to the unfamiliar roads. And then Rob let out a strange, strangled noise and she glanced over to see him stabbing at the phone's keypad.

'Emer – we have to head home. There's something wrong with Mom – listen.'

As Emer pressed on the accelerator, Rob switched his phone to loudspeaker and hit his voicemail again. If he hadn't told her the message was from Siobhán then Emer wouldn't have recognised his mother, her voice sounded so faint and slurred.

'Rob? I'm not feeling well, love... can you come—'

And then through the tinny receiver came the sound of a crash, and then a hiss of static and then nothing at all.

Chapter Twenty-Four

NEW YORK

1926

Annie turned into the narrow, leafy street and pulled her jacket more tightly around her shoulders. The temperature had dropped sharply now that fall was here – she instinctively called it 'fall' now, after more than two years in America, and had to be careful to remember to write 'autumn' in her letters home. The brown tweed jacket was a cast-off from Miss Jemima and much too big for her, but she had accepted it with gratitude when her young employer had offered it for today's trip to the city, not just because it would keep her warm but also because it was so obviously expensive and unlike anything a maid would wear. It was now more than three months since she had left the Chateau for the coast and she hadn't heard a word from Seánie Lynch in all that time, but the Irish population in New York was a large and gossipy one and Annie was terrified he'd find out she was visiting the city again. With any luck, the jacket would act as sufficient disguise to let her enjoy just one carefree afternoon.

She pulled the directions to Meg's house from her pocket

and checked them again, then crossed the street, counting the houses as she walked. The invitation to tea had been issued the previous week, relayed over the telephone to Edward, the Harbour View butler, and then conveyed to Annie in a note written in his copperplate handwriting. Edward hadn't hidden the fact that he felt himself above acting as a social secretary for mere maids, but Annie had pretended not to notice and had accepted the invitation with great excitement. The idea of a half day away from Harbour View had been exciting enough – it was a beautiful house, but Annie missed the bustle of the city and although the other maids were friendly enough, she hadn't found a friendship that came near to replicating the one she shared with Noreen. More enticing still, however, was the prospect of meeting Meg and Simone again and spending more time in their company. Annie had been unable to forget the looks that passed between them in the café, that brief but tender touch, it was as if a curtain had been pulled aside for a moment and she hungered now to discover what was really on the other side. And if what she suspected about Meg and Simone's relationship was true, then maybe she could even ask their advice about Elena – the very notion of it seemed at times preposterous, at others, tantalisingly within reach.

Miss Jemima had, once again, been unable to refuse Meg's request to 'lend' her her maid for the day but hadn't been particularly enthusiastic about doing so and had only dropped Annie at the edge of the city this morning, pleading a prior appointment, and telling her she'd have to find her own way from there. Now Annie found herself wondering if she had in fact taken a wrong turn after all, as the homes in this part of New York were so small and shabby it felt inconceivable that a woman such as Meg could live around here. Just as she was about to consult her map again, however, the front door of the smallest house of all opened and a tiny figure emerged.

'Over here, Annie! Oh, we're so pleased you came! Meg has been pacing the floors this last half hour, she was worried, you see, that you wouldn't be able to get away...'

Simone's wave of words carried Annie up the pathway and into the home which was indeed tiny in comparison to the New York mansions Annie had grown accustomed to, but so prettily furnished she decided she would rather be mistress here than at the Chateau or even Harbour View. The hall floor was wooden, highly polished and covered in tightly woven rugs which led the way into a small sitting room stuffed to bursting with a sofa and several mismatched chairs. A door at the top of the room opened onto a small kitchen area from which Meg called out to her.

'It's good to see you, Annie! Make yourself comfortable and I'll be out presently.'

Simone indicated a seat on the sofa next to her but Annie remained standing, and looked around the room for a moment before her hostess guessed the reason for her unease.

'Of course, after such a long journey you will want to make yourself comfortable. Please – if you go upstairs you'll find everything you need.'

It really was a tiny house, Annie thought as she ascended the wooden stairs and emerged onto a small landing which led onto only three doors. The first stood wide open and as Annie walked past, the maid in her couldn't help but notice the mounds of clothes flung carelessly onto the floor and the piles of books stacked untidily on both sides of the bed. The next door was shut and she pushed it open, hoping to find the bathroom, but found herself instead in another bedroom, the polar opposite of the first, which seemed to contain only a neatly made bed and a locker with a dry dusty glass on top.

As Annie looked at the glass, a wave of something akin to relief washed over her, as well as a rising sense of excitement. It hadn't been her imagination after all! Having finally located the bathroom – and resisting the urge to pick several towels up off the floor – she paused for a moment before going back downstairs. It was true, then. Meg and Simone really were... Annie didn't have the language to express what she was trying to say, not even to herself. But they were like her. Like her and Elena. And that meant they weren't alone in the world. Back down in the living room Simone looked up at her with a broad smile.

'Did you find everything you needed?'

'Yes thank you. I did indeed.'

As Meg slopped tea all over the tray and forgot first the butter and then the knife for the scones, Annie itched to restore order but Simone brushed away all her offers.

'You sit beside me, Annie, and we can get to know each other.'

Meg, clearly flustered, poured another cup of tea.

'I put in three spoons – was that right? I can never remember.'

'That's because you grew up with servants, my dear. It's really not so difficult when you get used to it, isn't that right, Annie?'

Annie took the proffered cup and poured in some milk before answering.

'I suppose so. It took me a while to learn to make coffee when I moved over here, mind you, it was all tea at home.'

'Oh, it was the same where I come from!'

Simone smiled.

'My father would bring a twist of tea home from the store and my mother sure made that little packet last.'

'And where did you grow up?'

Annie flushed, still unsure if she could ask questions of someone like Simone but the other woman answered easily enough.

'I'm from the Midwest, I'm one of twelve children. My father was a farmer and my mother taught school – we certainly didn't have anyone waiting on us! I'm the eldest girl, I had to learn to cook or we would all have starved.'

Meg, who was finally sitting down on a chair opposite Annie, let out a theatrical sigh.

'Simone is trying to teach me to cook but I'm not an easy study. It's so complicated – all those steps.'

'Oh come on, Margaret Anne.' Simone tutted. 'You can write articles in the newspaper and interview all those people. Of course you can make a stew, it's just following instructions!'

As the two women continued to tease each other, Annie felt for all the world as if she was back in Ballydrynawn, listening to her mother laughingly scold her father about having put yet another hole in a sock she had recently darned. That sense of being in a family home lent her courage to ask another question.

'Twelve children! We have families of that size at home

but I've never heard of it in America. Do you see much of them now? Did any of your brothers and sisters move to the city?'

It had been, she thought, an innocuous enquiry but all the joy went out of Simone's face suddenly and when she answered, her voice was sad and distant.

'No. I don't see any of them any more.'

Unsure of what she had done wrong, Annie cast about for something else to say and then all three women looked up in relief as a sharp knock came at the door and Simone rose to answer it. When she returned she was accompanied by a middle-aged, portly man with long grey sideburns and an unbuttoned dark coat revealing a waistcoat which was fighting a losing battle to stay fastened over a linen shirt. The newcomer was red-faced and somewhat dishevelled, but so obviously a gentleman Annie had to restrain herself from getting to her feet and heading into the kitchen to prepare more refreshments. Meg, however, shook her head and indicated she should stay where she was.

'You are very welcome to our home, Mr Robinson. Were the directions I sent you adequate?'

The man removed a handkerchief and mopped the shining dome of his forehead.

'Quite adequate, my dear, although it is warm today and I perhaps didn't leave myself enough time – a glass of water, perhaps, if one were available?'

Annie twitched in her chair but Meg rose.

'I'll get that for you now. You relax and we can all get acquainted!'

The next few minutes were spent distributing drinks and settling the visitor into a chair and finally Annie found herself with a fresh cup of tea in one hand and a plate containing another of Meg's dry scones in the other. She hesitated for a moment but there was no table within her reach so she placed the plate on the floor and sipped at the tea, which was weak and needed sugar. Mr Robinson looked much revived and gazed around him with a satisfied, rather kind smile.

'So, this is our author then?'

Annie waited for Meg to respond in the affirmative and then realised, with amazement, that the other three were looking at her.

'This is Annie.'

Meg sounded a little like a mother, Annie thought, parading her young child in front of relatives at a children's party. She still had no idea who the man was or what, indeed, was the purpose of his visit, and then her hostess introduced him in a manner that did little to settle her confusion.

'Mr Robinson is a publisher, Annie. I showed him some of your work and he was so excited he wanted to meet you right away.'

'My... work?'

For a second Annie wondered if this was a joke, a very unkind joke set up by Meg and Simone to humiliate a poor Irish servant. She had been beginning to think of them as friends, but maybe that had been foolish of her? After all, who ever heard of society women making friends with a 'Bridget', even if these particular women seemed to live a far less conventional life than most? But Meg, sensing her confusion, lifted a magazine from a pile on a side table.

'I showed him the article I wrote, and your contribution.'

It must have been clear by the look on Annie's face that she had no idea what Meg was talking about and the other woman tutted in frustration.

'Heavens, did Jem not show it to you? I posted a copy to her especially, and called her up to remind her to pass it on.'

'I didn't see any magazine, miss.'

Annie stared at Meg, completely at a loss as to what she meant. An article? Smiling, Meg rose, and handed the magazine to her.

'Turn to page five, my dear girl, then you'll see what I'm talking about.'

Annie did as she was told, and then it was as if the room simply faded away, and with it Meg's irritation and Simone's kindness and even Mr Robinson's inquisitive expression. There was nothing in front of her now other than rows of neatly printed words and the headline, 'A Maid on Fifth Avenue'.

I came to America in 1924. I had never left my county, let alone my country before but—

Annie gasped and looked over at Meg.

'But this – this is my letter!'

Meg nodded, her eyes shining.

'I know! Isn't it thrilling? I wrote my story too, it's on the other page, look...'

Annie briefly took in rows of neatly printed text and the name 'Meg Abernathy' perched on top in darker letters but she couldn't stop her eyes from returning to her very own words which were in the centre of the page, printed in squiggly writing to let the reader know they had originally been part of a personal letter.

...and I was lucky enough to find a place in a large house in New York City.

She let her eyes skip over the next few lines, then found the section she was looking for:

Some mistresses in America are very kind and allow their staff two half holidays, however others seem to feel that hours off are a luxury and not to be granted until all of the household work is completed. I know of maids who are forced to walk the streets after dark, forgoing an evening's rest because it is the only time they can get a breath of fresh air or catch up with friends from home...

The pages fell to Annie's lap as she pressed her hand against her mouth, her heart racing. Had she really meant to sound that critical? What if the Cavendishes learned of her treachery? But Meg leaned over and patted her on the arm.

'You're not to worry, Annie. I took out your name and any reference to the Cavendishes or their address. No one will have any idea who wrote the piece. But it's so much more interesting and truthful than anything I could have written third hand. My story has the facts and the figures, how many girls are in New York, that sort of thing. Your words bring us right to the heart of the situation. It's quite simply better than anything I could have done myself.'

Annie reached out a fingertip then smoothed it over the

words, as if afraid they were about to disappear under her touch.

'But I only meant it for you, Meg – ma'am. To answer your question, to help you with what you wanted. I never dreamed you would use my words like this!'

'But it's so good!'

Meg crossed the room and sat down lightly on the arm of Annie's chair.

'Your writing is so fresh and truthful. This paragraph here...'

She pointed over Annie's shoulder.

'The piece about how much you do in the course of a day. I don't think anyone who lives in those houses really considers how the work gets done around them. Why, you said it yourself, the servants' staircases are carpeted to make sure you can't be heard running up and down, some families even built hidden doors so you can appear to glide in and out of a room like magic. It's like you opened a door yourself, and our readers loved it.'

'Your readers?'

'Oh yes!'

Meg nodded.

'The article appeared in the women's section but the paper got so many letters about it the editor said he regretted not putting it in the main paper. He's very pleased with my work too.'

Her smile widened and she glanced across at Simone.

'He says next time I can pitch for space in the news pages just like any other reporter. I'm so pleased – but you, Annie! All of New York is talking about you!'

Annie felt a sudden burn of shame leap from her throat.

'What I said... I wasn't very... complimentary in places.'

'Oh, fiddlesticks!'

From across the room, Simone threw her head back and laughed.

'That paragraph about how women like to talk about feminism while ignoring the women who butter their bread and lace their shoes? It's wonderful, just wonderful. I can't tell you the number of people who have quoted it back to me since it was published! We have meetings, you know, in the village on Saturday afternoons. All sorts of women join us, and some men too who care about women and equality – we call them "feminist gatherings". I know it sounds highfalutin, but I think you could contribute something really valuable if I could persuade you to join us!'

'Ahem!'

The three women looked across the room at Mr Robinson who looked rather like an elderly cat as he coughed again to remind them of his presence. Meg was the first to gather herself and gave him a warm smile.

'I'm sorry, Mr Robinson. As you can see, Annie wasn't quite aware of our plans.'

The man folded his rather small hands over his waistcoat and nodded graciously.

'Well, if you could permit me to explain?'

He took their silence as a cue to continue.

'As Miss Abernathy said, Annie, your article – your *letter* has attracted quite a bit of attention. I myself had it passed on to me by no fewer than three people and, when a group of people are all saying the same thing about a piece of writing, well I have to admit it gets one thinking. I run a publishing house, Annie...'

Annie's attention had wandered, she was too busy looking at her words – her words! Right there on the page. But as Mr Robinson continued, the meaning of what he was saying finally started to filter through.

'I run a publishing house, Annie, and I think there might well be a market for a book from you.'

'A book? By Meg, you mean.'

'By you!'

Mr Robinson was smiling broadly now.

'*A Maid on Fifth Avenue*. It's a fine title, very evocative. You'd need some guidance of course, to finesse the work – although I was very impressed with your original letter, there must be a fine education system in Ireland, very fine indeed – or did you receive extra tuition over here?'

Annie bristled slightly, thinking of Master O'Donoghue, who sat behind the battered desk at the top of Ballydrynawn's one-roomed classroom and made sure that every child, whether they were headed for the secondary school in town or back to feed the family's few chickens, had the same basic grounding in Euclid and English grammar. But this was not the time, she knew, to take offence and she put her head to one side, trying to take in the meaning of the man's words even though it was hard to believe he was saying them at all.

'... most definitely a market for it. I'm not sure about keeping you anonymous, we will have to discuss that. Any book would have much more weight if you could be photographed, or interviewed for the newspapers—'

'Oh I'm not sure about that!'

It was Meg who spoke but her words echoed Annie's thoughts.

'Annie still needs to work, Mr Robinson, and no employer would agree to hire a maid who had written such a volume!'

'Well she mightn't need to work for much longer!'

Mr Robinson sat back, a pleased look on his face, aware that he finally had the full and absolute attention of the three other people in the room.

'We would pay an advance on sales, of course, I can't promise a kings' ransom, we are after all a small publishing house.'

He was enough of a salesman to pause, and then name a figure Annie was sure she had misheard. Pleased at her reaction, Mr Robinson allowed himself a quiet smile before continuing.

'Yes, we would pay in the region of that sum in advance and then, after that, if sales are satisfactory, I would imagine you could earn, well, quite a bit more.'

This time the sum of money he suggested made Annie's heart throb in her chest, a loud, insistent throb that spelled out a name.

El-ena. El-ena.

It would take her years to earn that sort of money if she stayed working for the Cavendishes. To receive it now would change two lives overnight: hers, and the woman she adored. No more hiding and saving, they could leave the city straight away, and settle somewhere quiet, somewhere away from Elena's family and Seánie Lynch's cruelty. Somewhere they could be happy, and free. Maybe there would be a small house in their future even, with a guest bedroom that nobody ever used... Her voice, when she replied, was as steady as if she had been planning for this moment for all of her life.

'What do I need to do?'

Mr Robinson looked impressed by her composure and pointed at the paper in her hand.

'Just write, my dear! More of this. Concentrate. Bring me some more pages in, shall we say a month's time? And if I like what I see, then we shall speak again. But now...'

He was also enough of a showman to know when an exit was needed.

'I shall take my leave of you lovely ladies. You have my details, Miss Abernathy. I shall await your response with interest.'

'I'll send you more pages as soon as I can.'

'You see that you do!'

The three women embraced and then Annie left the house, walking down a street that looked shabby no longer. Meg had offered to call a cab to bring her to the station – she would have plenty of her own money soon, she joked, to spend on such things – but Annie had refused. Her head was fuzzy, both from the unexpected news and the bottle of wine Simone had opened to toast her good fortune and although the women had been extraordinarily happy for her, she needed some time alone to fully absorb what was going on. A book, with her words inside and her name on the cover? It seemed too good to be true. But Meg had clinked her glass against Annie's and assured her she wasn't dreaming.

'If I didn't like you so much I'd hate you, child. I've been writing for years and never had such an offer. But you deserve it, Annie Thornton from County Kerry, you have real talent. I'll just be happy if I can play a small part in bringing it to light.'

Annie reached the subway station and began her descent into the bowels of the city, noting with pleased surprise how comfortable she felt doing so. She might still be 'Annie Thornton from Co. Kerry' but these days she moved around her adopted city like a real New Yorker and, importantly, was starting to feel like one on the inside, confident and in charge of her own destiny. There was a train departing for the coast at seven thirty, she would catch it, she decided and walk back to Harbour View from the station. That would give her plenty of time to clear her head and properly digest the news.

But that train would also leave her with three hours to spare in the city, and there was only one way she wanted to spend that time. Annie hadn't planned on visiting Elena today, she was still terrified that doing so would somehow lead Seánie to her and she had, in fact, decided to stay away from her altogether until she had saved enough money to make a proper plan for their future. But as the subway station names rolled by outside her window she realised how close she was to the restaurant and suddenly found she could not countenance leaving New York again without at least trying to make contact. Her pulse quickened as she thought of it. This was a city where two women could live together as husband and wife, and where a simple maid from the far side of the world could publish an article in a newspaper that anyone could read. In a world where anything was possible, surely she could spend just one hour with Elena, with her love? And after all, Annie told herself firmly as she alighted from the train, this book would be for

Elena, everything was for Elena now and what was the use of having all this good fortune if she couldn't even tell her what had transpired?

The feeling that she was doing the right thing increased as Annie found herself back in the New York she adored. Every storefront held a memory – here was the place where she bought fat teddy bears for her nieces and nephews, there was the cake shop where she and Noreen used to buy the most delicious pastries, waiting until just before closing time so they could get them at half price. Annie would have loved to share her news with Noreen today too, but she was also following her dream and had written to Annie some weeks previously to tell her she had finally left the city for the West Coast. She had secured a position in a hat shop, she said, but it was a shop frequented by costume designers from the movie world and surely it would just be a matter of time before she joined that world herself? Annie had grinned when she read the letter and knew that if any Mayo woman was going to make it onto that silver screen then Nora Carey was the woman to do it.

But now she was at the restaurant. For the first time since she had left Meg's house, nerves made Annie's feet falter but she forced herself onwards. Just a quick visit, that was all she needed, just long enough to let Elena know their future was secure. The alleyway to the side of the building was deserted and, heart hammering, Annie gave a sharp knock on the metal door, praying for some more good fortune. But it was one of the cooks who answered, not Elena, a tall, heavyset man who looked at her with suspicion.

'Yeah?'

'I was wondering...'

His scowl did not invite conversation but Annie coughed and tried again.

'I was wondering please if Elena is here?'

The man stared at her for so long, Annie was starting to doubt he even spoke English but then he lit a cigarette, exhaled and squinted at her through the smoke.

'Who am I, a messenger boy?'

But she had anticipated this response and pulled coins from her coat pocket and then, when his face remained blank, a dollar bill.

'I would really appreciate any help you could give me on this matter... sir.'

She could almost see him struggle for a moment but the 'sir', coupled with the money, seemed to win him over and he took the bill from her hand before placing it in his pocket. And then his face broke into a smile that was somehow even more intimidating than the scowl that had gone before.

'You at a loose end tonight, honey? What do you want the girl for, maybe you'd like to come walking with me instead?'

The look on his face was so laden with meaning, it was all Annie could do to stop herself from turning and running away, but then she suddenly thought of Noreen, and how she acted when she needed men to do her a favour. Putting her head to one side, Annie mustered as wide a smile as she could.

'Thank you for the invitation. I'm afraid I only have a short amount of time free this evening. But if you could please tell Elena that her friend Annie is here, I would be ever so grateful.'

'Ever so grateful, huh?'

The man shut the door without another word. As Annie stood in the dank alley she felt her courage drain away. Would the man run off with her money? Or worse, would he warn Elena's father, or Lorenzo even, that there was someone looking for her? And then the door opened again and the dear face of the person she loved more than anyone else in the world emerged, confusion turning to shock when she saw who was in the alleyway.

'Come with me, please. I have so much to tell you. Just one hour.'

'I thought you were never coming back.'

It had taken a lot of talking – and another precious dollar bill – but finally Annie had persuaded the cook to send Elena on an 'errand' that could not be postponed and their precious hour was secured. As they walked towards the corner of what Annie still thought of as 'their' park, however, the Italian woman seemed lost in thought and didn't speak to Annie until they had found their clearing at the centre of the trees.

'You didn't write to me.'

Annie took off her jacket and lowered it onto the ground for them to sit on as Elena continued.

'You said you'd write and you never did.'

'I was afraid.'

Elena pulled her knees towards her and hugged them tightly.

'I was afraid too, afraid you were never coming back.'

Hearing the anger in the other woman's voice, and worse

than that the hurt, Annie felt all of her earlier joy and excitement drain away.

'I told you what was going on, Elena. I told you about Seánie, I had to get away from him and I was terrified that he would find out about our friendship.'

But Elena's voice remained cold.

'You told me you were afraid of a man and so you ran away. What about me, Annie? I am afraid of Lorenzo and I have to see him every day.'

'Oh, my love...'

Annie reached out her hand but Elena flinched and kept her arms wrapped tightly around her knees. Fear made Annie speak in a whisper.

'Has he hurt you again?'

She waited for one long painful moment before Elena shook her head.

'Not in that way. He is being nice to me now, most of the time. But that is not a good thing; he is determined to marry me, he told my father he wants us to wed in the spring.'

'Well then by spring we shall be gone!'

Annie turned so her body was facing Elena's on the small patch of ground. Speaking as quietly as she could for fear of alerting any passers-by she told Elena everything that had happened that morning, the meeting with Mr Robinson, the suggestion of a book, the glorious promise of an advance payment. Slowly Elena relaxed her grip on her knees and looked at her.

'But this is a fairy story, surely.'

'No, it's true. It's all true.'

'And if you earn that money, you will send it home to your parents?'

'No.'

Annie thought back to the last letter from her mother, how settled the family was now, how happy they were that she was making her own way in the world. They didn't make any demands on her and she loved them for it.

'No, Elena. It will be our money, for you and me. To allow us to go away together, to have our own home.'

'But that's not possible.'

And then Annie revealed her second piece of news, handing it over like a jewel under their woodland canopy. About Meg and Simone's home, their relationship, the love for each other that was clear for anyone to see.

Elena's eyes grew wide with wonder.

'You told them about us?'

'No – not yet. But I feel that if I did, they would understand. I'm sure they would love to meet you – they will meet you one day, please God.'

'I'm dreaming, I must be.'

'It's not a dream. We can have our own little house, in the Midwest somewhere...'

Annie had only a vague notion of what the 'Midwest' meant but she knew it was far from Lorenzo and Seánie and that would be good enough for them.

Elena shook her head.

'And when could all this happen?'

'I just need a few more weeks.'

Annie reached over, plucked at Elena's sleeve.

'Believe me, Elena, this can happen. There will be money – Mr Robinson said I just have to write a few chapters and then he will pay me.'

Finally, Elena allowed Annie to take her hand.

'I think of you all the time.'

'I know. I know.'

'All of the time. Every morning and every night, you are with me, Annie.'

Their fingers were interlinked now and to Annie it felt as if they shared one pulse now, one heartbeat. But Elena's voice remained low and serious.

'I thought there was something wrong with me. I went to mass, I prayed for forgiveness. I couldn't tell the priest what I was thinking because I was too afraid of what he would say but I prayed, I prayed that I could change...'

Annie raised their joined hands to her lips.

'I don't want you ever to change.'

She could feel Elena shudder under her kiss, but her eyes still looked troubled.

'This must be wrong...'

'Does it feel wrong?'

She had been so scared before, but what Annie had seen in Meg's house that morning had lent her courage and she kissed Elena's hand again before pulling her towards her.

'We are not alone, there are others like us. And they are not bad people.'

Deeper kisses were punctuating her words now.

'We are not bad people.'

And then the weeks of waiting, of missing each other and longing for each other, bubbled over and they were in each other's arms. Soft kisses gave way to urgency, the delicious pressure of mouths, of bodies. Clothes became an encumbrance as they sought each other out, exploring each other as they had done in their dreams. And threaded through it all came joy. Laughter, and great joy.

Afterwards they brushed dust and leaves from each other's clothes and hair then walked back towards the park gates, physically separate but utterly in harmony. Annie's skin was so alive the material of her dress felt too rough against it and she pushed up her sleeve, almost expecting to see it glow from inside. It was late, too late, they hadn't noticed the time passing and there was no time for a proper goodbye. But Annie gave her lover a fleeting kiss on the cheek and whispered it again, their prayer.

'I will return for you. Wait for me, my love. Wait for me.'

Chapter Twenty-Five

WEST KERRY

2022

'She won't pick up.'

It felt as if the car was about to rise onto two wheels as Emer took the corner, the speed limit a mere memory as she followed Rob's directions on the back roads towards his home. And even if she was stopped by the guards, Emer thought, well maybe that would be no bad thing because Rob was onto the emergency services himself, having failed multiple times to get his mother to pick up the phone. When the operator answered he had to fight to keep his voice steady.

'She called me, yes, and said there was something wrong and there was a sound, like she had fallen and...'

Emer listened as he went through the story, her concern receding slightly at the thought that the professionals would soon be involved. But the emergency operator, although sympathetic, informed Rob that all available ambulances were attending to an accident further out the Tralee road, and predicted it would take at least forty-five minutes for help to reach his mother. He hung up, then stared at the phone in frustration as if it could somehow give him a clue as how to proceed. They had hit a patch of heavy traffic now, it was a sunny afternoon and half the county, it seemed, had decided to head for one of West Kerry's glorious beaches. As Emer tailgated a glistening white SUV, its back window stuffed with bodyboards and beach toys, she started to fret that they wouldn't get to Siobhán any quicker than the ambulance. And then a thought occurred to her.

'Alison! If she's in the flat, maybe she could check on her?'

Rob's frown cleared slightly.

'Of course! Jesus, I'm not thinking straight...'

But Alison's phone went straight to voicemail too and now, looking at the long line of happy daytrippers that stretched out ahead of her, some of whom were actually slowing their cars to a crawl to take photos of the scenery, Emer felt a surge of panic. And then Rob scrolled through his phone again and tried another number. The sound of an actual human voice answering was, Emer thought, the most joyful thing she'd heard all day.

'Cian? It's Rob, man. No, not good. Look, I think something has happened to Mom...'

Their conversation was short and just as businesslike as Rob needed it to be and, when he finished, he looked at Emer with something approaching relief.

'Cian's at the guesthouse, he's going to head over there now. He has a key to the back gate, he came over to use the Wi-Fi a couple of times when he was teaching from home during the pandemic. You know Mom, she has some sort of special booster, he was able to sit in the garden and still get a strong enough connection to teach the kids...'

You know Mom.

His voice faded away but the words seemed to clog up the car's stuffy interior and Emer opened the window, hoping the rush of fresh air would focus their minds. She did know Siobhán, knew her well enough at this stage to understand that hearing her sound so vulnerable had been completely shocking but there was no point in panicking now. They just needed to get home.

Gerry was standing at the doorway of his shop and Emer was vaguely aware of his startled face as she sped through the village, but what of it? All going well there would be an ambulance tearing past in a short while too and she didn't care what gossip it provoked as long as the day's story eventually became a good one, a 'weren't they lucky they got there in time' anecdote instead of the other kind. She was so close to her destination she didn't need Rob's directions any more but he muttered them anyway, hunched forward in his seat.

Moving quickly, but steadily – there was no point in them crashing, that wouldn't help anyone – Emer drove out of the village, past the clearing that led to the Fairy Tree and then took the now familiar left at the crossroads, slowing the vehicle as the road narrowed. And although she had grown to love this place and understand Siobhán's desire for privacy, she felt a sudden jolt of frustration at how narrow the road was, how impractical the location. Branches scraped against the door as she drove and she had to pull in twice to make room for oncoming traffic, Rob twitching with tension as the minutes ticked by. He had the clicker out of his pocket long before they reached the wooden gates, pushing it multiple times before they were ever within range and when they finally opened, he barely waited for Emer to drive through before unfastening his seatbelt and leaping out of the car. As Emer brought the car to an inelegant halt and jumped out herself, Cian emerged from the kitchen, shaking his head and telling them he had searched the ground floor and found no sign of Siobhán.

They split up then, she and Rob running upstairs while Cian headed off to comb the grounds. As they ran, Rob dialled his mother's number repeatedly but Siobhán always kept her phone on silent and it was almost comical, Emer thought, while at the same time not funny at all, the way they had to freeze every couple of seconds, like statues in a children's game, to try and hear even the slightest vibration before beginning their search again. They checked Siobhán's bedroom, next the exquisite sitting room and then, as they were making their way back out on to the landing Rob dialled his mom again and Emer finally heard it, a low buzzing sound coming from a guest bedroom. It was the room closest to the landing and afterwards she wondered if poor Siobhán had simply tried to find the nearest bed when she began to feel ill. But she hadn't even made it that far because when they found her she was sprawled on the floor of the en-suite bathroom, her leg at a stomach-churningly awkward angle, blood pooled on the floor from the cut on her forehead, sustained when she struck the sink.

Rob's lifeguard training overcame his panic and he checked his mother's pulse while dialling the ambulance again. Yes, there was a pulse, but it was thready and weak. Yes, her airway was clear, but her skin was clammy. No, she wasn't able to speak to them...

Conversation over, he sagged back against the bath and

held the tips of his mother's fingers as if afraid that by grasping her hand he'd cause her more pain. Emer stood in the doorway, unable to get any closer.

'Will they be here soon?'

Rob shook his head miserably.

'Not soon enough. They were on the far side of Ballydrynawn when I spoke to them.'

And then his phone rang again and his face, already pale, turned grey.

'No, there's no way round that top road at all. Not a hope of getting through there. You'll have to turn around – yes, and leave it at the bend. My friend Cian is here, I'll send him down to ye.'

He hung up and looked at Emer, tears of frustration in his eyes.

'That fucking road. Get Cian, will you? The ambulance can't get up here – they've tried the back way too and nearly got stuck, they've been driving around for twenty minutes. Tell Cian to meet them at the bend, he can help sort out the traffic...'

Emer ran and relayed the instruction to Cian who was waiting in the kitchen and looked relieved to have something practical to do. As he jogged off down the driveway she grabbed two glasses of water, not sure if they were needed but anxious to do anything to alleviate this dreadful, impotent waiting. Carrying them back to the guest room she heard, for the first time since they had returned, Siobhán's voice.

'I tried to call you...'

As Emer entered the room, however, her initial relief that Siobhán was awake evaporated. It was clear Rob's mother was in terrible pain and seemed barely aware of what had happened to her or, indeed, where she was.

'Where the fuck are they?'

Rob spoke through gritted teeth, turning his head away so his mother couldn't see the panic on his face as Siobhán began to cry.

'I fell, Robbie, I'm not well, can you help me? It's sore... I need something for the pain...'

It took twenty long minutes for the paramedics to arrive, Siobhán all the while moaning in discomfort on the cold, hard bathroom floor. Although they moved her as gently as they could, she screamed in pain as they lifted her onto a stretcher, then manoeuvred her out of the room and down the steep wooden stairs. Even the gravel driveway seemed endless as the stretcher bumped across it, out through the gates and onto the road until they reached the corner where they'd been forced to abandon the ambulance.

Rob went with his mother, leaving Emer behind, and it took ten minutes, but felt much longer before she finally heard the clang of ambulance doors shutting and the sirens begin to wail.

Chapter Twenty-Six

NEW YORK

1926

'Oh, this is impossible.'
Muttering to herself, Annie tossed the page aside with frustration and sank back onto her pillows. In the bed on the other side of the room her young French roommate gave a sudden start, and then settled down into a deep slumber again. Annie looked at the low lamp burning on her bedside table and wished more than anything that she could go to sleep too, but she had promised Meg she'd send her some pages this weekend and so far all she had to show for her work was a pile of crumpled paper and cramped, ink-stained fingers.

She was exhausted too from her long day's work, but although her eyes were gritty, every time she closed them the number of tasks still undone seemed to swell inside her and deny her rest. She must have been out of her mind, she thought gloomily as she surveyed the box of writing paper, she must have been actually insane to think she could write a book, or anything like it. Oh, it had been fine well sitting in Meg's house listening to Mr Robinson and his grand plans, but now the job was right in front of her, she reckoned it would be easier to row herself back to Ireland in a currach than fill those blank pages. She was a maid, when all was said and done, not a writer. Just a maid, with notions above her station.

Sighing, she reached and lifted the box of writing paper on to her lap. Maybe a fresh sheet would prove inspirational? She saw the envelope poking out from under the stack of paper and pulled it out, feeling more downcast than ever. Her family back home were owed a letter but she didn't have time for that now – then she paused, and looked at the blank pages again. The thought of writing a book was impossible, even starting one seemed far beyond her. But she could write letters, wonderful letters, everyone told her so, and after all, wasn't it a letter that Miss Meg had seen fit to put in her newspaper?

She picked up her pen, uncapped the nib and made the first strokes.

Dear...

Annie hesitated. Pretending to write to her parents wouldn't do, what would be the point of telling them her life story when they already knew so much of it? And then a bolt of excitement shot through her as her mind wandered, as it so often did, to her last meeting with Elena. She hadn't seen her since that day in the park but she had written to her, care of Salvatore the cook, enclosing another dollar bill to ensure the message was delivered safely. It had just been a short note, to tell Elena she was thinking of her, nothing specific that could betray them but she had wanted to say so much more. And maybe she could, in this way?

Dear Elena

Maybe writing to her would ease the pain of separation too. So Annie began, not a book, but a letter to her love and as she did so, finally the words began to flow. She wrote down everything she could think of, in whatever sequence the images arrived in her mind. Her first day at school in Ireland, her first time shopping in a New York store, even the first time she used a mechanical carpet sweeper that sucked up dust from the rugs like magic – all of the memories from pleasurable to mournful and even astonishing spilled out onto the pages. Annie wrote about Seánie Lynch too, but in an oblique way, musing about how difficult life could be for women on both sides of the Atlantic if they were not allowed to live in peace. She wrote about things she found boring but which Meg had assured her Americans would want to read about; all of the daily, mundane tasks involved in running a house like Harbour View. Not all of what she wrote came from her own experience, maids in New York liked to talk when they got together and Annie found she could remember quite a store of anecdotes gleaned at dances and after masses, including how some ladies took no part in the running of their households and delegated everything to housekeepers, while others tried to organise everything themselves and ended up creating a greater mess. She relayed stories too of houses where the doors were locked at nine p.m. and any servant who found herself outside after that time, even on a permitted night off, would have to take shelter in an outhouse until the sun rose the following morning. How a maid's happiness could depend on exactly who was in charge.

Sometimes Annie wrote in her bedroom, but it wasn't always possible to find peace there with the French girl sighing over a magazine or trying to engage her in conversation to practise her English. But in a house the size of Harbour View there was always somewhere to hide and at night when her work was done, or on her half afternoons, Annie sought out corners and folded herself away with her thoughts. Some nights she wrote in the ballroom, using a dust-sheeted drum as a table. Once she tried working in the library itself but a guest in the house had called in to look for a book and took so much interest in what she was doing, perching himself on a seat right beside her and leaning over her shoulder to 'check her handwriting' that she ran from him, fearful he would report her to Miss Cavendish.

And then one evening Annie remembered the boathouse, a brightly painted structure down by the shore which was only used once a week or sometimes even less, depending on Miss Jemima's moods. It was a grand, comfortable place, with an equipment locker just the right height to be used as a writing desk and a small stool that had been dragged down from the kitchen one day for some forgotten purpose and never returned.

Annie wrote and wrote on that stool, the pile of notepaper growing beside her, and while her ache for Elena didn't ease, writing to her in this way made the loneliness easier to cope with. Writing a book was like building a house, she found – too daunting to attempt all on one day but if you put it together, brick by brick, word by word, then slowly the paragraphs would form. A month later, after working around the clock and getting very little sleep, Annie finally decided she had enough material to send to Meg. She read over the pages one last time, striking out words here, rewriting there, then parcelled the document up in brown paper and string and carried it to the post box in the hall. There was a letter waiting for her there and after she had deposited her parcel she picked it up, smiling when she saw May's handwriting. A treat, beautifully timed to reward her now her hard work was done.

Annie carried that letter around all day in her pocket and it made the long hours easier to think of the pleasure of reading that lay in store. She even hummed a little as she dusted the blue dining room and Florence, who was walking past, wondered if whatever had been preoccupying her best worker over the past few weeks and had left her so pale and drawn had finally been resolved. When the last of the dinner dishes had been cleared away and the rest of the servants were sitting down to their own supper, Annie took a slice of bread and cheese down to what she now thought of as 'her' boathouse and curled up on top of a pile of ropes and old cleaning materials that had been left in the corner. So lovely to have the smell of the sea in her nostrils, all the better to read the news from home.

And then as she absorbed that news, her world tumbled in on itself.

My dear Annie

I trust this letter finds you well. We are all in good health here TG. Harry had a bad chest but we did not have to call the doctor and he is much recovered now. Well there is much change here Annie. My husband Seán Lynch is returned from America TG. God saw fit to send him home to us. He arrived back three weeks since and we all thought he was dead but he is not dead. He was beyond in America this past three years but now he is home. I could not believe it when I saw him walking the fields towards us. He is not afraid any more to stay, he says. The trouble is over now and everywhere is very peaceful and he is back at home and says he will not leave again. The children found it strange to begin with but I am sure they will be pleased to have their father here again. Thank the Lord he is home safe and well.

That is all I have time for Annie but I think of you every day and pray for your intentions. As I hope you pray for mine.

Yrs affectionately your friend May

Ps Maybe it was God's will Annie but I did not pray for him to come back.

Annie dropped the letter onto her lap and then noticed the envelope which it had come from was not quite empty. Her fingers shaking, she reached inside and withdrew another piece of paper. This time the handwriting belonged to her sister, Eve.

Dear Annie. This is only a note, I am visiting Mam today and we passed May on the road and she told us she was on her way to post a letter to you. I persuaded her to come back to the house while I wrote you a note. She thinks I am just taking the opportunity to write to you

but oh Annie, we are all so dreadfully worried about her.
She will have told you Seánie is back. It has only been
a month but already our dear friend is gaunt and pale.
Little Muireann has been missing school and when I saw
Harry yesterday he had a bruise on his temple although
May did her best to hide it. But what can we do? A man's
place is in his family home and Seánie Lynch is back
there now. I am glad May is writing to you although
I'm not sure how honest she will be. She is such a loyal
person and so good. But I can't help but thin his return
will not be in her best interest. Maybe I am wrong and
I pray that I am. But I want you to pray too, Annie, for
your friend and mine.

   Your loving sister Eve

He went back. Annie buried her face in her hands and
rocked backwards and forwards, the full horror of the
situation unfolding in her mind. Seánie Lynch had gone
back to Ireland. After all those months she had spent
fretting, worrying that he would follow her to Harbour
View or hunt her down in New York City, the truth had been
far more terrifying. He was home. Back in Ballydrynawn,
back with May, back with the children. Back to torture her
beautiful friend.

And it was all her fault.

The wind had picked up outside but Annie couldn't hear
anything over the thrumming of blood in her ears. It was
all her fault, all her stupid, selfish fault. She had refused him
the money, had chosen flight over appeasement. She had
decided that her life with Elena, their happiness, was more
important than giving him what he wanted and in making

that choice had driven him straight back into the arms of May. Her beautiful friend, and her beautiful children.

And now she had to make things right. Her legs numb from sitting in one position for too long, Annie stumbled back towards Harbour View, ignoring the stares of Miss Jemima and her mother who were seated on the veranda enjoying coffee and the evening view. She kept running, through the kitchen where the rest of the staff were finishing their tea, and up the stairs to her bedroom. Alone now, Annie shut the door then reached into the small hole she had made in the underside of her mattress. There was a substantial ball of notes there now, life was quiet at Harbour View and every cent she made went towards the future she had been dreaming of. But now those cents were needed for another purpose. Slowly, Annie began to count the money. She loved Elena more than anything on the earth but right now, May needed her more.

'You have to promise you will return to us.'

Annie drew her feet up under her skirts and curled up on the large, shabby fireside armchair. From across the room, Meg leaned forward to make her point again.

'You must return, Annie, your home is here. Promise?'

'I will. I do.'

When Annie had handed in her notice to the Cavendishes, telling them she had an emergency to attend to at home, she had hoped she would be able to spend her final night in New York at the Chateau. Mrs Cavendish, however, had not taken kindly to the speed of her departure and had informed Annie that as she was not fully working out her notice she was under no obligation to accommodate her. Annie had been too weary to argue, had even contemplated heading straight to the docks and spending the night in the open air, feeling she was unlikely to sleep anyway. But once Meg had caught wind of what happened she had sent a cab to bring her straight to Brooklyn, had fed her dinner and finally, gently but thoroughly, extracted from her the reason for her sudden departure.

And in that tiny sitting room, where the warmth of Meg and Simone's affection for each other was stitched into every cushion, Annie allowed herself, for the first time in many years, to relinquish control. Meg poured her tea and Simone sat and listened as she talked, and explained and finally cried about Seánie, and May, and how worried she was about her friend. She had savings, she told them – her voice cracking again as she remembered their original purpose – and going back to Ireland would use most of them up, but she would work hard to build up her little store again.

It was then that Meg left the room, returning moments later to press a bundle of notes into Annie's hand.

Annie looked at her, not understanding.

'I can't take your money.'

'It's your advance.'

As Meg settled back beside Simone, Annie shook her head.

'Mr Robinson said the advance would not be paid for months, I don't have anything like enough of the pages ready.'

'Well call it an advance on the advance, then!'

Meg forced a smile.

'Technically, this is my money but it will be yours soon

enough. I just want to make sure that you come back to us, Annie. I know how strongly you feel about having to travel and I respect that, I really do, but you belong here in New York. Why, we've watched you blossom these past few months – haven't we, Simone?'

The other woman nodded in agreement.

'Think of it as a loan from both of us, Annie. Why, it will be like a form of insurance! You have to come back to us now, don't you see?'

The warmth in their voices brought forth more tears.

'A good cry, that's what my mother calls it.'

Meg tried her best to sound practical.

'I don't always agree with her sayings but that one is useful, I think. Have your good cry, but you'll have to get some rest too, you have a long journey ahead of you tomorrow.'

She exchanged a quick glance with Simone and then, as if they had come to an agreement, spoke again.

'You can take the spare bedroom, at the top of the stairs.'

The room was almost fully dark now, lit only by the dying embers of the fire and the dim light and the warmth made Annie feel she could say anything.

'I would really appreciate your spare room. Thank you.'

She was surprised to see a flicker of relief in Meg's answering smile.

'We weren't sure how to broach certain topics with you. You are our friend, but we didn't want to make you in any way uncomfortable. I know that apart from anything else you might have a strong religious faith...'

For the first time since she had sat down that evening Annie allowed herself a small smile.

'My faith isn't something that concerns me any more, not faith like going to mass anyway. But I have great faith in what I have seen in this house. You have both made me so welcome. And besides...'

It was easy now to imagine she was speaking to herself.

'I also have a friend, a friend whom I love very dearly. Leaving her tomorrow will be the worst thing I have ever had to do but being here with you, seeing what you have together – it gives me courage, and makes me think that some day I will see her again.'

There was a moment's silence and then Meg crossed the room and embraced Annie in a tight, fierce hug.

'You will always find a welcome in this house, I promise you. You, and your friend. You will come back to us.'

The light was almost gone but Annie could have sworn that even the sturdy Simone had tears in her eyes.

Exhaustion ensured she was able to get a couple of hours of rest, but when Annie woke before dawn she knew by the swirling of thoughts in her mind that she had no chance of getting back to sleep. Her hostesses' door was shut tight and she crept out of the house, unwilling to wake them. The evening before had been too perfect, she didn't want to say a grim morning goodbye.

She walked around the city streets for an hour, watching her beloved New York wake to a new morning. Took it all in, the cries of the newspaper boys, the thud of boxes onto pavements as they were unloaded from delivery carts, the smell of fresh bread wafting out of the Jewish bakery just a few blocks from the Chateau. The bagel she bought for breakfast was so fresh out of the oven she had to toss it from hand to hand for a moment to cool it down before breaking open the firm surface and pulling out the soft doughy centre. She ate as she walked, afraid to miss even a second of her final hours in the place she loved most in the world.

There was a smell of bacon in the side alley at Elena's restaurant when she reached it, just before nine. She could have called to see her any time in the previous week but something had prevented her from doing so – fear of what Elena would say, most likely. Fear that she would persuade her to stay. Elena herself answered her knock but Annie's joy at seeing her was immediately shattered when she saw how wretched she looked. Her face was pale, her eyes shadowed. Even her beautiful hair hung lank around her tired and drawn features.

'Dear Lord – what has happened?'

Not answering, Elena stepped instead past Annie into the alleyway, taking shelter behind the large metal bin. The stench was almost unbearable but the space was a haven nonetheless, the bin tall and broad enough to ensure no one from the restaurant would see them if they looked out. As gently as she could, Annie explained to Elena where she was going and why she had to leave.

'But not for long. I'll be back, I promise you.'

Instead of protesting however, Elena simply hung her head.

'It's too late.'

'Elena, I know this is not what we planned—'

'Lorenzo knows.'

Annie felt the words like a blow to her stomach.

'Knows? Knows what?'

Elena had lost so much weight, Annie noticed now, that her apron strings were wrapped twice around her waist. She continued in the same flat tone.

'That letter you sent, that was meant for me? Salvatore gave it to him. He asked me for more money and when I didn't have any he gave it to Lorenzo.'

Annie's head began to throb.

'But there was very little in it to upset him, surely?'

But Elena just gave a small, defeated shrug and the sight of her thin sloping shoulders caused Annie's heart to fracture.

'He knows that we are friends, that you miss me.'

'But he doesn't know, he doesn't know that we...'

Annie reached out her hand but the other woman flinched away.

'It doesn't matter. He knows we are friends and that I have a life outside of here and that was enough. He told my father you are a bad person who led me astray.'

'Oh, my love.'

And then Elena stretched out her own hand, palm upwards, then slowly turned it over. The alleyway was so dark there was no glint from the tiny stone but Annie could see that the gold band was too tight and that the poor sore flesh was raised and red around it. Her hand flew to her mouth.

'You are engaged?'

Elena nodded miserably.

'He said that if we marry then he will forgive my past behaviour, and that my parents will always have a home. He was going to put them on the street! He says they are slow and that he could easily get young people to do their jobs. But they wouldn't survive away from here, Lorenzo owns the building they live in. When my father heard what he was planning, he begged me to go along with it. He says Lorenzo will be kind, once I am his bride—'

Elena's voice finally cracked on the final word and she took her hand back, as if it was somehow not entirely part of her, and used it to wipe her tears away.

'Come to Ireland with me?'

But even as she said the words Annie knew they were useless. Elena looked so broken, she doubted she would make it as far as the quays.

'I can't. I've tried to fight him and I can't. Maybe, if you had stayed in New York I might have been braver, if I had been able to see you, to talk to you. But you were gone, and I was alone. And maybe...'

She made a terrible attempt to compose herself then.

'Maybe it won't be so bad, you know? Being his bride. I won't have to worry about my parents any more...'

But the fear in her words belied their bravery and Annie clasped her own hands together, squeezing them tightly in the hope that the pain would ground her. She had a sudden image of Elena, her beautiful Elena, those brown eyes solemn above a sea of white, walking away from her and towards a life that, despite her brave words, would bring her nothing but sorrow. It must not happen. It could not happen. She took one sharp intake of breath then looked directly at her.

'Give me a little more time.'

'What good will time do?'

Elena sounded exhausted.

'This book, my work – I know it's hard to explain but give me some more time and I will come for you. Can you do that, can you wait for me?'

'I don't think I have the strength, Annie, not any more.'

'Well then let me be brave for both of us.'

They looked at each other for one long moment and there was a lifetime of love in that look, and the flickering promise of happiness. Then a figure rounded the corner and Elena dropped Annie's hand and shrank backwards into the shadow of the bin. But her fiancé had seen all he needed. The shove sent Annie sprawling onto the ground, her head striking the edge of the bin so hard it left her dizzy and by the time she looked up again Lorenzo was dragging Elena back towards the kitchen.

'Go, Annie, just go. It's better if I don't see you again.'

The worst part of all, Annie thought afterwards, was that Elena didn't cry out. She had learned by then not to make a sound.

Chapter Twenty-Seven

WEST KERRY

2022

'Hey. You didn't have to wait here all this time.'
'Yes, I did.'

As Rob sank into the hard plastic hospital chair, Emer reached over and enfolded him in a one-handed, awkward but heartfelt hug. He smelled of hospitals, of antiseptic and sweat and worry and looked as if he could have been a candidate for admission himself but none of that mattered now, because Siobhán was alive. Weak, and still in terrible pain, but alive. Rob leaned into Emer's embrace for a moment, seeming to draw strength from it, then straightened up and ran his fingers wearily through his hair.

'She's just woken up there, and sipped some water. They had to put a pin in her hip and she'll be off her feet for a good while but they think that's the worst of the damage looked after.'

'Poor Siobhán.'

Emer released him then pulled her chair closer to his so they could speak without being overheard by the others in the waiting room.

'And do they have any clue yet what happened?'

Rob shook his head.

'A mini stroke, maybe? They're still waiting for test results. I had a chat with her there just now but she's so groggy it's hard to know what she remembers, or if any of it is in the right order, even. She says she was just after having a coffee and was sending a few emails when she felt lightheaded. She thinks she decided to go upstairs and lie down but she can't really remember anything other than waking up on the floor of the guest room and us two being there. And the pain...'

He swallowed, looking sightly sick himself.

'Mom never complains, I mean never. I've seen her coming home from the dentist, after having wisdom teeth out and all sorts and she just sits on the sofa and sends emails and complains that nothing will get done if she takes a day off. If she says she was in pain it must have been really, really bad.'

Emer slipped her hand into his and squeezed it gently.

'I know. It was horrific. But they've given her something now?'

'Ah yeah.'

Rob managed a weak smile.

'She's off her head on morphine, says it's great stuff altogether. But it'll be a long road back for her, she'll have to do physio and all sorts. She won't be able to drive for a good while either, she'll hate that...'

His voice cracked, and he swallowed before continuing.

'She's comfortable now, that's the main thing. She needs a few bits brought in from home but they said it'll do to bring them in in the morning. Will you go in and see her, before we head away?'

Emer bit her lip.

'Oh, I'm not sure if I should—'

'She's asking for you.'

Rob leaned over and kissed her gently on the cheek.

'She says she remembers you being there, this afternoon. Wants to thank you herself, I think. Go on through, she's in a room at the end of the corridor. I'll meet you back here.'

Nervously, Emer pushed open the heavy swing doors and followed the signs for St Alice's Ward. It was past nine at night now and away from the fluorescent buzz of the waiting room bulbs the hospital seemed to have fallen asleep. The lights were dimmed in every room she passed and the only sign of activity came from the nurses' station at the centre point of the corridor where a woman of around her own age with a bouncy ponytail and clear, fresh skin directed her onwards.

'Rob said you might drop in. Just for a minute, all right? It's the second door on the right, down there at the end of the corridor.'

Oh, Rob told you, did he? Hiding a smile, Emer wondered if the nurse learned the names of all of her patients' family members so quickly. One of the lights at the far end of the corridor was broken and flashed intermittently, creating an otherworldly, eerie feeling and when she pushed open the door of the room at the end it was empty, apart from an elderly lady in the bed by the window. Emer hesitated, sure she'd been sent the wrong way, and then the old woman stirred and Siobhán's eyes looked out from her lined and weary face.

'Ah, Emer, you came.'

The voice was exhausted and blurred by drugs but it

was Siobhán all right, although a Siobhán who seemed to have aged twenty years since Emer last saw her. There was no one else in the room but it seemed appropriate, still, to speak in a whisper.

'I won't stay long.'

'You're grand!'

Siobhán patted the side of her bed weakly.

'Sit down here for a minute. I wanted to thank you, for everything you did earlier. Ye got back so quickly, I don't know what would have happened if ye hadn't found me...'

Her eyes filled with tears and she patted the bed again. But Emer was afraid of hurting her and looked around the room for a moment before spotting a chair and dragging it across.

'How are you feeling now?'

Siobhán turned her head towards Emer, taking care to keep the rest of her body very still.

'Shite, to be honest with you. Well, floating now, thanks to the drugs but lousy underneath it and I'd say I'll be worse tomorrow.'

She was dressed in a hospital gown, Emer noticed, and was pleased to think of something practical to say.

'Can I get you some pyjamas? I could be back in an hour if it's urgent...'

'No no, not tonight. They won't want me moved again tonight. I asked Rob to bring a few bits in tomorrow but there's no rush then either. He looks wrecked, God love him, and you must be tired too, so take it easy on the road, OK? We don't want another accident.'

Her voice slurred on the last word and her eyelids drooped but just as Emer felt sure she had drifted off to sleep Siobhán opened her eyes again and looked directly at her.

'And my laptop, will you bring that in as well? It'll be still in the kitchen.'

Emer shook her head, gently.

'Ah now, Siobhán, I'm sure you won't need that in here. Whatever it is it can wait a few days, surely?'

'No!'

The note of urgency in the other woman's voice alarmed her and Emer glanced over her shoulder, wondering if the perky nurse was nearby. Then Siobhán reached over and laid one pale, thin hand on her arm.

'Please, Emer. I haven't been very nice to you, I know that...'

Sensing Emer was about to argue, she shook her head.

'I haven't. Look, I can be a bit protective of Rob, I know it, and it's awful foolish, the size of him!'

She managed a weak smile.

'But I've been thinking about it and we have a lot in common, you and I. You've built your own business, I admire that. So I'm asking for your help now, one businesswoman to another. Please get me my computer. I need to jot down a few things. To put things in order.'

In order. It was such a strangely specific thing to say that Emer leaned closer, attempting to reassure her.

'There's no rush with anything now, surely. I know you got an awful fright but it's a broken hip, nothing more serious. I know the cut on your head looks bad but the doctor said you only needed a couple of stitches—'

'I can't remember.'

Tears rushed into Siobhán's eyes.

'I can't remember what happened to me. I don't want to bother Rob but I'm worried, Emer. The hip I can cope with, it's a nuisance but these things happen, it'll heal. It's the rest of it is the problem; it was like my mind just went somewhere without me and I'm terrified it might happen again. Did Rob tell you that my mom, his granny, had dementia?'

Emer shook her head.

'No, he didn't say.'

'He was in Australia at the time.'

The lines of pain on Siobhán's face deepened but she was speaking clearly now, making perfect sense.

'I didn't want to upset him so I didn't tell him how bad it got. But it was bad, Emer, and it was sudden. One day she was baking and maybe just losing her glasses or something but a few months later my dad found her wandering out on the road with no clue how she got there. She didn't remember any of us in the end...'

Emer shivered, thinking of the powerhouse that was her own mother, and indeed Siobhán herself, and how devastating it would be if anything happened to those sharp witty minds.

'I'm so sorry.'

'It was horrendous. And it started when she was younger than I am now.'

Emer stayed quiet as it dawned on her where the conversation was going.

The older woman shifted in the bed, the action causing a gasp of pain.

'I just can't help wondering if it's happening to me? This isn't the first time, either. A few months ago, I found myself down at the Fairy Tree with absolutely no recollection of getting down there. I was terrified – I must have walked past the cliffs too, do you know how dangerous that could have been?'

Emer nodded, speechless now as she thought back to her first day in Ballydrynawn and the glimpse she had caught of the distraught Siobhán.

'I'm afraid, Emer. I'm terrified that what happened to my mother is happening to me. I want to get my affairs in order, update my will while I still can and I need my computer and phone in here to do it. Will you bring them in for me? Please?'

'I'm sure you have plenty of time...'

But Siobhán's eyes were darting around the room now.

'I want to make changes...'

Then, as if the effort of speaking had been too much for her, she let her head sink into the pillow again.

'You're a good girl, Emer, I knew I could ask you. Not fair on Rob. But there's Alison to consider now and I need to make changes...'

Her eyelids fluttered but she forced them to stay open.

'That young girl has had a tough road, maybe she was meant to come over here and find us. Maybe it was all for the right reasons.'

Emer swallowed, wondering what Rob would say if he was here. Wondered, indeed, what Paudie would say, his theory about Alison was coming to pass, and in a very dramatic fashion.

'... and I have to get rid of that damn tree.'

'What?'

Startled, Emer forced her mind back to the hospital room

and the woman lying on the bed, her face now as pale as the pillow under her head.

'I've been made so many offers for the land over the years and always turned them down. Dad always said not to touch that tree and I wanted to keep that promise for him. But look at where it got me today? I could have died up there if that ambulance had taken much longer – don't look at me like that! You were there, you saw it. Changes.'

She fought a yawn, failed.

'Maybe it's time to make a lot of changes.'

This time when Siobhán's eyes closed she didn't open them again.

Chapter Twenty-Eight

WEST KERRY

1927

'Ah, Annie Thornton, you're welcome home, child, as welcome as the flowers of May. Your poor mother must be so pleased, to have you home, God love her.'

'Thank you, Mrs O'Neill.'

Annie wanted to keep on walking but the woman was blocking her path, a toothless smile emerging as she pushed the heavy woollen shawl away from her face. Although some of the women in the village, Annie's mother Eileen among them, had modernised their clothes since she had been away, most of the older generation still wore the long shawls beloved by their grandmothers and Annie found the sight of them disconcerting, as if she had never left Ireland at all.

'And you must be happy yourself to be back?'

The woman cocked her head to one side, a curious magpie pecking for information. Annie smiled, but didn't answer. She hadn't even told her parents why she had returned, and so was hardly going to divulge her secrets to Mrs O'Neill.

'It's lovely to be back and see my parents, and the children.'

Many would have been satisfied by the answer but Bridie O'Neill was a tougher bird.

'And tell us now, what brought you all the way back to Ballydrynawn?'

'I...'

She should, Annie realised belatedly, have come up with a decent answer to the question because God knows, it wouldn't be the last time she was asked it. But she couldn't think of one reason that made any sort of sense. Other than the truth, of course, but that wasn't for Mrs O'Neill's ears. And then a figure passed by on the opposite side of the road and the older woman pulled the woollen curtain across her face again.

'I'll bid you good day now, Annie, and send my blessings to your poor mother.'

In a moment she was gone, walking far more quickly than she should have been able to, given her advanced years. Annie glanced across to where the other person was now moving, equally briskly, in the opposite direction. But that woman's head wasn't covered and Annie recognised Mary Ross who had been a couple of years ahead of her in school. Or Mary O'Neill as she had since become... ah.

Annie paused to allow both women to disappear from sight and then began to walk home herself, moving slowly as she teased out what had just occurred. Mary Ross had married Felim O'Neill, a cousin – or was it a nephew? – of Bridie's husband Gerard. And although the war that had torn the country apart had officially ended almost five years ago, Annie had gleaned enough from her father's letters to know that many of the scars it had left on the boreens of the country were far from healed. Felim O'Neill had been a Free Stater who had joined the National Army after the signing of the treaty between London and Dublin, while Gerard O'Neill and the rest of his family had remained firmly on the side of the Republicans. Ireland and its politics had moved on since then but it seemed that declarations of peace and even the sight of old enemies sitting side by side in the new Irish parliament had not brought about reconciliation in families like the O'Neills.

There were other changes too, Annie mused, her thoughts carrying her on the road towards home – or her parents' home which was how she had come to think of it in the days since she had returned. Ireland was its own country now, or twenty-six counties of it at least, and despite the wariness she could feel in the air – or the out-and-out hostility, in the case of people like the O'Neills – Annie noticed a whisper of something more positive too. Not confidence, that was too strong a word, but a sense of forward momentum. After all, if looking backwards was too painful then maybe forwards was the only option. It was clear the country had come through great and painful change and this added to her feeling of alienation from it, she was an observer now, could not empathise with what had gone on in her absence, in truth, didn't want to.

She had reached the turnoff for the lane that led to the house where her mother would now be adding her name to the pot for dinner but kept walking straight ahead instead, taking the road to the cliffs. Her family had been delighted to see her, of course, but settling back into life under her parents' roof was proving anything but straightforward. Annie knew part of the problem lay within herself, it was just too hard not to compare Ireland with America, to watch her mother light the lamp in the evening and not immediately think of the electric lights in every room at the Chateau, or at Harbour View. There, a telephone sat in the hallway for the family's use, while here, news still came via the weekly paper – or sometimes, she thought wryly, via Mrs O'Neill – and the family dinner was still cooked in the same old black pot they'd been using on the morning she left for Cobh. There was very little physical room for her at home now too; like water into a puddle, the family had flowed into the gap she had vacated and it was proving as difficult for her to fit back in as it would be to siphon that water from the muddy ground.

Eve was long gone, she was a married mother of two now, but Annie's younger sister Bríd had taken her place as the local schoolteacher and was more than deserving of the small bedroom at the back of the house. Her parents still had their own room, of course, and the extension, once occupied by their grandmother, now held Emmet and James, who would be taller than any of them soon. The boys, as their family would always call them, were still identical in looks but differences between them, almost invisible in early childhood, had grown more acute as the years had gone by. There was a wariness about James now Annie couldn't warm to while his brother had retained the guilelessness of a child. Annie knew Eileen prayed that there would always be a place for Emmet at his brother's table, he was unlikely to ever start a family of his own but once he was shown kindness, he would be loyal forever.

All of this movement and growth meant Annie was currently sleeping on a makeshift mattress in front of the fire, not retiring until the rest of the family had gone to bed and up with first light, but this did not upset her in the slightest. She was not home for good, no matter what Mrs O'Neill thought. She had a task to complete and then she would leave for New York again. Home. Wherever Elena was, was home.

She could feel the wind in her face now and saw the Fairy Tree straight ahead, one part of Ballydrynawn that hadn't changed since she had left. As she climbed, Annie's hand went instinctively to the envelope in her pocket. Meg's dollars had been sitting there for a month now, during those blank, dreadful three weeks at sea when she told her bunkmates she was too ill for conversation, and during her first few days at home when her mother had pushed questions at her, and soup when she wouldn't answer them. They were still there now and, although Annie didn't believe in prayer any more or even the foolish notion of a magic tree, she believed in their crispness and knew they represented her future. These dollars would get rid of Seánie Lynch once and for all. And once she was sure he was really gone, she had enough left over, thanks to Meg, to pay her own fare back to America again. Back to Elena, back to her love.

'You're the Yank.'

The voice seemed to come from the tree itself. Annie jumped, and then grinned as a pale face emerged from behind the leaves. With her blue eyes and pretty, freckled face there was no doubting that the girl was May's daughter but whereas her friend had been always smiling as a child, this child's face was thin and solemn, her shoulders stooped as if she was carrying too heavy a load for her size. Annie waited for her to walk around the tree and then knelt down until they were eye to eye.

'You must be Muireann Lynch.'

The girl frowned suspiciously and Annie smiled.

'You won't remember me, you were a very small girl when I left. But your mammy has been writing to me and telling me all about you, she says you are a great girl for your reading.'

The girl blossomed so quickly under the praise, it was obvious to Annie that she was in dire need of kind words this morning. She reached out then and touched the soft, curly hair.

'Does your mammy ever mention me?'

The girl nodded, eyes wide.

'All the time, before. You sent us presents, clothes and a teddy bear. And she made us write to you to say thank you. I mean...'

Annie laughed at her obvious embarrassment.

'You did, they were lovely letters and I treasured them. And is your mammy in today?'

'She is.'

Muireann nodded solemnly.

'My daddy is gone to town so she's on her own. She sent me to ask you to visit us. I was supposed to call to your own house but you are here instead.'

'I am indeed.'

Annie rose and began to follow the girl across the fields. She had already made two attempts to visit May since returning home, but on the first occasion the farmhouse had been empty and on the second, Seánie had met her at the door and told her, with a sneer, that his wife was far too busy to 'socialise'. Now it seemed they would finally be able to have a precious moment together. From outside, the Lynches' farmhouse looked to have changed little. Still whitewashed, still with that bright red door, although a patch of flowers in the yard outside looked like they had been recently trampled on and Annie hoped it was childish negligence rather than adult spite that had destroyed May's hard work. The door was open and she followed the little girl inside to find her friend folding clothes on the kitchen table. May looked up, joy mixed with anxiety on her weary face.

'You came!'

'I've missed you...'

Tears flowed as they folded each other into a warm hug, holding on tightly until Annie felt a tug on her arm. The tiny boy had Seánie's eyes but his mother's frown as he gazed up at her, utterly seriously. Then his big sister appeared from behind him.

'Did you bring us presents this time?'

'Muireann...'

But Annie shushed her friend and grinned down at the children.

'I did, but I have them back in my own house, I didn't know I was going to be visiting today. Will ye walk back with me later maybe and collect them?'

'I will.'

The children nodded and, still solemn, the boy released his grip and ran off out of the room. May wiped her eyes and sighed.

'They're a pair of divils. I'm sorry, Annie.'

'Would you go away with your sorry.'

Sah-rry. Annie hadn't thought she had absorbed any of the American accent while she was away but she heard it now in the dimly lit kitchen, sah-rry, and it added to her discombobulation, that feeling of being neither here nor there. May returned to her laundry.

'Sit down here now and talk to me while I do this.'

But Annie couldn't countenance sitting while her friend worked so stood beside her instead, helping her fold the clothes, noting how beautifully sewn and darned each item was. May paused for a moment, then arched her back with a sigh.

'It hasn't stopped raining in days, I thought I'd never get them dry.'

'I had forgotten how much it rains over here.'

'Are you telling me it doesn't rain in America?'

'Ah it does, but it's different.'

'Warm rain, I suppose!'

'Yes!'

They laughed, and continued talking, the inconsequential chatter helping them feel their way back into their former, easy friendship. And then Annie turned to May, her face serious.

'Seánie went into town?'

'He did. I'm not sure when he'll be home.'

May's gaze darted towards the centre of the table where a pot of potatoes stood, peeled but uncooked.

'I'd a mind to put the spuds on but I'm not sure when he'll need his dinner.'

Annie shrugged.

'Sure stick them on now. Won't the children need to eat anyway?'

But May didn't move.

'He likes them to be hot when he comes in. I just have to think... when would be best...'

Annie thought of the children's thin pinched faces and tried to keep her voice calm.

'But if he won't tell you when he'll be back...'

May shivered.

'I'll be wrong whatever happens.'

'Oh, May...'

Annie dropped the sheet she was holding and reached across the table but the woman shied away from her touch.

'I might boil up the water anyway, just to be on the safe side.'

She bustled over to the far side of the kitchen, but not quickly enough that Annie couldn't see how her hands shook as she hung a pot of water above the fire. Annie folded a final blouse, then looked around the kitchen. It was spotlessly clean – almost too clean for a house with such young children. The only item out of place was a ragged work jacket which had been left hanging on the back of a chair. May followed her gaze.

'I'm sorry about the mess. Seánie was out in the fields this morning, I told him I'd wash that for him but I haven't had a minute—'

'Would you sit down, May. You look worn out.'

'The potatoes ...' May stood in the centre of the room, looking from fire to jacket and back to the fire again, frozen into indecision by the fear of doing the wrong thing.

Annie made another attempt to find a solution.

'Stick the potatoes on, I'll keep an eye on them and if he's not here we can keep them warm—'

'I'm hungry!'

The voice came from the doorway that linked the kitchen

to the hall. Annie looked up to see the little boy again, his lower lip trembling.

'Go away and play, Harry, and I'll call you when supper is ready.'

'But I'm hungry—'

'Who's that whinging?'

She had been too busy thinking of May and her children to listen out for the footsteps and Annie's heart gave a fearful double thud now as the back door opened. Seánie had drink taken, she could tell that by his high colour and glittering eyes and he walked straight towards the jacket and flung it on the floor.

'Sitting around here chatting all day, I suppose, rather than doing the one job I asked you to.'

'Seán...'

May's voice was shaking as she looked towards the jacket and then over to the potatoes, which were still sitting, uncooked, on the table.

'I didn't expect you home.'

'Oh, you didn't expect me, was it?'

He strode towards the table and the only thing Annie could be thankful for was that the little boy had fled on his approach, although she had no doubt that Seánie's roar could be heard all over the house, if not further afield.

'The one thing I asked you for is a clean coat and a bit of dinner but that was too much trouble for you, was it?'

'No, Seánie...'

May clutched at her throat as if she could somehow locate the right words to mollify him.

'I'll stick the spuds on now, they'll be ready before you know it and I'll get to work on your coat—'

'Forget about it!'

Seánie strode across to the fire and picked up the pot of water. Briefly, Annie wondered if she had the strength to tackle him, because the water was boiling now and hot enough to cause serious injury. But as she watched Seánie carried it across to the table and then, slowly and deliberately, poured the water all over the pile of dry clothes.

'Maybe you'll think twice next time about putting me at the bottom of your list, lady. You were alone too long, got to thinking you were the mistress of the house. Well I'm back now, you slovenly bitch, and you'd do well to know your place!'

Annie looked from Seánie's red-rimmed eyes to May's terrified ones and made a decision. Walking towards him, she kept her voice as calm as she could.

'Come for a walk with me, will you, Seánie? It was you I came to see, not your wife. Come on now, we'll let May get on with things in here.'

Despite his drunkenness, he was so surprised that he did in fact follow her, heading out into the evening leaving May standing silently in the kitchen behind them. The wind had picked up since she had been inside but Annie kept her shoulders straight and didn't allow herself to shiver as she led him towards the barn at the back of the house, out of sight and earshot of the others. They stopped then and Seánie turned to her.

'So you have something to say to me?'

'I do—'

But the breath was taken from Annie's lungs then as Seánie lunged and shoved her backwards against the cold stone wall of the barn. The ground was damp underfoot from recent rain and Annie struggled to remain upright on the slippery stones.

'Seánie, I—'

'Do you think you can order me around, ha?'

A sudden sharp slap to her face sent her head pounding against the wall. Annie's ears rang and she fought against the blackness that threatened to cloud her vision.

'No—'

But when he hit her again she understood, with sudden and devastating clarity, just how much she had underestimated him. She had been a fool, she realised, and thought again of those pale faces in the house, the cowed expressions.

'I'll teach you to come into my house and order me around.'

He reached out and grasped her by the shoulder and she flinched as the alcohol on his breath hit her face, but there was worse to come as his other hand dipped towards his trousers and began to unbutton his flies.

'Seánie—'

'I think you want it, you Yankee bitch.'

He was panting now, but not from exertion, she could see that the violence had excited him and she was in more trouble now than she ever could have realised.

'People were talking about you over there, you know. You and that stuck-up red-headed tart. Thinking ye are too good for the likes of us, no time for decent Irish men. Well I'll show you, Annie Thornton...'

His knee was between her legs now and he used it to pin her against the wall as he continued to fumble with his britches.

'I'll show you...'

'I have money!'

He wasn't expecting her to speak and his surprise bought her just enough time to drop her hand into her skirt pocket and withdraw the envelope. Paying him off had been her plan all along but she had visualised a negotiation, a conversation, not this assault. But she still had the dollars and she could see, even now, the power they held over him. Struggling not to cry, she opened the envelope just wide enough for him to see inside. Seánie was suddenly very sober.

'You didn't earn that type of money as a skivvy. Oh, I see...'

He laughed, a deep disturbing chuckle and then his fingers were probing again, moving inside the waistband of her skirt, poking and tearing until she thought she would be sick, but she made one final effort then pushed him away.

'It's yours, Seánie, if you leave now. More than you'd earn in two years here.'

He stopped, looked at her.

'You don't have your fine Republican friends to help you now.'

She shook her head.

'No. But I have this. And what is here for you anyway, Seánie Lynch?'

Despite himself he took a quick glance over his shoulder, back at the house where poor May was no doubt trying once again to dry her pile of sodden clothes.

'A house full of squalling brats – you said it yourself, Seánie, it's a very dull existence. I bet you miss New York.'

He attempted a sneer but Annie could see in his eyes that she had made a connection and pressed the point home.

'You could use this money to go back, start again. You had friends over there, maybe there was a woman...'

The sudden glance he gave her showed her she was on the right track.

'This is no place for you now. Sure I'm the same way, you think you can come home but it's never the same. But there's enough here for a lovely life across the water.'

He paused, then shook his head and spat on the ground.

'And why didn't you give this to me over there, when I asked you? You could have saved the two of us a lot of bother.'

'I'm sorry about that.'

Apologising to him made her feel ill but it was working, he had taken a step backwards from her now, his attention focused on the small brown envelope.

'Things got a bit mixed up – I had to go to the coast for a while. But this is yours if you want it; you can have it today if you promise to go and leave May alone.'

He snorted.

'And you'll move in with her, I suppose? Take the man's place. That's what they say about you, Annie Thornton. That you don't want a man of your own.'

Her stomach clenched at how close to the truth he was and how her life would be ruined if he continued to spread his poison, but she was so close to winning now, she had to press through.

'Just take it, Seánie. Go back. Think of it, New York. It's a great town if you have a few bob in your pocket. There's enough here to set yourself up in a little business. Think of the life you could have over there inside of sitting here, fretting over oil lamps and boiling water over a pot. Think of the life you could have...'

It was so close to her own dreams for her future she felt her voice wobble but forced herself to continue.

'Go, Seánie, take the money and go back to America. There is nothing for you here.'

Annie shoved the money into his hand then darted past him, ready to run, but Seánie made no attempt to block her path. Head down, she kept moving until she was sure he wasn't following then climbed the path to the Fairy Tree and sank to the ground at its branches, her breath coming in ragged gulps. Had she done enough to save May? And those beautiful children... and then Elena's face replaced all others in her mind. She had kept enough money back to pay her fare to America but that was the end of it then, she'd have to start saving all over again. Their little house, their freedom, was as far away as ever. But if they could be together, that would be enough. Annie leaned back in the shadow of the tree then and, without realising what she was doing, began to mutter the closest thing she had to a prayer.

'Wait for me, Elena. Wait for me, my love.'

Chapter Twenty-Nine

WEST KERRY

August 2022

'I'll just get you inside...'

'Jesus, Rob, mind the step!'

'Sorry, Mom...'

Rob winced as he manoeuvred the wheelchair over the lip of the door and into the kitchen.

'I should have got someone out really, to sort out a ramp or something...'

But his mother looked up from her wheelchair and sighed.

'No, I'm sorry, love, I'm being a bitch. I just wasn't expecting to feel so bloody helpless, that's all.'

'It can be tough, getting out of hospital. But you'll soon get into a routine!'

Emer, who had been hovering in the kitchen waiting for their return home knew even as they left her mouth that the words sounded patronising, and Siobhán must have felt the same way because she remained silent as her son eased her into the centre of the room.

Behind her back, Rob shook his head, mouthing 'anything I do is wrong'.

'Will I get the walker out of the car, Mom? You know you have to start doing those exercises they set for you. And I must show you the bedroom we've set up. Emer and Alison were a great help to me—'

'Sleeping in the study, I never thought I'd see the day, but it'll do for a while, I suppose.'

Siobhán's voice wobbled as she continued.

'I suppose I might as well go to bed anyway, I'm no use to anyone around here.'

'Actually, Siobhán, I was hoping you'd help me with something?'

Alison had been in the house all morning too and had kept herself busy making cupcakes, which now stood cooling on a wire tray on the counter, before making a few final adjustments to the downstairs room they had prepared for Siobhán to use while she was off her feet. She had cared for her father throughout his terminal illness, she explained to Emer, and had grown used to living with someone who needed extra care. She walked over to Siobhán now, her expression open and hopeful.

'It's my brother, in LA – I've been trying to help him with his business, I used to do it all the time at home and I was trying to keep it up while I was over here, but I've got myself into a mess with some spreadsheets and he needs it sorted today. This is very cheeky, I know, but I just think I've done something stupidly obvious and if there was any way you could take a quick look…?'

Rob raised his hand in protest but Siobhán shushed him, and turned to Alison.

'What business did you say your brother was in, again?'

'He's a mechanic, he runs a small garage. I drew up this database, it was supposed to link each client with repair work they had done, it should be really simple but I've pressed something stupid and...'

Siobhán's mouth twisted.

'Do you know, Alison, it sounds to me like you're trying to butter up an old lady, maybe you think giving me a project would cheer me up or something?'

The other three froze, waiting for an explosion. And then the older woman's face relaxed into a grin.

'But I've missed being busy, to be honest with you. Come on! We'll go into the study – or the bedroom, I suppose I have to get used to calling it – and have a look at it there.'

She nodded at Alison.

'Give me a push, will you? And maybe Rob could bring us coffee, and one of those delicious-looking buns?'

The request, flung over her shoulder at Rob, was delivered in a voice so close to Siobhán's normal one that Emer could almost see some of the tension lift from his shoulders.

'She's only in the door and she's ordering me around. I might bring you a plate of them, so?'

'Do that. They'd have you starved above in that hospital...'

As the kitchen door closed behind his mother and Alison, Rob turned to Emer, something approaching relief on his face.

'Jesus, fair play to Ali. I'd never have thought of putting Mom to work but it looks like it was the best call she could have made.'

'Yeah, great!'

Emer tried to sound cheerful, but her attempt at a smile failed and she turned away, busying herself by filling the kettle so he wouldn't sense her unease. Of course Alison was just trying to be helpful, she had nursed an ill parent before, she knew exactly what she was doing.

But what about the will?

She put the kettle on and began to root in the press for mugs but couldn't distract herself from her worries. Siobhán hadn't mentioned her will since that first night in the hospital, indeed Emer wasn't completely sure if the older woman remembered the conversation they had had, she had been so dozy on pain relief at the time. But Emer had delivered her computer to her the following day, as instructed, and there was no reason to believe she hadn't followed through with her plan to remember Alison in her will.

Then again, what if she had? Emer poured the boiling water into the teapot, a little annoyed with herself that she was so invested in the entire situation. So what if Siobhán did want to give Alison a few bob, hadn't she enough of it to go around? After all, Alison had been incredibly helpful while Rob's mom was in hospital, doing extra shifts in the surf school to free him up for visits, even cooking meals to bring into Siobhán when she couldn't face another day of hospital food. She had been kind, obliging and unintrusive, just the type of person you would want around in a crisis.

It just all seemed a little – convenient. Emer added milk to the mugs and placed two on a tray before walking across to fetch some of the cupcakes. Alison had turned up in Ballydrynawn, declared herself a missing relative and then, lo and behold, Siobhán had an accident and decided to change her will. It just all seemed a little bit far-fetched for a family in 2022, even if the head of that family was rich enough to give Bill Gates a dig out if he was stuck. It was also, of course, absolutely none of Emer's business. She handed the tray to Rob then slid back onto her stool and sipped her own tea. Nothing that happened within these gorgeously appointed four walls were any of her concern, not really. She was Rob's summer girlfriend, his fling, that was the beginning and end of her role in the affair. Her ticket back to the States was booked for the end of August, just a couple of weeks away, and once she got on that plane Ballydrynawn would become nothing but a memory.

Disturbing her thoughts, Rob returned and took a seat on the stool beside her. He looked tired, Emer thought; it was hard to be an only child in a scenario like this one. Her own brother was next to useless but at least Niall was another human being to call or text or just give out to when there was anything wrong at home. Rob, however, had neither father nor sibling and it was clear the last few weeks had taken a significant toll.

'I had a chat with the doctor this morning before we left.'

'Oh?'

Emer felt a sudden dart of panic when she saw the serious look on his face.

'There's nothing else wrong, is there? Other than the broken hip, I mean?'

'No, no, nothing new. But that's the strange thing really. They actually couldn't find anything wrong, there was no sign of Mom having had a stroke or anything.'

Rob glanced across at the kitchen door but it remained firmly shut, both Siobhán and Alison well out of earshot.

'They couldn't find anything at all to indicate why she fell. And that's what's worrying them. The doctor asked me – well, he asked me if she takes any medication regularly. Any sedatives.'

'Sedatives? Your mom?'

Emer almost smiled at the thought of the dynamic Siobhán Lynch taking anything designed to slow her down. But Rob's frown deepened.

'Yeah. They found something in her blood, the night she was admitted. A sedative is what the doctor called it, a strong one. And when they asked what she had taken – well, she refused to say.'

'How do you mean, refused?'

'Exactly that. Mom told them that she might have taken something on the plane, she wasn't sure, that it had been a long journey. The doc said she got kind of upset then and wouldn't say any more. He asked me if I knew anything, sure I didn't have a clue. So anyway, in the car on the way home just now I asked her about it again and she was, I don't know, really funny about it? Wouldn't say yes or no. So I asked her would she have taken something on the plane, maybe, to help her sleep and she lost her head altogether, said she'd been travelling the world since before I was born and "If I needed your advice, Robert Henry Lynch, I'd bloody well ask for it!" I let it go then, but what I can't understand for the life of me is, why she wouldn't just come out and tell us if she had taken something strange? It would make everything a hell of a lot more straightforward.'

Because she simply can't remember, Emer thought but couldn't say. Her heart ached for Rob but she felt sorry for his mother too, who clearly hadn't mentioned her fears about her memory loss to her doctors or anyone else. Only Emer knew the truth.

But again, none of this was her business.

Avoiding Rob's gaze, she looked around the kitchen for a moment, a place that had become as familiar to her as any home she had ever lived in. But all that would have to change now that Rob's mom was back in residence. This was Siobhán's home, and Rob's, and even Alison had more of a claim to it than Emer did, in more ways than one. A summer fling, that was all they had promised each other. In a fortnight's time she'd be back in LA and then what? A few video calls, a string of WhatsApp messages, fretting over the time difference when a blue tick didn't immediately appear? That would be a miserable way to end things between them. This had been a perfect summer, where Rob was concerned at least, and when the break came it would have to be perfect too. She looked across at him now and came to a decision.

'Are you working today?'

'Yeah, I'm heading down to the strand now. Do you want to come along?'

'No, I'm going back to the Tigín, I've a few bits to do. And Niall's baby is due any minute, I want to be near the phone if anyone is looking for me.'

'Of course. Will I see you later so?'

'No.'

Emer took a final sip of tea then climbed off her stool.

'I'm actually going to head into Limerick this afternoon. My cousins have been on at me to visit and I was thinking today might be a good day. Look, you've enough going on...'

She could see confusion on his face and began to speak more quickly.

'You've enough on your plate, your mom's home, you've a nurse coming later. You don't need me hanging around. The cousins have invited me to dinner, I'll be late enough coming back. So I'll give you a shout tomorrow, OK?'

She leaned forward and brushed her lips against his cheek, warding off any protest.

'Tell your mom I was asking for her, I won't disturb her now.'

She stepped backwards then, avoiding his eyes.

'She's lucky to have you, Rob. I'll give you a shout later.'

She'd been lucky to have him too. But now it was time to begin the break away.

Emer had her own zapper for the gates now and exited through them as quickly as she could, waving cheerfully into the camera as they slid shut behind her. But when she reached the turnoff that would take her to Ballydrynawn she found that she couldn't face going any further. Instead she pulled into the lay-by – the lay-by where they'd parked after that first night in the pub, Christ that seemed like forever ago – and stilled the engine.

Climbing out of the car, she locked it behind her then stood tight beside it as another car drove past, far too quickly. The bite in the afternoon air was a reminder of how close she was to the sea and the cliffs but it was also impossible now not to also think of how narrow the roads were around here, how impractical, how dangerous all of this beautiful isolation had been on the night of Siobhán's accident. Rob's mom hadn't mentioned her will to anyone else, but had she thought any further about tearing down the tree, building a proper driveway? A couple of weeks ago Emer couldn't have imagined such a thing, but a lot had happened since then.

Rob had left a spare Breaking Waves fleece in the car and she slipped it on, then locked the car behind her and began to climb. God, she was indistinguishable now from any of the other summer workers down on the beach in her cargo shorts, sensible sandals and branded fleece but it was a holiday uniform, that was all. The path was steep but Emer climbed quickly, her muscles coping easily with the gradient. She had never felt so fit as she did this summer, the surfing had done more for her than two decades of sweating in gyms on two different continents. But the surfing was also part of the holiday, of Kerry, this time out of real life. Technically, she could keep it up when she returned to the States, but somehow she knew that this passion would also come to an end when the holiday did.

The tree stood as it always had, guarding the cliffs, with the hedge that marked the perimeter of Siobhán's house just a couple of metres behind. A tourist would never spot it, but then again, wasn't that all she was really? A tourist, a visitor. A fling. She moved into the shadow of the tree and watched the leaves move as the breeze grew stronger. It had been a wonderful holiday but now it had to come to an end. The only trouble was, she didn't want it to.

She pushed the sleeves of the fleece higher up on her arms. Oh, it was time to admit the truth, even if only to herself, and the truth was that she had only bloody gone and fallen in love with Rob Lynch, the one thing she swore she wouldn't do. It had just all been so perfect, the beach and the sea and the sun and the sand and the man – and she had let her guard down and, by doing so, ruined everything. Emer would have thumped herself on the forehead if that hadn't been such a cliché but wasn't that what she was, really, when all was said and done? A walking, breathing, surfing cliché, dreaming of romance after the holiday ended. It wasn't Rob's fault, he hadn't made any promises and they'd had the summer of a lifetime, just as they had planned. But now here she was, wearing a jumper that smelled of his aftershave and with tiny grains of sand trapped where he had folded the sleeves back to help it fit her better. She could take the fleece back to LA with her, she supposed, and one day she'd try it on and those grains would fall onto the floor and crunch against her toes and she would think of Rob Lynch. But he wouldn't be thinking of her at all.

She could cry, but she didn't even want to allow herself that luxury. Instead Emer walked around the tree and looked out onto water that was almost black this afternoon, grey clouds massing overhead. Even the seagulls seemed to have disappeared and the air was so heavy it felt like you could almost squeeze the rain from it. Rob would have to cancel his afternoon classes, she thought, if the wind got any stronger, and then felt a pang at how well she knew him, how intertwined his days had become with hers.

She turned to the tree again then, wondering how many women had hung their hopes on its branches over the years. Poured out their hearts, asked for a husband, or a baby, or freedom, maybe. But wasn't she as bad as any of them now, having told a man her heart wasn't on offer and then losing it to him anyway? There was a sharpness to the breeze now and when she dug her hands into her pockets for warmth Emer's fingers brushed against a strip of velvet ribbon. She pulled it out, remembering a collection box shoved at her while she was doing her shopping in town. Distracted, she had given a euro to the woman and barely noticed the token proffered in return but here it was now, a tiny strip of navy velvet thanking her for her contribution to a charity whose function she couldn't even remember. Well, maybe everything did happen for a reason, Emer thought, reaching out and hanging the ribbon from the tree, laughing at herself because it was less humiliating than crying. So many wishes had been made at this tree but surely this was the first time someone had wished for a relationship to end, for lovers to part as friends.

'Go easy on me.'

Emer wasn't sure if she was talking to the tree, or to Rob, or to herself maybe, but she only allowed herself one more minute of pure misery, then turned and set her shoulders to the wind. The cousins could wait, she thought, she needed time to herself tonight. A hot shower, a movie, time alone. Time to get used to being alone.

And out at sea the storm rose.

Chapter Thirty

WEST KERRY

1927

'You'll have time for a bit of lunch before you go, surely?'

'I won't, thank you. May is expecting me.'

Annie yawned, then pulled her jacket around her shoulders.

'I told her I'd give young Muireann a hand with her reading. I'll most likely stay over there for dinner too.'

Eileen walked over to her eldest daughter and stroked her face gently.

'You'll drive yourself into an early grave, you know. Up all night scribbling in that oul notebook, I don't know what you're doing but surely to God it's not worth losing your health over.'

'It's important to me.'

Annie did her best to keep the frustration out of her voice. She hadn't told her family she was writing a book – it was hard enough for her to believe in the idea herself, let alone the rest of them – but she had told them that the work she was doing was connected with her old life back in America.

Then again, she thought as she headed for the door, all going well they wouldn't be able to see what she was doing for much longer. Seánie Lynch had left for Cobh the previous day and was due to sail – she checked her grandmother's small wristwatch that had never failed to keep the time – in just a couple of hours. She and May had put down a difficult week as he prevaricated over whether or not to leave but thankfully Annie's dollars had finally done their job and persuaded him his life would be better spent on the far side of the ocean. She herself would give it a few weeks, she decided, just to make sure that May was coping well alone and then she would book her own passage. Back to America, back to Elena. Cheered by the thought, she turned to her mother with a genuine smile this time.

'Don't be worrying about me, I'm grand.'

'You're still my daughter, Annie Thornton. I'll worry about you until the day I die, that's my job.'

'You didn't worry about me when I was in America, did you? Sure you hadn't a notion what I was up to over there.'

'No.'

Eileen's face grew sombre again.

'But I knew you were happy then. Don't ask me how, but I knew, a mother always knows. And I don't sense any of that happiness now. Go away with you, child, with my blessing and I hope that whatever you are doing brings you the peace you deserve.'

Annie kissed her mother and left the house, Eileen's words still ringing in her ears as she made her way across the fields towards the Lynches' farm. She hadn't told her family she was planning to go back to New York but she knew they wouldn't stand in her way and that thought gave her more comfort than they would ever know. In fact their love, and those pages she was writing, were the only things that were keeping her sane throughout the long sleepless nights on the hard mattress in front of the fire. Annie was missing Elena more, not less, as the days went by, her absence a physical ache in her gut that made her fear sleep because to wake was to experience even more violent pain. Writing her book, which she still thought of as a letter to her lover, at least brought the Italian woman a little closer, and allowed Annie to wallow in memories of America, its sights and sounds. But now Seánie was gone and May was safe and Annie could begin to dream of a life with Elena again. It wouldn't be easy, Annie knew – once she had booked her passage across she'd be next to penniless again – but she would be in the same city as the woman she adored and that would give her the courage to start over.

Desperate to keep in touch, but afraid of creating any more trouble Annie had only written one real letter to Elena since she had come back to Ireland. Conscious that her words could be intercepted by Salvatore the cook or even by Lorenzo himself, she had kept them brief and bland, merely telling her, as one friend to another, that her business in Ireland would soon be concluded and she intended to sail back to the US again.

I remain, your friend…

Annie had kissed the envelope before she handed it to her father to be brought to the village and smiled now as she imagined it travelling on the boat, and arriving in New York. Would her kiss travel all that way? Into the postman's bag, all the way through the crowded city streets. Maybe Elena herself would greet the postman at the door of the restaurant, her fingers landing on the very square inch Annie had sealed.

'Annie!'

She was so lost in thought she didn't hear her brother call her name, and jumped when the footsteps pounded on the damp grass behind her.

'Annie! I was shouting and shouting.'

Emmet's round, pleasant face was red with exertion.

'Daddy said to catch you before you went to the Lynches. A letter is after coming for you, will you keep the stamp for me?'

He handed her the envelope but did not let go of the edge.

'It's from America and I don't get stamps any more now you are home.'

'Of course I will, pet.'

Annie smiled at her brother, who was still in so many ways a small child.

'I might have a few more back in the house too, I'll dig them out for you later.'

'Thanks, Annie! I'll go back to Daddy so, we are working in the bottom field.'

Emmet scampered away and Annie took the letter, holding it in her hand as she made her way out onto to the road. And then she opened it and felt the rest of the world recede as she took in the address, the sender's name and then the two wavering lines, written on cheap, almost transparent paper.

My daughter Elena is dead.
Do not write to this address again.

★

'Annie! I wasn't expecting you until… Children, go outside and play.'

'But you told me—'

'Run away now! I'll call ye when the dinner is ready.'

Muireann, who had been sweeping the kitchen floor, looked curiously at the stricken face of their visitor but an offer to abandon her chores was not to be taken lightly and her curiosity was forgotten as she skipped out into the garden, calling out to her brother to follow.

May grabbed Annie's arm and led her to the chair closest to the fire. Her friend was shaking uncontrollably, her face grey.

'Annie, are you ill? Is there something wrong over beyond – is it your mother?'

'She's dead… I've lost her…'

'Your mother? Oh Lord above.'

But Annie gave another violent, uncontrollable shiver.

'Not Mother. Don't leave me, May.'

At a loss as to what had caused it, but devastated by the pain on her best friend's face, May knelt down and took Annie's two pale hands in hers.

'It's all right, a stór. Calm yourself now, catch your breath.'

'I abandoned her, and now she's dead.'

May only half understood it, but kept tight hold of Annie's hands as a story tumbled out about a woman in New York and how Annie had hoped she would wait for her. It didn't make sense, May thought as her knees grew numb on the cold earth floor, to have Annie sobbing like a jilted bride over some friend she had made in that faraway city which May would never visit, but she was wise enough not to question what her friend was saying and simply pulled Annie towards her and let her sob on her shoulder.

'She's dead and I'll never see her again...'

'Hush now. It's all right, it's all right. Whatever it is we'll get it sorted out, you have me here and your family all around you. We'll look after you, whatever it is. Hush now...'

They were both so wrapped up in Annie's grief that they didn't notice the front door open. When the draught fell on her face, May looked up sharply.

'Muireann Lynch, I told you to stay outside—'

But it was Seánie Lynch and not his daughter whose figure darkened the doorway. May dropped Annie's hands.

'No...'

The fear in her voice cut through Annie's misery and she too looked up, then froze as she saw the malicious and terribly familiar sneer.

'And isn't this a fine sight to greet a man who has returned to his family.'

May scrabbled backwards on the dirt floor. Her mouth gaped open but no words came as she stared up at her husband.

'You weren't long taking my place, Annie Thornton. I had my doubts about you all along, you unnatural bitch, and this just proves them, ha? You thought you'd get rid of me and get your feet under my table—'

'No.'

Annie's voice was still thick with tears but she found the strength to pull herself up on the chair.

'I told you to leave. I paid you—'

'You did, did you? You're a witch, Annie Thornton, and you thought your few dollars could buy my family. Well, they are not for sale.'

He took a step forwards, and Annie rose to meet him but he strode past her to the other woman who was now cowering on the floor.

'This is my wife—'

A kick brought forward a hopeless moan.

'This is my home, my family, and you have no right to it.'

Another kick, and then Seánie grabbed May by the hair and began to haul her upwards.

'This is my family and you are not welcome here, Annie Thornton!'

There was a poker by the fire and Annie lunged for it but Seánie was too quick for her and, letting go of May's hair, grabbed it instead.

'You're not going to get rid of me now, girleen.'

He was standing above her now, his face triumphant.

'If you want to take a man's place then get up here and fight me like a man.'

The first blow was aimed at the side of her head. Annie ducked just in time but still yelped in pain as the poker hit the side of her shoulder. Her eyes darted around the kitchen but there was nowhere to run, Seánie stood between her and the door and the fear that he would chase after May, or God forbid one of the children, made her stand and face him. And maybe, Annie thought as he raised his hand again, his eyes gleaming with savagery, maybe this was what she deserved. She had abandoned Elena, left her to die – maybe it was only right that her own story should end now too.

Chapter Thirty-One

WEST KERRY

2022

'Ah, Mam, that's terrific news. And you're sure everything is OK?'

'Amn't I after telling you it is! Sadie is fine, the baby is gorgeous, your brother is in flitters but he'll come around. It was quick enough in the end, she was only six hours in the hospital. Your father had to drive her home, of course, Niall didn't know his own name at that stage.'

'And have they a name picked?'

The phone fell silent and Emer wondered for a second if the connection between Kerry and Sydney had failed. And then her mother answered, sounding, for the first time in her life, a little overwhelmed.

'Well, they've given her my name as a second name. It was all her idea – Sadie said I've been so good to her this past while.'

'That's lovely! A baby Maura, I'm delighted for you. And her first name?'

There was another brief silence before her mother answered.

'Aurora. Isn't it pretty?'

'Aurora – Maura?'

'Yes.'

There was a definite note of defiance in her mother's voice now, a 'don't you argue with me' tone that Emer knew of old.

'Isn't it gorgeous? Unique.'

It is that, thought Emer, wondering what blissful combination of drugs had come together to ensure that nominative pairing. At least, she supposed, they hadn't gone the whole way and thrown an 'Alice' in at the end as well. But there was no denying the joy in the new grandmother's voice and Emer took care to keep the grin out of her own as she continued.

'I can't wait to see photos, Mam, will you send me a few?'

'I will, of course, actually your brother has put a few up on the book-face already if you want to check there?'

'I'll do that, so. Get some rest now, Mam, and I'll talk to you later.'

'I will, I will. And how are you getting on yourself? Not going out of your mind with boredom, I hope? And tell us, have you seen much of Siobhán Lynch's son?'

I've seen all of him, Emer thought, but kept that little detail to herself.

'I'm having a ball, Mam, but listen, ye all must be exhausted. Tell them I was asking for them, all right?'

'All right, sweetheart. Bye now. Bye…'

After roughly another minute of bye bye bye byes, Emer ended the call and walked over to the kettle. Then again, it wasn't every day she became an auntie. There was a bottle of Prosecco in the fridge that she'd found on offer in Lidl and she opened it, filled a glass, then brought both glass and bottle back to the sofa. It really was fantastic news, and Maura's joy had been contagious – or should have been. Emer sipped the fizzy liquid thoughtfully. She had just never expected her brother to reach such a major life milestone before her – or any milestone really.

A sudden shower of rain pelted the windows and made her jump, but the Tigín was well insulated and after a moment Emer settled back down with her fizz again. It was the ultimate grown-up thing to do though, wasn't it? Having a child. Niall would have to cop on now, even the redoubtable Maura couldn't continue mammying him now he was a parent himself. And Emer was delighted for him, of course she was. It was just all making her feel a little… untethered.

Anxious for distraction, she pulled her laptop towards her, and opened Facebook to see if her brother had updated his feed with photos. But the only image Niall had posted so far was a rather fuzzy one of a pink blanket topped by a whorl of blonde hair. Once Emer had liked and gushingly commented on the snap there was very little else she could do, so she poured another glass of Prosecco and sat back again. She hadn't bothered going into Limerick in the end, heavy rain had been forecast and she had used the weather as an excuse to postpone the visit to her cousins, although the truth was she really just felt like a night alone. Now she was here, however, she was annoyingly short of things to do. There was nothing on telly, and she had tried and failed to start two books earlier that evening. Finally, she turned back to the computer and opened her mail, deciding she might as well do a virtual tidy-up now she had time on her hands. Taking another, smaller, sip from her drink she began to delete a mixture of spam and out-of-date messages, swiping deftly, finding a surprising amount of comfort in the online slash and burn. In fact she got into such a rhythm – click, swipe, delete, click, swipe, delete, that she almost missed the message marked *Thought you might find this interesting*, coming perilously close to deleting it unread before she clocked the name of the sender. Marco Jaunuz had produced several commercials Emer had worked on over the past few years and they had even won an award for the last one, a tender story of the love between one man and his spicy chicken pizza. When she opened this mail, however, all thoughts of greasy fast food disappeared. Marco's daughter, he said, had used lockdown to write a short film. He would produce it, they had secured finance and maybe, just maybe, Emer might like to direct?

The evening had turned quite chilly now and Emer walked to the closet, picked up a cardigan and shrugged it on before returning to the computer and the wine. But the email didn't get any less interesting on a second read. Marco's daughter had been working on this script for months, he said, and maybe it was parental bias but he didn't think it was half bad. Would she take a read? No obligation, of course, but he had so enjoyed working with her in the past...

Emer lifted her fingers from the keyboard. Marco was no eejit, he had been working in the business for over twenty years and, daughter or not, he wouldn't be pushing this script unless he thought it had real potential. Ignoring the wind, which was really picking up now, Emer opened the attachment and began to read.

The noise of the phone reverberated around the bedroom and Emer scrabbled for it, but it was lost somewhere in the duvet and rang out before she could get to it. There wasn't something wrong with the baby, surely? Her mam had sent her a few more pictures just before she fell asleep and everyone had looked healthy and happy. Panic mounting, she finally located her phone under the pillow just as it began to ring again. But it was Rob's name, not her mother's that glowed on the screen.

'Hello?'

'Hey.'

Rob sounded a lot more alert than she did although that wasn't, Emer thought, particularly difficult.

'I was just wondering if everything is all right over there?'

Emer pulled herself up on the pillows and croaked out a reply.

'Sure. Why wouldn't it be?'

A soft chuckle came from the other end of the phone.

'You really do sleep like the dead, don't you? I mean the storm – we got battered up here. I texted you a couple of times during the night to see if you needed anything but I couldn't drive down, I was too afraid to leave Mom and the nurse here on their own.'

'The storm...'

Emer rose and carried the phone to the window. Once she had finished the script – had read through it twice, actually – she had finished the Prosecco too and fallen into a deep and surprisingly restful sleep. Now Rob mentioned it, she did remember getting up to go to the loo and hearing the wind rattling the windows but the Tigín was in a dip, sheltered by trees and far less exposed than Rob and Siobhán's coastal home, and she hadn't paid any particular heed to the noise before falling back asleep again. She squinted through the raindrops that were clinging to the French doors but the only thing out of place was one of the garden chairs, which seemed to have migrated to the far end of the garden.

'All's fine here, I think. How about yourselves?'

'Not great.'

Rob sounded rattled, she noticed now she was properly awake.

'I was up most of the night, to be honest with you. Mom was uncomfortable and the night nurse was freaked out by the weather. I ended up making both of them tea and then I couldn't get back to sleep afterwards. The house took a serious pounding. I think we might have lost a few slates, I heard an unmerciful bang around half three.'

Despite her vow to start cooling things off, Emer found herself anxious to check Rob was OK.

'Do you want me to drop over?'

'Would you?'

Rob sounded halfway between embarrassed and grateful.

'The nurse is heading off soon and I don't want to leave Mom on her own while I check the place over. But I could call Alison if you're busy…'

The mention of the American girl – who hadn't, Emer noticed, lost any time in becoming the Lynches' right-hand woman – made up her mind.

'I'm on my way.'

★

She had assumed Rob's concern had been heightened by exhaustion but as Emer drove west it became clear that the storm, which had had such a minimal impact on her own little house, had been much stronger, and more destructive, closer to the coast. She passed hedgerows almost bent double by the gale, two lost wheelie bins and even a stray trampoline which must have taken flight during the night and had ended up in the middle of a field, being gazed at by a couple of curious sheep who seemed to be debating having a quick bounce themselves. It had just turned ten and she turned on Radio Kerry, expecting to hear about power outages all over the county, but the weather story was surprisingly far down the news bulletin and it was clear the storm had been confined to a very small area – a 'freak weather occurrence' was how it was eventually described. When the news bulletin ended, she turned off the radio and allowed her thoughts to bounce unrestricted around in her mind.

The script she had read last night had been amazing. And it wasn't just loyalty to Marco that made her think it. It was sharp, witty, poignant, everything a short film should be, in fact, and as soon as Emer had finished it she had found herself planning a shot list and even engaging in a bit of fantasy casting. Emer had always longed to direct a feature and this short would be the perfect starting point, she reckoned. It was exactly the type of story that would play well at festivals and she'd give anything to have her name attached to it. Despite the Prosecco, her brain felt as if it was firing on all cylinders this morning. The vague emptiness she had felt when speaking to her mother the previous night was completely gone, replaced by enthusiasm for this project, for getting back to work again. Ideas were pulsing through her mind now and, alongside them, memories of her apartment in LA, her incredibly expensive computer with its editing software, the local bar where she could meet up with Marco and his daughter to discuss the script, the joy of working as a team, of creative people united in passion for a project – she wanted to go back. The thought appeared in Emer's mind so suddenly she almost slammed on the brakes. She wanted to go home. Ballydrynawn had been amazing and yes, she had fallen head over heels for Rob Lynch and would miss him dreadfully. But this was his place, not hers. It was time, finally, for the holiday to end.

Rob was in the kitchen drinking coffee when she arrived and he rose to kiss her but Emer moved away at the last moment, leaving his lips brushing against her cheek instead. His eyes narrowed slightly but he didn't comment and Emer couldn't help noticing how exhausted he looked.

'Do you want me to go see your mom?'

'There's no need.'

Rob rubbed his eyes wearily.

'I've just been in to check on her, she's out for the count. She was in awful pain, God love her, but whatever the nurse gave her seems to finally have kicked in. There'll be no budging her for a couple of hours – I'm sorry if I called you out here for nothing.'

'Not at all. Will I come with you for a quick look around the grounds, so? Make sure everything is all right?'

'That would be great.'

The morning was warm now, the air cleared by the storm,

and although Siobhán's wildflower meadow had taken a battering, there appeared to have been no major damage done to either the house or the gardens. They walked to the end of the garden then Rob turned, looked up at the roof and frowned.

'I could have sworn I heard something fall but it looks fine.'

'Well that's the main thing, isn't it?'

''Tis.'

As they continued their journey down the garden and out along the cliffs Rob reached out and took Emer's hand in his, a gesture that felt so natural she couldn't resist it. And after all, being around him should be even easier now she had something in mind for her own future. They could enjoy the short amount of time they had left and then part as friends, just as they had always planned it. The way his thumb was circling her palm right now didn't feel very friendly though, nor did the little darts of pleasure pulsing up through her arm—

'Oh my God.'

It only took a moment to see what had caught his attention, and then Rob dropped her hand and started to run. The top of the Fairy Tree should have been visible from here, but today there was nothing on the other side of the hedges clear blue sky. As Rob punched the security code into the fencing and ran through, Emer followed close behind then stopped dead when she saw the full extent of the damage. The lightning had done a clean but remorseless job. The Fairy Tree, which had guarded this place for over a century, had been split right down the middle. One large branch was lying on the ground, another huge section had completely disappeared, presumably over the cliff and into the sea. She started to walk forward, but Rob grabbed her arm.

'Be careful. We don't know if it's stable.'

He was right, of course, and they picked their way around the wreckage carefully then, checking for loose branches. Rob walked one way and Emer the other, her heart sinking even further when she saw the white heartwood achingly vulnerable and exposed to the elements. She heard Rob cry out, and hurried around to join him. And that's when Emer too saw the bones.

Chapter Thirty-Two

WEST KERRY

2022

'Right so.'
Rob parked the car but didn't move, and Emer reached over and gave his hand a squeeze.

'Long day.'

'The longest. Thanks for coming here with me though. I really appreciate it.'

'No bother.'

It took him a while to locate phone keys and jacket before climbing out of the car but they were both moving slowly today, the stress of the morning taking its toll. After they had found the bones – a concept Emer was still finding it hard to process – they had called the Gardaí, and then the day just seemed to pick up speed, like a rogue travelator, and dragged them along. Two guards arrived, a young guy who looked as if he could still have been on work experience and an older, stocky woman with a helmet of auburn hair and an expression that said she was absolutely not going to be impressed by millionaires or their mansions. They placed crime scene tape at the bottom of the cliff road before asking Rob and Emer to come back to the house for what the young guy described as 'a quick word' and his older colleague 'witness statements'.

Anxious to help, she and Rob had trooped back to the kitchen to tell the guards all they knew but their usefulness as witnesses, Emer thought, could be described as dubious, at best. Once they had described where and when they had found the bones, there was little else to say. They hadn't heard of anyone going missing in the parish, either recently or further back, and there had certainly, Rob confirmed, never been any talk in the family of a burial up by the tree.

The cops had questioned Alison too, who said she had been asleep in her apartment all night and that the white noise app on her phone had meant she hadn't even heard the storm. Then they had woken Siobhán who had done her best to hide her distress and insisted on being helped to get out of bed and dressed before telling them that she too was utterly baffled by what had been found. The guards then told them they would go back to the nursing home to speak to Rob's grandfather, as the previous owner of the property. But when Rob had called the station later to see if there was any news the younger officer, finally free from the steely gaze of his superior, had admitted the meeting with the old man hadn't gone well at all.

'They weren't even sure if he took in what they were saying to him,' Rob told Emer now, as he locked the car.

'Garda Horan told me Granddad didn't get upset, even, just stared straight ahead of him and didn't say a word. He asked me if there was anything wrong with his hearing but sure, Granddad could hear the grass grow.'

Emer looked at him sympathetically.

'He was probably just in shock.'

'More than likely.'

Rob led her through the car park and towards the nursing home.

'I'm glad they're letting us see him now though, I need to make sure he's OK. Cian said he saw a television crew on the road earlier so there's bound to be something on the six o'clock news and I don't want there to be any chance of Granddad watching that on his own. Mom is really worried about him too, she'd have loved to come in herself but she's not up to it.'

They reached the door and Emer rang the buzzer, then smiled into a security camera in a way she hoped did not betray how utterly freaked out she was by the direction the day had taken.

'Will Siobhán be OK up at the house on her own?'

'Oh, she's not on her own.'

They both watched as a fuzzy white uniform materialised through the blurred glass door.

'The night nurse is due at eight and Alison said she'd sit with her till then, or until we get back, whichever is first. Mom is more worried about Granddad than herself anyway, he was so adamant that nothing should happen to that tree— Ah, Katya!'

The Ukrainian nurse was all smiles as she ushered them inside. Emer and Rob followed her along the corridor, her shoes squeaking on the recently washed floors.

'Did you hear what happened?'

The young nurse shrugged.

'I know the police called to see Harry. Is everything all right with your family?'

'It is, thank you.'

Rob glanced at Emer.

'Well, as far as I know anyway. How's his form?'

Katya frowned.

'Well, that's the funny thing. He was great yesterday and this morning, ate his breakfast, even let me take him for a little walk in the grounds. But when the police came...'

She paused before leading them down a second corridor.

'Oh I don't know. He didn't seem well after that but I know he'll be glad to see you.'

She lifted her head, smiled and raised her voice cheerfully.

'Here are your visitors, Harry!'

Then, in an aside...

'It's good that you can sit with him for a while. Even if he doesn't feel like talking, he'll be happy to know you are here.'

Harry was in bed but lying on top of the covers, a tartan dressing gown buttoned around his bony frame. Staring straight ahead, he didn't even seem to notice them come in. A television flickered in the corner of the room and Rob moved to turn it off, mindful that it was almost time for the evening news. Then, from the bed, came a firm order.

'Leave it.'

Rob gave Emer a quick look before they took their seats, both careful not to block the screen. Rob leaned towards to the old man.

'You had visitors earlier, Granddad.'

'I did.'

The face was pale, almost grey, and the eyes watery but the voice was steady and fully alert. This was not, Emer thought, the elderly, almost incapable person the Gardaí had described. Rob must have felt the same way because when he spoke again his voice was conversational and utterly normal.

'And do you remember what they told you?'

'They said they found the bones.'

The bones. The back of Emer's neck prickled, it was clear from Harry's matter-of-fact tone that the discovery hadn't come as any surprise to him. She opened her mouth to speak and then shut it again, the atmosphere in the room so charged she felt that one wrong sentence, one wrong word might stop him from saying anything else. From the chair opposite her, Rob squeezed his grandfather's hand.

'I hope they didn't upset you? The guards.'

But again, the old man remained utterly calm.

'I suppose I always knew they'd call some day.'

He shifted slightly in the bed as if to continue, but then the picture on the TV set changed and Emer followed his gaze to see the opening credits of the evening news light up the screen. Harry pointed at it.

'Turn it up there, Rob, like a good boy.'

But Emer was nearest and she reached for the remote control, fiddling with the volume. Almost immediately, pictures from just a few miles down the road from where they were sitting filled the screen.

'*Gardaí are investigating the discovery of a body...*'

A body. Emer shivered, despite the heat of the room. All day she had been thinking of their discovery as 'bones' but the use of the word 'body' was a reminder that, no matter how long those bones had been there, they had been a body once, and before that, a person. There was another reporter on the television now, standing at the lay-by – where love stories began, Emer thought wryly – with the road to the cliffs rising behind her. The crew had clearly been prevented from going any further and Emer felt thankful that Siobhán's privacy wouldn't be compromised, not today at least. The young reporter's hair whipped around her as she spoke but she too had nothing much to add to what they already knew. The state pathologist would carry out a full investigation, but Gardaí were working on the assumption that the find was a historical one. The newscaster thanked her, then moved smoothly on to the dreadful ongoing conflict in Ukraine and Rob beckoned to Emer to turn down the TV.

'You knew about it so, Granddad. Before today, I mean.'

The old man nodded.

'I did. I do.'

'But you didn't tell the guards anything.'

'Rude woman.'

Harry extended one long, brown-spotted hand and began to pluck at the edge of his bed sheet.

'The boss woman. Shouting at me as if I was deaf. Or stupid.'

Rob gave Emer a look.

'I think we met her all right. And why didn't you tell her what you knew?'

'Because my mom didn't know I saw them.'

My mom... the old man's voice cracked and Emer felt a rush of sympathy for him, ninety-eight years old and still thinking of his mother. Harry was looking at Rob now, his hands shaking.

'Did I do the right thing, Robbie? I wanted to talk to you first, before I said anything.'

The room felt airless suddenly, and far too warm, and Emer half rose from her seat.

'I could leave you two alone...'

But Harry made a trembling attempt at a smile.

'You might as well stay, my darling, this lad will tell you everything anyway, he has a very high opinion of you. Look, Robbie, I can talk to the guards, of course I can. I just wanted to get things straight in my head first.'

His grandson bent towards him.

'We're here, Granddad, talk away. We can worry about the guards after. But let us know what's bothering you, first. You knew the bones were there?'

'I did.'

'And do you know who they belonged to?'

Harry inhaled, and the subsequent exhale was almost a groan.

'My father. Seánie Lynch.'

Rob's face was soft with pity now.

'I'm sorry, Granddad, but that can't be true. Seánie Lynch went to America, you said so yourself. We have letters above in the house from him and everything, he never came back again. You remember I was telling you about Alison?'

He looked across at Emer then, his face stricken. Maybe Harry's mind was a lot more feeble than they had assumed.

'Alison is Seánie's great-granddaughter, she was born in the States. He's buried over there, she told us—'

'No!'

The word was loud – and rock steady. Harry looked, Emer thought, like a man who had been carrying a heavy burden for a long time and had finally put it down.

'Seánie Lynch died in our house and was buried up at that tree. I know. Because my mother killed him and Annie Thornton helped her.'

Chapter Thirty-Three

WEST KERRY

1927

Annie lifted her hand to ward off the blow but when it fell it merely glanced off her shoulder. She heard a grunt and looked up to see May hanging off her husband's arm.

'I'll kill you too, you bitch!'

Seánie raised his hand again to try and shake off his wife but May had given her the time she needed and Annie scrambled to her feet, then steadied herself and kicked Seánie as hard as she could between the legs. He moaned and doubled over, and as he did so May grabbed the poker from his hand. For a fraction of a second she stood, motionless, then seemed to come to a decision and brought it down as heavily as she could on his head. Seánie stumbled forwards, seemed almost to recover, then lost his footing and fell heavily and the sound of his head striking the edge of the cooking pot reverberated around the kitchen.

The women looked at one another, May's eyes wide with fear.

'Jesus, Annie, what if I've killed him?'

But Annie had no time for remorse now.

'What if you haven't?'

Too wrapped up in the horror of what was happening, they didn't notice the little face that peeped through the doorway at the back of the room. Then that face disappeared, just as Annie Thornton took the poker from her friend and brought it down again, and again, and again, until there was no more uncertainty left at all.

Seánie was a stocky man but not a tall one and, buoyed by adrenalin, the women managed to drag his body from the house and leave it in the small lean-to shed at the back where various pieces of farm equipment were stored. May was sobbing now, barely coherent, but Annie was stony-faced and utterly calm.

'You'll have to listen to me now, May Lynch. We are going to feed the children their dinner, do you understand? And put them to bed.'

May could only manage a groan.

'You have to stay calm, May, do you hear me? We can manage this between us, but you have to help me. Can you do that?'

'But Seánie...'

Annie reached out her hand and tipped her friend's face towards her.

'Seánie is gone, May, you have to understand that now, he's gone. We just have to look after a few things. Stay with me now. Then you'll be free of him.'

Her friend was so shaken it was as if her nerve endings lay naked on the surface of her skin and it was clear to Annie that if she didn't remain strong the other woman would dissolve under the pressure of what needed to be done. So Annie made sure to keep her busy, keep her moving. First they boiled another pot of water and cleaned the kitchen, then called the children in and fed them their supper. They put them to bed then and if little Harry was unusually compliant, curling up in a ball and shutting his eyes without complaint, well Annie was unable to take on board another worry and simply left him to sleep off whatever was bothering him. Finally, when the house was quiet and night had fallen, May looked out of the kitchen window into the blackness.

'We have to tell the police.'

But Annie walked up behind her and spun her around.

'And have me arrested, or you, and have those children lose both their parents?'

May shook her head, helplessly.

'But what else can we do?'

'We'll...'

Annie paused and then the answer came to her out of the darkness.

'We'll bury him at the Fairy Tree.'

May stared at her but didn't say anything as Annie continued.

'It was raining earlier, the ground will be soft enough to dig and there will be no one out walking at this hour.'

'But the man deserves a Christian burial, at least.'

Annie reached out and gently lifted her friend's hair away from her shoulder then pulled at the collar of her blouse, revealing a necklace of bruises, some new and livid, others faded to yellow.

'And was it Christian, what he did to you? And would it have been Christian, if he treated his children the same way?'

A flicker of pain crossed May's face and Annie narrowed her eyes.

'Or maybe he had already started.'

Between them, they bundled his body into a sack and dragged it the short distance to the tree. Rain was falling again, a misty dampness that didn't hamper the digging yet ensured no one would be out walking that evening and Annie couldn't help but take the weather as a sign that they were doing nothing wrong. When they had finally finished they trampled the ground underfoot, covered it with leaves then stood for a moment to catch their breath. It was too black to see the water but they could hear the waves and Annie fancied they carried with them echoes of laughter and joy from the other side of the ocean. Laughter she would never hear again, joy that would never be hers now that Elena was gone. Maybe it was her own grief that had numbed her this evening, kept her panic in check, helped her work so calmly. Maybe. May was steadier now too, the physical work having settled her nerves.

'What will we do now, Annie?'

'We'll say he went back to America. Sure wasn't he in town last night on his way to the boat?'

'But what if someone finds him here?'

Annie took a deep breath.

'We will just have to hope that they won't.'

Of all the pleas made to the tree, had there ever been one as fervent? May nodded and then turned to Annie, tears streaming down her face.

'You won't leave me, will you? '

Annie looked at her, and then back at the blackness that contained the ocean. New York would be a bleak and silent city without Elena, but it was her home, and now the fear of Seánie coming back had been removed from it. Lonely as she would be without her love, there might be some sort of a life over there for her, if she sought it out. Meg was over there, and Simone, they would make her very welcome if she returned. And then Annie thought of the two children, asleep in their beds back in the farmhouse. May was exhausted, she'd never be able to keep this secret on her own.

It had stopped raining now but the breeze from the ocean was strong, and cleared her head. Across that water lay America and the future. Her friends, her book, her only hope of some sort of happiness. But May needed her now. Seánie was gone, they had killed him and Annie's punishment would be to stay here and make sure he was never found.

Chapter Thirty-Four

WEST KERRY

2022

'Jesus, that was some story.'
    'I know. But I believe him, don't you?'
'Yeah, I do.'

The afternoon sun had heated the car to a ridiculous temperature while they had been inside with Harry and, given that her mother's car wasn't equipped with anything as fancy as air conditioning, Emer rolled down the window as she drove. But the fact that Rob now had to shout to be heard didn't make the astonishment in his voice any less obvious.

'So, are you going to tell the cops what Harry said?'

He nodded. 'Of course. There's no way they can blame Granddad for this, surely, he was only a kid when he saw what happened, a baby, really. And everyone else involved is long gone, his mom and this Annie person. And I guess it's time this Seánie fella had a proper burial, no matter how much of a dick he was.'

Despite the glorious sunshine, Emer was careful to stay well under the speed limit, aware that fallen debris from the storm still littered the road. Her voice, too, was cautious when she spoke again.

'You know what this means – if your granddad's story is true. About Alison, I mean?'

Rob looked blank for a moment and then Emer saw recognition dawn.

'Alison isn't our cousin.'

'Well she can't be, can she? When did she say her grandmother was born, 1930s? According to Harry, Seánie was dead years at that stage and certainly not floating around California having an affair with anyone's great-granny.'

'Jesus, you're right. What about those letters though? The ones Mom found, with the American address?'

Emer shrugged.

'Haven't a clue. We'll have to tell the guards everything, I suppose, see what they can work out. But Alison was definitely wrong about you guys being related. Do you think…'

She paused. Emer knew how fond the Lynches had become of the young American woman and, despite her own suspicions, she didn't want to sound in any way triumphant.

'Do you think she just made a mistake?'

Rob's face was non-committal.

'Well it's a common name, John Lynch, it'd be easy to mix them up. And sure at the end of the day, what harm? Alison came over here looking for a family, unfortunately we're not it and that's all there is to it.'

But Emer, thinking of photos and envelopes, had a sick feeling in her stomach now.

'Rob, had your mother …'

She swallowed. This all felt like far too intimate a conversation to be having with someone she might never see again after her holiday was over. But it would be very unfair of her not to share what she knew with Rob.

'Had your mother ever mentioned anything about giving money to Alison?'

'Money? What, like wages? No, sure I'm paying her from the surf school—'

'Not wages.'

Emer's heart was thumping now.

'She made me swear not to tell you at the hospital, she was so upset. But I thought she might have said something.'

'What do you mean?'

Rob sat motionless in the car then as Emer sketched out what Siobhán had said that first night in hospital, or as much as she could without compromising the older woman's privacy. It wasn't her place, she felt, to share with Rob his mother's fears about her memory, but she told him how Siobhán had asked her to bring in the laptop, and how adamant she had been about 'settling her affairs'.

'Right.'

Rob looked out of the car window for a moment, then turned back to Emer.

'I need to talk to her.'

Emer suddenly felt very cold.

'Rob – you don't think she's already changed her will, do you?'

'I don't know. But when Mom gets an idea in her head...'

'Yeah.'

Emer tried to concentrate on the road but her head felt crammed with thoughts now, most of them too fantastic to make sense on this small country road with the purple mountains rising to one side and the cliffs dropping away on the other. Then again, Paudie had been worried too, hadn't he? He'd had his suspicions about Alison. And then there was that whole thing about the doctors, and the drugs Siobhán may or may not have taken. Oh, she was probably being ridiculous, Emer thought, Alison was more than likely just who she said she was, one of millions of Americans who came back to Ireland looking for their roots, no harm done. Except these roots had turned out to be made of solid gold. Despite the soggy leaves under the tyres, Emer found herself easing the car up towards the speed limit. It would be good to get back to Siobhán all the same, just to check that she was OK.

Chapter Thirty-Five

WEST KERRY

1946

'The cinema? Right, so.'

Calling a goodnight to her mother over her shoulder, Rita Rafferty shut the front door behind her and didn't try too hard to hide her disappointment. James Thornton had said he'd call for her at seven and, given that there was a dance on in the new hall in town, she had washed her hair and kept it pinned up all day so that it now fell perfectly onto the collar of her sister's best blouse. But after all that effort, when James had arrived at her door, out of breath after cycling all the way from Ballydrynawn, he had announced he had bought tickets for the pictures instead.

'It's a lovely evening!'

'It is.'

Rita took James's proffered arm but didn't bother to continue the conversation. She knew James loved the films but she herself could never understand what was so special about sitting in the dark and watching made-up stories, when you couldn't even ask a question about what was going on without someone telling you to shush. She and James had been walking out together for more than six months now, surely it would be nicer to be whirled around the dance floor in his arms, a sign to everyone in town they were getting serious about each other? In the cinema, the best Rita could hope for would be that James would maybe hold her hand. It wasn't as if she wanted him to go any further, or anything, not really, but it would be nice, Rita thought with a scowl, it would be nice if he at least looked like he wanted to try.

To make matters worse, James was in marvellous form this evening, all talk about some actress from Co. Mayo who was starring in the film. Apparently his sister had known her beyond in America, or so she said anyway. From Mayo, would you mind. Rita tossed her beautifully curling hair as they queued up for the tickets. She had been to Mayo once for a funeral and thought it an awful barren place, nothing but mountains and hedges, worse than Ballydrynawn even, and James Thornton would want his head examined if he thought they bred film stars up there alongside the sheep.

Liz Casey was taking the tickets this evening but Rita ignored her and kept her head down as she followed James into the auditorium. 'Twas well known that one only came to work in the evenings for the sake of the gossip she could bring home. Her spirits lifted a little when it became clear James had paid for the decent seats, and produced a box of chocolates too, but just as Rita was starting to think the night mightn't be a total disaster she spotted a familiar figure two rows in front of them and her heart plummeted again. That awful old maid Annie Thornton. James's sister, on her own, as usual.

Thankfully the lights were turned off before James got a chance to greet her, but there was no hope of Rita getting comfortable now, not with Annie sitting just inches away. She was a dreadful creature, with her long sad face and mannish clothes, living up there in Ballydrynawn with her two brothers, just the three of them now since the father had died and the mother went to live with the married sister beyond in Limerick. Rita took a chocolate toffee and chewed it thoughtfully, not in the slightest bit interested in the news reel that was now unspooling on the screen. It wasn't a bad house, mind you. James and his father had added a few rooms to it over the years and there was a fair bit of land attached to it now as well. It had – what was that word her father was fond of using? *Potential.* And, Rita had to admit as the screen darkened and then lit up with some nonsense, James could be said to have *potential* too. Unlike his poor brother. He and Emmet were twins, but different as night and day. Emmet, the craythur, was soft in the head and although he was the older brother there was no chance of him bringing a wife back to Ballydrynawn any time soon. James, on the other hand, was a handsome man in his own way, or would be if he smartened up a bit. Or somebody smartened him.

James reached into the box of chocolates then but Rita slapped his hand away. She needed something to get her through this film, which she already knew she wouldn't be able to make head nor tail of. Of course, any woman coming into the Thorntons' place would have to put up with Emmet, and droopy drawers Annie herself, moping around the place. Back when they were in school, Rita remembered, she and a few of the other children used to shout things at

Annie in the street, just to see if she would react. She never did though, never let on she heard them at all, just walked around with her nose in the air as if her mind wasn't in Ballydrynawn at all but somewhere else entirely. James still wouldn't have a word said against her, said she had been as good as a second mother to him and his brother since she came back from America all those years ago. America. Rita sniffed. There was certainly no trace of the Yank in Annie Thornton now, to look at her you'd swear she'd never gone further than the bend in the road.

The film wasn't bad, in the end, a simple enough oul yarn about a maid in a mansion on Fifth Avenue in New York City who fell in love with the son of the house and dreamed of running away with him. His mother was having none of it though, and rightly so, in Rita's opinion anyway. The mother was played by that actress James had been going on about, but surely he must have been mistaken, because the woman, Noreen Delamare, was no more from Mayo than she was from the moon. She was a beautiful woman, not young, but with the most fabulous long hair and clear, unlined skin. You wouldn't find the likes of that in a bog in the west of Ireland, she told James after the movie ended but he just shook his head, half laughing.

'She is Irish! Annie told me. Noreen Delamare – well, she was Cotter, at one stage and Carey way back before that again. She has been married a few times anyway. They say she might get a big award for this film, an Oscar.'

An Oscar, was it? Well, Mayo or not, 'twas far from Oscars the Thorntons had been reared. The cinema emptied out quickly but as they were leaving, Rita could see that Annie Thornton was still sitting on her own, stock-still in the centre of the row. James moved as if to say hello to her but Rita grabbed his arm and made him keep walking. She always thought the woman was half cracked but this evening only confirmed it. Sitting there with tears rolling down her face, right in the centre of the picture house where anyone could have seen her. God, you'd be mortified to be seen talking to her, let alone be related to her... and then James turned and smiled, and something about the way he looked at her, and the way the light streaming in from the foyer caught his eyes made Rita look at him a second time. And a third. He really was a fine-looking man when he made an effort, and he had made an effort this evening all right. James held out his arm then and Rita took it and was gracious enough to throw Liz Casey a smile as they sailed past. Liz had always had a soft spot for James, a few of the girls in school had, actually. It was not yet dark, and still warm when they left the cinema and James greeted a few people they knew and then looked at her, thoughtfully.

'I was thinking – we might take a wander up to the dance hall now, if you're not too tired, I mean?'

It really was a lovely house, Rita thought, just a few minutes from the strand. And the tiresome brother and sister would have to make way, surely, if James brought a bride home.

'No. I'm not too tired at all.'

Chapter Thirty-Six

WEST KERRY

2022

The crime scene tape was still waving at them from the lay-by but Emer took the left-hand turn instead, heading up the narrow road that led to the wooden gates of Siobhán's home. She hadn't told Rob what was on her mind, in fact she wasn't sure, really, why she was so anxious to get back. It had just been such a mad day; first the grim discovery at the tree and then Harry's extraordinary revelations, it was no wonder she was feeling a bit antsy. She brought the car to a halt and watched Rob unfasten his seatbelt. Quick cup of tea and all would be well again.

'Stick the kettle on, will you?'

Rob gave her a thumbs up as he walked towards the kitchen door, but it seemed to be shut tight and he returned to the car a moment later, frowning.

'Give us a hand with this, would you, please? I can't seem to get the doors open, and Mom never locks up down here, not when the big gates are shut.'

A quick check confirmed that the kitchen door was

indeed locked today. Sighing, Rob dug around in his pocket for his keys.

'Must have been the nurse or someone told her to do it, it's ridiculous. There is no need to lock these when we have the security gates... Oh.'

His key jammed halfway into the lock and refused to turn. Emer walked a couple of steps away and peered through the window, then beckoned him over and showed him what she had spotted. The door had been locked from the inside and the key was still in it, preventing anyone outside from gaining access.

'Oh that's just...'

Rob swore then jogged around to the front of the house, but returned almost straight away as that door too appeared to have been jammed.

'I'll give her a call.'

He took his phone from his pocket but Siobhán's phone went straight to voicemail.

'I told her not to let that phone run out of charge, or out of her hand. Jesus, she's never off the thing when she's well, so now she's laid up she decides not to answer it?'

'She might be asleep.'

Emer tried to make her words sound more reassuring than she felt, then grabbed her own phone from the car.

'I'll just give Alison a shout, see what the story is.'

But that phone too rang out without an answer, and Rob's face tightened.

'I don't know what the hell is going on but I need to get in there.'

He looked around for something to break through the

kitchen window, but the flowerpot he found just banged off the toughened reinforced glass.

'I'll have to—'

Before he could finish the sentence, however, Emer's phone pealed and she was relieved to see Alison's name on the screen.

'Hey there – can you come out to the kitchen, please? There seems to be a problem with the door.'

Alison's surprise was evident even through the handset.

'I'm not in there, I'm down in the village just waiting for my order. Didn't Siobhán say?'

'Say what?'

Sensing Rob's frustration, Emer pushed the phone onto loudspeaker and held it out to him, as Alison continued.

'I'm down in the village collecting the Chinese, Siobhán let me take her car.'

Rob grimaced.

'Alison – I thought the deal was that you'd sit in with Mom till we came back?'

'Yeah but she was starving.'

He looked ready to explode but Emer made what she hoped was a 'calm down' gesture, and answered instead.

'There was plenty of food in the house surely?'

The American girl laughed.

'Yeah, I know, but Siobhán said she had, like a craving for Chinese. It was Peking duck or nothing—'

'You weren't supposed to leave her!' His thin reserves of patience exhausted, Rob bellowed into the phone. 'Peking bloody duck? Jesus, Alison, she's just out of hospital, she's not supposed to be alone.'

'But she's not alone!'

The American girl sounded completely taken aback by his anger.

'She was expecting a visitor, she told me to go to Ballydrynawn and they'd let themselves in—'

'Over here!'

While Rob was glowering, Emer had been taking a closer look at the house and finally spotted what she had been hoping for, a small window jutting out a short distance away from the main kitchen block. It was the laundry room window, she realised, and when she pulled it forward she found, just as she had hoped, that it was unlocked and she was able to ease it forwards. There was no hope of Rob's bulk being able to fit through but he helped her upwards and Emer managed, with some wriggling and a prayer of thanks to her new-found flexibility, to ease her way inside. Calling out to Siobhán as she went, she dashed back into the kitchen and unlocked the door, standing back to allow Rob to storm inside. They ran into the hall but, despite the tremendous racket they were making, the house, when they paused to listen, remained eerily silent. It was all so similar to the day of Siobhán's accident that Emer found herself on the verge of panic, but this time, when they burst into her room Rob's mom was not on the floor or in any way injured, but lying peacefully on her bed.

'Thank God – Mom!'

And then Rob's relief turned to terror as the woman in the bed did not turn towards him or give any indication that she had heard them come in.

Rob raced to her side, placed a shaking hand on her neck then looked at Emer in disbelief.

'There's a pulse there but only barely. Ring an ambulance,

tell them it's urgent. Jesus, I can't believe this has happened again!'

Emer dialled the number, her hands shaking, and gave the now familiar instructions. No, the road wasn't wide enough but yes, she would come down to the bend and meet them… after she had finished the call she looked across at Rob.

'It'll be at least twenty minutes, OK? They said to keep talking to her.'

'I think there's an oxygen monitor in the bathroom.'

Rob's face was grey with worry.

'Mom bought it to keep an eye on her O_2 levels when she had Covid the first time. I'm pretty sure it's in there.'

'I'll check.'

Happy to have something practical to do, at least, Emer rose and headed to the small bathroom located next door to the study, forcing her mind into action mode. As soon as she found this oxygen machine, whatever the hell it looked like, she'd leg it out onto the road, ready to greet the ambulance when it arrived. Her head was so full of practicalities it took her a moment to register the figure standing behind the bathroom door and when she did, he was so familiar she almost smiled.

'Cian! What are you—'

The breath was expelled from her lungs as Cian pushed past her. He tried to make it as far as the bedroom door but Rob jumped up and barred his way.

'What the hell, man—'

It was then Emer saw the glint of the razor in Cian's hand. Her scream distracted Rob just long enough to allow the other man to pounce, and then there was another scream, and a roar and Emer looked up to see a spatter of bright red blood on the white bedroom walls.

Chapter Thirty-Seven

WEST KERRY

1946

It was a long cycle home from the cinema but Annie didn't mind, savouring the rare chance to be alone. She was happy living with her brothers but it did mean she rarely had a minute to herself. Emmet, in particular, was as much a child as he had ever been and stuck closely to her side, whether at home or on the weekends when they went as far as Ballydrynawn for mass, or a bit of shopping. Annie knew some of the children in the village laughed at him, they laughed at her too but she had grown used to deflecting their insults with a cheery smile or simply by walking past and pretending she hadn't heard. Emmet, on the other hand, took their teasing to heart and every incident, no matter how small, seemed to end with him retreating even further into himself.

She raised herself up onto the pedals and began to breathe more heavily as the road rose before her. James had been at the cinema tonight too, with that Rita Rafferty one. It wouldn't be long, she supposed, before James would marry and start a family of his own, maybe even bring her back to Ballydrynawn to live. Emmet wouldn't take kindly to that, he hated change but Annie would take care of him. There was a small outbuilding on Lynch's land that May said she would help convert into a little cottage if Annie ever needed it. May could well afford to help them, she had proved herself a resilient businesswoman over the years and had invested in the creamery in town as well as employing several men out here in Ballydrynawn. They never spoke about what had happened all those years ago but Annie knew her friend would never see her homeless, and there was great comfort in that. Besides, neither of them could ever move too far from the Fairy Tree.

She reached the top of the hill now and sank gratefully back down onto the saddle as the bike picked up speed. Keeping house for Emmet, God bless him, would be no real trouble but tonight a few of the lads he had known at school had persuaded him to go to the dance in town and Annie had to admit she was looking forward to a little time alone. She would build up the fire and there was a new library book in her bag that she hadn't even started yet. As nice an evening as she could hope for.

It had been lovely to 'see' Noreen again this evening, even if just on a screen. Annie did her best to watch all of her movies, but this was the first time the Mayo woman had had such a big part and Annie had been tempted to stand up at the end and applaud or do something mad like turn around and tell everyone that the beautiful star up there on the screen had once been her best friend. Then again, she smiled to herself, most of Ballydrynawn thought she was half cracked already, it was probably best not to give them any more ammunition.

When she had found out Annie was intending to stay in

Ireland, Noreen had written to her many times, pleading with her to come back to America, warning her she'd 'waste away' on what she always referred to as 'that wet and windy rock'. But Annie, although she never told her why, made it clear that wasn't an option so finally the Mayo woman had stopped asking and wrote instead of cheerful, airy things, and it gladdened Annie's heart to read that one of them, at least, had followed their dreams. Noreen had only been a couple of months in the hat shop before she had been called for a screen test at one of the big studios. She had played many parts since then, usually the best friend or the big sister of the main character and once – and how it had amused Annie to see it! – once she had even been a housekeeper in a New York mansion, although she had cut a far more glamorous figure than Mrs O'Toole.

And Noreen had also been a true friend to Annie when she needed her. She was nearing the house now and Annie depressed the brakes, slowing the bike, allowing herself to remember, something she rarely did any more. Without asking for an explanation Noreen, God bless her, had sent letters and postcards addressed to 'Mrs John Lynch' from all over California, and when they arrived back in Ballydrynawn every one of them had been proof that Seánie was alive and well and living in the USA. His children, who had never seen his real handwriting, even collected the stamps, God bless their innocence, as proof of their father's adventures. Noreen had never asked why Annie needed such a strange thing but she must have guessed the importance of it because once she even asked for a photo of Seánie, to give to the young Mexican maid who cleaned her apartment. The girl was in trouble, she explained to Annie in a letter, and the cause of that trouble was in jail, and it would help her out greatly if she had a photograph of a fine Irishman to show to her parents, a respectable-looking fellow who could at least look like someone who might marry her one day.

Annie had reached her own garden now and paused for a moment to deadhead a flower, and compose herself again. Meg, too, had tried for a while to stay in touch but Annie, feeling awful about having never finished the book, had been too ashamed to write back to her, and she hadn't heard from her now for many years. She had saved up money to repay the advance though, and sent it off in a postal order, although she had no way of knowing if it had ever been redeemed. Annie thought about Meg often though, and Simone of course, and hoped they were still together in that gorgeous, warm, welcoming home. She sighed now as she straightened up, the ache in her back the only real reminder she had of her life in America. But oh, what a beautiful life it had been. Sometimes late at night Annie's dreams would carry her back to the corner of a dusty city park, the feeling of Elena's soft lips on hers, the crackle of skin when they touched, the urgency of their desire. But she always woke alone.

She propped her bicycle against the wall, patted her skirts for her key. It was best, really, not to think of these things any more. She had a life here in Ballydrynawn now and kept herself as busy as she could. It was a quiet life, a lonely life, very far from actresses and Oscars and further still from the softness of a woman in her arms but it was a life without Seánie and that was the best she could hope for. A home and a fire and a new book every Saturday. Maybe, Annie often thought, maybe it was as much as she deserved.

Chapter Thirty-Eight

WEST KERRY

2022

'And you're sure you are up to this, Granddad?'

'I'm grand.'

The old man was sitting up in bed, hands neatly folded on his lap, and the nurse looked at him for a moment before nodding at Rob, calmly.

'Harry has been listening to the radio all morning, waiting for news. I think you might as well tell him yourself what happened, he'll drive himself mad otherwise!'

Drive himself *med*. Katya had a distinct Kerry edge to her accent now, Emer noted with amusement. Between that and the way she coddled her charges it was no wonder Rob's grandfather adored her. She was right though, Harry deserved to learn the full story.

As Rob lowered himself onto the chair beside his grandfather's bed, Emer tried to avoid looking at the massive bandage on his forehead, held in place by what looked like half a roll of medical tape. He had been incredibly lucky, the hospital had told him, that Cian's wild swipe with the razor had missed any significant artery or vein. Instead the cut to his forehead, which had bled profusely, would heal within weeks, although it would probably leave a significant scar. After he had been discharged from hospital and Emer was helping him into the car ahead of the drive home Rob had attempted to make a joke about how she mightn't want to be seen with him any more if he looked like a Bond villain. For the first time since all of the madness had begun Emer had burst into tears and then kissed him in a manner that wasn't jokey at all.

Cian had been in custody by then, of course. Despite Rob's injury, he and Emer had been able to restrain him until the paramedics had arrived and they, once they had gotten over the shock of the unexpected bloodbath in Siobhán's tastefully appointed bedroom, had called the Gardaí for back-up. Their neighbour was due to appear in court on charges of assault and, Emer hoped, attempted murder too. Because it *had* been attempted murder. Rob coughed and began to tell Harry the story, as gently and efficiently as possible.

'You know Mom had an accident? Well it turned out it wasn't an accident at all, Cian drugged her. Cian Thornton from over the road—'

His voice cracked on the last word and Emer had a sudden, painful image of that first conversation in the pub, and how important Rob's friends had always been to him.

'His grandmother was a Rafferty.' It was a brief interjection from Harry, but it gave Rob a moment to compose himself and after a moment, he resumed his story.

'It was all about right of way, land, all that sort of mad stuff.'

He glanced at Emer.

'Cian's family have been living around here as long as we have, and his dad built their guesthouse up on the cliffs years ago, on the site of the original family home. Well, it turns out they've been wanting to extend for ages and Cian's dad has been on at Mom to sell him the field between the two houses, to allow for a proper access road. The plan was to build a five-star place, a spa type retreat to make use of those views, but Mom was having none of it.'

'She'd have never cut down the tree, you see. I made her promise that.'

Harry looked pleased to have made the connection and Emer sat up straighter in her chair, determined that if the ninety-eight-year-old could figure out what was going on that she could too. It was a very complicated story to take in though, particularly after a second night spent on the hard chair of the local A and E department. But Siobhán was safe, and recovering from her ordeal, and Rob had finally felt able to leave her side that morning and come to tell his grandfather what had been going on.

'That was where Annie Thornton lived, originally,' Harry said, appearing to address the room in general.

'Annie and her brother Emmet, but neither of them had children, of course. So when James married, he moved in there, with his wife, Rita Rafferty. The Raffertys would squat in your ear if they were let. She'd be Cian's grandmother, you see.'

'Well anyway...'

Rob took gentle charge of the conversation again, afraid, Emer reckoned, that Harry was going to amble down a completely different path.

'Cian told Mom everything yesterday, after he broke in.

He was ranting and raving but she said he was determined
to tell her what was going on, or more to the point how
hard done by he felt. It all makes sense, you see, in his head.
He said he's sick of teaching and that his family could make
a fortune if they built a posh hotel. He kept going on about
Alison too. Apparently he asked her out a few weeks ago
and she said no, and he's convinced if he had more money
he could persuade her to hang around. But of course the
Thorntons would never get planning or build any sort of a
decent place up there without cutting the tree. Sure, we all
know that, isn't our own house built backwards because of
it? Cian got some mad idea that if Mom got sick then maybe
she'd realise how stupid it was not to have a proper road
up to the house and knock the tree down herself. There'd
be nothing stopping her then from selling the land to Cian's
dad. So he started messing with her head—'

'With her head?'

They had all forgotten Katya was there and she blushed
when they all turned round but Rob simply nodded.

'I know, it's insane, isn't it? Mad stuff, but Mom explained
it all to me last night. We gave Cian a key to our house,
you see, during Covid, so he could use the Wi-Fi for the
home schooling and that. It looks like he held onto it and
when Mom was away he started moving stuff around in
the house, just to throw her off balance. Taking things like
her wallet or her passport, then leaving them back the next
day, just to freak her out. Then he put sleeping tablets in the
oat milk, you know how much coffee she drinks, she gets
through buckets of the stuff. Just enough to make Mom
think there was something really wrong with her. And for

some stupid reason she never told me, or anyone else, that she wasn't feeling well.'

Now it was Emer's time to blush. She and Rob hadn't slept much the previous night, had sat up instead and pieced the whole story together between them. She knew he was hurt that his mother hadn't confided in him about her fears for her memory but that was something they'd have to talk about another day.

Harry was still silent but it was clear he was following the conversation intently as Rob continued.

'It was something Mom remembered yesterday finally made her figure out what was going on. Alison was up at our house but had to nip back to her own place to grab her phone. Mom was looking out the window and when she saw her go past she remembered seeing Cian running away from the house the day she had the fall. Now, if she had any sense...'

Rob exhaled sharply before continuing.

'If she had any sense at all in her head she would have called me at that stage. But you know Mom, has to be in charge. She wasn't even sure if Cian had done anything wrong, even, she just had this sort of uneasy feeling about the whole thing. So she called him and asked him to come over, then sent Alison into the village to pick up a Chinese. She had no real plan other than to ask Cian if he had been up at the house that day and what he'd been doing. But when she confronted him—'

His voice cracked and Emer took over the story.

'He started shouting at her at her, telling her that the Lynches had been controlling the lives of everyone in

Ballydrynawn for years and that they couldn't be allowed to get away with it forever.'

She looked at Harry before continuing, to make sure he wasn't getting upset but the old man just nodded gently.

'Siobhán reached for her phone to call the guards then and Cian must have just panicked because he grabbed a pillow and tried to suffocate her. She hadn't a hope of fighting him off, she couldn't move. She doesn't remember much after that until she woke up in the ambulance, and it was all over...'

'We disturbed him.'

Rob coughed to steady his voice before continuing.

'If we hadn't got there when we did – well.'

'And what is going to happen now?'

Katya's face was grim as she looked from Emer to Rob.

'Cian is in custody now, they'll question him for another few hours and then I suppose he'll be charged.'

Rob looked as if he was struggling to remember the right terminology.

'The guards have been really good at keeping us informed; it'll be assault, probably, and maybe attempted murder. And it'll be all over the news – I'm sorry, Grandad.'

Harry shook his head.

'No need to be sorry on my account, Robbie. I'm just glad they caught the bastard. And how is your mom?'

'She's good actually!'

Rob attempted a smile.

'She was so worried she was going doolally it's actually a relief to her that there was something physical causing it. That'll teach her to keep stuff to herself though. If she had talked to a doctor in the first place about the memory problems she was having we might have got to the bottom of this a lot sooner.'

'And the tree?'

Rob moved closer to the bed and took his grandfather's hand.

'It's gone, Granddad. The council have cleared it. It would have been too dangerous to leave the roots up there. We need to talk to you as well about what you want to do with... well, your father's remains. But we don't need to go into all that straight away.'

For the first time that day Harry's voice sounded shaky.

'I just want to be sure that bastard stays in the ground.'

Katya walked across to him and held his wrist lightly.

'I think you are getting tired, Harry?'

The old man put up little resistance.

'I might take a little rest all right.'

The nurse looked relieved.

'I will give you a couple of minutes to say goodbye and then you have to sleep.'

Emer stood up and began to gather her belongings, but Harry tugged Rob's hand gently.

'Before you go, son, I have something I want to give you both. Over there, in the bottom of the wardrobe.'

There was a large unit on the far wall and, following Harry's instructions, Emer walked over to it and found, in a compartment at the bottom, a large cardboard box. She carried it back to the bed where Rob, moving as gently as he could, was helping his granddad up on the pillows. The box was stuffed with exactly the stuff Emer knew her own mother could consider important: old pamphlets, address books and even a miraculous medal, and then

Harry reached in and pulled out a brown envelope which he handed reverentially to his grandson.

'This was Annie Thornton's. She gave it to me many years ago, when she went into hospital for the last time. Go on, open it...'

Rob eased the envelope open to find reams of thin paper, covered in neat blue handwriting.

'Take it with you.'

Harry gave a weak wave.

'Take them away with you, read them when you get a chance. She was a good woman, Annie. She used to call these her "pages"; she was writing about her time in America, I think. Some of them got lost over the years but you might find them interesting.'

'I will, Granddad,' said Rob. He slid the pages back into the envelope but it snagged on something at the bottom and he withdrew them again, anxious not to rip the precious paper. Carefully, he reached in a second time then pulled out a small metal disc, incongruously modern among the yellowing sheets.

'I think this got mixed up.'

'I put it in there for safe keeping,' said Harry with a soft chuckle. 'You'll understand why. I'm going to shut my eyes now.'

Rob bent over to kiss him, and Harry was asleep before they left the room.

Back in the car Rob placed the envelope in the back seat but held the badge on his palm, looking at it with something close to wonder. Emer glanced at it but the slogan, written in Irish, meant nothing to her. Rob sensed her confusion and smiled.

'It says "Tá, Comhionnannas". "Yes, Equality". Tá for Grá, they used to say, vote yes for love. I forgot you weren't here for the referendum. The marriage one.'

'No, no I wasn't.'

Emer had watched the coverage online, of course, had sobbed her heart out at the scenes in Dublin Castle on the day Ireland ratified same-sex marriage by means of a public vote. But she couldn't imagine why the day had been so special to an old man like Harry, or why he had kept the little token so safely.

'We'd better read his pages,' Rob said softly as she started the car.

'He said something to me just before I left and I want to know what he meant.'

'What did he say?'

'He said: "You young ones think you invented love. But we had it right here in Ballydrynawn all the time."'

Chapter Thirty-Nine

WEST KERRY

1946

Night was falling and it was only when she smelled the freshly burning turf that Annie looked up and saw smoke rising from the chimney. Concerned, she pushed open the door to find May standing by the fire, a broad smile on her face.

'I thought I'd light it, make the place cheerful for you both.'

You both?

Her friend said nothing, just stepped aside and it was only then that Annie saw the woman sitting on the chair on the far side of the room. The woman... but it couldn't be true. She opened her mouth to speak but no words came and when she tried to walk her legs would not obey her. The newcomer seemed equally overwhelmed until May came to their rescue.

'Come over here, Annie, and say hello to your visitor. She has come a long way to see you!'

'I hope you don't mind.'

It was the voice that finally told Annie she wasn't

dreaming. The hair was grey now, though still curly, and the skin around her eyes lined with fatigue. But those eyes were the same deep brown and that voice, American in tone but with the Mediterranean sun still shining through its vowels – that voice hadn't changed at all.

'You're here.'

Elena rose to her feet.

'I'm here.'

Annie couldn't remember deciding to cross the floor but suddenly she found herself in Elena's arms. She was only vaguely aware of May's smile and then the sound of the door shutting gently behind her.

Many minutes passed and then Annie stepped back to look at Elena properly.

'I wrote to you – your father said you died!'

'For a long time I wished I had.'

They gazed at each other for a long moment and then Annie took Elena by the hand and led her to the two-seater settee on the other side of the room.

'I'm so sorry I couldn't come back to America. You have no idea...'

Elena gave a watery smile.

'I had a little talk with May before you got here. She says you saved her life, Annie. That's all I need to know for now.'

'I wanted to save you.'

Elena shrugged.

'Maybe you did, in a way. It turned out I was braver than I thought, you see, and when it became clear you weren't coming back I knew I had to save myself. So I ran away.'

It was impossible to miss the note of quiet pride in her voice.

'But your father –and Lorenzo?'

'I had some money saved and I just took the train away from New York early one morning. I started in Chicago and then took a bus from there – I travelled for days. It was very lonely and I was very scared. But not as scared as I was at the thought of being his bride. I think my father told everyone I was dead because it was easier than admitting what had really happened.'

Annie reached up and stroked the lines around Elena's eyes, wondering at the experiences that had etched them there.

'How long were you gone?'

'The day I got the boat to come here to Ireland was the first time I set foot back in New York.'

Elena shook her head.

'I don't even know if my mother or father are still alive. My heart aches for them every day but I could not contact them and risk Lorenzo finding me. I changed my name, got a job as a cook in a boarding house – we have so much to tell each other, Annie! But I was safe. I thought about you every day. I thought about writing to you but I was worried you might come looking for me then, and that wouldn't be safe for you. And then came the war... there was so much in our way. But finally, a few months ago, the man I was working for died and I was going to have to find a new job, and a new place to stay. I knew then it was time to move on. I didn't know if you would want me here, but I had to try.'

'Want you? Oh, Elena, you have been on my mind every day, every hour for twenty years. But how on earth did you find me?'

Elena laughed and the deep, genuine chuckle made Annie's heart swell with love.

'I remembered the name Ballydrynawn, it's not a very big place! I got the train from – is it Cove? To Tralee and then hired a man to drive me.'

She looked at Annie then, her eyes dancing.

'I think, Annie, a lot of people in the village will know I am here, it might be hard to keep me a secret.'

Annie was laughing now too at the thought of every oul biddy in Ballydrynawn wondering who this beautiful Yank was and what on earth she wanted with mad Annie Thornton. They would get even more of a surprise, she thought, when mad Annie announced that the beautiful Yank was here to stay.

The words tumbled out as they arrived in her brain.

'You will stay?'

'I will, Annie, for as long as you will have me. You can tell them I am a cousin, maybe? Or a friend from America who has fallen on hard times. I hope it won't cause any difficulty for you. But now that I have found you…'

It may have been twenty years but when they kissed it was as if they had parted only hours ago. And then Annie pulled Elena even closer and whispered the rest of the sentence into her soft curls.

'I will never let you go again.'

Chapter Forty

WEST KERRY

2022

'It looks very bare, doesn't it? With the tree gone.'

'Miserable.'

Rob was sitting with his legs dangling over the edge of the cliff. The small ledge just beneath where he was sitting meant his perch wasn't as dangerous as it looked from behind but Emer still hesitated before lowering herself down beside him. Sensing her nervousness he laughed, then put an arm around her shoulders.

'You're grand.'

He expanded his chest, deepened his voice to a drawl.

'I'd sacrifice myself for you, ma'am.'

Emer rolled her eyes.

'You would all right.'

But she nestled into his embrace anyway, relishing the solidity of him, the warmth. It was breezy up here on the cliffs today, especially with the tree gone, and even as she sat, Emer found herself consigning the moment to memory, a memory she could bring back to America along with the others.

They sat like that for several minutes, looking out to sea. Once the bones had been excavated the council had done a good job of removing the rest of the tree and the area where it had stood was a clearing now, ready and waiting for whatever Siobhán decided to do with it. Some of the locals had made noises about having a plaque put up to Seánie Lynch but Rob and his family had batted away their opinions and held a small and very private burial in the local graveyard. Alison had been there too, having shyly asked permission to attend. Siobhán had made her welcome, but there was an awkwardness now between the American woman and the Lynches. Following the discovery of Seánie Lynch's remains, Alison was no closer to solving the mystery of her own ancestors, but she had told Emer she would be leaving Kerry at the end of the month and might travel to Mexico before going home.

Harry had professed himself too unwell to attend the service, but Rob had snuck a naggin of whiskey into the nursing home that evening and they had drunk a toast, not to Seánie Lynch but to his wife May and her friend Annie Thornton whose actions had had such an impact on all of their lives.

'So.'

Rob shuffled backwards a little and looked at Emer.

'Are you looking forward to going back to America?'

She nodded. 'I am.'

The waves were foaming beneath them now. They would go for a surf later, she thought, and tried, as she had been doing all week, not to think of it as the fourth, or the third or the second last time she would do so. She had promised Rob she'd keep surfing once she got back to

LA but could already imagine her resolve slipping away under the onslaught of deadlines and cramped edit suites. Marco had secured funding for the film, he had told her in an excited email, but it would need to go into production months earlier than they had planned to fit the deadline and Emer would be busy from the moment she arrived. She didn't mind, she felt energised by the project and tremendously excited. But it did mean that her old life would be left behind her as soon as the plane wheels left the ground.

'I'm delighted for you.' Rob was grinning now. 'This is what you wanted, isn't it? A movie? For feck's sake. Have you the Oscar dress picked out already – or I suppose the designers will contact you, isn't that how it works?'

'Ah now.'

Emer gave him a light shove but she was laughing now too. Thrilled that he was thrilled for her, that he knew her so well.

He pulled her closer again.

'You'll be amazing.'

'Thank you.'

The kiss was so gentle it felt like goodbye. Tears rushed into Emer's eyes and she blinked them back, furious with herself. This had been the plan all along, a summer fling, no strings, so why was she so gutted now it was over? Despite all of her efforts one salty drop escaped and Rob reached over, capturing it with his thumb.

'Don't cry, darlin'. We had some summer, didn't we?'

She nodded, unable to speak or indeed staunch the flow of tears now, and for a moment they just sat there, shoulder to shoulder, gazing out onto the ocean and the life beyond.

I wished for you, Emer thought to herself. But I wished for a movie too. It would be greedy, to ask for everything.

'Hey.' She sniffed, gathered herself. 'I had something else I wanted to discuss with you, actually. Would you mind if I took a copy of Annie's notes home with me?'

If Rob was surprised by her use of the word 'home' he didn't let it show.

'Sure! Granddad gave them to both of us. What were you thinking of doing with them?'

Emer felt suddenly shy.

'I'll be busy with the film for the next few months but you know I always wanted to try my hand at a screenplay myself. I was wondering, if you and Siobhán wouldn't mind – I think Annie's story needs to be told and I'd love to have a crack at it.'

'That would be amazing!'

Rob's enthusiasm was genuine.

'She always intended to write a book, Granddad said, but it never worked out for her. It would be incredible if you could get her story out there.'

'It would, wouldn't it? I might be useless at it, mind you, but I'd like to try.'

'I can't imagine you being useless at anything,' Rob told her and kissed her again. And then he sat back. There was no ghost wink now, no half smile, in fact if she didn't know him so well, Emer would swear he was looking pensive. But this was Rob Lynch. He didn't do serious, did he?

'Do you like living in California?'

Emer shrugged.

'I do, actually. It's not as beautiful as here, though.'

And now the grin reappeared for a second.

'Well *obviously*.'

'But it's a great place to live. Beaches, scenery, great bars. Amazing weather.'

This time the kiss was serious, too.

'I was thinking. I could always come out to visit, like.'

Her head jerked around and a dark blush rose underneath the tan and the stubble.

'Sorry, I mean only if you wanted me to, of course. But look, if you are happier just heading off – I mean that was the deal.'

She intertwined their fingers then, pulled his hand onto her lap.

'I would like that. But what about the fling? I thought—'

'Yeah. I thought too. But these last few weeks, with Cian and everything… well. It was a lot, you know? And you were amazing and I was starting to think I'd be an eejit just to let you go.'

Emer's heart was thumping now but she kept her tone light.

'And you're no eejit.'

'So they say!'

Rob squeezed her hand.

'In fact I was thinking – if you don't mind I mean, that I could stay for a bit? Maybe even look for work…'

'You? Leave Kerry?'

The smile was fully back now.

'Well yeah. I do have a passport, you know?'

'I know. I just can't imagine… can't imagine you anywhere but here really.'

But I can imagine you with me. She didn't say the words. But it was she who kissed him, this time.

After a moment he pulled away and looked at her.

'So how would you feel if I came over for a while? Maybe for a good while?'

Another kiss. That taste of salt and sea and Rob that she couldn't imagine ever forgetting.

'I'd really like it. But you know America, you can't just come and stay indefinitely. It can take ages to get a Green card—'

'Emer.'

'Yeah?'

'I know it has been a mad few months but do you remember what I told you? About where I was born?'

'Where you were... Oh!'

And now the kiss was flirtatious.

'You're an American citizen!'

'Dual citizenship, ma'am.'

The mocking drawl was back.

'I could probably sing you the "Star-Spangled Banner" if I had to.'

'So you can travel over – whenever you want.'

'Whenever I want, yeah.'

They were punctuating their answers with kisses now.

'If that's OK with you.'

Kisses, and smiles.

'It is. Have you thought about what you might do, though? You'd go mad if you weren't busy.'

'Well, I could be way off the mark here but I've heard there might be the odd bit of work for surf instructors in California, like.'

'Oh – yeah. Quite a few waves in California, as it happens.'

'I could give that a go, so. And don't worry, I won't crowd you. Mom has a place in Santa Barbara.'

This time it was Emer's turn to laugh.

'Of course she does. Is it nice?'

''T'isn't bad. And it's two blocks from the beach, so the commute would be manageable.'

The next kiss was harder, more urgent, and she could see him now, blond curls bobbing, heading for the beach with his board under his arm. In California. With her.

'So we could hang out there if you like. Or at yours, I don't mind.'

'Rob?'

'Yeah?'

'I live in a studio apartment, where you can lie in bed and put a pizza in the oven at the same time. I reckon we'll probably do more hanging out at your place.'

'You wouldn't mind then? If I come over for a bit?'

The wind was full in their faces now and although the Fairy Tree was gone, Emer could have sworn she heard the rustle of its leaves.

'I wouldn't mind at all.'

Acknowledgements/
Author Note

Surfing, West Kerry, New York City, a good bottle of wine – this book drew together many of my favourite things and was a joy to research. Of course the writing was harder than the research but at least I wasn't alone. And so to the Thank Yous...

To my agent Sara O'Keeffe and editor Rosie De Courcy, who loved this story from the beginning and made it so much better.

To copy editor Liz Hatherall for keeping me and my multiple timelines on the straight and narrow.

To Bianca Gillam and all at Head of Zeus for the work on the book, and the gorgeous welcome when I visited.

To Dr Will Murphy for his historical expertise, all errors are my own!

To Beth Lewis for her expertise.

To Andrew, Conor and Séamus for being the best travel companions, and especially for a wonderful week in Kerry that inspired much of this book.

To Caroline Stynes, for fabulous book chats and even better nights out.

To Liz Nugent and Jane Casey, I couldn't – no, wouldn't – have kept going without your support.

To the wider book community, especially Catherine and Colin, you make media social.

To my former RTE colleagues, who became my friends, keep doing what you're doing.

To Mags, Ciara and Treasa, and more than thirty years of friendship. We'll always have Vegas.

And finally to my grandmothers, Mary Anne Lyons and especially Bridget Crowley who travelled to New York and back again. This is not her story but she was, nonetheless, an inspiration.

About the Author

SINÉAD CROWLEY'S three DS Claire Boyle
crime novels were all nominated for Irish
Book Awards with the first two becoming
Irish Times bestsellers. Her most recent
novel, *The Belladonna Maze,* spent three
weeks in the *Irish Times* top ten. She lives
in Dublin with her family.